False Colours

Georgette Heyer, author of over fifty novels, was
seventeen when she started writing her first book,
The Black Moth, to amuse her convalescing
brother. It was published in 1921 and is still
selling. Although she is known primarily for her
historical novels set in Regency London, she also
wrote eleven detective stories, relying on her
husband, a barrister, for the plots. She died in
July 1974, at the age of seventy-one.

Georgette Heyer

False colours

Pan Books
London and Sydney

First published 1963 by The Bodley Head Ltd
This edition published 1973
by Pan Books Ltd,
Cavaye Place, London SW10 9PG
9 8 7 6
© Georgette Heyer 1963
ISBN 0 330 23763 2
Printed in Great Britain by
Richard Clay (The Chaucer Press) Ltd, Bungay, Suffolk

For Susie

I

It was past two o'clock when the job-chaise turned into Hill Street; and, as the watchman wending his way round Berkeley Square monotonously announced, a fine night. A full moon rode in the cloudless sky, dimming the street-lamps: even, as the solitary traveller had noticed, in Pall Mall, where gas-lighting had replaced the oil-burners. Linkmen, carriages, and light streaming from an open door on the east side of Berkeley Square indicated that not all the members of the ton had left London; but at the end of June the Season was drawing to a close; and it did not surprise the traveller to find Hill Street deserted. It would not have surprised him if the knocker had been removed from the door of a certain house on the north side of the street, but when the chaise drew up a swift scrutiny reassured him: the Earl of Denville's town residence had not yet been abandoned for the summer months. The traveller, a young man, wearing a tasselled and corded Polish greatcoat, and a shallow-crowned beaver, sprang down from the chaise, dragged a bulging portmanteau from the floor of this vehicle, set it down on the flagway, and pulled out his purse. The postboys paid, he picked up the portmanteau, trod up the steps to the front-door, and gave the iron bell-pull a tug.

By the time the last echo of the clapper died away the chaise had disappeared, but no one had responded to the bell's summons. The traveller gave it a second, and more vigorous, tug. He heard it clanging somewhere in the nether regions, but was forced to conclude, after waiting for several minutes, that it had failed to rouse any of my lord's servants.

He considered the matter. It was possible, though unlikely, that the household had removed from London without taking the knocker from the door, or shuttering the windows. To verify that the windows had not been shuttered he retreated to the flagway, and scanned the house, perceiving that not only were all the windows unshuttered but that one of them, on the entrance-floor, had been left open a few inches at the top. This gave, as he knew, on to the dining-room; and to reach it presented a lithe and determined young man with no insuperable difficulty. Divesting himself of his greatcoat, and trusting that no watchman would come down the street in time to observe his clandestine entry, he proceeded to demonstrate to the uninterested moon that Colonel Dan Mackinnon, of the Coldstream Guards, was not without a rival in the art of perilous climbing.

No such thought entered the Hon. Christopher Fancot's head: he was not acquainted with Colonel Mackinnon; and he did not think the feat of reaching the desired window-sill either dangerous or difficult. Once there it was easy to thrust up the lower sash, and to swing himself into the room. A couple of minutes later he emerged into the hall, where, upon a marble-topped side-table, he found a lamp burning low, with an unlit candle in a silver holder standing beside it. Observing these objects with an intelligent eye, Mr Fancot concluded that their noble owner had told his servants not to wait up for him. The subsequent discovery that the front-door was unbolted confirmed him in this belief. As he opened the door, to retrieve his belongings from the porch, he reflected, with an inward chuckle, that when his lordship did come home at last he would find his bed occupied by a most unlooked-for visitor, and would in all probability think that he was a great deal boskier than he had supposed.

On this thought, which appeared, from the mischievous

smile which played about the corners of his mouth, to afford Mr Fancot amusement, he kindled the candle at the lamp's low flame, and made his way towards the staircase.

He went softly up, the candlestick held in one hand, his portmanteau in the other, and his greatcoat flung over his shoulder. No creaking stair betrayed him, but as he rounded the bend in the second flight a door opened on the floor above, and a voice said anxiously: 'Evelyn?'

He looked up, seeing, in the light of a bedroom-candle held aloft in a fragile hand, a feminine form enveloped in a cloud of lace, which was caught together by ribbons of the palest green satin. From under a nightcap of charming design several ringlets the colour of ripe corn had been allowed to escape. The gentleman on the stairs said appreciatively: '*What* a fetching cap, love!'

The vision thus addressed heaved a sigh of relief, but said, with a gurgle of laughter: 'You absurd boy! Oh, Evelyn, I'm so thankful you've come, but what in the world has detained you? I've been sick with apprehension!'

There was a quizzical gleam in the gentleman's eyes, but he said in accents of deep reproach: 'Come, come, Mama –!'

'It may be very well for you to say *Come, come, Mama,*' she retorted, 'but when you faithfully promised to return not a day later than –' She broke off, staring down at him in sudden doubt.

Abandoning the portmanteau, the gentleman shrugged the greatcoat from his shoulder, pulled off his hat, and mounted the remaining stairs two at a time, saying still more reproachfully: 'No, really, Mama! How *can* you be so unnatural a parent?'

'*Kit!*' uttered his unnatural parent, in a smothered shriek. 'Oh, my darling, my *dearest* son!'

Mr Fancot, receiving his widowed mama on his bosom, caught her in a comprehensive hug, but said, on a note of laughter: 'Oh, what a rapper! *I'm* not your dearest son!'

Standing on tiptoe to kiss his lean cheek, and dropping

wax from her tilted candle down the sleeve of his coat, Lady Denville replied with dignity that she had never felt the smallest preference for either of her twin sons.

'Of course not! How should you, when you can't tell us apart?' said Mr Fancot, prudently removing the candlestick from her grasp.

'I *can* tell you apart!' she declared. 'If I had expected to see you I should have recognized you instantly! The thing was, I thought you were in Vienna.'

'No, I'm here,' said Mr Fancot, smiling lovingly down at her. 'Stewart gave me leave of absence: are you pleased?'

'Oh, no, not a bit!' she said, tucking her hand in his arm, and drawing him into her bedchamber. 'Let me look at you, wicked one! Oh, I can't see you properly! Light all the candles, dearest, and then we may be comfortable. The money that is spent on candles in this house! I shouldn't have thought it possible if Dinting hadn't shown me the chandler's bill, which, I must say, I wish she had not, for what, I ask you, Kit, is the use of knowing the cost of candles? One must have them, after all, and even your father never desired me to purchase tallow ones.'

'I suppose one might burn fewer,' remarked Kit, applying a taper to some half-dozen which stood in two chandeliers on the dressing-table.

'No, no, nothing is more dismal than an ill-lit room! Light the ones on the mantelpiece, dearest! Yes, that is much better! Now come and tell me all about yourself!'

She had drifted over to an elegant day-bed, and patted it invitingly, but Kit did not immediately obey the summons. He stood looking about him at the scene he had illumined, exclaiming: 'Why, how is this, Mama? You were used to live in a rose-garden, and now one would think oneself at the bottom of the sea!'

As this was the impression she had hoped to create when, at stupendous cost, she had had the room redecorated in varying shades of green, she was pleased, and said approvingly: 'Exactly so! I can't think how I endured those commonplace roses for so long – particularly when poor Mr Brummell told me years ago that I was one of the few females whom green becomes better than any other colour.'

'It does,' he agreed. His eyes alighted on the bed, and crinkled at the corners as he saw that the billowing curtains were of gauze. 'Very dashing! Improper, too.'

An enchanting ripple of laughter broke from her. 'Fudge! Do you think the room pretty?'

He came to sit beside her, raising her hands to his lips, and planting a kiss in its palm. 'Yes, like yourself: pretty and absurd!'

'*And* like you!' she retorted.

He dropped her hand, not unnaturally revolted. 'Good God –! *No*, Mama!'

'Well, absurd, at all events,' she amended, thinking, however, that it would have been impossible to have found two more handsome men than her twin sons.

The Polite World, to which they belonged, would have said, more temperately, that the Fancot twins were a good-looking pair, but by no means as handsome as had been their father. Neither had inherited the classical regularity of his features: they favoured their mother; and although she was an accredited Beauty dispassionate persons were agreed that her loveliness lay not so much in any perfection of countenance as in her vivacious charm. This, asserted her more elderly admirers, was comparable to the charm of the Fifth Duke of Devonshire's first wife. There were other points of resemblance between her and the Duchess: she adored her children, and she was recklessly extravagant.

As for Kit Fancot, at four-and-twenty he was a well-built young man, slightly above the average height, with good shoulders, and an excellent leg for the prevailing fashion of skin-tight pantaloons. He was darker than his mother, his glossy locks showing more chestnut than gold; and there was a firmness about his mouth which hers lacked. But his eyes were very like hers: lively, their colour between blue and gray, and laughter rarely far from them. He had her endearing smile as well; and this, with his easy unaffected manners, made him a general favourite. He was as like his brother as fourpence to a groat, only those most intimately acquainted with them being able to tell them apart. What difference there was did not lie perceptibly in feature or in stature, unless they were stood side by side, when it could be seen that Kit was a shade taller than Evelyn, and that Evelyn's hair showed a trifle more burnished gold than Kit's. Only the very discerning could detect the real difference between them, for it was subtle, and one of expression: Kit's eyes were the kinder, Evelyn's the more brilliant; each was more ready to laugh than to frown, but Kit could look grave for no reason that Evelyn could discover; and Evelyn could plummet from gaiety to despair in a manner foreign to one of Kit's more even temper. As children they had squabbled amicably, and turned as one to annihilate any intruder into their factions; during boyhood it had been Evelyn who inaugurated their more outrageous exploits, and Kit who extricated them from the consequences. When they grew to manhood circumstances separated them for long stretches of time, but neither physical separation nor mental divergence weakened the link between them. They were not in the least unhappy when apart, for each had his own interests, but when they met after many months it was as though they had been parted for no more than a week.

Since they had come down from Oxford they had seen little of one another. It was the custom of their house for a younger son to embrace a political career, and Kit entered the diplomatic service, under the patronage of his uncle, Henry Fancot, who had just been rewarded for his labours in the ambassadorial field with a barony. He was sent first to Constantinople; but as his appointment as a junior secretary coincided with a period of calm in Turkey's history he soon began to wish that he had persuaded his father to buy him a pair of colours; and even to wonder, with the optimism of one who had not yet attained his majority, whether it might not be possible to convince his lordship that he had mistaken his vocation. Stirring events were taking place in Europe; and it seemed intolerable to a spirited youth already dedicated to the service of his country to be thrust into a backwater. Fortunately, since the late Earl was quite the most unyielding of parents, he was transferred to St Petersburg before the monotony of his first appointment had goaded him into revolt. If he had owed his start in diplomatic life to his uncle, it was his father who was responsible for his second step: Lord Denville might be inflexible, but he was sincerely attached to Kit, and not altogether unsympathetic. His health was uncertain, and for several years he had taken little part in politics, but he had some good friends in the administration. Kit was sent, at the end of 1813, to join General Lord Cathcart's staff, and thereafter had neither the time nor the inclination to complain of boredom. Cathcart was not only ambassador to the Tsar, but also the British Military Commissioner attached to his armies, and in his train Kit saw much of the successful campaign of 1814. For his part, Cathcart accepted Kit unenthusiastically, and would have paid no more heed to him than to any of his other secretaries if his son had not struck up an instant friendship with him. George Cathcart, a very youthful lieutenant in the 6th Dragoon Guards, was acting as his father's military aide-de-camp. Much of his time was spent in carrying despatches to the several English officers attached to the Russian armies, but whenever he returned to what he insisted on calling headquarters he naturally sought out his only contemporary on the ambassadorial staff. Inevitably, Kit came under his lordship's eye, and soon found favour. Cathcart thought him a likeable boy, with a good understanding, and easy manners: exactly the sort of well-bred lad who was invaluable to an overworked and elderly diplomat obliged to entertain on the grand scale. He had tact and address, and, for all his engaging lightheartedness, an instinctive discretion. When his lordship journeyed to Vienna to attend the Congress there, he took Kit with him. And there Kit had remained. Lord Castlereagh, noticing him with aloof kindness for his uncle's sake, introduced him to the newly-appointed ambassador, who happened to be his own half-brother, and Lord Stewart took a fancy to him. What Kit thought of Stewart, whom the irreverent at the Congress dubbed Lord Pumpernickel, he kept to himself; and if he was sorry to leave Cathcart he was glad not to be sent back to St Petersburg when the war was over. By then he had not only recovered from envy of George Cathcart's rare good fortune in having been appointed to Wellington's staff in time to have been present at Waterloo, but had become so much interested in the tangled policies of the Peace that St Petersburg would have seemed to him almost as remote from the hub of international affairs as Constantinople.

He had met Evelyn abroad twice in the past two years, but he had only once visited England, to attend his father's funeral.

Lord Denville had died, quite suddenly, in the early spring of 1816; and since that date, some fifteen months previously, Lady Denville had not set eyes on her younger son. She thought at first that he had not altered at all, and said so. Then she corrected herself, and said: 'No, that's silly! You look older – of course you do! I am remembering how you were used to look, or trying to. The thing is, you see, that Evelyn is older too, so I've grown accustomed. You are still exactly like him, you know. Dearest, I wish you will tell me how it comes about that you're here so suddenly! Have you brought home a dispatch? *Do* you carry dispatches, like officers?'

'No, I'm afraid not,' he answered gravely. 'King's Messengers are employed on that business. I'm here to attend to – to urgent private affairs.'

'Good gracious, Kit, I never knew you had any!' she exclaimed. 'Oh, you're trying to hoax me! Now, why?'

'But I have got urgent private affairs!' he protested. 'You must know I have, Mama! I've become a man of substance, in fact: what you might call a well-breeched swell!'

'I shouldn't call you anything so vulgar! Besides, it isn't true.'

'How can you say so, when my godfather was so obliging as to leave his fortune to me?' he said reproachfully.

'Is *that* what you mean? But it isn't a fortune, Kit! I wish it were – and I must own I thought it would be, for Mr Bembridge was always said to be very well to pass, only it turns out to be no such thing, and he was possessed merely of what Adlestrop, detestable creature, calls a *competence*. Poor man! I dare say it was not his fault, so you mustn't blame him!'

'I don't! A pretty easy competence, Mama!'

'A competence,' stated her ladyship, with conviction, 'cannot be described as *easy*! You are talking like Adlestrop, and I wish you will not!'

Kit was aware that the family's man of business had never been a favourite with his mother, but these embittered references to him seemed to call for explanation. 'What's Adlestrop done to offend you, Mama?' he asked.

'Adlestrop is a – Oh, let us not talk about him! Such a screw, and so *malignant*! I can't think why I mentioned him, except that he told me, when Mr Bembridge died, that there was no occasion for you to come home, because there are no estates in question, or anything you might be obliged to attend to yourself – nothing but those detestable *Funds*, whatever they may be – and pray don't tell me, Kit, for you might as well talk gibberish! I perfectly understand that they are *holy*, and must on no account be touched; and, for my part, I would never invest my money in anything so stupid!'

'Of course you wouldn't!' agreed Kit. 'It would never stay in your purse long enough to be invested in anything!'

She considered this for a moment, and then sighed, and said: 'No; that's true! It is the most lowering reflection. I have frequently tried to cultivate habits of economy, but I don't seem to have the knack of it. None of the Cliffes have! And the dreadful thing is, Kit, that such habits only lead to *waste*!'

He gave a shout of laughter, but, although her eyes twinkled sympathetically, she said earnestly: 'Yes, but they *do*! I purchased a cheap gown once, because Papa cut up stiff over one of Céleste's bills, but it was so horrid that I was obliged to give it to Rimpton, without *once* wearing it! And when I gave orders for an economical dinner Papa got up from the table, and went straight off to the Clarendon, which is quite the most expensive hotel in London! Yes, you may laugh, but you have no experience of such matters. I assure you, the instant you begin to practise economy you will find yourself spending far more than ever you did before you embarked on such a ruinous course!'

'No, shall I? Perhaps I had better sell out of the Funds immediately, and start wasting the ready!'

'Nonsense! I know very well you haven't come home to do *that*! So what *has* brought you home, dearest? I'm persuaded it wasn't to look after these prodigious affairs of yours, so don't try to bamboozle me!'

'Well – not entirely,' he admitted. He hesitated, colouring a little, and then said, meeting her look of inquiry: 'To own the truth, I took a notion into my head – stupid, I dare say, but I couldn't be rid of it – that Evelyn is in some sort of trouble – or just botheration, perhaps – and might need me. So I made my prodigious affairs serve as a reason for wanting leave of absence. Now tell me I'm an airdreamer! I wish you may!'

She said instead, in a marvelling tone: 'Do you still get these feelings, both of you? As though one's own troubles were not enough to bear!'

'I see: I am *not* an airdreamer. What's amiss, Mama?'

'Oh, nothing, Kit! That is to say – well, nothing you can cure, and nothing at all if Evelyn returns tomorrow!'

'Returns? Where is he?'

'I don't know!' disclosed her ladyship. 'No one knows!'

He looked startled, and, at the same time, incredulous. Then he remembered that when she had first seen him, and had mistaken him for Evelyn, she had sounded disproportionately relieved. She was not an anxious parent; even when he and Evelyn were children their truancies had never ruffled her serenity; and when they grew up, and failed to return to the parental home at night, she had always been more likely to suppose that she had forgotten they had told her not to look for them for a day or two than to wonder what accident could have befallen them. He said in a rallying tone: 'Gone off upon the sly, has he? Why should that cast you into high fidgets, Mama? You know what Evelyn is!'

'Yes, I dare say I shouldn't even have *noticed* that he wasn't here, at any other moment! But he assured me, when he left London, that he would return within a sennight, and he has been away now for *ten days!*'

'So –?'

'You don't understand, Kit! *Everything* hangs upon his return! He is to dine in Mount Street tomorrow, to be presented to old Lady Stavely, and she has come up from Berkshire particularly to make his acquaintance. Only think how dreadful if he were to fail! We shall be at fiddlestick's end, for she is odiously starched-up, you know, and I collect, from something Stavely said to me, that already she doesn't like it above half.'

'Doesn't like *what* above half?' interrupted Kit, quite bewildered. 'Who is she, and why the deuce does she want to make Evelyn's acquaintance?'

'Oh, dear, hasn't Evelyn told you? No, I dare say there has been no time for a letter to reach you. The thing is that he has offered for Miss Stavely; and although Stavely was very well pleased, and Cressy herself not in the least unwilling, all depends upon *old* Lady Stavely. You must know that Stavely stands in the most absurd awe of her, and would turn short about if she only *frowned* upon the match! He is afraid for his life that she may leave her fortune to his brother, if he offends her. I must say, Kit, it almost makes me thankful I have no fortune! How could I bear it if my beloved sons were thrown into quakes by the very thought of me?'

He smiled a little at that. 'I don't think we should be. But this engagement – how comes it about that Evelyn never so much as hinted at it? I can't recall that he mentioned Miss Stavely in any of his letters. You didn't either, Mama. It must have been very sudden, surely? I'll swear Evelyn wasn't thinking of marriage when last I heard from him, and that's no more than a month ago. Is Miss Stavely very beautiful? Did he fall in love with her at first sight?'

'No, no! I mean, he has been acquainted with her for – oh, a long time! Three years at least.'

'And has only now popped the question? That's not like him! I never knew him to tumble into love but what he did so after no more than one look. You don't mean to tell me he has been trying for three years to fix his interest with the girl? It won't fadge, my dear: I know him too well!'

'No, of course not. You don't understand, Kit! This is not one of his – his *flirtations!*' She saw laughter spring into his eyes, tried to keep a solemn look in her own, and failed lamentably. They danced with wicked mirth, but she said with a very fair assumption of severity: 'Or anything of *that* nature! He has outgrown such – such follies!'

'Has he indeed?' said Mr Fancot politely.

'Yes – well, at all events he means to reform his way of life! And now that he is the head of the family there is the succession to be considered, you know.'

'So there is!' said Mr Fancot, much struck. 'What a gudgeon I am! Why, if any fatal accident were to befall him *I* should succeed to his room! He would naturally exert himself to the utmost to cut me out. I wonder why that should never before have occurred to me?'

'Oh, Kit, must you be so odious? You know very well –'

'Just so, Mama!' he said, as she faltered, and stopped. 'How would it be if you told me the truth?'

2

There was a short silence. She met his look, and heaved a despairing sigh. 'It is your Uncle Henry's fault,' she disclosed. 'And your father's!' She paused, and then said sorrowfully: 'And mine! Try as I will, I cannot deny that, Kit! To be sure, I thought that when your Papa died I should be able to discharge some of my debts, and be perfectly comfortable, but that was before I understood about jointures. Dearest, did you know that they are nothing but a *take-in*? No, how should you? But so it is! And, what is more,' she added impressively, 'one's creditors *do* know it! Which makes one wonder why they should take it into their heads to dun me now that I am a widow, in a much more disagreeable way than ever they did when Papa was alive. It seems quite idiotish to me, besides being so unfeeling!'

He had spent few of his adult years at home, but this disclosure came as no surprise to him. For as long as he could remember poor Mama's financial difficulties had been the cause of discomfort in his home. There had been painful interludes which had left Lady Denville in great distress; these had led to coldness, and estrangement, and to a desperate policy of concealment.

The Earl had been a man of upright principles, but he was not a warm-hearted man, and his mind was neither lively nor elastic. He was fifteen years older than his wife, and he belonged as much by temperament as by age to a generation of rigid etiquette. He had only once allowed his feelings to overcome his judgement, when he had succumbed to the charm of the lovely Lady Amabel Cliffe, lately enlarged from the schoolroom to become the rage of the ton, and had offered for her hand in marriage. Her father, the

19

Earl of Baverstock, was the possessor of impoverished estates and a numerous progeny, and he had accepted the offer thankfully. But the very qualities which had fascinated Denville in the girl offended him in the wife, and he set himself to the task of eradicating them. His efforts were unsuccessful, and resulted merely in imbuing her with a dread of incurring his displeasure. She remained the same loving, irresponsible creature with whom he had become infatuated; but she lavished her love on her twin sons, and did her best to conceal from her husband the results of her imprudence.

The twins adored her. Unable to detect beneath their father's unbending formality his real, if temperate, affection, they became at an early age their mama's champions. She played with them, laughed with them, sorrowed with them, forgave them their sins, and sympathized with them in their dilemmas: they could perceive no fault in her, and directed their energies, as they grew up, to the task of protecting her from the censure of their formidable father.

Mr Fancot, therefore, was neither surprised nor shocked to discover that his mother was encumbered by debt. He merely said: 'Scorched, love? Just how does the land lie?'

'I don't know. Well, dearest, how *can* one remember everything one has borrowed for years and years?'

That did startle him a little. 'Years and years? But, Mama, when you were obliged to disclose to my father the fix you were in – three years ago, wasn't it? – didn't he ask you for the sum total of your debts, and promise that they should be discharged?'

'Yes, he did say that,' she answered. 'And I didn't tell him. Well, I didn't *know*, but I'm not trying to excuse myself, and I own I shouldn't have done so even if I had known. I can't explain it to you, Kit, and if you mean to say that it was very wrong of me, and cowardly, *don't*, because I am miserably aware of it! Only, when Adlestrop wrote down everything I said –'

'What?' exclaimed Kit. 'Are you telling me he was present?'

'Yes – oh, yes! Well, your father reposed complete confidence in him, and it has always been he, you know, who managed everything, so –'

'Pretty well, for one who set so much store by propriety!' he interrupted, his eyes kindling. 'To admit his man of business into such an interview –!'

'I own, I wished he had not, but I dare say he was obliged to. On account of its being Adlestrop who knew just what the estate could bear, and –'

'Adlestrop is a very good man in his way, and I don't doubt he has our interests at heart, but he's a purse-leech, and so my father should have known! If ever a grig was spent out of the way he always behaved as if we should all of us go home by beggar's bush!'

'Yes, that's what Evelyn says,' she agreed. 'I *might* have been able to have told Papa the whole, if he hadn't brought Adlestrop into it – that is, if I had known what it was. Indeed, I had the intention of being perfectly open with him! But whatever my faults I am not a – a *mawworm*, Kit, so I shan't attempt to deceive you! I don't think I *could* have been open with Papa. Well, you know how it was whenever he was displeased with one, don't you? But if I had known that my wretched affairs would fall upon Evelyn I *must* have plucked up my courage to the sticking-point, and disclosed the whole to him.'

'If you had known what the whole was!' he interpolated irrepressibly.

'Yes, or if I could have brought myself to place my affairs in Adlestrop's hands.'

'Good God, no! It should have been a matter between you and my father. But there's no occasion for you to be blue-devilled because your affairs have fallen on Evelyn: he must always have been concerned in them, you know, and it makes no difference to him whether my father discharged your debts, or left it to him to do so.'

'But you are quite wrong!' she objected. 'It makes a great deal of difference. Evelyn *cannot* discharge them!'

'Stuff!' he said. 'He has no more notion of economy than you have, but don't try to tell me that he has contrived, in little more than a year, to dissipate his inheritance! That's coming it too strong!'

'Certainly not! It isn't in his power to do so. Not that I mean to say he would wish to, for however *volatile* your father believed him to be, he has no such intention! And I must say, Kit, I consider it was most unjust of Papa to have left everything in that uncomfortable way, telling your uncle Henry that he had done so because Evelyn was as volatile as I am! For he never knew about the two worst scrapes Evelyn was in, because *you* brought him off from his entanglement with that dreadful harpy who got her claws into him when you both came down from Oxford – and how you did it, Kit, I have *long* wanted to know! – and it was *I* who paid his gaming debts when he was drawn into some Pall Mall hell when he was by far too green to know what he was doing! I sold my diamond necklace, and your papa knew nothing whatsoever about it! So why he should have told your uncle that –'

'You did *what*?' Kit interrupted, shaken for the first time during this session with his adored parent.

She smiled brilliantly upon him. 'I had it copied, of course! I'm not such a goose that I didn't think of *that*! It looks *just* as well, and what should I care for diamonds when one of my sons was on the rocks?'

'But it was an heirloom!'

'I have no opinion of heirlooms,' said her ladyship flatly. 'If you mean to say that it belonged to Evelyn, I know it did, but, pray, what *use* was it to him, when what he needed, quite desperately, poor love, was the money to pay his gaming debts? I told him about it afterwards, and I assure you he made not the least objection!'

'I dare say! And what of *his* son?' demanded Kit.

'Dearest, you are too absurd! How should *he* raise an objection when he won't know anything about it?'

'Have you – have you disposed of any more heirlooms?' he asked, regarding her with awe, and some reluctant amusement.

'No, I don't think so. But you know what a wretched memory I have! In any event, it doesn't signify, because what's done is done, and I have more important things to think of than a lot of hideous family jewels. Dearest, do, pray, stop being frivolous!'

'I didn't mean to be frivolous,' he said meekly.

'Well, don't ask me stupid questions about heirlooms, or talk nonsense about its being as easy for Evelyn to pay my debts as it would have been for your papa. You must have read that hateful Will! Poor Evelyn has no more command over Papa's fortune than you have! Everything was left to your uncle's discretion!'

He frowned a little. 'I remember that my father created some kind of Trust, but not that it extended to the income from the estate. My uncle has neither the power to withhold that, nor to question Evelyn's expenditure. As I recall, Evelyn was prohibited from disposing of any part of his principal, except with my uncle's consent, until he reaches the age of thirty, unless, at some time before that date, my uncle should judge him to have outgrown his – his volatility (don't eat me, Mama!), when the Trust might be brought to an end, and Evelyn put in undisputed possession of his inheritance. I know I thought my father need not have fixed on thirty as the proper age: twenty-five would have been a great deal more reasonable, and in no way remarkable. Evelyn was vexed, of course – who wouldn't have been? – but it made very little difference to him, after all. You've said yourself that he has no intention of wasting his principal. You know, Mama, the income is pretty considerable! What's more, my uncle told him at the time that he was prepared to consent to the sale of certain stocks, to defray whatever large debts Evelyn had incurred – particularly any post-obit bonds – since he thought it not right that the income should perhaps be reduced to a monkey's allowance until they had all been paid.'

'Yes,' she agreed. 'He did say that, and it quite astonished me, for, in general, he's as close as wax, Kit!'

'No: merely, he doesn't live up to the door, and certainly not beyond it. But the thing is, Mama, that he didn't wish Evelyn to succeed my father under a load of debt, and if you had but told him of the fix *you* were in I'm persuaded he would have settled your debts along with the rest.'

She gazed at him incredulously. '*Henry*? You must be out of your mind, Kit! When I think of the way he has always disapproved of me, and the rake-down he gave Evelyn, whose debts were *nothing* compared to mine – Oh, no, no! I had liefer by far put a period to my existence than cast myself on his mercy! He would have imposed the most humiliating conditions on me – condemned me to live the rest of my days in that horrid Dower House at Ravenhurst, very likely! Or worse!'

He was silent for a moment. Knowing that Henry, Lord Brumby, considered his charming sister-in-law incorrigible, he could not help feeling that there was some truth in what she said. His frown deepened; he said abruptly: 'Why the devil didn't Evelyn tell him? He could have handled my uncle so much more easily than you could!'

'Do you think so?' she said doubtfully. 'He never *has* done so. Besides, he didn't know just how things stood with me, because I never thought to tell him. Well, how was I to guess that nearly every soul I owed money to would suddenly start to dun me, and some of them in the rudest way, too? Not that I should have teased Evelyn with my difficulties when he was already in hot water with Henry on his own account. I hope you know me better than to suppose I should do such a selfish thing as that!'

A wry smile twisted his lips. 'I'm beginning to, Mama! I wish you will tell me how you expected to settle matters, though, if you didn't tell Evelyn?'

'Well, I didn't know *then* that I should be obliged to,' she explained. 'I mean, I never *had* done so, except now and then, in a *gradual* way, when I was particularly asked to, so you can imagine what a shock it was to me when Mr Child positively refused – though with *perfect* civility – to lend me £3000, which would have relieved my immediate difficulties, and even begged me not to overdraw the account by as much as a guinea more – just as if I hadn't paid the interest, which, I promise you, I *did*!'

Mr Fancot, considerably bemused, interrupted, to demand: 'But what's this talk of Child, Mama? My father never banked with him!'

'Oh no, but *my* father did, and your Uncle Baverstock does, of course, now that Grandpapa is dead, so I have been acquainted with Mr Child for ever – a most superior man, Kit, who has always been so very kind to me! – and that is how I come to have an account with him!'

Mr Fancot, his hair lifting gently on his scalp, ventured to inquire more particularly into the nature of his mama's account with Child's Bank. As far as he could ascertain from her explanation, it had its sole origin in a substantial loan made to her by the clearly besotted Mr Child. Something in his expression, as he listened in gathering dismay, caused her to break off, laying a hand on his arm, and saying imploringly: 'Surely you must know how it is when one finds oneself – what does Evelyn call it? – oh, *in the basket*! I collect that has something to do with cock-fighting: so disgusting and vulgar! Kit, haven't *you* got debts?'

He shook his head, a rueful gleam in his eyes. 'No, I'm afraid I haven't!'

'*None?*' she exclaimed.

'Well, none that I can't discharge! I may owe a trifle

here and there, but – oh, don't look at me like that! I promise you I'm not a changeling, love!'

'How can you be so absurd? Only it seems so *extraordinary* – but I expect you haven't had the opportunity to run into debt, living abroad as you do,' she said excusingly.

He gave a gasp, managed to utter: 'J-just so, Mama!' and went into a fit of uncontrollable laughter, dropping his head in his hands, and clutching his chestnut locks.

She was not in the least offended, but chuckled responsively, and said: 'Now you sound like yourself again! Do you know, for a moment – only for a moment! – you looked like your father? You can't conceive the *feel* it gave me!'

He lifted his head, wiping his streaming eyes. 'Oh, no, did I? Was it very bad? I'll try not to do so again! But tell me! When Child would give you no credit didn't you *then* tell Evelyn?'

'No, though I did think I might be obliged to, till it darted into my mind, in the middle of the night, to apply to Edgbaston for a loan. Isn't it odd, dearest, how often the answer to a problem will flash upon one in the night?'

'Applied to Lord Edgbaston?' he ejaculated.

'Yes, and he agreed to lend me £5000 – at interest, of course! – and so then I was in funds again. Oh, Kit, don't frown like that! Are you thinking that I should rather have applied to Bonamy Ripple? I couldn't, you see, because he had gone off to Paris, and the matter was – was a little urgent!'

For as long as Kit could remember, this elderly and extremely wealthy dandy had run tame about his home, regarded by himself and Evelyn as a fit subject for ridicule, and by their father with indifference. He had been one of Lady Denville's many suitors, and when she had married Lord Denville he had become her most faithful cicisbeo. He was generally supposed to have remained a bachelor for her sake; but since his figure resembled nothing so much as an over-ripe pear, and his countenance was distinguished only by an expression of vacuous amiability and the snuff-stains on his fat cheeks, not even the more determined brewers of scandal-broth could detect anything in his devotion but food for mockery. The twins, inured to his frequent appearances in Hill Street, accepted him with much the same contemptuous tolerance as they would have felt for an over-fed lap-dog which their mama chose to encourage. But although Kit would have hooted with ribald laughter at the suggestion that any impropriety attached to Sir Bonamy's fidelity he was far from thinking it desirable that his mother should apply to him for help in her financial difficulties, and he said so.

'Good gracious, Kit, as though I hadn't often done so!' she exclaimed. 'It is by far the most comfortable arrangement, because he is so rich that he doesn't care how many of my bonds he holds, and never does he demand the interest on the loans he makes me! As for dunning me to repay him, I am persuaded such a notion never entered his head. He may be absurd, and growing fatter every day, but I have been used to depend on him for years, in all manner of ways! It was he who sold my jewels for me, and had them copied, for instance, besides –' She stopped abruptly. 'Oh, I wish I had never mentioned him! It has brought it all back to me! *That* was what made Evelyn go away!'

'Ripple?' he asked, wholly at sea.

'No, Lord Silverdale,' she replied.

'For the lord's sake, Mama –!' he expostulated. 'What *are* you talking about? What the deuce has Silverdale to say to anything?'

'He has a brooch of mine,' she said, sunk suddenly into gloom. 'I staked it, when he wouldn't accept my vowels, and continue playing. Something told me the luck was about to turn, and so it might have, if Silverdale would but have played on. Not that I cared for losing the brooch, for I never liked it above half, and can't conceive why I should have purchased it. I expect it must have taken my fancy, but I don't recall why.'

'Has Evelyn gone off to redeem it?' he interrupted. 'Where is Silverdale?'

'At Brighton. Evelyn said there was no time to be lost in buying the brooch back, so off he posted – at least, he drove himself, in his phaeton, with his new team of grays, and he said that he meant to go first to Ravenhurst, which, indeed, he did –'

'Just a moment, Mama!' Kit intervened, the frown returning to his brow. 'Why did Evelyn feel it necessary to go to Brighton? Of course he was obliged to redeem your brooch – Silverdale must have expected him to do so! – but I should have supposed that a letter to Silverdale, with a draft on his bank for whatever sum the brooch represented, would have answered the purpose.'

Lady Denville raised large, stricken eyes to his face. 'Yes, but you don't perfectly understand how it was, dearest. I can't *think* how I came to be so addlebrained, but when I staked it I had quite forgotten that it was one of the pieces I had had copied! For my part, I consider Silverdale was very well served for having been so quizzy and disobliging about accepting my vowels, but Evelyn said that it was of the first importance to recover the wretched thing before Silverdale discovered that it was only a copy.'

Mr Fancot drew an audible breath. 'I should rather think he might say so!'

'But, Kit!' said her ladyship earnestly, 'that is *much* more improvident than anything I should dream of doing! I set its value at £500, which *was* the value of the real brooch, but the copy isn't worth a tithe of that! It seems to be quite wickedly extravagant of Evelyn to be squandering such a sum on mere trumpery!'

Mr Fancot toyed for a moment with the idea of explaining to his erratic parent that her view of the matter was, to put it mildly, incorrect. But only for a moment. He was an intelligent young man, and he almost instantly realized that any such attempt would be a waste of breath. So he merely said, as soon as he could command his voice to say anything: 'Yes, well, never mind that! When did Evelyn set forth on this errand?'

'Dear one, you cannot have been attending! I *told* you! Ten days ago!'

'Well, it wouldn't have taken him ten days to accomplish it, if Silverdale was in Brighton, so it seems that he can't have been there. Evelyn must have discovered where he was gone to, and decided to follow him.'

She brightened. 'Oh, do you think that is what happened? I have been a prey to the most *hideous* forebodings! But if Silverdale has gone to that place of his in Yorkshire it is very understandable that Evelyn shouldn't have returned yet.' She paused, considering the matter, and then shook her head. 'No. Evelyn didn't go to Yorkshire. He spent one night at Ravenhurst, just as he told me he would; and then he drove to Brighton. That I *do* know, for his groom accompanied him; but whether he found Silverdale there or not I can't tell, because, naturally, Challow doesn't know. But he returned to Ravenhurst the same day, and stayed the night there. I thought he would do that – in fact, I thought he must have stayed for several days, for he told me that he had matters to attend to at home, and might be absent from London for perhaps as much as a sennight. But he left Ravenhurst the very next morning, and under the most *peculiar* circumstances!'

'In what way peculiar, Mama?'

'He took only his night-bag with him, and he sent Challow back to London with the rest of his gear, saying that he had no need of him.'

'Oh!' said Kit. His tone was thoughtful, but not astonished. 'Did he tell Challow where he was going?'

'No, and that is another circumstance which makes me very uneasy.'

'It need not,' he said, amusement flickering in his eyes. 'Did he send his valet back to London too? I take it that Fimber is still with him?'

'Yes, and that is *another* thing that cuts up my peace!

He wouldn't take Fimber to Sussex: he said there was no room for him in the phaeton, which is true, of course, though it set up all Fimber's bristles. I must own that I wished he might have found room for him, because I *know* Fimber will never let him come to harm. Challow is very good too, but not – not as *firm*! It is the greatest comfort to know that they are both with Evelyn when he goes off on one of his starts.'

'I'm sure it is, Mama,' he said gravely.

'But that's just it!' she pointed out. '*Neither* is with him! Kit, it's no laughing matter! I'm persuaded that some accident has befallen him, or that he's in some dreadful scrape! How *can* you laugh?'

'I couldn't, if I thought it was true. Now, come out of the dismals, Mama! I never knew you to be such a goose! What do you imagine could have happened to Evelyn?'

'You don't think – you don't think that he did see Silverdale, and quarrelled with him, and – and went off alone that day to *meet* him?'

'Taking his night-bag with him in place of a second! Good God, no! You *have* put yourself into the hips, love! If I know Evelyn, he's gone off on a private affair which he don't want you to know anything about! You would, if he had taken Fimber or Challow with him, and he's well aware of that. They may be a comfort to you, my dear, but they're often a curst embarrassment to him! As for accidents – fudge! You'd have been apprised of anything of that nature: depend upon it, he didn't set out to visit Silverdale without his card-case!'

'No, very true!' she agreed. 'I never thought of that!' Her spirits revived momentarily, only to sink again. Her beautiful eyes clouded; she said: 'But at such a moment, Kit! When so much hinges upon his presenting himself in Mount Street tomorrow! Oh, no, he *could* not have gone off on one of his adventures!'

'Couldn't he?' said Kit. 'I wonder! I wish you will tell me a little more about this engagement of his, Mama.

You've said that there has been no time for him to tell me about it himself, but that's doing it very much too brown, my dear! There might have been no time for a letter to have reached me, telling me that he had come to the point of offering for this girl; but he never mentioned her name to me in the last letter I had from him, far less the possibility that he would shortly be married; and that, you know, is so unlike him that if anyone but you had broken this news to me I should have thought it a Banbury story. Now, I know of only one reason which would make Evelyn withhold his confidence from me.' He paused, his eyelids puckering, as though he were trying to bring some remote object into focus. 'If he were in some fix from which I couldn't help him to escape – if he were forced into doing something repugnant to him –'

'Oh, no, no, no!' cried Lady Denville distressfully. 'It is *not* repugnant to him, and he was *not* forced into it! He discussed it with me in the most reasonable manner, saying that while he was resolved on matrimony, he believed it would suit him best to – to enter upon a contract in the oldfashioned way, without violence of feeling on either side. And I must say, Kit, that I think he is very right, for the females he falls in love with are *never* eligible – in fact, excessively *ineligible*! Moreover, he is so very prone to fall in love, poor boy, that it is of the first importance to arrange a match for him with a sensible, well-bred girl who won't break her heart, or come to points with him, every time she discovers that he has a *chère amie*.'

'Of the first importance –!' he exclaimed. 'For Evelyn, of all men! I collect that if she is sufficiently indifferent and well-bred nothing else is of consequence! She may be bran-faced or swivel-eyed or –'

'On the contrary! It goes without saying that there must be nothing in her appearance to give Evelyn a disgust of her; and also that each of them should be ready to like the other.'

He sprang up, ejaculating: 'Oh, good God!' He glanced

down at her, his eyes very bright, but not with laughter. '*You* made such a marriage, Mama! Is that what you wish Evelyn to do? Is it?'

She did not answer for a moment; and when she did speak it was with a little constriction. 'I didn't make such a marriage, Kit. Your father fell in love with me. The Fancots said he was besotted, but nothing would turn him from his determination to marry me. And I – well, I was just seventeen, and he was so handsome, so exactly like the heroes schoolgirls dream of –! But the Fancots were right: we were very ill-suited.'

He said, in an altered tone: 'I didn't know – I beg your pardon, Mama! I shouldn't have spoken to you so. But you haven't told me the truth. All this talk of Evelyn's being *resolved on matrimony*, as though he were four-and-thirty rather than four-and-twenty –! Flummery!'

'I have told you the truth!' she declared indignantly. She read disbelief in his face, and amended this statement. 'Well, *some* of it, anyway!'

He could not help smiling at this. 'Tell me all the truth! A little while ago you said it was my uncle's fault – also your fault – but in what conceivable way could either of you make it necessary for Evelyn to contract a marriage of convenience? Evelyn doesn't depend on my uncle for his livelihood, nor is he answerable to him for anything he may choose to do! The only power my uncle has is to refuse to permit him to spend any part of his principal – if he should wish to do so!'

'But that is just what he does wish to do!' she replied. 'At least, I can't suppose that he *wishes* to do it precisely – except that it would be a great relief to him to be rid of all the worry and bother of my debts.'

'Your debts! But – Is Miss Stavely an heiress? and is Evelyn crazy enough to imagine that he will be able to dispose of her fortune as he pleases? It isn't possible!'

'No, and he wouldn't dream of doing such a thing, if it were! He means to settle my debts out of his own fortune.

He says – and you did too, Kit! – that Papa should have done so, and that it is just the same as if he had. And also he says that he is determined your uncle shall know nothing about it. So he went to see him, to try if he couldn't prevail upon him to end the Trust – putting it on the score of his age, and how much he dislikes being treated as though he were a schoolboy. Which is true, Kit!'

'Yes, I know it is. What had my uncle to say to that?'

'Well, he didn't say very much to Evelyn – only that he would be glad to be rid of the Trust, and would willingly end it the instant Evelyn had finished sowing his wild oats. But afterwards he came to see me, and although he was very stiff, I do him the justice to acknowledge that he discussed the matter with far less of that reserve of his which I find so *daunting*! He spoke very kindly of Evelyn, saying that he has many excellent qualities, and that in spite of being far too heedless and rackety he doesn't commit horrid excesses, or frequent low company, which (Henry says) has become the fashion amongst a certain set of young men. And then he said he would be happy to see him married to some female of character, since he had been brought to believe that marriage would be the making of him, and cause him to become more settled and responsible – though not, he fears, such a pattern-card as *you*!'

'Much obliged to him! What can have possessed him to say anything so foolhardy? Did you give him snuff?'

She laughed. 'No, I was more inclined to embrace him for holding you in esteem. Besides, I know it to be true. Oh, I don't mean that you are a pattern-card of *virtue*, so you needn't look so – so –'

'Dog-sick?' suggested her ungrateful offspring.

'*Odious* creature! All I meant to say – and your uncle too! – was that you are more – more *dependable* than Evelyn. You always were. I wish you will stop funning: this is a *serious* matter!' She looked up at him, smiling ruefully. 'I know I'm lightminded, Kit, but not when it is a question of my sons' welfare, I promise you! I would make *any* sacrifice – indeed, I have been wondering whether I ought not to change this room again, and make it all blue, or pink, or straw-coloured, no matter how commonplace it would be. They say that green is an unlucky colour, you know, and there's no denying that my luck has been quite out for months, which is not the least helpful to poor Evelyn. I thought that if only I could win a fortune all his troubles would be over. Well, they would have been, but the luck hardly ever runs my way. Yes, and that puts me in mind of something that has me in a puzzle! One is for ever hearing of persons who have *lost* their fortunes at gaming, but one never hears of anyone who has *won* a fortune. It seems very odd to me. Where *do* all the lost fortunes go to?'

'Never into your pocket, love – that's all I know! So don't, I implore you, change this room! I dare say *that* would cost a fortune.'

'Yes, but I shouldn't grudge a penny of it!' she said earnestly. She added, with a touch of asperity: 'And I am quite at a loss to understand why you should go into whoops!'

'Never mind, Mama!' he said unsteadily. 'Only don't – don't m-make sacrifices for Evelyn! I'm persuaded he won't appreciate them as – as he ought!'

'I don't care for that. But it's of no consequence! I wasn't thinking of fortunes and debts when I told you it was a serious matter: indeed, I can't imagine how we come to be talking of such trivial things! Kit, I would not say so to your uncle, but from you I need conceal nothing! You think it is mercenary of me to arrange an eligible marriage for Evelyn, but it isn't! It can't be mercenary to wish him to be comfortable, which he will be, because Henry says the Trust shall be wound up as soon as he is safely married. He disclosed to me that he had never thought it right of Denville to create it, but considered himself bound in honour to abide by his expressed wish. Well, it would be nonsensical to deny that it is of the greatest importance for Evelyn to be free to do as he chooses with his inheritance, but that wouldn't have weighed with me if I hadn't felt the force of Henry's words. Indeed, I wasn't even thinking about it!' She hesitated, a crease between her arched brows. 'No one understands Evelyn as well as you, Kit, but you have been abroad for so long that I fancy you don't know – are not quite aware – Oh, dear, it is so very difficult to explain it to you!'

All trace of laughter had vanished from his eyes. They became suddenly intent, searching her face. He sat down again beside her, and took one of her hands in a reassuring clasp. 'I know. *I* find myself unable to explain to *you* the feeling I've had – oh, for a long time now! – that something is amiss. But what it may be I've never discovered, which has made me think it could be nothing of a serious nature.'

'Oh, no!' she said quickly. 'But he's so restless, Kit, and so wild! No, that's not the word. *He* calls it being always ripe for a spree, but it has sometimes seemed to me that he commits extravagant follies because he is bored, and can find nothing else to do. And when Henry spoke of his becoming settled, and responsible, I suddenly knew that he was perfectly right. I mean, if he were suitably married, and had the estates to manage, besides setting up his nursery – and however disagreeable the thought of being a grandmother may be I am determined to bear it – he would be more – more content. He would have things to occupy him, and you know what he is, Kit! – he can never be happy unless he is *doing* something! And, situated as he is, he has nothing to do but get into mischief, which I shouldn't care a straw for, if only it amused him! But I don't think it does, except for a very little while, do you, Kit?'

'No. That is, I don't know, but I understand what you mean!'

She squeezed his hand gratefully. 'I knew you must! And you will understand that when Harry said that, about marriage being the making of Evelyn, I began instantly to cast about in my mind, and naturally hit upon Cressy.'

'Cressy?'

'Cressida – Miss Stavely! In every respect what one would wish for, Kit! A young woman of the first consideration – not a schoolroom chit, full of romantic notions! She has what Henry calls a well-regulated mind, though she is not, I assure you, a blue-stocking. I don't say she is a *beauty*, but I think her very pretty, and with a good deal of countenance, besides having a well-formed figure, and truly *exquisite* taste! She will fill her position to admiration – better by far than I ever did! – for she conducts herself with perfect propriety, and will never give Evelyn cause to blush for her!'

'And how comes it about that this highly finished piece of nature is on the shelf?' he asked sceptically.

'She is *not* on the shelf! To be sure, she is twenty, which might lead you to suppose that she had never received any eligible offers, but that is not the case at all! She received several offers when her grandmama brought her out, but she refused them all, because she thought it her duty to remain with her papa. She *said* she had met no one she liked better than Stavely, but the fact is that she is his only child, and she has kept house for him since she was sixteen. He was used to dote on her, too.'

'What caused him to stop doting on her?'

'Oh, I daresay he still does so, but he would be afraid for his life to betray it! What must he do, when one would have supposed him to be past the age of such folly, but form an attachment for a female not very much older than Cressy, and marry her! Well, I never had a very high idea of his understanding – he formed a passion for me, you know, when I was first out, and behaved like a perfect moonling – but I thought he had grown to be quite rational! But to have allowed himself to be caught by Albinia Gillifoot –! He must be about in his head! She keeps him dancing attendance on her, which will very soon make him regret his imprudence; and she's as jealous as a cat, particularly of poor Cressy.'

'Oh, so that's why poor Cressy is willing to accept Evelyn, is it?'

'Of course it is! Really, nothing could have been more providential!'

'I hope she thinks so!'

'No, but I do, and so does your uncle! When I mentioned Cressy to him he almost *approved* of me!' Her eyes danced. 'He said he had never looked for so much good sense in me! *Unexceptionable*, he called her, and one with *strength of character*!'

'And what does Evelyn call her?' inquired Kit, in a voice of polite interest.

'Evelyn told me that he believed she might be the very thing he had in mind. You mustn't think I urged him in any way, Kit! Indeed, I begged him not to make her an offer if he felt he could not like her; but he assured me that he does like her. He is not very well acquainted with her, for although she has frequently visited me, and I have chaperoned her to balls now and then, because I am her godmother, her mama having been a particular friend of mine, he has never paid her any extraordinary attention.'

'Not his style, eh?'

'If you mean she is not in the style of the girls he tumbles in and out of love with, no, and a very good thing too! He believes they may deal very comfortably together, and so do I. *He* won't feel leg-shackled, and *she* won't fall into a grand fuss over his little *affaires*. She must be accustomed to such things. I could furnish you with the names of at least three of Stavely's mistresses, and you may depend upon it that Cressy is well aware of his being quite a man of the town. Kit, I know you don't like it, but I must tell you that Evelyn's mind is made up: he is *determined* to marry. I needn't tell *you* how impossible it is to turn him from his purpose when he gets that *obstinate* look in his face. I don't know what passed between him and Cressy, when he popped the question, but he told me afterwards he thought himself very fortunate. Nothing was farther from his intention than to cry off! Why, he even said that he meant to return from Ravenhurst in good time to adonize himself for the encounter with old Lady Stavely! And if he doesn't return tomorrow his tale will be told, for Lady Stavely is bound to take a pet – and small blame to her! Only think how brass-faced it would be of him! And then he would offer for some girl not nearly as suitable, and be wretchedly uncomfortable for the rest of his life! Oh, Kit, what am I to do? If he hasn't suffered an accident, I have the most lowering fear that something has happened to put his engagement in Mount Street out of his mind. You can't deny that he *does* forget things!'

Since very much the same explanation of his twin's continued absence had long since occurred to him Mr Fancot made no attempt to deny it, merely saying, in a heartening tone: 'Well, if he doesn't return in time to attend this party you must inform Stavely that he has been taken ill suddenly.'

'I thought of that myself, but it won't do, Kit! If Evelyn could send me a message, he could send one to Mount Street as well.'

'Too ill to write!' he said promptly. 'One of the servants brought the news to you!'

'Well, of all the bird-witted suggestions!' she exclaimed. 'If that were the case I should be compelled to post off to Ravenhurst immediately, and I don't mean to do any such thing! What's more, Kit, if I were to set that story about, Evelyn would drive into London the very next day, as sure as check! Looking as bright as a button, and exchanging greetings with half-a-dozen persons, and very likely more!'

He grinned. 'Yes, very true! That would make mice-feet of the whole business, wouldn't it?'

'Oh, Kit, don't joke me! I am going *distracted*!'

He put his arm round her. 'No, no, don't go distracted, Mama! If the worst comes to the worst I can always take Evelyn's place, can't I?'

3

These lighthearted words, uttered with no other purpose than to banish the woebegone expression from Lady Denville's face, were productive of an unexpected result. She had relaxed within Kit's arm, leaning her head on his shoulder, but his frivolous speech acted on her like a powerful restorative. She sat up suddenly, and, staring at him with widened eyes, breathed: '*Kit*! The very thing!'

Startled, he said: 'I was only funning, Mama!'

She paid no heed to this, but embraced him warmly, saying: 'I might have known you would come to the rescue! How *could* I be such a ninnyhammer as not to have thought of it myself? *Dear* Kit!'

Mr Fancot, realizing too late that he had committed an error of judgement, made haste to retrieve his position. 'You didn't think of it because it's an absurdity. I said it only to make you laugh! Of course I couldn't take Evelyn's place!'

'But you *could*, Kit! Why, you have frequently done so!'

'When we were hey-go-mad boys, kicking up larks! Mama, you must surely perceive that this is a very different matter! Setting aside all other considerations, how could I hope to fob myself off as Evelyn at such a gathering?'

'But nothing could be easier!' she responded.

'Mama, do, pray, consider! I apprehend this party is to be composed of the various members of the family. Well, I know Stavely, admittedly, but not another soul should I recognize – least of all the girl to whom I should be supposed to be betrothed!'

She disposed unhesitatingly of this objection. 'You will recognize Cressy, because she will receive you, with Stavely and his new wife. As for the rest, Evelyn doesn't know them either.'

'And Miss Stavely herself?' he demanded. 'Can you believe that she wouldn't detect the imposture?'

'Oh, I am persuaded she won't!' responded her ladyship blithely. 'Recollect that she is not closely acquainted with Evelyn! The only occasion on which they have been alone together was when he proposed to her. Then, too, she doesn't *expect* to see you instead of Evelyn. That is *very* important!'

'Of course she doesn't expect it! But –'

'No, no, you don't understand what I mean, dearest! It won't occur to *anyone* that you are not Evelyn, because no one knows that you've come home. It would be a very different matter if you resided here, when people would be accustomed to find themselves talking to the wrong twin. You can't have forgotten how it was before you went abroad! Why, persons who had known you from your cradles were used to say, when either of you came into the room: 'Now, which of them is this?' *Then* there was always the possibility that the one who was thought to be Evelyn would presently be found to be you, so that people naturally stared very hard at you, trying to decide which of you it was. But you have been abroad now for three years, and no one wonders any more if Evelyn is *really* Evelyn. He couldn't be you, because you are in Vienna. My dear, *providence* must have caused you to arrive at this ridiculous hour, and without a word of warning! Not a soul has the smallest suspicion that you are not still in Vienna!'

Mr Fancot was much inclined to think that not providence but his evil genius had been at work, but he kept this reflection to himself, applying his energies instead to the task of pointing out to his parent the various reasons which made her scheme impossible. He was singularly unsuccessful. The more Lady Denville dwelled on it the more enamoured of it did she become; and when Kit told her that it was fantastic, she said enthusiastically: 'Yes, isn't it? That's what makes it so excellent! Nobody would ever dream we should dare do anything so out of the way!'

'Not out of the way! *Outrageous*!'

She looked at him with misgiving, and said: 'You know, Kit, I never did quite like it when you joined the diplomatic service. I had the greatest dread that you might grow to be like Henry, and I was right! Dearest, I hate pinching at you, but I couldn't *bear* it if you became prim and prosy!'

'Oh, dear!' said Kit, dismayed. 'Am I prim and prosy? I'd no suspicion of it!'

'No, love,' she replied, patting his hand. 'Naturally you had not, which is why I feel it to be my duty to drop a word of warning in your ear, so that you may overcome the tendency. You're not like Henry *yet*, but when you said *outrageous*, in that condemning way, you did put me in mind of him. You didn't care a rush about doing outrageous things before he pushed you into being a diplomat, and never would you have raised all the foolish objections!'

'I was three years younger then, Mama.'

'So was Evelyn, but *he* hasn't changed! In your place he wouldn't hesitate for a moment, *or* think about propriety, *or* be afraid to take a trifling risk or two! I can't think what has come over you, Kit!'

'The diplomatic service, and a want of dash. Alas that you should have given birth to a pudding-heart, Mama!'

'That I would never believe!' she declared.

'Thank you, love! It pains me to disillusion you, but when I think of coolly walking into Stavely's house, and palming myself off as Evelyn, I find myself shaking like a blancmanger!'

She laughed. 'Oh, no, Kit! That's coming it too strong! You never did so in your life. I know very well you are not afraid, but you do seem to me to be sadly *cautious*!' She put up her hand to his cheek, compelling him to turn his head fully towards her. 'Don't banter me, but tell me the truth, wicked one! Do you think you couldn't do it?'

He hesitated. Then he said bluntly: 'No. For one evening, amongst a set of persons who are not well enough acquainted with Evelyn to know his mannerisms, I'm pretty confident I could do it. And, in certain circumstances, I'm not yet so prim and prosy that I shouldn't enjoy doing it!'

'There!' she said triumphantly. 'I knew you couldn't have changed so *very* much!'

'No, Mama, but this isn't a matter of playing a Canterbury trick on people who would think it a very good joke if they found me out. But to cut such a sham to gain an advantage is quite another pair of shoes. And only think, Mama, what a humiliating insult I should be offering to Miss Stavely!'

'I don't see that, Kit. For one thing, she won't know it; and, for another, she would be much more humiliated if you *didn't* take Evelyn's place. Do but consider! Can you conceive of anything more – more *annihilating* than to be obliged to tell all the relations who have been invited to meet one's betrothed that he has excused himself from attending the party? For my part, I should be *grateful* for the masquerade!' She caught his hand, and pressed it. 'Kit, for Evelyn's sake! He would do it for you!'

That was undeniable. Evelyn would do it, and revel in it, thought his twin, with a gleam of amusement.

'Only for one day!' urged Lady Denville.

'If we could be sure of that! What if it should prove to be very much more than one day? I couldn't maintain such an imposture: I should be bound to run against his cronies – some, perhaps, whom I shouldn't even recognize!'

'Oh, if Evelyn doesn't come back in a day or two, we shall say you are unwell, or have been obliged to leave town on business! But he will, Kit! Indeed, I have a feeling that he will return tomorrow.'

'I hope to God he does!' said Kit fervently.

'Yes, but we must be *provident*, dearest, and be ready to meet any mischance. And, do you know, I have suddenly thought that it might be a good thing if you *should* be obliged to go to the party in his stead! I very much fear that old Lady Stavely has heard tales about him which have made her suspect him of being rather wild – in fact, quite ramshackle, which is untrue, of course, or, at all events, grossly exaggerated! And although he means to behave with the greatest propriety I can't help thinking that you would deal with her much better, through being a diplomat, and knowing how to look grave and sober at formal parties, which Evelyn hasn't the least idea of. I won't conceal from you, Kit, that if Cressy's aunts and uncles and cousins are a set of dead bores, which is extremely likely – only consider one's own relations! – I have the liveliest fear that Evelyn will say something outrageous, or excuse himself far too early in the evening, which would be *fatal*!'

'If Evelyn does not return tomorrow,' said Kit, with feeling, 'I'll wring his neck the instant I set eyes on him! And if he does return neither he nor you, my very dear Mama, will persuade me to take his place at this party! Nothing short of the direst necessity would induce me to do so!'

'No, dear, and we must hope there won't be any necessity,' she agreed cheerfully. 'But just in case there should be you won't object to pretending you are Evelyn for a *little* while, will you? I mean, until he arrives, which I dare say he will, for even he couldn't be quite so forgetful, do you think? But if he doesn't it would be most unwise to let the servants know the truth.'

'Good God, Mama, do you imagine they won't recognize me?'

'Well, the maidservants won't, and the footmen won't, and Brigg won't either, because he is getting so short-sighted and deaf. We ought to engage a younger butler, but when Evelyn only *hinted* to him that he should retire on a *very* handsome pension he was thrown into such gloom that Evelyn felt obliged to let the matter drop.'

'And what of Mrs Dinting?' interposed Kit.

'Why should she suspect anything? If you were to encounter her, you have only to greet her, as Evelyn would, quite carelessly, you know. Depend upon it, she won't even wonder if you're Kit, because she would never believe you would come home after all these months and not pay a visit to the housekeeper's room to have a chat with her. Then, too, she will have been told that Evelyn is home, and why should she call it in question?'

'Who is going to tell her this whisker? You?'

'No, stupid! The servants will see that the candle that was set on the hall-table for Evelyn has gone, and the whole household will know that he has returned before you are even awake.'

'Including Fimber! I collect he won't recognize me either? Mama, *do* come out of the clouds! A man who valeted us both when we were striplings!'

'I am not in the clouds!' she said indignantly. 'I was about to say, when you interrupted me, that we must take him into our confidence.'

'Also Challow, your coachman, the second groom, all the stableboys, –'

'Nonsense, Kit! Challow, perhaps, but why in the world should the others be told?'

'Because, my love, there is a phaeton and four horses to be accounted for!'

She thought this over for a moment. 'Very true. Oh, well, we must trust Challow to do that! You can't think he won't be able to: recollect what *convincing* lies he was used to tell when Papa tried to discover from him what you had been doing whenever you had slipped away without telling anyone where you were going!'

'Mama,' said Kit, 'I am going to bed! I haven't given back – don't think it! – but if I argue with you any more tonight I shall end with windmills in my head!'

'Oh, poor boy, of course you must be fagged to death!' she said, with ready sympathy. 'Nothing is so fatiguing as a long journey! That accounts for your perceiving so many difficulties in the way: it is always so when one is very weary. Go to bed, dear one: you will feel much more yourself when you wake up!'

'Full of spunk – not to say effrontery, eh?' he said, laughing. He kissed her, and got up. 'It's midsummer moon with you, you know – but don't think I don't love you!'

She smiled serenely upon him, and he went to retrieve his belongings from the half-landing, and to carry them into Evelyn's bedroom.

He was so tired that instead of applying his mind to the problems confronting him, as he had meant to do, he fell asleep within five minutes of blowing out his candle. He was awakened, some hours later, by the sound of the blinds being drawn back from the windows. He raised himself on his elbow, wondering, for a moment, where he could be. Then he remembered, and lay down again, rather mischievously awaiting events.

The curtains round the bed were pulled apart with a ruthlessness which was a clear sign to the initiated that the supposed occupant of the great four-poster was in his devoted valet's black books. Kit yawned, and murmured: ''Morning, Fimber: what's o'clock?'

'Good morning, my lord,' responded Fimber, in arctic accents. 'It is past ten, but as I apprehend that your lordship did not return until the small hours I thought it best not to wake you earlier.'

'No, I was very late,' agreed Kit.

'I am aware of that, my lord – having sat up until midnight, in the expectation of being required to wait on you.'

'Stupid fellow! You should have known better,' said Kit, watching him from under his eyelids.

The expression of cold severity on Fimber's face deepened. He said, picking his words: 'Possibly it did not occur to your lordship that your continued absence would give rise to anxiety.'

'Lord, no! Why should it?'

This careless rejoinder had the effect of turning the ice to fire. 'My lord, where have you been?' demanded Fimber, abandoning his quelling formality.

'Don't you wish you knew!'

'No, my lord, I do not, nor it isn't necessary I should know, for what I *do* know is that you wouldn't have been so anxious not to let me go with you if the business which took you off had been as innocent as you'd have me believe. Nor you wouldn't have sent Challow home! You should think shame to yourself, staying away all this time, and never sending her ladyship word to stop her fretting herself to ribbons! For anything she knew you might have been dead! Now, just tell me this, my lord, without trying to tip me a rise, which you know you can't do! – are you in a scrape?'

'I don't know,' replied Kit truthfully. 'I hope not.'

'So you may well, my lord! At a time like this! If it's serious, tell me, and we'll see what can be done.'

'I can't tell you what I don't know, Fimber.'

'Indeed, my lord?' said Fimber ominously. 'I *should* have thought that your lordship knew I could be trusted, but it seems I was mistaken.' He turned away, deeply offended, and walked across the room to where Kit's open portmanteau stood. Kit had done no more than drag his night-gear out of it, considerably disarranging the rest of its contents. Muttering disapproval to himself, Fimber stooped to unpack it. He lifted up a waistcoat, took one look at it, and turned swiftly to find Kit watching him quizzically. He stood staring for an incredulous moment, and then gave a gasp. 'Mr Christopher!'

Kit laughed, and sat up, pulling off his night-cap. 'I thought you were the one person we couldn't hoax! How are you, Fimber?'

'Quite stout, thank you, sir. And you wouldn't have hoaxed me for long! To think of you taking us all by surprise like this! Does her ladyship know?'

'Yes, she heard me come in, and got up, hoping to see my brother.'

'Ay, no wonder! But I'll be bound she was glad to see you, sir. Which I am too, if I may say so.' He glanced critically at the waistcoat he was holding, and sniffed. 'You never had this made for you in London, Mr Christopher. You won't be wearing it here, of course. Is that foreign man of yours bringing the rest of your baggage after you?'

'No, it's coming by carrier. I haven't brought Franz with me. I knew I could depend on you to look after me.' Receiving no immediate response to this, he said, surprised: 'You're not going to tell me I can't, are you? Fimber!'

The valet emerged with a start from what bore all the appearance of a profound reverie. 'I beg your pardon, sir! I was thinking. Look after you? To be sure I will!' He added, as he laid the condemned waistcoat aside, and picked up the greatcoat which Kit had flung across a chair: 'And time I did, Mr Christopher! These Polish coats are gone quite out of fashion. Nor you can't wear that shallow in London: the present mode, sir, is for high crowns.'

'Never mind my dowdy rig!' said Kit. 'What the devil is my brother doing?'

'I don't know any more than you do, sir, and it's got me all of a twitter! It might be that he went off in one of his distempered freaks, and yet I don't think it, somehow. My lady will have told you that he's in a way to become buckled?'

'She did, but *he* has never so much as given me a hint of it,' replied Kit grimly. 'Something damned brummish about the business! Well, if anyone knows the truth you do, so tell it to me, without any hiding of the teeth! Is he turning short about?'

'No, that I'll go bail he's not!' Fimber replied. 'No one knows better than me the sort of bobbery he'll get up to when he's in high leg, but he wouldn't play nip-shot now – not when he's made the young lady an offer! What's more, he wasn't poking bogey when he told me, and her ladyship too, that he would be back within the sennight, for he bid me to be sure to engage the barber to come to trim his hair today. He will be here, sir, at noon.'

'And what, pray, has that to do with me?' asked Kit, eyeing him with misgiving.

'It occurs to me, sir, that you are wearing your hair too long. His lordship favours more of a Corinthian cut.'

'Oh, does he? Now, you may stop pitching your gammon, and tell me this! – Are you thinking that I might take my brother's place tonight?'

'Well, sir,' said Fimber apologetically, 'the notion *did* cross my mind! It seems as if it was *meant,* you coming home without a soul's being the wiser, and not bringing that foreigner with you – and no need to worry about your baggage, for you may leave it to me to see it safely stored. No need to worry about your clothing either, because his lordship has enough and to spare for the pair of you. Nor it wouldn't be the first time you've changed shoes with him, not by any means it wouldn't be!'

'The circumstances were very different. I've told my mother that already.'

Fimber turned a shocked countenance towards him. 'You told my lady you wouldn't help his lordship to bring himself home? Well! Never did I think to see the day when you would not be ready to through stitch in *anything* for his sake, Mr Christopher! As he would for you, no matter what might come of it!'

'I know that. Nor would I hang back an instant, however much against the pluck it might be, if I were convinced it was what he wished me to do. But that's where the water sticks, Fimber: I've a strong feeling that there's nothing he wishes less than to marry Miss Stavely. If that's so, I should be better employed trying my possible to bring him safe off.'

'You can't do that, sir! Why, he's offered for her! You wouldn't have him play the jack, putting such a slight on the poor young lady – no, and he wouldn't do it! I don't say he hasn't often set people in a bustle with his starts, but I've never known him behave ungentlemanly, not in all the years I've served you both!'

'I was wondering rather if I couldn't contrive to get Miss Stavely to cry off. I wish you will be open with me! Don't try to persuade me that he isn't blue-devilled: I *know* he is!'

'Well, sir, since you ask me, in my opinion he wasn't near as blue-devilled when I saw him last as what he has been ever since –' Fimber broke off in embarrassment.

'Ever since when? Go on, man!' said Kit impatiently.

Fimber began with finicking care to fold the despised waistcoat. His reply was evasive. 'It is not my place, Mr Christopher, to speak of the circumstances which might have caused his lordship to offer for Miss Stavely, but he didn't make up his mind to it in the twinkling of a bed-post, as you might say. So don't you get to thinking that he did it on the spur of the moment, and was sorry for it after, because that's not so. I'm not saying it was what he'd have chosen to do, for often and often he's told me that he's got no fancy to become a tenant-for-life, never having met any female he didn't think a dead bore after a month or two. Well, I didn't pay much heed to that, not at first, thinking he'd get to be more sober when he was older, like you have, sir.' He paused, looking undecidedly at Kit. Then he said, as though impelled: 'Mr Christopher, there's not a soul I'd say this to but yourself, but the truth is I've been regularly worried about him! Let alone that he's been going the pace more than he should, he's more rackety than ever he was when it was to be expected that he should always be prime for a lark, and he's beginning to take to the muslin company – which is what has me in a worse fret than all the rest!'

Kit nodded, but said frowningly: 'It sounds to me as if he were bored, or out of spirits. That always made him resty. But why?'

'I couldn't say, sir, not to be sure. Unless it might be that he's lonely.'

'*Lonely*? Good God, he has a host of friends!'

'In a manner of speaking, sir. But I wouldn't call them

intimate friends – not such as he'd tell his mind to, the way he would to you. He's never been quite the same since you went away, though it's hard to explain what I mean, and no one that didn't know him as well as I do would notice it. I dare say it comes of being a twin. You was always so close, the pair of you, that you never wanted any other cronies. His lordship never took anyone into his confidence but you, and it's my belief he won't, except, maybe, his wife. It may be otherwise with you, but –'

'No,' Kit said slowly. 'I hadn't considered it, but it isn't otherwise. But I have a good deal to occupy me, and he hasn't.'

'Exactly so, Mr Christopher, and that's where the mischief lies, as I don't doubt her ladyship would tell you.'

'She has told me. But whether the remedy lies in marrying him to a girl he don't care a rap for I strongly doubt.'

'Well, sir, it isn't what one would have chosen, but the way he's carrying on now he never will be married. What's more, if my Lord Brumby was to discover the sort of company he keeps he wouldn't end that Trust a day before he was obliged to. If you'll pardon my saying so, sir, your father may have meant it for the best, but he served his lordship the worst turn he could, when he put that slight on him!'

'Took it very much to heart, didn't he? That was the only time he ever buttoned up against me. He barely spoke about it. I was afraid it would rankle.'

'Yes, sir, and so it has! It wasn't a bit of use trying to persuade him that the thing to do was to prove to my Lord Brumby that he was very well able to manage his affairs. Well, you know what he is when he's been put into a real flame, Mr Christopher! Not a bit of interest will he take in his estates: it's seldom he even visits them, which isn't surprising, for he's got no power to do a mortal thing without he has his uncle's leave, and I know well he feels downright humiliated.'

'As bad as that, is it? Damnation! I wish I had been

at home! I might have been able to bring him and my uncle together. They never liked one another, but my uncle would have been willing to have given Denville a pretty free hand in the management of the estates, had he wished for it.'

'That wouldn't have done for his lordship, sir. It's all or nothing with him.'

Kit was silent for a minute or two. 'So, to put him in possession of his estates we help him into this loveless marriage, do we?'

'You may take it that way if you choose, sir, but there's many such marriages which have turned out well. From all I hear, Miss Stavely is a very agreeable young lady, not one of the giddy sort, but with a head on her shoulders. It wouldn't surprise me if his lordship grew to be fond of her.'

'That would be something indeed!'

'Yes, sir, it would. I'll fetch your breakfast up now, for we don't want to run any risks, and it might occasion remark if you was to be seen downstairs before Mr Clent has given your hair a different cut. One comfort is that we shan't have to get his lordship's coats altered to fit you, which would have presented us with a difficulty, being so pressed for time as we are.'

'Well, that would no doubt be a comfort to my brother,' retorted Kit, 'but it's none at all to me!'

4

Shortly before eight o'clock that evening, my Lord Denville's town carriage, an impressive vehicle which bore its noble owner's arms emblazoned on the door-panels, drew up in Mount Street to set down its solitary, and extremely reluctant occupant.

No one, observing this gentleman's composure, could

have guessed that it had taken the united efforts of his mother and his brother's valet to coax and coerce him into lending himself to what he persisted in calling an outrageous masquerade.

Fimber and Mr Clent had done their work well. Mr Clent, a dedicated artist, had given Mr Fancot a modish Corinthian cut, accepting without question the explanation offered him that the length of his supposed lordship's glowing locks was due to his prolonged absence from London; and Fimber had spent a full hour teaching him how to tie his neckcloth in the intricate style favoured by his lordship. He told him that it was known as the Trône d'Amour, a piece of information which drew from the exasperated Mr Fancot the acid rejoinder that it was a singularly inappropriate style for the occasion. Mr Fancot also took exception to the really very moderate, though highly starched, points of his collar, saying that it seemed to him that his brother had become a damned dandy. But Fimber, treating him firmly but with great patience, described in such horrifying detail the height and rigidity of the very latest mode in collar-points, that he subsided, thankful that at least he was not obliged to wear these uncomfortable 'winkers'. He added that if he had known that he would be expected to rig himself in raiment more suited to a ball than to a family dinner-party nothing would have induced him to yield to his mama's persuasions. Lady Denville, striving to impress upon him the need to treat with the greatest formality an old lady who could be depended upon to take an instant dislike to any gentleman arriving at an evening party in pantaloons, did nothing to reconcile him to the ordeal awaiting him; but Fimber, deeming it to be time to put an end to such contrariness, speedily reduced him to schoolboy status by telling him severely that that was quite enough nonsense, and that he would do as he was bid. He added, as a clincher, that Mr Christopher need not try to gammon him into believing that he wasn't in the habit of wearing full evening-dress five days out of the seven. Furthermore, neither he nor her ladyship wished to listen to any further gibble-gabble about walking to Mount Street: Mr Christopher would go in the carriage, as befitted his station.

So Kit, driven in state to Mount Street, entered Lord Stavely's house looking complete to a shade. Not only was he wearing the frilled shirt, the longtailed coat, the knee-breeches, and the silk stockings which constituted the fashionable attire of a gentleman bound for Almack's: he carried a chapeau-bras under one arm, and one of his brother's snuff-boxes in his pocket, Fimber having thrust this upon him at the last moment, with an urgent reminder that my lord was well-known to be a snuff-taker.

Having relinquished the chapeau-bras into the tender care of a footman, Mr Fancot trod up the stairs in the wake of the butler, and entered the drawing-room on that portly individual's sonorous announcement.

At first glance, he received the impression that he was being scrutinized by upwards of fifty pairs of eyes. He discovered later that this was an exaggeration. His host, who was the only person whom he recognized, was chatting to a small group of people; he moved forward a step to greet the guest, and so also did two ladies. Fancot realized that he had been imperfectly coached: he had no idea which of them was the lady to whom he was supposed to have offered his hand. For one agonized moment he thought himself lost; then he saw that the taller of the two, a fashionably attired woman with elaborately dressed fair hair and a rather sharp-featured but undeniably pretty face, was in the family way; and barely repressing a sigh of relief, he bowed to her, and shook hands, exchanging greetings with a cool assurance he was far from feeling. He then turned towards her companion, smiling at her, and carrying the hand she extended to him to his lips. He thought that that was probably what Evelyn, a practised flirt, would do; but even as he lightly kissed the hand he was assailed by a fresh problem: how the devil ought he to address the girl? Did Evelyn call her Cressy, or was he still on formal terms with her? He had had as yet no opportunity to take more than a brief look at her, but he had received the impression that she was a little stiff: possibly shy, certainly reserved. Not a beauty, but a goodlooking girl, gray-eyed and brown-haired, and with a shapely figure. Well enough but quite unremarkable, and not at all the sort of female likely to appeal to Evelyn.

At this moment, and just as he released Miss Stavely's hand, one of the assembled company, an elderly spinster who had been observing him with avid curiosity, confided to a stout matron in the over-loud voice of the deaf: '*Very* handsome! That I *must* own!'

Startled, and far from gratified, Kit looked up, involuntarily meeting Miss Stavely's eyes. They held a look of twinkling appreciation; and he thought suddenly that she was more taking than he had at first supposed. He smiled, but before he could speak Lord Stavely interposed, saying: 'Come, Denville, my mother is anxious to make your acquaintance!'

He led the way across the room to where the Dowager Lady Stavely was seated in a large armchair, grimly watching their approach.

Listening to his mama's daunting description of the Dowager, Kit had insensibly formed the impression of a massive lady, with a hook nose and a commanding bosom. He realized that his imagination had misled him: the Dowager was small, and spare, with a straight nose and a flat bosom. She had a deceptive air of fragility, and her thin fingers were twisted by gout. Her expression was not that of one anxious to make Lord Denville's acquaintance. When her son rather obsequiously presented Kit, she said: 'H'm!' in a disparaging tone, and looked him over critically from head to foot before holding out her hand. That tickled his ready sense of humour, and brought a dancing smile into his eyes. He said demurely: 'I am honoured, ma'am!' and bowed politely over her hand.

'Fiddle!' she snapped. 'So you are William Denville's son, are you? You're not as goodlooking as your father.'

Lord Stavely cleared his throat deprecatingly; a faded lady of uncertain age and a harassed demeanour, who was standing beside the Dowager's chair, looked imploringly at Kit, and uttered a faint, twittering sound. He was aware of tension amongst the assembled members of the family, and began to be very much amused. He replied: 'Oh, no! But, then, my father was exceptionally goodlooking, wasn't he, ma'am?'

She glared at him; and, in another attempt to put him out of countenance, said: 'And, by what I hear, you're not as well-behaved either!'

'He was exceptionally well-behaved too,' countered Kit.

Someone behind him gave a smothered guffaw; the faded lady, blenching, said, in the voice of one expectant of a blistering set-down: 'Oh, *pray*, Mama –!'

'Pray what?' demanded the Dowager sharply.

Lord Stavely, jerked out of paralysis by a nudge from his wife's elbow, hurried into the breach, saying: 'I must make you known to my sister Clara, Denville! I believe you have not previously met, though you are acquainted, I fancy, with my eldest sister, Lady Ebchester.'

Kit, casting a swift glance round the room, saw that one of the middle-aged ladies present was favouring him with a slight smile, and an inclination of her turbaned head, and said promptly: 'Yes, indeed! But –' drawing a bow at what he believed to be a fairly safe venture – 'I have not hitherto had the pleasure of making Miss Clara Stavely's acquaintance. Your servant, ma'am!'

'And my brother!' said Stavely, edging Kit away from the Dowager's vicinity. 'You must let me present Mr Charles Stavely to you, Denville!'

'Overdoing it, George!' said Mr Stavely, in a caustic undervoice. 'I've been acquainted with Denville since his come-out.' He nodded to Kit, and gave him two fingers, observing that he hadn't seen him in the club lately.

Kit, realizing that he had placed rather too much reliance on his mother's airy assurance that Evelyn was not acquainted with any other of his betrothed's relations than her father, now knew that it behoved him to tread with even greater wariness than he had foreseen. He responded that he had lately been out of town, and passed on, to be presented to two ladies, one of whom said that they had met before, though no doubt he had forgotten the occasion. Since any gentleman, accustomed, as Kit was, to a succession of routs, balls, and official receptions, was familiar with this gambit, he dealt with it easily enough. He was then spared any further introductions by the intervention of Lady Ebchester, who shook hands with him in a very robust way, adjuring her brother in a pungent aside to stop trying to addle the poor boy's brains by presenting him to every member of the family.

'They all know who he is,' she said trenchantly, 'and if he don't know who we are, so much the better for him! If I had guessed you meant to invite the whole family, stock and block, I wouldn't have come here tonight, and nor, I dare say, would he. Anyone but a chucklehead would have known that it would only serve to make Mama as cross as crabs!' She waved him aside, and addressed herself to Kit, saying: 'No need to take fright! *I* don't know what maggot my brother got into his head, but very likely you'll never set eyes on most of these old quizzes again. How does your mother do?'

'Very well, ma'am, and desired me to convey her compliments to you.'

'Mighty civil of her – or of you!' she replied. 'We've never been on better than bowing terms. So you're going to marry my niece! I wish you happy: it won't be her fault if you're not.'

'Then we shall be, ma'am, for I am determined it shan't be mine.'

'You're full of pretty speeches,' she said, putting him

forcibly in mind of the Dowager. 'I see young Lucton wanting to edge in a word. Heaven knows what he's doing here, for he's the merest connexion! However, I dare say you're glad to see a face you do know!'

She nodded dismissal, and he turned away to confront a young gentleman of dandified appearance, who was hovering close at hand, and who greeted him with a broad grin, and drew him a little apart, saying: 'I *warned* you, Den! Devilish, ain't it? Dashed nearly sherried off to Brighton this morning: can't think why I didn't!'

'A want of nerve!'

'No, no, that wasn't it! The old lady don't take a particle of interest in me. Fact is, I wanted a word with you. You haven't forgotten that little matter I broached to you, have you?'

'No, but to own the truth I've been too busy to think about it.'

'What a fellow you are!' said Mr Lucton. 'No wish to press you, but you said you'd give me an answer within a day!'

'Oh, lord, did I?' said Kit, thankful for the first time in his life for his twin's well-known forgetfulness. 'I was called away suddenly, and it went out of my mind.'

'Ay, I guessed as much, so I've done nothing about it. Don't want to press you, Den, but I wish you will tell me one way or the other!'

'Yes, but not at this moment!' protested Kit. 'It's neither the place nor the occasion.'

'Oh, very well!' said Mr Lucton discontentedly. 'I'll give you a look-in tomorrow, then. Though I must say –'

He was interrupted by the sound of the dinner-gong, and, as Lady Stavely came up at that instant to take possession of Kit, the rest of the sentence remained unuttered.

Kit found himself placed between his hostess and Miss Cressida Stavely at the dinner-table. He was relieved to see that the length of the table separated him from the

Dowager; had it separated him from Cressida he would have been profoundly thankful.

For the first ten minutes his attention was fully engaged by Lady Stavely, who regaled him with a flow of vivacious small-talk. This presented him with no difficulty, since she allowed him little opportunity to speak, and asked him only such commonplace questions as anyone would have been able to answer. She was, mercifully, more anxious to show herself off than to draw out her guests, but he found her empty, incessant titter of laughter irritating, and was not altogether sorry when she turned from him to converse with Mr Charles Stavely. Sooner or later he would be obliged to talk to Cressida; he thought that to do so at the dinner-table might be the best way of avoiding a tête-à-tête. He glanced at her. Her head was turned a little away, as she listened to what her other neighbour was saying to her. It struck Kit that she had all the unconscious assurance lacking in her stepmother. Lady Stavely was overacting the part of Society hostess; she had been for too long the daughter who had failed to catch a husband to slip easily into her new position. It was not difficult to understand why she should be jealous of Cressida, so quietly poised, so well-accustomed to the management of her father's establishment, and to the entertainment of his guests. She appeared to be absorbed in her conversation with her neighbour, but she must have noticed that Lady Stavely had transferred her attention to her brother-in-law, for she brought her conversation to a natural conclusion and turned towards Kit, saying, with a faint smile: 'I wish this were not such a dull party: you must be dreadfully bored!'

'Not at all!' he replied.

She looked quizzically at him. 'A high treat, in fact!'

'Well, I shouldn't describe it in quite those words,' he owned, 'but the truly boring parties, you know, are the formal squeezes, when one is obliged to do the polite to all the people one would least wish to talk to.'

She was surprised. 'But I thought you never attended such parties!'

'Not when I can avoid them,' he said, retrieving the slip.

'Which, in general, you find yourself able to do! And when you are not so able,' she added thoughtfully, 'you take care not to become bored by arriving late, and leaving early, don't you?'

'A gross aspersion upon my character!'

She laughed. 'Did you think that because I am not very much in the habit of attending such squeezes that I don't know your reputation? You are the despair of hostesses!'

'You have been listening to slanderous reports.'

She smiled, but shook her head. 'You will be able to leave this party early, at all events. My grandmother doesn't keep late hours. I am afraid, however, that she will wish to hold further conversation with you. Can you bear that?'

'Easily! I consider she has been much maligned. I will allow her to be disconcerting, but by no means the petrifying Gorgon I was led to expect.'

'Not by me!' she said quickly. 'I never said that of Grandmama!'

Mr Fancot, whose courage had been strengthened by the excellent food and drink offered him, replied coolly: 'Oh, yes! If not in actual words, by inference! Can you deny it?'

She exclaimed instead: 'What an odd, unexpected creature you are, my lord! Can *you* deny that you looked forward to this party with the gravest misgivings? You told me that the very thought of running the gauntlet of my family put you into a quake!'

'That was because I had been misled,' said Kit brazenly.

She looked at him, amused, yet with a puzzled crease between her brows. 'But you weren't in a quake – even before you decided that you had been misled. I own, I thought Grandmama would have put you out of countenance, but she didn't.'

'To be honest with you, she did, but I thought it would be fatal to betray my embarrassment.'

'Yes, very true: she despises the people she can bully. You gave her a homestall, and she may very likely have taken a fancy to you.'

'Can she bully you?' he asked.

'Oh, no! That is, I shouldn't let her do so, but the occasion hasn't arisen: she is always very kind to me.' She fell silent for a few moments; and when she spoke again it was in a more formal tone, and as though she were carefully picking her words. 'Lord Denville, when you did me the honour of asking me to marry you, we discussed the matter – we *began* to discuss the matter quite frankly. But we were interrupted, as I expect you will recall, and there has been no opportunity since that day to resume our discussion.' She raised her eyes to his face. 'I should like to be able to do so before coming to an irrevocable decision.'

He had been regarding her over the rim of his wine-glass, but he set the glass down at this, saying involuntarily: 'I thought you *had* come to a decision! How is this?'

She answered apologetically: 'I'm afraid I gave you reason to think so. And indeed, at that moment, I believed I *had* done so. I can't explain it to you tonight. I had hoped to have seen you again before this party, but you had gone into the country, and Albinia – Lady Stavely – sent out the invitations without telling me.'

He cast a swift glance towards his hostess, to assure himself that her attention was still being claimed by her brother-in-law, before asking bluntly: 'Do you wish to cry off, Miss Stavely?'

She considered the question, frowning. 'You will think me a perfect wet-goose, Denville, but the truth is that I don't know! If Albinia had not come into the room when she did –'

'Unfortunate!' he agreed.

'Yes, and so stupid, if she but knew it, poor thing! To be sure, there was some awkwardness attached to our discussion, but we were on the way to an understanding – or, so I believed. I have felt ever since that a great deal was left unsaid. You too, I dare say. When Albinia came in you had just said there was one stipulation you must make – but you weren't granted the opportunity to tell me what that may be.'

'Good God, did I really say anything so uncivil?' he asked, startled.

'No, no, you were not uncivil! Remember that I begged you to be plain with me – not to stand on points!'

'I seem to have taken the fullest advantage of that request, if I did indeed talk about stipulations!'

'I thought that was the word you used, but I might be mistaken, perhaps. Yet –'

'I fancy you must have been, for I haven't the smallest recollection of it.'

'But you can't have forgotten that you said *something* of that nature!' she objected, considerably surprised.

He laughed. 'But I have forgotten, which proves that it can't have been a matter of much consequence. If only we had not suffered that untimely interruption –!'

'Exactly so! You must feel as I do that it left us uncomfortably situated. Would it be possible for you to visit me tomorrow, a little after eleven o'clock? We may be secure against another such interruption, for Albinia means to go shopping with her mother directly after breakfast, and my grandmother never leaves her room until noon.' She thought he hesitated, and added, colouring slightly: 'I ought not to suggest it, perhaps, but my situation is a trifle difficult. Surely it can't be thought improper in me – at my age, and in such circumstances – to receive you alone?'

'Improper! Of course not!' he said immediately. 'I shall present myself at – a quarter past eleven? Unless I find a carriage waiting at the door to take up Lady Stavely, when I shall conceal myself behind a lamp-post until I see her drive away.'

'Thus investing a morning-call with the trappings of an intrigue!' she said, laughing.

Her attention was then claimed by the cousin who sat on her other hand; and in a very few moments Kit was once more engaged by his hostess.

When the ladies withdrew, and the cloth was removed from the table, Lord Stavely came to sit beside Kit, unconsciously rescuing him from Mr Lucton, who had formed the same intention. Conversation became general; and as Lucton was too shy to raise his voice amongst so many seniors, and Mr Charles Stavely, in his late forties, had only a casual acquaintance with young Lord Denville, no pitfalls awaited Kit. He would have been happy to have remained in the dining-room for the next hour, but Lord Stavely was under orders not to allow the gentlemen to linger over their wine, and he very soon declared it to be time to join the ladies.

In the drawing-room, the supposed Lord Denville had inevitably been the subject of animated discussion. Opinions were varied, one party, led by Lady Stavely, extolling his air and address; another warning Cressy that she would be very unwise to marry a man so notoriously volatile; and a third, headed by Lady Ebchester, stating that it was a very good match, and that Cressy, at the age of twenty, and with a dowry of only £25,000, would be a fool to draw back from it.

This brought Lady Ebchester under the Dowager's fire. Sitting forward in her chair, and leaning on her ebony cane, the old lady looked like the popular conception of a witch. She fixed her daughter with a gleaming eye, and snapped: 'Besides what I may leave her!'

Lady Ebchester was rather taken aback by this, but she said: 'Oh, well, Mama, that is a matter for you, of course, but you will hardly leave any great sum to Cressy when you have sons who have nearer claims on you. Not to speak of your daughters – though, for my part, I expect nothing, and nor, I dare say, does Eliza. As for Caroline, however, and poor Clara –'

'Oh, pray don't, Augusta!' begged Miss Clara Stavely, tears starting to her eyes. 'So very improper – so disagreeable for dear Cressy!'

'Don't cry, Aunt!' said Cressy cheerfully. 'If Grandmama leaves her fortune to me, I'll engage to give it back to the family immediately.'

The Dowager uttered a cackle of mirth. 'Do you want to start a civil war, girl?'

'Not in the least, ma'am – and if Aunt Augusta doesn't know that there won't be any occasion for me to do so, I do!' retorted Cressy, twinkling at her.

At this point, the deaf cousin, who had formed a very imperfect impression of what had been said, nodded at Cressy, and stated in the voice of one prepared to go to the stake in defence of her beliefs: 'Well, dear, I said it before, and I'll say it again: he's *very* handsome!'

As this declaration coincided with the arrival of the gentlemen, Kit, ushered first into the room by his host, was once more privileged to hear this tribute. He managed to preserve his countenance, but his eyes met Cressy's across the room, and he was obliged to grip his lips tightly together. Cressy retreated to the end of the room, her shoulders shaking; and the Dowager, having informed the deaf cousin that she was a fool, commanded Kit to come and sit beside her.

He obeyed her, drawing up a chair. The Dowager tartly adjured Clara not to hang about her, and told the rest of the company that they were at liberty to indulge in their usual bibble-babble. Correctly interpreting this as a prohibition on any attempt to intrude into her conversation with the principal guest, her relations meekly drifted away, to form small groups in various parts of the room.

'Gabblemongers, all of 'em!' said the Dowager, sardonically observing their efforts to maintain a flow of small-talk. She brought her piercing gaze to bear on Kit's face, and said 'Well, young man? What have you to say for yourself?'

'I don't think I have anything to say for myself, ma'am, and I stand in too much dread of being thought a gabble-monger to say it if I had,' he replied.

'Balderdash!' she said. 'You've a mighty ready tongue in your head, sir!'

He smiled at her. 'Well, what do you wish me to say, ma'am? You can't expect me to recite a catalogue of my vices, and as for my virtues, would you really think better of me if I puffed them off to you?'

'Have you any?' she demanded.

'Yes, a few, and quite a number of good intentions,' he replied.

'So your Uncle Brumby seems to have told my son. But I have a very good memory, and I recall that he once told *me* that your brother was worth a dozen of you!'

This speech, had it been shot at him before dinner, would have shaken him badly, but he was now sufficiently fortified to be able to answer it with smiling ease. 'Yes, my uncle has a great kindness for my brother. Kit is his protégé, you know, ma'am.'

She seemed to be satisfied with this response, for she abandoned the subject, and said, after considering him for a few moments: 'Well, it's my way to open my budget, so I'll tell you to your head that I'm not mad after this marriage. Mind, I don't dislike you! In fact, you're better than I looked for. But whether you're the man for my granddaughter is another pair of shoes.'

Knowing Evelyn as he did, he found himself in agreement with her, and might have added that Miss Stavely was not at all the sort of girl to attract Evelyn's roving fancy. He said: 'I can only hope, ma'am, that I may be able to prove you wrong. It will be my endeavour, I promise you.'

'I'll say this for you,' she remarked dryly, 'you have excellent address! That's in your favour – or it is to persons of my generation. I detest the scrambling manners some of you younger men affect! Brumby tells my son you have no faults that won't be cured by a suitable marriage, but from all I hear, Denville, you're a here and thereian! I put it no more strongly than that, though, to use words with no bark on 'em, there are those who don't scruple to say you've libertine propensities.'

'Are there?' Kit said, his brows drawing together. 'I didn't know it, ma'am, – and it is untrue!'

'No need to fire up!' she replied. 'I set no store by reports of that nature. How old are you? Four-and-twenty? Lord, what's the world coming to if sprigs of your age ain't to be allowed a few petticoat affairs without a parcel of windsuckers setting it about that they're loose-screws? I've no patience with such prudery!'

He laughed. 'Why, thank you, ma'am!'

She directed another of her piercing glances at him. 'All very well, young man, but if you marry my granddaughter you'll put a period to your philandering! She's a rational girl, and a well-bred girl, and I don't doubt she'd take it with composure, but she wouldn't like it, and I don't mean to have her made uncomfortable, *that* you may depend on!'

'Nor do I, ma'am – and that *you* may depend on!' he retorted, a little stir of anger in his heart. His twin might have been going the pace rather too rapidly; he might be careless, even lightminded; he was certainly forgetful; but he was not insensitive; and Kit was ready to swear that if he married Miss Stavely he would never use her unkindly, or wound her pride by blatantly pursuing some other female. Whether he would remain faithful to her was another and more doubtful matter; but he would conduct his *affaires* with discretion. Presumably Miss Stavely, no schoolroom miss, but a rational woman, entering openly

65

into a marriage of convenience, was prepared for some divagations, and would demand no more of Evelyn than the appearance of fidelity.

The Dowager saw the flash in Kit's eyes, and was pleased. All she said, however, was: 'Easy to say, Denville!' She relapsed into silence, staring grimly ahead. After a long pause, she said abruptly: 'When I was young, our marriages were arranged for us by our parents. I could name you a dozen females who were barely acquainted with their bridegrooms. I don't know that it was a good thing.' She brought her gaze back to Kit's face. 'If you're expecting me to give you my blessing because you've a glib tongue and engaging manners, you're out in your reckoning! I want to know you better before I do that, and I want Cressy to know you better too. I'm tired now: tell my daughter Clara I'm ready to go to bed! And you may tell your mother to come and visit me one morning! Good night!'

5

Mr Fancot returned to Hill Street, on foot, shortly before midnight, and just in time to witness the arrival of his parent, borne down the street in her own sedan chair, and attended by three middle-aged gallants, and one very much younger gentleman, who walked as close to the chair as possible, and bore all the appearance of one who was equally a prey to adoration and jealousy.

Mr Fancot, awaiting the cortège in the open doorway, was deeply appreciative of the scene, which was certainly impressive. My lady was carried by two stalwarts dressed in neat livery; and her chair, when it came into the lamp-light, was seen to be of particularly elegant design, and to be lined throughout with pale green velvet. The gallants were plainly men of mode, and when the chair was set down one opened the door, the second tenderly helped her to alight, and the third stood waiting to offer his arm for her support up the few shallow steps to her front-door. Her young worshipper, quietly elbowed out of the way when he had tried to be the first to reach the door, was left disconsolate, gazing hungrily after the goddess. But she paused before she reached the steps and looked back, exclaiming in her soft voice: 'Oh, my fan! I must have dropped it in the chair. Mr Horning, will you be so *very* obliging as to see if it is there?'

Mr Horning's drooping spirits revived magically. He dived into the chair, found the fan, and presented it to her ladyship, with a low bow, and a smile which Kit thought perfectly fatuous. She thanked him prettily, gave him her hand to kiss, and said: 'Now you must all go home, for here is Denville waiting for me, and we have a great deal to discuss. You know, he has been out of town lately.'

Kit had by this time recognized two of the elderly beaux, and exchanged greetings with them; and Lady Denville put him in possession of the third's name by saying: 'Here is Lord Chacely, wanting to know why you weren't at Ascot. Wicked one, you were to have joined his party!'

Kit clapped a hand to his brow. 'Good God, I forgot to write to you, explaining why I was obliged to fail! I *beg* your pardon, sir!'

'Humbug, you young rascal!' Chacely said. 'You forgot the engagement altogether!'

'No, no!' Kit protested.

'But, Chacely, did you think he wouldn't?' asked one of the other gentlemen.

At this, the third gentleman added his mite to this badinage. It was evident that no suspicion that they were roasting Kit, and not Evelyn, crossed their minds: a circumstance which made Lady Denville say, when the door was shut upon them: 'You see, Kit! I told you how it would be! I dare say that Newlyn and Sir John Streatley have been acquainted with you since you were in short coats, and if *they* never guessed the truth you may be easy!'

'I am not at all easy,' he retorted. 'But as for *you*, love, I wonder how you dare address *me* as "wicked one"! Mama, you are incorrigible! Who the devil is that mooncalf you've enslaved?'

Her infectious ripple of laughter broke from her. 'Isn't he ridiculous, poor boy? But one must be kind to him: you see, he is a *poet*!'

'Ah, that, of course, explains everything!' said Kit cordially. 'I expect you are his inspiration?'

'Well, just at present I am,' she acknowledged. 'It won't last – in fact, I think that at any moment now he will fall desperately in love with some chit – probably *quite* ineligible! – and forget that I ever existed. Which, I must own, will be in one way a great relief, because it is dreadfully tedious to be obliged to listen to poetry, even when it has been composed in one's honour. But in another – oh, Kit, you won't understand, but to be three-and-forty, and *still* able to attach foolish boys, is *such* a comfort!'

'Mama, you must never make such an admission again! No one would believe you to be a day older than three-and-thirty – if as much!'

This was true, but Lady Denville, after considering the matter, said: 'No, but one must be reasonable, Kit, and everyone must *know* I can't be a day younger than three-and-forty, when all the world knows that you and Evelyn are four-and-twenty! It is the most *lowering* reflection! But never mind that! What happened tonight, in Mount Street? I was in such a fret of anxiety all the evening I left *my* party early!'

'Oh, was that the reason? I must tell you that I was knocked acock when I perceived that the sumptuous chair being carried down the street *before midnight* was yours!'

'Yes, I don't think I have ever left a party so early before – particularly when I was winning!' she said naively.

'No, were you? But I was very much shocked, Mama! What has become of your most handsome *cavaliere ser-*

vente? How comes it about that he permitted another – *four* others! – to squire you home tonight? Don't tell me his passion has waned!'

She went into another ripple of laughter. 'Oh, poor Bonamy! How can you be so unfeeling as even to *think* of his walking all the way from Albemarle Street? He must have dropped dead of an apoplexy, had he made the attempt! As for his passion, I have a melancholy suspicion that I share it with his cook: he was boring on for ever tonight about a way of serving teal with poivrade sauce! Now, stop funning, and tell me what happened at *your* party!'

'Oh, a very handsome dinner, and the company – er – the pink of gentility! Not quite in my style, perhaps, but certainly of the first respectability!'

'Were they excessively fusty?' she said sympathetically. 'I did warn you that they would be!'

'You did, but you did *not* warn me, dear Mama, that two of the number are acquainted with Evelyn!'

'No! Who, Kit?'

'Mr Charles Stavely, who appears to be –'

'Oh, *him*!' she interrupted. 'Very likely he may be, but so slightly that it is not of the least consequence!'

'Very true, but if Evelyn doesn't return in time to save me from Lucton I shall be totally undone. Is he one of Evelyn's bosom-bows?'

'Young Lucton? Good gracious, no! You don't mean to say that *he* was invited to the party?'

'That is precisely what I do mean to say, Mama! Furthermore, I apprehend that Evelyn has entered into some sort of an undertaking with him. What it may be I haven't the least guess, and something seems to tell me that you haven't either.'

She shook her head. 'No, indeed! How excessively awkward for you!'

'Yes, isn't it?' he agreed. 'Particularly when one considers that he is coming to visit me tomorrow – to learn what is my decision! That's what I call having a wolf by the ears!'

'Most vexatious!' she said sunnily. 'But there's no need to be in a worry, dearest! Perhaps Evelyn will have returned – or Fimber may know what it is that stupid creature wants. And if he doesn't know, Brigg will say that you are not at home. I see no difficulty in evading Lucton.'

'No, love, I've no doubt of that! But not even my abominable twin could agree to receive a man on a matter of business and then say that he was not at home!'

'But, Kit, how foolish of you!' she said reproachfully. 'You should have fobbed him off!'

'So I might have, if it had not been made very plain to me that he thinks himself pretty ill-used at having been fobbed off for over ten days already. Oh, well, I dare say I shall be able to brace it through! What has me in a far worse worry is that Miss Stavely has asked me to visit her tomorrow morning, to resume an interrupted discussion she had with Evelyn, on the day that he proposed to her.'

'Now, that *is* tiresome!' she exclaimed, dismayed.

'Very much more than tiresome, Mama. It's one thing to masquerade as Evelyn at a party, but quite another to receive Miss Stavely's confidence under false pretences.'

'I see what you mean,' she agreed, wrinkling her brow. 'But very likely you are making a piece of work about nothing! I should be astonished to learn that she has anything of a *very* confidential nature to say to Evelyn, because she is not at all well-acquainted with him, besides having a great deal of reserve. Depend upon it, it will prove to be nothing to cause you embarrassment. Indeed, the more I think about it the more positive I feel that it can only be a triviality, because Evelyn said nothing to me about having been interrupted. And, what is more, Kit, if he had thought that Cressy had something of importance to say he would *not* have left London without seeing her again!'

'She seemed to think it was he who had something important to say. He appears to have told her that he had a stipulation to make.'

'A *stipulation*? What in the world can he have been thinking of? He must have taken leave of his senses! Unless –' She broke off, her eyes widening. Then she said: 'I know what he was going to say, and I am very glad he *was* interrupted, for I told him he was on no account to do so. He is set on us all living together, which I have *no* intention of doing, because such arrangements very rarely answer. It was used to be quite the thing, you know, and I always thought it such a fortunate circumstance that your papa's parents were both dead when I married him. If Cressy brings the matter up, say that you have changed your mind, or have forgotten, or that she misunderstood you!'

'I can hardly do that, Mama,' he objected. 'It is clearly not what Evelyn would say.'

'It is what *I* say!' she replied spiritedly. 'I mean to give him a *very* severe scold – and if you look at me in that odiously quizzy way I shall give you one too! Tell me about old Lady Stavely! Did she frighten you?'

'She wanted to do so, but I tried the effect of giving her a civil set-off, which answered very well.'

Lady Denville was awed. 'Kit, how *brave* of you!'

'Yes, wasn't it? But, there, Mama! you know me! Pluck to the backbone!'

She laughed. 'Well, *I* should never have dared to do such a thing!'

'You must make the attempt: she'll bullock you if you don't!'

'Oh, I mean to keep out of her way! She came to London to make your acquaintance, and now that she has done so I dare say she will return to Berkshire within a day or two!' returned her ladyship blithely.

'You're out, love!' said Kit, grinning wickedly at her. 'She remains in London until next month, when she means, according to what Lady Ebchester told me, to go to Worthing for the summer, taking Cressy with her. She charged me with a message for you: you are to visit her one morning!'

'*No!*' she ejaculated, in the liveliest horror. 'Kit, you're shamming it!'

'I am not. Those were her very words.'

'Oh, you abominable creature! Why didn't you tell her I was sick – gone into the country – *anything*? She never liked me – indeed, when Stavely was dangling after me she did her utmost to dissuade him from making me an offer! Not that there was the least necessity, for your grandfather would never have countenanced the match when so many *far* more flattering offers were being made for me! Oh, Kit, how *could* you subject me to such an ordeal? She will annihilate me!'

'No such thing! You have only to bear in mind that Evelyn is a matrimonial prize of the first water, and that will give you an immeasurable feeling of superiority!'

But Lady Denville, while agreeing that Evelyn might look as high as he chose for a bride, refused to be comforted. She informed Kit that when a redoubtable old lady had known one from the cradle such considerations counted for nothing. She added tragically, gathering the shimmering folds of her cloak about her, as she prepared to mount the stairs: 'I have it on the *best* authority that she described me once as *a pretty widgeon*! And when she looks at me, in that beady way of hers, I shall *feel* like a widgeon!'

'But a very pretty one!' her son reminded her.

'Yes, but much she will care for that!' replied her ladyship. She paused on the half-landing, to add: 'And don't put yourself to the trouble of telling me that I am of higher rank than she is, because she won't care for that either!'

On these embittered words, she resumed her progress up the stairs. He caught up with her as she reached the second floor, and told her in shocked accents that if she meant to go to bed without kissing him good night he would be unable to sleep a wink. That made her give a choke of laughter; and when he pointed out to her that the ordeal awaiting her was as nothing when compared to the ordeal to which he had been subjected, she melted completely, saying: 'No, indeed! My poor darling, you may rely on me to lend you all the support I can! There is *nothing* I would not do for *either* of my beloved sons!'

Embracing her with breath-taking heartiness, he mastered a quivering lip, thanked her gravely, and parted from her on the best of terms.

Fimber was waiting for him in his own room. As he eased him out of Evelyn's longtailed coat, he asked, in the voice of one to whom the answer was a foregone conclusion, if anyone had recognized him. Upon being told that no one had, he said: 'It was not to be expected that anyone would, sir. When you passed out of my hands this evening the thought crossed my mind that even I should not have known that you were not his lordship. You are, if I may say so, the spit of him, Mr Christopher!'

Questioned about Mr Lucton, he said austerely: 'A very frippery young gentleman, sir – what one might term a mere barley-straw!'

'You may term him anything you please,' said Kit, stripping off his neckcloth, 'but do you know what was the proposal he made to my brother, to which he expected an answer within a day?'

After a frowning pause, during which Fimber divested Kit of his waistcoat, he said: 'No, sir, his lordship made no mention of it to me. But from what I know of Mr Lucton I would venture the guess that he may have been wishful to sell his lordship one of his hunters.'

'Who wants to purchase a hunter at this season?' demanded Kit sceptically. 'Not my brother!'

'No, sir; as you say! But his lordship is known to be very goodnatured: one who finds it difficult to say no; and Mr Lucton is frequently in Dun territory. We will discover what Challow may know about the business, when he comes for orders tomorrow morning. I should inform you,

73

Mr Christopher, that I have taken it upon myself to apprise Challow of what has occurred here. I trust you will think that I did right.'

'Much you'd care if I didn't!' observed Kit. 'It's to be hoped that he does know what Lucton expects of my brother! If he doesn't I shall find myself lurched!'

But Challow, presenting himself on the following morning, did not fail his harassed young master. He was a stocky individual, with grizzled hair, and the slightly bowed legs of one bred from his earliest youth to the saddle. He had taught the twins to ride their first ponies, had rescued them from innumerable scrapes, besides putting his foot down on some of their more dangerous exploits; and while his public demeanour towards them was generally respectful, he treated them, in private, as if they were the schoolboys he still thought them. He greeted Kit with a broad grin, responded to an invitation to tip a mauley by grasping the hand held out to him, and saying: 'Now, that's enough, Master Kit! How often have I told you to mind your tongue? A nice thing it would be if her ladyship was to hear you using such vulgar language! And who'd bear the blame? Tell me that!'

'You would – at least, so you always told us, though I don't think either my mother or my father ever did blame you for the things we said! Challow, I'm in the devil of a hank!'

'That's all right, sir: *you'll* never be bum squabbled!' replied Challow cheerfully. 'Not but what things are in a rare hubble-bubble, which I don't deny. But don't you fall into the hips! I'll lay my life you'll get there with both feet. Well, there's no reason why you shouldn't, let alone you always was a sure card! If Fimber hadn't of told me, I wouldn't have known you wasn't his lordship – well, not right off I wouldn't!'

'I wish to God I knew what had become of my brother!'

'You don't wish it no more than I do, Master Kit. There's times when I've worried myself sick, fancying all

74

kinds of things; but then I get to thinking that his lordship is like a cat: fling him anyway you choose, he'll land
on his feet! And now I've seen *you* in tolerable spirits I'll
take my affy-davy he's safe and sound!' He cocked an
intelligent eye at Kit, and gave a chuckle. 'Lor', sir, what
kind of a clodpole do you take me for? Me, that knew
you when you wasn't out of leading-strings! If his lordship
was in trouble, or – or worse, which *has* crossed my mind
– you'd know it! Ain't that so?'

Kit nodded. 'Yes – I think. I haven't said so to my
mother, but I could have sworn, about a week ago, that
he had met with some accident. That's what brought me
home so suddenly. I'd meant to come, for I haven't been
easy – Well, never mind that! I think something *did*
happen to him, but it wasn't fatal. I am as certain of that
as I am of anything. If he were dead, or in desperate straits,
I should know it.'

'That's just what I thought,' agreed Challow. '*He* ain't
dead! In mischief, more like! I never ought to have let
him go off like he did, but he properly bamboozled me,
Master Kit. Nor I didn't think he'd go off on one of his
starts when he's in a way to be buckled. Oh, well, we'll just
have to bear a hand until he comes back, sir, and that's
all there is to it! Now, if you wish to ride today, there's
a neatish bay hack would suit you pretty well. Or there's
the curricle, and a pair of prime 'uns: beautiful steppers,
they are: just the thing for showing off in the Park! Or you
could have his lordship's new tilbury: quite the rage these
tilburies have got to be!'

But Kit, pithily informing him that nothing could be
farther from his intention than to show himself off in the
Park, or anywhere else, declined these offers, and demanded
instead to be told what, if anything, Challow knew about
Mr Lucton's mysterious business.

'Him!' Challow said scornfully. 'Trying to sell his lordship a horse which we don't want: not in our stables we
don't!'

'If his lordship doesn't want the animal, why didn't he tell Mr Lucton so?'

'You know what his lordship is, sir! Too easy by half! Not but what Mr Lucton ain't one to take no for an answer: a proper jaw-me-dead he is! He waved to us in the Park, so his lordship pulled up, and then he started in to puff-off a flat-sided chestnut he hunted last season, trying to slumguzzle my lord into believing it was the very thing for him. Let alone no one would want a horse Mr Lucton had hunted, that chestnut ain't worth the half of the price he's set on it. "A perfect fencer," he tells my lord. "Jumps off his hocks," he says. Yes, I thought to myself, I wish I may see it! So I give his lordship a nudge, and he tells Mr Lucton he'll think it over, and let him know next day, meaning, as he told me, to write him a civil note. I dare say it slipped his mind, for it was the next day that we went off to Ravenhurst. There's no call for you to trouble yourself, Master Kit.'

'Oh, isn't there? Mr Lucton is coming here today, to get my answer! I shall have to buy the creature, I suppose. What's the figure?'

'Master Kit! You won't never! £160 is what he told his lordship, and dear at £80 is what I say!'

'I'll offer him £100, and if he refuses, so much the better. I can't say I don't want the horse when the man's been kept waiting for a fortnight! I'll give him a draft on my bank – Oh, the devil! I can't do that, can I? Well, you must go to the bank for me, Challow, and draw the money in bills. I'll give you a cheque. I'd better make it out for £200, for I shall be needing some pitch and pay for myself. Don't get robbed!'

'It's you that's going to be robbed, sir!' said Challow, deeply disapproving.

'Not I! I'm buying this horse on my brother's behalf – and serve him right!' said Kit.

He set forth a little later to walk to Mount Street, nattily attired in the correct town-dress of a gentleman of fashion. His coat of dark blue superfine was the very latest made for Evelyn by Weston, and never yet worn by its owner; his stockinette pantaloons were knitted in the newest and most delicate dove-colour; his cambric shirt was modishly austere, with no ruffle, but three plain buttons; his waistcoat combined opulence with discretion; and his hat, set at an angle on his glowing locks, had a tall and tapering crown, smoothly brushed, and very different from the low, shaggy beaver to which Fimber had taken such instant exception. Only his Hessian boots were his own. Within ten minutes of forcing his feet into Evelyn's shoes Kit had straitly commanded Fimber to retrieve from his baggage his own foot-wear. Fimber, obstinately prejudiced against Kit's Viennese valet, had eyed his Hessians with contempt, but there was really no fault to be found either in their cut, or in their unsullied brilliance. Starched shirtpoints of moderate height, a Mathematical Tie, dogskin gloves, an elegant fob, and a malacca cane completed Mr Fancot's attire, and caused his mama to declare that he was precise to a pin. Thus fortified, he set forth with tolerable composure to keep his appointment with Miss Stavely.

Halfway up John Street this composure was shaken by an encounter with a total stranger, who demanded indignantly what he meant by giving him the cut direct. He extricated himself from this situation by pleading a brown study; but as he had no clue to the stranger's identity, nor any knowledge of the latest on-dits to which this Pink of the Ton made oblique references, the ensuing conversation severely taxed his ingenuity. It culminated in a pressing invitation to him to join a gathering of Evelyn's cronies at Limmer's Hotel that evening. He declined this, on the score of having promised to escort his mother to a ton-party; and parted from his insouciant new acquaintance imbued with a resolve to seek refuge at Ravenhurst without any loss of time.

It had been forcibly borne in upon him that a prolonged sojourn in the Metropolis would not only be extremely wearing, but would infallibly lead to his undoing.

He was admitted to Lord Stavely's house by the butler, who came as near to bestowing a conspiratorial wink upon him as his sense of propriety permitted, and was conducted to a parlour, at the back of the house. Here Miss Stavely awaited him, becomingly attired in a morning dress of jaconet muslin, made up to the throat, its sleeves tightly buttoned at the wrists, and its hem embellished with a broad, embroidered flounce. As he bent ceremonially over her hand, the butler, surveying the scene with a fatherly and sentimental eye, heaved an audible sigh of great sensibility, and withdrew, softly closing the door behind him.

There had been constraint in Miss Stavely's manner, but the butler's sigh brought the ready twinkle into her eyes, and she said involuntarily: 'Oh, dear! Poor Dursley is convinced that he is assisting in a romantical affair! Don't be dismayed! The thing is that he, and all the upper servants, have, most unfortunately, taken it upon themselves to champion what they imagine to be my cause!'

'Unfortunately?' he said.

'Why, yes! I should be a monster if I were not very much touched by their loyalty, but I wish with all my heart they could be persuaded to accept Albinia as my successor! You can't conceive how awkward they make it for both of us! Do what I will, they persist in coming to me for orders, even of referring *her* orders to me! I do most sincerely feel for her: her situation is insupportable!'

'What of yours?' he asked. 'Is that not insupportable?'

'Yes,' she acknowledged, with a wry smile. 'You know that! It was – is! – my reason for – for entertaining your proposal, my lord.'

'That's frank, at all events!' he remarked.

Her eyes responded to the smile in his. 'We were agreed, were we not, that only candour on both our parts could make our projected alliance tolerable to either of us? Your reason for wishing to be married is your very understandable desire to become independent of your uncle; mine is – is what I feel to be an urgent need to remove myself from this house – from any of my father's houses!'

'Having made the acquaintance of your mother-in-law – having *furthered* my acquaintance with her,' Kit said, smoothly correcting himself, 'I perfectly comprehend your feeling – and sympathize with you!'

'No, no, don't misunderstand me!' she said quickly. 'You should rather sympathize with Albinia! It must be hard indeed for her to come into a household which has been managed for years by a daughter-in-law so little removed from her in age. Then, too, I have been in some sort my father's companion since my mother's death, and – and it is difficult to break such a relationship. Albinia feels – inevitably – that she is obliged to share Papa with me.'

'And you?'

'Yes,' she said frankly. 'I feel the same – perhaps more bitterly, which – which quite shocks me, because I had never dreamt I could be so horridly ill-natured! Between the two of us poor Papa is rendered miserably uncomfortable! I detest Albinia as much as she detests me, and – to make a clean breast of it! – I find I can't bear playing second fiddle where I have been accustomed to being the mistress of the house!' She added, with an effort at playfulness: 'You should take warning, Denville! I have lately learnt to know myself much better than ever I did before, and have come to the dismal conclusion that I am an overbearing female, determined to rule the roast!'

He smiled at her. 'I'm not afraid of you. But tell me this! – if I should ask it of you, would you find it irksome to share a home with my mother?'

She stared at him, and then exclaimed, as enlightenment dawned on her: 'Was *that* the stipulation you spoke of? Good God, how could you be so absurd? Did you think that I should require you to thrust her out of her home?

What a toad you must think me! My dearest, most adorable Godmama! Let me tell you, my lord, that my hope is that she will receive me into your household with as much kindness as she has always shown me!'

'Thank you!' he said warmly. 'But I must tell you that she straitly forbade me even to suggest such an arrangement to you. She says it *never* answers. Indeed, she informed me that she had always regarded it as a most fortunate circumstance that her own mother and father-in-law were dead before she married my father!'

Her eyes danced. She said appreciatively: 'I can almost hear her saying it – perfectly seriously, I make no doubt! Do, pray, assure her that I should not so regard *her* death!'

'I shan't dare to disclose that I mentioned the matter to you. She promised me a severe scold if I did so!'

'No wonder you should be in a quake!' she agreed. 'One always dreads the ordeal of which one has no experience!'

He laughed. 'Now, how do you know I have not that experience, Miss Stavely?'

'I don't think my understanding superior,' she replied, 'but I *have* cut my eye-teeth!' She looked curiously at him. 'May I know why I have sunk to be *Miss Stavely* again? You called me Cressy when you proposed to me – but perhaps you have forgotten?'

'By no means!' he said promptly. 'Merely, your habit of addressing me as *my lord* led me to fear that I had gone beyond the line.'

'What a whisker!' she remarked. 'I recall that Grandmama told me last night that you had a ready tongue.'

'I wish I could think that she meant it as a compliment!'

'With Grandmama one can never be quite certain, but she did say that she had been agreeably surprised in you!'

'Come, that's encouraging! May I hope that she will consent to our marriage?'

'I don't know. I haven't asked her, you see, and all she

has said so far is that she wants to know you better.'

'I wish you will tell me, Cressy, whether you mean to be ruled by her decision?'

She shook her head. 'No. I make my own decisions.' She thought for a moment, and then said, with a gleam of mischief: 'I might make her decision my excuse!'

'Oh, no, I don't think you would! You're no shuffler,' he responded coolly.

'How can you know that?' she asked, meeting his eyes with a surprised question in her own.

He smiled. 'It isn't difficult to know it: no extraordinary intelligence is necessary to enable one to perceive that your mind is direct. You don't talk flowery commonplace, and you're not afraid to come to the point.' He paused. 'That being so, tell me what it is you wish to say to me! I fancy you didn't invite me to visit you only to discover what my *stipulation* was.'

'No,' she acknowledged. Her colour was a little heightened; she said, with a touch of shyness: 'I hardly know why I did ask you to come. You will think me very far from direct! You see, when you proposed to me, I was in a horrid quarrel with Albinia – a vulgar pulling of caps, as women do! I wished of all things to go away from here, not only because I was hurt and angry, but because I saw that it wouldn't do for me to remain. Albinia is anxious to be rid of me, and I can't blame her, for I find I am becoming one of those detestable people who are for ever picking out grievances, or coming to cuffs over trifles. And when I made the really shocking discovery that I was hoping that Albinia's child, which she is so certain will be a son, will be a daughter – just to take the wind out of her eye! – I knew that I *must* go away.' She pressed her hands to her flushed cheeks. 'So *ignoble!*' she uttered, in a stifled voice.

'But very natural,' Kit said. 'A son to put your nose out of joint, eh?'

She nodded. 'Yes, that was it. But to allow oneself to be put into a flame by such a cut – spoken in a mere fit of crossness, too –!'

'I consider it stands greatly to your credit that you didn't divulge your ignoble wish.'

She forced a smile. 'I'm not quite as direct as that.'

'You may put it so, if you choose: *I* should have said that you are not so wanting in conduct!'

'Thank you: that was kind in you!'

'No, only truthful. Were you in a passion when I proposed to you? I didn't guess it.'

'Oh, no, not then! Merely determined to put an end to a miserably uncomfortable situation, and unable to think how it could be done.' She hesitated, and continued, with a little difficulty: 'I had never meant to have remained here when my father was married again. I thought – hoped – that Grandmama would have invited me to live with her. She didn't, however. I dare say you'll understand that I didn't care to ask her.'

'Readily! Also, that, Grandmama having failed to come to the scratch, *my* arrival on the scene was providential!'

'Yes, that's the truth,' she said frankly. 'I don't mean that I would have accepted *any* offer. But although I was so little acquainted with you I liked you very well, and I knew, from what Lady Denville told me, that you were kind, and good-natured, and –'

'Stop!' he interrupted. 'My poor girl, how *could* you allow yourself to be so taken-in? If you mean to accept me at my mother's valuation a shocking disappointment awaits you! She is the most dotingly fond parent imaginable, and can detect no fault in either of her sons.'

She laughed. 'Oh, I know that! But *you* are dotingly fond of *her,* and so charmingly attentive to her that I don't know how she should detect your faults. I liked that in you too. And although I shouldn't have thought of marriage if Grandmama had invited me to live with her I knew that it wouldn't be easy to do that, because I had discovered by then that when one has held the reins for four years, as I did here, and at Stavely, it is the most difficult thing in the world to become a mere young lady, obedient to the decrees of her elders. You see, I never *was* that! So when you offered for me, Denville, it did seem to me that I should be a ninnyhammer to refuse you, only because I was not in love with you, or you with me. You were not disagreeable to me: I dearly love your mama; and you offered me not only your hand but the – the position to which I am accustomed.' She paused, and after thinking for a moment, said: 'And to be honest with you, having endured several taunts on my age, and being at my last prayers, I was strongly attracted by the notion of catching one of the biggest prizes on the Marriage Mart!'

He shook his head. '*Very* ignoble!'

'Yes, wasn't it?' she agreed, answering the laughter in his eyes with one of her merriest twinkles. 'But understandable – don't you think?'

'Well, never having regarded myself in that flattering light –'

'Oh, what flummery!' she interjected. 'You must be well aware of it! But it's all nonsense, of course: when you had left me that day, and I had leisure to reflect, I knew it.' She scanned his face, her brow puckered. 'I don't know how it is, but when you came here last night I – I had almost decided to tell you it would not *do*. Thinking about it, not seeing you again after that interrupted talk – which was attended by a good deal of awkwardness, was it not? – and having had leisure to reflect more calmly – I had misgivings – began to think that we should not suit – that I had accepted your offer in a distempered freak! Then, last night, I met you again, and –' She stopped, her frown deepening. He waited, speechless, and she said, with one of her open looks: 'I liked you much better than ever before!'

He still said nothing, for there was nothing he could think of to say. Various thoughts chased one another through his head: that Evelyn was more fortunate than he knew; that the part he himself was playing was even more odious than he had foreseen; that he must remove himself from her vicinity immediately; that when she saw Evelyn again she must surely be conscious of his superior qualities.

'And now I don't know!' she confessed. 'I was never in such a – such a bumble-broth in my life, and how I come to be so stupid as not to know my own mind I can't imagine! Such a thing has never happened to me before, for, in general, I should warn you, I *do* know it!'

'I can believe that,' he said. 'You have a great look of decision! I conjecture that once your mind is made up there can be no turning you from it!'

'Yes, I fear that's true,' she replied seriously. 'I hope I may not be arrogant: one of those overmighty women, who grow to be like poor Grandmama!'

'I don't think there can be any fear of that!' he said, amused.

'I trust you may be right! I have certainly given *you* no cause to think me anything but a woolly-crown! But I must hold you accountable for that,' she said, in a rallying tone. 'I fancy you must have odd humours, perhaps! You make me feel one day that I have a pretty just notion of your character, and the next that I know nothing about you, which is very disconcerting, let me tell you!'

'I beg your pardon! And so?'

'And so I feel that Grandmama is right, when she says I ought to know you better before I make up this skimble-skamble mind of mine.' Her eyes were hidden from him; she was engaged in the occupation of twisting a ring round and round upon her finger; but she raised them suddenly, squarely meeting his. 'Will you grant me a little more time for consideration? To become better acquainted – each of us with the other? I dare say you mean to go to Brighton now that London is getting to be so thin of company: that's your custom, isn't it?'

'Why, yes! I have been very much in the habit of escorting my mother there! This year, I find myself obliged to go to Ravenhurst – I don't know for how long, or whether Mama means to accompany me,' he replied.

'Oh! Well, Ravenhurst is not so far from Worthing, is it? The thing is, Denville, that I am going to Worthing with Grandmama next week, to spend the summer there, and I thought that perhaps you would drive over to visit us now and then.'

'So that we may learn to know one another? You may be sure I shall do so. I must hope that you will find it such a dead bore at Worthing, amongst all the dowagers, that it will weigh the scales down in my favour.'

'It might well do so,' she acknowledged, with a grimace. 'But I must warn you that I am inured to that particular boredom: I go there every year!'

'I can safely promise that if you marry me you will never set foot in the place again!' he said, laughter springing to his eyes as he tried to picture his twin in that respectable resort.

6

Mr Fancot arrived on his own doorstep just as his mother's youthful adorer was being ushered out of the house by Brigg. Mr Horning, who was dressed with a studied negligence which included a handkerchief carelessly knotted round his neck, and unstarched shirt-points, checked, and uttered dramatically: 'My lord!'

'How do you do?' said Kit politely. His appreciative gaze took in every detail of the poet's attire. He saw too, with unholy amusement, that Mr Horning was looking slightly belligerent, and concluded that Evelyn had not encouraged the dazzled youth's infatuation. So he said, with immense affability: 'Did you come to visit me? Do tell me how I may serve you!'

Somewhat taken-aback, Mr Horning said, with a challenging look: 'I have been visiting Lady Denville, my lord!'

'No, have you?' said Kit. 'But how kind of you!'

'Kind?' repeated Mr Horning blankly.

'As long as she didn't find your visit rather too much for her. At her age, you know, and troubled as she is with the gout –'

'I collect, my lord, that you have some objection to my visits!' interrupted Mr Horning, glaring at him.

'Not the least in the world!' said Kit cordially. 'You have been reading to her, I dare say, and keeping her quietly entertained, which is an excellent thing! It is a hard matter to induce her to rest, but at her age, you know –'

'Lord Denville, I regard her ladyship as an *angel*!' said Mr Horning reverently.

'Oh, no, no, you take too melancholy a view of her case!' Kit assured him. 'We trust she may – with care – enjoy *several* more years of life, and tolerably good health!'

With these optimistic words he smiled sweetly at the stunned poet, and passed into the house.

Bent on regaling his mama with this passage, he looked into the drawing-room on his way upstairs, and was gratified to find her there, charmingly attired in a half dress of fawn figured silk, a treble pleating of lace falling off round the neck, and a cap of French lace, adorned with a cluster of flowers, set on her shining gold hair. She looked elegant, graceful, and absurdly youthful: circumstances which made Kit chuckle, as he said: 'I've just encountered your mooncalf, Mama! Next time he comes to visit you he won't bring a poem, but a gum-plaster!'

'Bring me a gum-plaster?' she said, astonished.

'Yes, love: for your gout!' he said mischievously. 'I told him that we hoped you would survive for a few years yet, however. That was when he called you an angel – and a more inappropriate description I never heard!'

She burst out laughing. 'Oh, what an abominable

creature you are! But come in, *Evelyn!* Bonamy and I were this instant talking about you!'

Having advanced a step into the room, and closed the door behind him, he had already seen that his mama was not alone: the enormous bulk of Sir Bonamy Ripple occupied almost the whole of a sofa placed opposite her chair. Kit shot a startled, questioning look at his mother, for although he did not rate Sir Bonamy's intelligence high, he could hardly believe that one who had known him and Evelyn from their cradles would detect no difference between them. But Lady Denville appeared to feel no misgiving. She smiled seraphically at Kit. 'Dearest, Bonamy tells me that proposed connexion with Cressida Stavely is one of the on-dits of London!'

'What, are the quizzes busy already?' Kit said, shaking hands with the visitor.

'Bound to be,' said Sir Bonamy, in a rich voice that accorded well with his massive person. 'How-de-do? Been out of town, I hear. Didn't see you at Ascot Races.' He scanned Kit's face, and added: 'You're looking better than when I saw you last. Told you it was time you went on a repairing lease. And now you're in a way to become riveted, are you? I wish you happy, my boy.'

'Thank you, sir, but you are a trifle previous! The matter is not yet decided, you know. Who set the rumour afoot, I wonder?'

'Lady Stavely, of course!' said his mother. 'Trying to force you both into it, meddlesome ninnyhammer that she is!'

Owing to the height and rigidity of his collar-points, and the depth of his Oriental Tie, Sir Bonamy could neither shake his head, nor nod it. When he wished to signify assent he was obliged to incline the upper part of his body in a stately manner which frequently exercised an unnerving effect upon strangers already awed by his size and magnificence. He did so now, but as the Fancots were well accustomed to his ways neither Kit nor his mama was dismayed. Lady Denville, indeed, stared very hard at him, and exclaimed: 'Bonamy! It's you who are making that creaking noise! Exactly like the Regent!'

He looked so crestfallen that Kit interposed to ask him how he had fared at Ascot. But although he was chagrined he was not in the least embarrassed by his hostess's forthright words. He said: 'Oh, tol-lol!' in answer to Kit, but told Lady Denville that in point of fact his new corset was a replica of the one worn by the Regent, only rather larger. 'For the truth is, Amabel, that I am growing to be a little too stout,' he confided earnestly.

Her eyes danced. 'How can you say so? I'll tell you what you must do: you must subsist wholly on biscuits and soda-water, as they say Lord Byron was used to do!'

He blenched perceptibly, but responded with great gallantry: 'Ah, my pretty, if I could hope to win you at last I would even do *that*!'

'If this is a proposal of marriage, I think I ought to go away,' said Kit.

'She won't have me,' said Sir Bonamy mournfully. He shifted his position ponderously, so that he could look at Kit, who had sat down out of the direct line of his vision. 'But I'll tell you this, Evelyn! you'll be a lucky fellow if you get yourself leg-shackled to Stavely's girl! They tell me she's a very amiable, pretty young woman. She can't hold a candle to your mother, of course, but I never saw the woman that could, which is why I've stayed a bachelor all my life. I could never fancy any other female. Never shall! That's why you see me now, a lonely man, with no one to care for, and no one to care a straw for me!'

As he presented the appearance of a comfortable hedonist, Kit was bereft of words. Lady Denville, however, was not so tongue-tied. With what her undutiful son subsequently informed her was an entire absence of propriety, she exclaimed: 'Well, of all the *plumpers* –! As though I didn't know about the – the birds of Paradise you've taken under your protection any time these five-and-twenty years!

And several of them, as I recall, were dashers of the first water – *far* more beautiful than I ever was!'

'No one was ever more beautiful than you, my lovely,' said Sir Bonamy simply. He heaved a deep sigh, which made the Cumberland corset creak alarmingly; but almost immediately grew more cheerful, as he disclosed to Kit that his object in coming to Hill Street was to beg him to bring his mama to a little dinner-party which he was planning to hold at the Clarendon Hotel, before he retired to Brighton for the summer months. 'They have a way of cooking semelles of carp which is better than anything my Alphonse can do,' he said impressively. 'You cut your carp into large collops, you know, and in a stew-pan you put butter, chopped shallots, thyme, parsley, mushrooms, and pepper and salt, of course – anyone knows that! But at the Clarendon something else is added, and devilish good it is, though I haven't *yet* discovered what it may be. It is *not* sorrel, for I desired Alphonse to try that, and it was not the same thing at all. I wonder if it might be just a touch of chervil, and perhaps one or two tarragon-leaves?' He slewed round to smile fondly upon Lady Denville. '*You* will know, I dare say, my pretty! I thought I would have it removed with a fillet of veal. We must have quails: that goes without saying – and ducklings; and nothing beside except a few larded sweetbreads, and a raised pie. And for the second course just a green goose, with cauliflowers and French beans and peas, for I know you don't care for large dinners. So I shall add only a dressed lobster, and some asparagus, and a few jellies and creams, and a basket of pastries for you to nibble at. That,' he said, beaming upon his prospective guests, 'is my notion of a neat little dinner.'

'It sounds delightful, sir,' agreed Kit. 'The only thing is –'

'Yes, yes, I know what you're going to say, my boy!' Sir Bonamy interrupted. 'It wouldn't do for a *large* party! But I mean only to invite three other persons, so that we shall sit down no more than six to table. And there will be side-dishes: a haunch of venison, and a braised ham, possibly. Or a dish of lamb cutlets: I must consider what would be most suitable.' A note of discontent entered his voice. 'I do not consider this the season for dinners of *real* excellence,' he said gravely. 'To be sure, few things are so good as freshly cut asparagus, to say nothing of a basket of strawberries, which I promise you, my pretty, you shall have! But only think how superior it would be if we could have some plump partridges, and a couple of braised pheasants!'

'Yes, indeed, but that wasn't what I was about to say, sir! Nothing would give me greater pleasure than to escort Mama to your party, but it so chances that I am obliged to return to Ravenhurst almost immediately.'

'Why, whatever will you find to do there?' asked Sir Bonamy, opening his small round eyes to their widest extent.

'A great deal, I promise you,' responded Kit easily. 'If Miss Stavely does me the honour to marry me, my uncle, as I dare say Mama has told you, means to wind up the Trust. There are arrangements to be made – a quantity of things to be done before I could venture to bring my bride to Ravenhurst!'

'But don't you mean to be in Brighton this summer?' demanded Sir Bonamy, greatly astonished. 'I thought you had acquired the same house on the Steyne which you rented last year!'

'Yes, so I have – and it is naturally at my mother's disposal. I expect I shall be joining her there presently. I don't know what her plans may be, but I can't think that she needs my escort to your party, sir! Her poet will be delighted to take my place!'

'If you mean that silly young chough I sent to the right-about not ten minutes before you came in, Evelyn, I won't have him at my party!' said Sir Bonamy, roused to unwonted violence. 'A fellow that knows no better than to come to visit a lady, dressed all by guess, and with a handkerchief knotted round his throat –! Ay, and what do you think he was doing when I walked in? *Reading poetry to her!* What a booberkin! I can tell you this, my boy: in *my* day we'd more rumgumption than to bore a pretty woman into a lethargy!'

'I was *not* in a lethargy!' stated her ladyship. 'No female of my age could be *bored* by poems written in her honour! Particularly when the poet has been so obliging as to liken her to a daffodil!' She observed, with sparkling delight, the revulsion in both gentlemen's faces, and added soulfully: 'Tossed like a nymph in the breeze!' She went into one of her trills of laughter, as the gentlemen exchanged speaking glances. 'Confess, Bonamy! you never said such a pretty thing to me!'

'Puppy!' said Sir Bonamy, his eyes kindling. 'A daffodil! Good God! Well, I've never written a line of poetry in my life: it is not my way! But if I *did* write about you I shouldn't call you a paltry daffodil! I should liken you to a rose – one of those yellow ones, with a deep golden heart, and a sweet scent!' said Sir Bonamy, warming to the theme.

'Nonsense!' she said briskly. 'You would be very much more likely to call me a plump partridge, or a Spanish fritter! As for your party, I should like it of all things, and it is most vexatious of Evelyn to go into the country again, for naturally I must accompany him. It is so *dreary* at Ravenhurst, if one is quite alone: not that I ever have been there alone, but I have often thought how melancholy it would be if I *were* obliged to stay there by myself. So you will drive over from Brighton to dine with us, if you please! I expect we shall be able to set ducklings before you, though not, I fancy, quails. But *certainly* lobsters and asparagus!'

This ready acquiescence in his resolve to seek refuge at Ravenhurst surprised Kit. It was not until Sir Bonamy had departed that he learned the reason for it. 'Dearest, did you *know*, then?' demanded his mother, when he returned from helping to hoist her admirer into his carriage.

'Did I know what, Mama?'

'Why, that your uncle Henry is coming to London, on a matter of business! Bonamy told me that he had heard someone say that he was coming, and he said that he would invite him to his party! To be sure, Bonamy couldn't recall *who* had told him of it, but I *wholly* believe it, because it is just the provoking sort of thing Henry *would* do! When anyone would have supposed that he would be fixed in Nottinghamshire – or do I mean Northamptonshire? Oh, well, it's of no consequence, and *you* will know! Wherever it was that he purchased a property when he retired! My darling, I know you have a kindness for him, but you must own that nothing could be more unfortunate than this ridiculous start! I don't feel that he can be *depended* on not to recognize you, do you?'

'On the contrary!' said Kit emphatically. 'He would know me within five minutes of clapping eyes on me! When is he coming to London?'

'Oh, not until next week!' she assured him. 'There's no need to be in a pucker, Kit!'

'No – not if I can get out of town!' he said. He looked at her, between amusement and exasperation. 'Mama, I don't think you can have the smallest notion of the dangers of this appalling situation! I met a friend of Evelyn's on my way to Mount Street, and gave him the cut direct! God knows who he is! I brushed through – said I had been in the clouds, and he swallowed it. But what if he'd guessed I wasn't Evelyn? A pretty case of pickles that would have been, wouldn't it?'

'Yes, but he *didn't* guess, and I'm persuaded no one will, except your uncle, or some particular friend of yours, and you may easily avoid them. However, I think you are very right to remove from London, for I perfectly understand that it must be very exhausting to be always on the watch for Evelyn's friends. Not that I believe any of them would suspect a take-in. Well, look at Bonamy! I did think that he might recognize you, and I let you come into the room just to see whether he would. It wouldn't have signified if he had, because I should have disclosed the whole to him, and he wouldn't have breathed a word to a soul, but he hadn't a notion!' Her eyes searched his face, trying to read his thought. She stretched out her hand, and when, with a faint, rueful smile, he took it in his, she said coaxingly: 'Dearest, why do you look like that? Are you not *enjoying* yourself? Not at all?'

'No, Mama, I am *not* enjoying myself!' he replied, with admirable restraint.

'Oh, dear!' she sighed. 'I thought you would! Why, you were used positively to revel in hoaxing people! Quite as much as Evelyn did! And if ever you were discovered it was always he who made the fatal slip, never you!'

His fingers closed round her hand. 'Do but consider!' he begged. 'In the old days we were just kicking up a lark: we never ran that rig for a serious purpose! Now, think, love! What if the fellow I met today had known me? You might trust Ripple with the truth, but how could I trust a stranger, who, for anything I know, may be no more than a chance acquaintance of Evelyn's? The story would have been all over town by now, and what would be Miss Stavely's feelings when it reached her ears?'

She thought this over, and nodded. 'Very true! It wouldn't do, would it? So awkward to explain it satisfactorily! You don't think Cressy suspects, do you?'

He shook his head. 'No, because she scarcely knows Evelyn. But she's no fool, Mama, and if she grew to know *me* – then she would recognize the imposture as soon as she met Evelyn again.'

'Yes, but she won't grow to know you. You shall leave for Ravenhurst immediately, and if Evelyn hasn't returned by then – though *surely* he will have done so? – I shall join you next week. It would look very particular, you know, if I were to leave London in a pelter.'

'Of course it would, and I beg you won't do so! You

need not come to Ravenhurst at all, love: you will be bored to death there!'

'Kit, how *can* you think me such an unnatural wretch?' she said indignantly. 'It is all my fault that you are obliged to air your heels in the country, and the *least* I can do is to bear you company! For it isn't as though you have a *chère amie* in England, which, of course, would be far more amusing for you – though I don't think you could take her to Ravenhurst, even if you had.'

'No,' he said unsteadily. 'I don't think I could!' His gravity broke down; he went into a fit of laughter, gasping: 'Oh, Mama, what next will you say? First it was Ripple's corset, and now my *chère-amie*! *Such* a want of delicacy, love!'

'Fiddle, Kit! What a wet-goose I should be if I thought you knew nothing about the muslin company! Of course you do, though not, I fancy, as much as Evelyn does, which I am excessively thankful for. Oh, Kit, what can have *happened* to Evelyn? Where *is* he?'

He stopped laughing, and put his arm round her, giving her a reassuring hug. 'Don't worry, Mama! I know no more than you do what can have happened to him, but I'm very sure he's safe and sound somewhere. As for where he is, it seems to me that since he was last heard of at Ravenhurst I may be able to discover a clue if I go there myself. So no falling into the dismals, if you please! Promise?'

She put up a hand to stroke his cheek, smiling mistily at him. 'You are *such* a comfort, dearest! I'll try to keep up my spirits, but it will be a struggle to do so when you've gone away. And when I recall that I shall have to visit old Lady Stavely I feel ready to sink!'

7

Leaving Fimber to follow him with such articles of his brother's wardrobe as Fimber considered indispensable, Kit drove himself down to Sussex in Evelyn's curricle, taking Challow with him. This individual lost no time in quashing the several plans he had formed for discovering Evelyn's whereabouts. He described these, with the freedom of an old and trusted servant, as caper-witted, adding, with some severity, that saving only his lordship he had never known anyone with more maggots in his head than Mr Kit. 'Being as you've set yourself up *as* his lordship, sir, there ain't nothing you can do to find him. A capital go it would be if you was to go round the countryside asking after him!'

Accustomed to the faithful henchman's strictures, Kit said mildly: 'I'm not really as bacon-brained as you think – not that that's praising myself to the skies! As far as inquiring after my brother goes I know very well I'm hamstrung. But –'

'Yes, sir, you are. And if you've taken a notion into your nous-box that I can do it for you, you're beside the bridge! In course, no one wouldn't think there was any havey-cavey business going on if I was to start asking after my lord when he's known to be at Ravenhurst! Oh, no! Not if I didn't ask any but whopstraws they wouldn't! And don't you humbug yourself into thinking everyone *won't* know it, Mr Kit, because there ain't anything that happens at Ravenhurst but what it's talked of all over! You'll have to show yourself abroad now-and-now, too, for you don't want it to look as if you was hiding yourself: that 'ud make you look brummish straight off!'

'Yes, I know all that,' Kit said. 'I was thinking of the toll-gates, and the pikes.'

'Well, sir, I don't deny I've thought of 'em myself,' confessed Challow. 'It's my belief it won't fadge to go asking questions there any more than it will anywhere else. Now, just you think! I *do* know that his lordship drove off through the main gates, but which way he took when he reached the lane I *don't* know, and even if I was to discover that, cunning-like, from Tugby, at the lodge, it's my belief it wouldn't do us a bit of good. If he turned left-handed, it looks like he was making for the London road, but I don't think he did, because I took that road myself, only a couple of hours after his lordship drove off, and the pike-keeper where you come out on to the post-road knows both him and me, and not a word did he say about having seen my lord when he opened the pike to let me through. Seems to me it's more likely he turned right-handed when he got to the lane, but that don't do us a bit of good neither. You know as well as I do, Mr Kit, that it's not more than five miles till you get to the end of the lane that way *and* only a step from the village. If I was to start inquiring after his lordship at *that* pike, we'd have the busyhead that keeps it flashing the gab in an ant's foot, which would send my lord up into the boughs when he got to hear about it.'

'There are other pikes and toll-gates on the road,' Kit said shortly.

'To be sure there are, sir, and a very busy road it is,' agreed Challow. 'Was you thinking of sending me to ask at all the gates and pikes up and down it, which ain't near enough to Ravenhurst for the keepers to recognize his lordship? Because it wouldn't fit, Master Kit! Who's going to remember one phaeton more or less a fortnight back? Ay, and even if I did get wind of his lordship how would I know whether he didn't perhaps turn off the post-road somewheres? I tell you, sir, it ain't no manner of use: he could be anywhere!'

'I'm well aware of that,' Kit replied, keeping his eyes on the road ahead. 'I don't know where to look for him, even if I weren't masquerading, because I don't know his habits, or the company he has been keeping. But don't *you* know,

Challow?' The groom did not answer; and, after a moment, Kit glanced at him, and saw that he was frowning. 'Come, man, unbutton!' he commanded. 'You surely can't suppose that my brother would want you to keep anything a secret from me!'

'It ain't that, Master Kit,' Challow said, shaking his head. 'The mischief is I *don't* know – not by a long chalk! That ain't to say I haven't had my suspicions, the same as Fimber has, but whenever his lordship goes off on one of his revel-routs he don't take either of us with him, nor he don't say where he's off to. It queers me why he should tip us the double like he does, because there's nothing *we* could do to stop him going the pace.'

Kit let this pass. He found nothing remarkable in Evelyn's desire to shake off his fond but censorious guardians when he was bent on adventures of which they would strongly and vociferously disapprove; but as no useful purpose would be served by entering into discussion of this he merely said: 'He may not tell you where he's off to, but I'll swear it's a guinea to a gooseberry that you know!'

'Not properly I don't, sir. I've got my reasons for thinking there's a ladybird in Brighton he used to have dealings with, and another one at Tunbridge Wells. It did cross my mind, when he went off alone from Ravenhurst, that that's where he was bound for. Well, I don't mind owning to you, sir, that when he didn't come home to London when he was looked for, what with her ladyship getting in a twitter, and him being engaged to dine at my Lord Stavely's, I took it upon myself to hop on to the stage, and see if I couldn't get news of him at the Wells. I didn't say anything about it to her ladyship, nor to you neither, Mr Kit, because I'll take my oath my lord ain't there, nor hasn't been. They hadn't seen him at the Sussex, nor the Kentish, nor even the New Inn: that's certain-sure! I got into talk with the ostlers, for if my lord had stabled his grays at any of the inns *they* wouldn't have been forgotten, even if *he* was! You ain't seen them yet, but I give you my word they're complete to a shade! Perfect in all their paces! Four of the tidiest ones you ever clapped eyes on, sir!'

'What about the livery-stables?' interrupted Kit.

'No, sir – not at any which my lord would have trusted with that team. Naturally I thought of that, when I got to wondering if perhaps he'd set his peculiar up private, and wasn't putting up at an inn at all.' He coughed discreetly, adding, on a note of apology: 'If I'm not speaking too free, Master Kit!'

Kit paid no heed to this, but said, frowning ahead of him: 'My brother wouldn't have remained with one of his peculiars at such a time as this.'

'*Just* what I think myself, sir!' said Challow. 'Not when he's made up his mind to step into parson's mousetrap he wouldn't! He's not of that cut – let alone the danger of it! Tunbridge Wells! Lord, I saw with my own eyes upwards of half-a-dozen people there that his lordship knew well!'

Kit nodded, and relapsed into silence. The problem of his erratic twin's whereabouts seemed insoluble; for the only explanation that occurred to him was that Evelyn, who had certainly gone off to redeem Lady Denville's brooch, must have found that Lord Silverdale had left Brighton, and had decided to follow him to his Yorkshire estates. But no sooner had he admitted this thought into his mind than he was struck by its improbability. If Evelyn, pressed for time, as he must have known he was, had undertaken such a journey, he would not have set forth in his phaeton. Nor could there have been any reason to account for his having taken such care to rid himself of his valet. It was equally unlikely that he would not have failed to apprise Lady Denville of his intention. He might well have driven himself to London – but why leave Challow behind? – and gone on from there by post-chaise; but that he had not done so was proved by the absence of his grays from their stable.

Kit was recalled from these ruminations by Challow, who

presented him with a fresh problem. 'Begging your pardon, Mr Kit,' said that worthy, 'but what was you meaning to *do* at Ravenhurst?'

'Do?' repeated Kit, whose only thought so far had been to escape from a locality so fraught with peril as London. 'I don't know – what should I do? Fish – shoot a few wood pigeons and rabbits!'

'Ah!' said Challow, in the voice of one who had foreseen this answer. 'I'm sure I wouldn't want to throw a rub in your way, sir, but if you want to gammon everyone into believing you're his lordship you won't go fishing! That ain't by any means his lordship's notion of sport!'

Kit, who had momentarily forgotten Evelyn's dislike of fishing, felt much inclined to damn his lordship. He quelled the impulse, but said, with a touch of exasperation: 'You've only to add that as I'm nothing like as good a shot as my brother, and must therefore not take a gun out, to tip me a final settler! Don't put yourself to the trouble of doing it, but tell me instead what the devil I *am* going to do!'

'Now, now!' responded Challow, indulgently chiding. 'There's no call for you to take a pet, Master Kit! All I'm saying is that if you do take a gun out you don't want anyone to go with you – no loader, nor Mr Willey, which is my lord's new gamekeeper. You ain't seen him yet, nor he won't know you from my lord, if he don't see you shooting.'

'Thank you!' said Kit, a reluctant grin banishing his frown. 'Stop depressing my pretensions, and tell me who *is* likely to recognize me at Ravenhurst!'

'I been thinking of that, sir, and it don't seem to me that anyone will, barring Mrs Pinner – and seeing as how she lives in the cottage by the west gates now I dare say you *could* keep out of her way.'

He sounded doubtful, but Kit had no doubt at all that there was no possibility of keeping out of his old nurse's way. He exclaimed: 'Keep out of Pinny's way? I don't mean to try! If I can't trust her, there's no one, not even my mother, whom I *can* trust!'

'That's true enough,' agreed Challow. 'What's more, sir, if anyone was to get a suspicion you wasn't his lordship – not that I think anyone will, for the new butler, which my lord engaged a year ago, when it got to be beyond old Mr Brigg to be jauntering up and down from London, ain't never laid eyes on you, and he don't know his lordship very well neither, for, barring the couple of nights we spent at Ravenhurst a fortnight back, my lord hasn't been next or nigh the place since he was here in November, with a party, for the shooting – however, if he *did* happen to be more of a downy one than I take him for, he won't think no more about it when me, and Fimber, *and* Mrs Pinner carry on as though everything was natural and above-board. Well, why should he, Master Kit? No one that didn't know you like we do would ever think of you taking it into your head to run a rig like this!'

Kit opened his mouth to refute the suggestion that he had ever taken any such idea into his head, but shut it again, as he remembered that it had been his own light-hearted words which had put it into his mama's head.

Perceiving that the unwonted frown had deepened on his young master's brow, Challow said encouragingly: 'Now, you don't need to get into the hips, sir, only because I've dropped a warning in your ear! You carry it with a high hand, and you'll do!'

It seemed, when they reached Ravenhurst, that he was right. Since his arrival was unexpected, he found the great gates shut. Tugby, whom he had known all his life, came out of the lodge, looking startled, when Challow blew a sharp summons on the yard of tin, but as soon as he saw Kit he hurried forward to open the gates, ejaculating, 'My lord! Well, I never did!'

'Didn't expect to see me again so soon, did you?' said Kit cheerfully.

'No, that I didn't, my lord! But I'm mighty glad you've come back. We don't see enough of you these days.' He set wide one half of the gate, and returned to pull back the other, looking up at Kit, and saying: 'And have you had word from Mr Christopher, my lord? I hope he's well?'

'Yes: he's in prime twig – and sends his remembrances to all his old friends here.'

'Ah, we want him home, don't we, my lord?' said Tugby. 'It don't seem right to see you here without him.'

Driving through the park, along the well-kept avenue, very much the same thought was in Kit's mind. Ravenhurst was the home of his boyhood, and he loved it; but all his memories of it were so inseparably linked with his twin that the place seemed empty without him, and even a little strange.

Half-ashamed to find himself sentimentalizing, he tried to shake off his depression, and to take pleasure instead in seeing that although it had seldom been visited since his father's death everything was in excellent order. But when he entered the house the feeling of emptiness was oppressive, and made him regret that he had come back to it alone. It had little to do with Evelyn, as he realized. When the family was in residence, upwards of twenty indoor servants were employed; and he could scarcely remember a time when no guests had been entertained there; and since the household had always known when to expect my lord and my lady he had never before found the saloons and the drawing-rooms shrouded in holland covers. He thought it was enough to cast the most cheerful person into gloom, and wondered for how long he would be obliged to remain there. He also wondered, and with a flicker of amusement, for how long his mother would bear it. She frankly disliked country life; and the only things that made her sojourns at Ravenhurst tolerable were a succession of visitors, and its proximity to Brighton.

His arrival threw the reduced staff into some disorder, but neither the new butler, nor his wife, showed the smallest disposition to question his identity. He said, quite in Evelyn's careless manner, that he supposed he must have forgotten to tell them that he meant to return within a few days; and added, by the way, that her ladyship would be joining him the following week. These tidings appeared to stun the butler; but Mrs Norton, her eyes kindling with housewifely fervour, instantly began to formulate a number of plans for my lady's reception, and to ask so many questions about the number of servants my lady meant to bring down with her from London, that Kit very soon escaped from the house, and walked across the park to visit his old nurse.

As he had expected, she recognized him, if not as soon as she saw him, the instant he spoke to her. She gave him a fond welcome; asked him several searching questions about his health, recalling to his memory various childish disorders which he had long since forgotten; and accepted, with no more than a shake of her head, and a disapproving click of the tongue, the intelligence that he was impersonating Evelyn. But when she discovered (after some still more searching questions) that the masquerade had been forced on him by the inexplicable disappearance of his brother, he found her far more sympathetic than any of the three other conspirators. She exclaimed: 'Oh, if ever there was such a whisky-frisky, downright *naughty* boy –! Never you mind, Master Kit-dear! I'll give him a good rakedown when I see him. The idea of him getting up to his tricks at his age, and just when he's going to be married, too! But don't you fret, my dearie: no one will know you; and, as for his lordship, you should know better than to get into the fidgets over *him*! If he's in a scrape, mark my words if he don't save his groats, and come safe home, bless him!'

Kit was not surprised to find that his nurse knew of Evelyn's matrimonial plans; but when he presently learned from Fimber, whom he found unpacking his valise in the bedroom in the west wing of the house, which Evelyn had inhabited a fortnight before, that the rest of the household was similarly well-informed, he could not help wondering whether any secret could be kept from servants, particularly such a perilous secret as his own. Fimber seemed to be untroubled by doubts; but he said, as he set out Kit's brushes on the dressing-table, that he had been thinking the matter over, and had reached certain conclusions.

Eyeing him with misgiving, Kit demanded: 'What conclusions?'

'Well, sir,' responded Fimber, 'it must be remembered that it has become extremely unusual for his lordship to visit Ravenhurst, so that your arrival today has given rise to a good deal of curiosity. In any ordinary circumstances, as I hope I don't need to assure you, I should instantly give the Nortons a heavy set-down, but in this case I felt it would be better to drop a hint to them.'

'A hint of what?' said Kit, with even greater misgiving.

'Of your approaching nuptials, sir – assuming that you are his lordship,' said Fimber, tenderly laying a pile of shirts on one of the wardrobe shelves. 'Naturally, rumours of the event had reached Ravenhurst some time since, but I had not previously confirmed these.'

'Oh, you hadn't?'

'No, sir,' said Fimber imperturbably. 'It is not my practice to go beyond the bounds of commonplace civility when conversing with the Nortons. Very respectable people, I dare say, but mere newcomers. I apprehended that they would try to discover from me what had brought you back to Ravenhurst, and I was prepared to meet with astonishment – not to say disbelief, Mr Christopher.'

'What the devil did you tell them?'

'That you wished to look into things here, sir – as was agreed before we left the Metropolis. It is perfectly well-known to everyone that it is my lord's uncle who holds the reins, and that my lord won't concern himself in any way with what he doesn't feel to be his own. So I was obliged, Mr Christopher, to drop a hint that there would shortly be Changes at Ravenhurst.'

'Did that satisfy the Nortons?'

'Oh, yes, sir! Quite excited they are, hoping that her *young* ladyship may take a fancy to the place, and persuade my lord to open up all the rooms, like they should be, and like they always were when his late lordship was alive – not that they know anything about that, except by hearsay. If I might make a suggestion, you should tell Mrs Norton to have her ladyship's apartments got ready for you to inspect – as if you was planning to refurnish them, sir.'

Kit raised no objection to this; but he looked suspiciously at Fimber, well aware that the precision of his speech, and the wooden manner he had assumed boded a further, and certainly less palatable suggestion. He said: 'I can do that easily enough, but you may as well tell me now as later what else you've got in mind.'

'I beg your pardon, sir?'

'Stop hiding your teeth!' commanded Kit. 'You don't ride on *my* back, so don't think it! What's up your sleeve?'

'I'm sure I don't know what you may mean, sir. It merely occurs to me that it would be a good thing if you was to send for your bailiff, to discuss all the business of the place with you. But no doubt you've already thought of that.'

'I've done no such thing!' said Kit forcefully. 'Send for Goodleigh – who is *not* my bailiff – to discuss my brother's affairs with him? Thank you! that would be beyond everything!'

'Then you'd as well turn tail at once, Mr Christopher, for nobody's going to believe you've come down to look into things if you *don't* look into them!' retorted Fimber, reverting to his usual manner. 'That would be just the very thing to set people wondering, that would! There's no need for such a humdurgeon. Why shouldn't you talk to Mr Goodleigh about the estate, and ride round with him, maybe? If you mean to tell me his lordship would take a huff, all I can say is that it ain't for you to accuse *me* of hiding my teeth, sir! You know as well as I do that his lordship would bid you do as you thought fit, and welcome!'

'Yes, I dare say, but –'

'You're blue-devilled, Mr Christopher: that's what's amiss!' interrupted Fimber bracingly. 'And no one could wonder at it, with the house like a tomb, and you missing his lordship, as I'll be bound you are. You'll feel more the thing when you've eaten your dinner. It seems his lordship didn't use any of the rooms but those in this wing when he was here, so I told Norton you'd do likewise. The library has been made ready for you, and dinner will be served you in the Green Parlour, so you go down, sir, and be comfortable!'

A short but excellent dinner certainly relieved Kit's depression, but it did nothing to lessen his reluctance to obtain access to the bailiff's records by what could only be regarded as a cheat. He would have found it hard to explain the repugnance he felt, for he had nothing to gain, and he knew even better than Fimber that so far from objecting to his conduct Evelyn would be very much more likely to demand to know what the devil he meant by imagining that he *could* object to it. The feeling of distaste lingered, however, and if his hand had not been forced he would have evaded an encounter with the bailiff.

But this worthy presented himself at the house before Kit had finished his breakfast on the following morning; and when his supposed employer joined him, perforce, in the library, he greeted him with a warm smile, and an apology for failing to wait upon him when he had visited Ravenhurst a fortnight earlier. He disclosed that when he had laid the quarterly accounts before Lord Brumby my lord had informed him (with gratifying condescension) that he had every expectation of being able, shortly, to resign his trusteeship; and had charged him to do all that lay within his power to put my Lord Denville in possession of every relevant detail that concerned the management of his Sussex estate. He added, beaming upon Kit, that if he had had warning of his previous visit he would not have failed to have waited upon him. 'For, if I may be permitted to say so, my lord, I – and, I believe, *all* who are employed at

Ravenhurst – have been eagerly awaiting the day when you would assume the control of your inheritance. Not that I, or anyone, would utter a word in disparagement of my Lord Brumby! No one could have been more punctilious in the execution of his duties than Mr Henry – Lord Brumby, I *should* say! – but it is not the same thing, sir! Not to those of us who watched you and Mr Kit grow up from your cradles! And how *is* Mr Kit, my lord?'

Mr Kit, resigning himself to the inevitable, said that he was very well; accepted gracefully felicitations on his twin's approaching marriage; and expressed his willingness to spend the rest of the golden summer's morning amongst the several forbidding tomes which Goodleigh had brought up to the house for his inspection. Fortunately, it did not occur to Goodleigh that his noble master was much more interested in the property bequeathed by the late Earl to his younger son than in his own vast inheritance.

During the next two days, Kit's boredom was enlivened by instructive rides round the estates with Goodleigh, and by a ceremonial visit from the Vicar of the parish. On the third day, the reduced staff at Ravenhurst was thrown into a state of excited expectation, and himself one of instinctive foreboding, by the arrival of two coaches from London, accommodating, amongst a number of lesser menials, the steward, my lord's and my lady's own footmen, and the extortionately paid, and vastly superior individual who held sway over the kitchens in my lord's town-house in Hill Street. These vehicles were followed some time later by a large *fourgon*, which was found to contain, besides a mountain of trunks, several housemaids, two kitchen-porters, two subordinate footmen, and such articles of furniture as my lady considered indispensable for her comfort. Later still an elegant private chaise swept up to the main entrance. The steps having been let down, a stately female, who bore all the appearance of a dowager of high estate but was, in fact, none other than Miss Rimpton, my lady's top-lofty dresser, alighted, to be followed, a moment later, by my lady herself, far from stately, but ravishing in a pomona green silk gown which clung to her shapely person, and the very latest mode in bonnets: a dazzling confection with a high crown, a huge, upstanding poke-front, pomona green ribbons, and a cluster of curled ostrich plumes. Mr Fancot, arriving on the scene just in time to hand this vision down from the chaise, was the immediate recipient of an unnerving announcement, delivered in an urgent undervoice.

'Dearest, the most *dreadful* thing!' said her ladyship, casting herself into his arms, and speaking into his ear. 'There was nothing to be done but to pack up immediately, and come down to support you! And don't, I implore you, try to law it in my dish, Kit, because I never foresaw it, and am wholly overset already!'

8

It was some time before Kit was able to detach his mama from the various senior members of the household who were either demanding, or receiving, instructions from her; but he managed to do it at last, and to withdraw with her to the library. Shutting the door upon the ominously hovering form of Miss Rimpton, he said, between laughter and anxiety: 'For God's sake, Mama, tell me the worst! I can't bear the suspense for another moment! *What* is the dreadful thing that has brought you here five days before your time? Why all those servants? Why so much baggage?'

'Oh, dear one, do but let me rid myself of this hat before you bombard me with questions!' she begged, untying its strings. 'It is giving me the headache, which is *too* vexatious, for it is quite new, and *wickedly* expensive! Indeed, if it had not been so excessively becoming I should have refused to purchase it. Except, of course, that when one owes one's milliner a vast amount of money the only thing to be done is to order several more hats from her. I bought the prettiest lace cap imaginable at the same time: you shall see it this evening, and tell me if you don't think it becomes me.' She removed the hat from her head, and looked at it critically. 'This does, too, I think,' she said. 'And what a *very* smart hat it is, Kit! It's what you, or Evelyn, would call *bang-up to the nines*! But it does make my head ache.' She sighed, and added tragically: 'There's no end to the troubles besetting me: first it's one thing, and then it's another! And all at the same moment, which quite wears down one's spirits.'

Accepting the situation as he found it, Kit replied sympathetically: 'I know, love! They come not single spies, but in battalions, don't they?'

'That sounds to me like a quotation,' said her ladyship mistrustfully. 'And it is only fair to warn you, Kit, that if you mean, after all I have endured, to recite bits of poetry to me, which I am not at all addicted to, even at the best of times, I shall go into strong convulsions – whatever they may be! Now, isn't that *odd*?' she demanded, her mind darting down this promising alley. 'One hears people *talk* of going into convulsions, but have you ever *seen* anyone do so, dearest?'

'No, thank God!'

'Well, I haven't either – in fact, I thought they were something babies fell into! Not that *my* babies ever did anything so alarming. At least, I don't *think* you did. I must ask Pinner.'

'Yes, Mama,' he agreed, removing the hat from her hands, and setting it down carefully on a table. 'But are you quite positive that this very beautiful bonnet is to blame for your headache? Might it not be the outcome of your journey? You never did like being shut into a postchaise, did you?'

'No!' she exclaimed, much struck. 'I wonder if you could be right? It *is* beautiful, isn't it?'

'Quite captivating!' he assured her. 'Did you purchase it to console yourself for all the troubles which have descended on you? What, by the way, was the particular trouble which brought you here in such a bang?'

'Kit!' uttered her ladyship. 'That terrible old woman is coming to visit us here next week, and she is bringing Cressy with her!' She waited for him to speak, but as he appeared to have been struck dumb, and merely stood staring at her, she sank into a chair, saying: 'I *knew* how it would be if I were obliged to visit her! Well, I knew that no *good* would come of it, though I didn't foresee such an ordeal as this. If I had had the smallest notion of it, I would have said I was going to stay at Baverstock – and, what's more, I would have done so, much as I detest your aunt! But I had already told her that I was coming here, and so the mischief was done. How *could* I say I wasn't coming here after all? You must perceive how impossible!'

'Mama!' interrupted Kit, finding his voice. 'Do you mean that Lady Stavely is going to give us a look-in on her way to Worthing?'

'No, no, what would there be in that to dash one down? She and Cressy are coming to spend a week or two here!'

'A *week* or two? But they can't! they mustn't be allowed to! Good God, what can have induced you to consent to such a scheme? You surely didn't *invite* them?'

'Of course I didn't!' she said. 'Lady Stavely invited herself!'

'But, Mama, how *could* she have done so?'

'Good gracious, Kit, I should have thought five minutes in her company would have been enough to show you that there's nothing she's not very well able to do! Besides, she led me into a trap. She is the most odious old witch in the world, and she *always* overpowers me, ever since I was a child, and positively dreaded her! Oh, she is too abominable! Would you believe it? – the *instant* she clapped eyes on me, she said that she saw I had taken to dyeing my hair! I was never more shocked, for it is *quite* untrue! It is not *dyeing* one's hair merely to restore its colour when it begins to fade a little! I denied it, of course, but all she did was to give the horridest laugh, which made me feel ready to sink, as you may suppose!'

'I don't suppose anything of the kind!' said Kit, roused to unwonted callousness. 'Why should you care a straw for anything Lady Stavely chose to say? It is too absurd!'

His mama's magnificent eyes flashed. 'Is it, indeed?' she said tartly. 'I marvel that you should have the effrontery to say such an unfeeling thing, when you know very well that *never* did your Great-aunt Augusta visit us but what she put you and Evelyn out of countenance within two minutes of seeing you!'

His formidable (and happily defunct) relative having been thus ruthlessly recalled to his mind, Mr Fancot had the grace to retract his unkind stricture. 'Less!' he acknowledged. 'I beg pardon, love! So then what happened?'

Bestowing a forgiving and perfectly enchanting smile upon him, Lady Denville said: 'Well, *then*, having made me feel as if I were a gawky girl – which, I do assure you, Kit, I never was! – she became suddenly quite affable, and talked to me about you with amazing kindness! Which shows you how cunning she is! For even if she did make me feel as if I were a silly chit I don't doubt she knew that if she had uttered one word in disparagement of *either* of my sons, I should – I should have *slain* her, and walked straight out of the room!'

On the broad grin, Mr Fancot interpolated: 'Bravo!'

Lady Denville received this applause with becoming modesty. 'Well, dearest, I should have been roused to fury, because nothing enrages me more than injustice! I may be a frivolous widgeon, but I am not so bird-witted that I don't know that no one ever possessed two such sons as mine! However, Lady Stavely said *nothing* about you to which I could take exception. Then she told me that although she perfectly acknowledged that Evelyn is a catch of the first water, she had come to perceive that marriages between persons who are not – not thoroughly acquainted with each other don't always lead to happiness. She said – not in the least exceptionably, but with true kindness! – that she was persuaded I must agree with her. Which I do, Kit! Then she confided to me that although she had wished very much to invite Cressy to live with her, when Stavely married Albinia Gillifoot – oh, Kit, she dislikes Albinia even more than I do! we had the most *delightful* cose about her! – she had not done so, because she is too old to take her to parties, and so what would become of Cressy when she dies? She said she would be obliged to live with Clara Stavely, and dwindle into an old maid. Which is why she wishes to see her suitably married. Then she said that she believed that, with all my faults, I was truly devoted to my children, and she was persuaded I must feel, as she does, that before coming to a decision Evelyn and Cressy ought to know one another better. Well, dearest, what *could* I do but agree with her? Especially when she told me that I must be the last person to wish to see my son make an unhappy marriage, for that was what I did myself. I must own, Kit, that I was very much touched!'

His pleasant gray eyes looked steadily down into hers, the suggestion of a smile in them. 'Tell me, Mama, *were* you so unhappy?'

'*Often!*' she declared. 'I have frequently fallen into fits of the most dreadful dejection, and if I were inclined to lowness of spirit I daresay I should have sunk under the trials that beset me. Only I can never stay for long in the dismals, for something always seems to happen which makes me laugh. You may say that I'm volatile, if you choose, but I do think you should be glad of it, because there is nothing so dreary as *ticklish* women, behaving like wateringpots at the least provocation, and being for ever in the hips! And in any event *my* sensibilities have nothing to do with the case! The thing is that as soon as I agreed that it would be desirable for Evelyn and Cressy to become better acquainted Lady Stavely *floored* me by saying that since I had the intention of joining you here she thought it would be an excellent scheme if she were to bring Cressy on a visit. I *hope* I didn't look no-how, but I fear I must have, for she asked, in that sharp way of hers, if I had any objection? Dearest, what *could* I say but that I thought it a delightful scheme, and only wondered that it hadn't occurred to me? I may be volatile, but I am not rag-mannered!'

'Couldn't you have made some excuse? Surely you must have been able to think of *something*, Mama?'

'I thought of several things, but they would none of them do. Indeed, I had almost said that one of the servants here had begun in the small-pox when it very fortunately struck me that if that had been so *you* wouldn't have come to the house. And though I did think of saying that it was you who had the small-pox, I couldn't but feel that it would be a shocking bore for you to be obliged to remain cooped up here for weeks and weeks – and we must remember, Kit, that Evelyn may come back at any moment! Well, you know what he is! We should never be able to persuade him to take your place in the small-pox.'

'Mama, why, in heaven's name, small-pox? Scarlet fever in the village would have been much better, if you had to make illness the excuse!'

'Yes, but I couldn't think of any other illness except the measles, and depend upon it Lady Stavely and Cressy have probably had them already.'

He began to pace up and down the floor, frowning heavily. After a pause, he said: 'I shall have to go away – back to Vienna, where, indeed, I must go pretty soon!'

'Go away?' she cried, in the liveliest dismay. 'You cannot do so, when the Stavelys are coming purposely to see you! It would be beyond anything!'

'It could be accounted for. I could be taken ill in Vienna, or suffer a serious accident – something very bad! No one would think it odd of Evelyn to go to me immediately!'

'Well, of all the hare-brained notions! Next you will say that no one would think it odd of me to remain in England under such circumstances!'

'Come with me!' he invited, pure mischief in his face.

It was reflected in hers. 'Oh, how amusing it would be!' she said involuntarily. Then she shook her head. 'No, we couldn't do it, Kit. Only think what a hobble we should all be in when Evelyn came back! He wouldn't know what had become of me, and he would be bound to search for me all over. That *would* fling the cat amongst the pigeons! Dearest, there is nothing for it but to make the best of it. And I must tell you that I have already done so – the best I *could*, at all events.'

'It won't do, Mama. Cressy and I should be thrown together in a way that must inevitably lead to a degree of intimacy which on all counts is to be avoided. Good God, that's why I left London – so that she should *not* become better acquainted with me!'

'Yes, and I perfectly understand how vexatious it is for you to be obliged to remain strictly upon your guard. But it won't be as bad as you anticipate! By the most amazing stroke of fortune I found Cosmo waiting for me in Hill Street when I returned from visiting Lady Stavely!'

'Cosmo?' he repeated blankly.

'Yes, Kit: *Cosmo!*' replied her ladyship, in a tone of determined patience. 'My *brother* Cosmo – your *uncle* Cosmo! Dearest, *must* you stand like a stock? You cannot have forgotten him!'

'No, of course I haven't forgotten him! But why you should think it a stroke of fortune to have found him in Hill Street is a matter quite beyond my comprehension!'

'Now, *that*,' said his mama triumphantly, 'shows that you are much more shatterbrained than I am! Because Cosmo is the very thing we need! And Emma, too, of course. My dear, he must have been sent by providence – which is a thing that frequently happens, I find, when one is in flat despair: like my recalling in the very nick of time, when I thought myself *wholly* ruined, that I might very well apply to Edgbaston for a loan. Naturally, when I was being driven home from Mount Street, I was racking my brain to think how, at this season, to assemble a *party* here, which I perceived was most necessary on *your* account, Kit: to save you from being thrown entirely into Cressy's company. I couldn't hit on anyone, except, of course, poor Bonamy, because even if there had been more time at my disposal – and one can't invite people all in a quack, you know, unless they are relations, or very close friends – no one *wants* to be in the country during the summer! Unless one is the sort of person who wishes to go on a tour, to observe mountains, and gorges, and the beauties of nature, which is the most exhausting and uncomfortable thing imaginable, I do assure you Kit! I cannot describe to you the miseries I endured when your father made me accompany him to Scotland once. I dare say it was all very fine, but when one has been jolted over *abominable* roads, and forced to put up at the most *primitive* inns, besides having to *walk* for miles and miles, one is in no case to admire scenery.'

'Do I understand, Mama,' said Kit, in a failing voice, 'that you have invited Cosmo, and my aunt, to come and stay at Ravenhurst?'

'To be sure I have!' she replied, with a brilliant smile. 'And it was exactly what he hoped I should do! At least, I fancy he meant to wheedle me into inviting him to visit us in Brighton, but you know what a nip-cheese he is, Kit! if he can but contrive to live at rack and manger *somewhere* he is content! In general, he goes to Baverstock in the summer, but it seems that he cannot do so this year, because your Aunt Baverstock won't have him. I must say, one can't blame her for not wanting him and poor Emma to be running tame about the house for weeks on end, however detestable one may think her. I have always avoided inviting them myself, though *not* as rudely as Amelia. But in this instance they are the very persons we need! Only consider, dearest! We scarcely ever see them, so they won't know you from Evelyn; and they play whist! For chicken-stakes, too, which will exactly suit Lady Stavely. So I told Cosmo he might come – I mean, I *invited* him and Emma to come, and I said that we should be delighted to welcome Ambrose as well. He may serve to entertain Cressy, perhaps.'

'I've nothing to say against having my uncle and aunt to stay: in fact, it's a good notion, love; but the last time I saw my cousin Ambrose he was the most odious little bounce I ever met in my life!' said Kit, entering a most ungrateful caveat.

'Yes, wasn't he?' agreed her ladyship, quite unruffled. 'But he was only a schoolboy then, after all! I dare say he may have improved. In any event, we are obliged to have him as well, because Cosmo says he means to keep him under his eye during the whole of the Long Vacation, poor boy, and not give him another groat to spend until he goes up to Oxford again in October, on account of his having run monstrously into debt. Or so Cosmo says, but I dare say it is no such thing, and he owes no more than a few hundreds. But what with that, and his having been rusticated last term, it does sound as if he must have improved, doesn't it? I don't know why he was rusticated – Cosmo primmed up his mouth when I asked him, so I collect there had been petticoat dealings – but I do know that you and Evelyn were, at the end of one Hilary term, and even your papa only thought it a very good joke!'

Mr Fancot, regarding her with a fascinated eye, drew an audible breath. 'No, Mama, I do *not* think it sounds as if he must have improved! On the contrary, it sounds as if he were growing to be a pretty loose fish! And let me inform you, love, that when Evelyn and I were sent down for the rest of the term, it was *not* because of petticoat dealings! Merely one of our hoaxes – as a matter of fact, the best rig we ever ran!'

'Well, never mind, dear one!' she said placably. 'No

doubt it is just as you say! I merely thought that if he is got into debt he does at least sound as if he were more of a Cliffe than Cosmo, who is such a scratch that one can't help but wonder whether he is not a changeling! It doesn't signify: indeed, we must hope that Ambrose hasn't improved too much, because it would never do if Cressy were to develop a *tendre* for him. You do perceive that things won't be so *very* bad, don't you?'

'To be sure!' he responded, with suspicious alacrity. 'You have behaved in the *nackiest* way, Mama, so that all we have to do now is to hope that Lady Stavely will find my uncle and aunt so intolerably boring that she will rapidly bring her visit to a close.'

She rose, and picked up her hat from the table. Brushing Kit's chin with its plumes, she retorted: 'On the contrary, there is a great deal more to be done – though I know very well *you* won't concern yourself with the preparations that must be made, horrid creature that you are! And though I dare say Lady Stavely *will* think Cosmo and Emma dead bores, she will be pleased to see Bonamy, don't you agree? She has been acquainted with him for ever, and he is a *very* fine whist-player!'

Kit gasped. 'Good God, I thought that was nothing but a bubble! You don't mean to tell me you've really persuaded Ripple to leave Brighton to come into the country, which he dislikes quite as much as you do, and play chicken-whist with a griffin like Lady Stavely?'

She lifted a saucy eyebrow at him. 'What makes you suppose there was any need of *persuasion*, Master Rudesby?'

'I *beg* your pardon, Mama! But this is devotion indeed!'

She chuckled. 'Yes, but the truth is that he is excessively goodnatured, besides having been in the habit for years and years of thinking he loves me better even than his dinner. He doesn't, of course, but I *never* let him suspect that I know it. Which reminds me that I must take care to see that his favourite dishes are set before him. Yes, and to speak to the cook about sending to Brighton *every* day to procure fresh fish. Then, since we *are* at Ravenhurst, I think we must hold a Public Day, which we didn't last year, because of being in mourning for Papa. Oh, dear, what a vast quantity of things must be attended to! I shouldn't wonder at it if I were prostrate by the time our guests arrive!'

For the following few days the household was certainly plunged into a vortex of activity, but my lady's part in all the preparations was confined to issuing a great many contradictory orders, forming and abandoning several ineligible plans for the entertainment of her guests, and sending the under-servants on errands which were afterwards discovered to have been unnecessary Tempers became frayed, but no one bore my lady the least ill-will, so charmingly did she give her orders, and so prettily did she thank anyone who performed a service for her. Instead, – and until Kit put his foot down, sternly informing the senior members of the staff that he wished to hear no more complaints from any of them – the London servants and the resident-servants blamed each other for every mistake or hitch that occurred; and a state of guerrilla warfare raged in the Room and in the Hall. The only two people to remain unaffected were Miss Rimpton, who held herself loftily aloof from any matter which did not immediately concern the care of my lady's wardrobe and her exquisite person; and the cook, who listened with the greatest civility to his mistress's orders and reminders, and continued to rule his kingdom exactly as he thought fit.

During this mercifully brief period of stress Kit was afforded a closer view of his parent's extravagance than had ever before been granted him. Before her arrival he had been surprised to discover that the smart new barouche which he encountered in the avenue was one of her latest acquisitions. It was drawn by a pair of good-looking bays; and the coachman, drawing up, and touching his hat, told him that he was just bringing them in after their daily exercise. Kit, mentally assessing the turn-out at £300, or more, was startled, for not only did he know that Lady Denville owned another, and even smarter, barouche, in which she was driven about London, but also that there were several carriages in the coach-house at Ravenhurst, one of which was a comfortable landaulet. It was later explained to him, by Challow, that since landaulets were now considered to be dowdy it was not to be expected that my lady would ride in one, even when staying in the country. Upon Kit's venturing to suggest to his mama that it was really a trifle wasteful to have purchased a second expensive carriage and pair merely for her use during her short and infrequent visits to Ravenhurst, she assured him that he was quite mistaken; and proved, to her own satisfaction, if not to his, that it was by far more economical to keep a second barouche and pair (with her own second coachman) at Ravenhurst, than to go to the trouble and expense of bringing her town equipage down to Sussex.

Since she had been assailed before leaving Hill Street by one of her fortunately rare fits of housewifely fervour, Mrs Norton, and Mr Dawlish, my lady's extremely competent cook, were astonished, and considerably affronted, by the arrival of the carrier, who disgorged from his ponderous wagon a staggering number of cases, which were found to contain, amongst other household necessities, forty-eight pounds of wax lights, and two casks of Genuine Spermaceti Oil, from the firm of Barret, of St James's, Haymarket; two Westphalian hams; several pounds of Hyson tea, Superfine Vanilla, and Treble-refined Sugar, from Peter Le Moine, at the sign of the Green Canister, in King Street; a large quantity of wafers, from Gunter's; and half-a-dozen strange but obviously costly pieces of furniture, presently identified by her ladyship as flower-stands, which she had happened to catch sight of on one of her shopping expeditions, and had instantly recognized as being Just the Thing for Ravenhurst. She explained the purchase of the candles and the groceries to Kit on very reasonable grounds: how could she have been sure that

Mrs Norton, who had been for so short a period house-keeper at Ravenhurst, had laid in a sufficient store of these commodities? Furthermore, she had been reared in the belief that true economy lay in buying the *best*, and as it was her ineradicable conviction that the best could only be obtained in London, or in Paris, the merest commonsense had prompted her to make good possible deficiencies in Mrs Norton's cupboards and stillroom. But since Mrs Norton prided herself on her competence and foresight her sensibilities were seriously ruffled, until Lady Denville explained, with her most engaging smile, that she had ordered all these groceries only because she knew how vexatious it was to be obliged to provide for guests at a moment's notice, and had been determined to spare her housekeeper as much trouble as she could. Mr Dawlish, far better acquainted with his mistress, received her excuses with a polite bow, but said that he preferred to make his own wafers – though the ones sent by Gunter would serve very well for the Public Day – and that if her lady-ship would be so obliging as to furnish him with the name and direction of the firm from which she had ordered a turtle he would write immediately to cancel the order, having already made his own arrangements for the delivery of a fine turtle at Ravenhurst. Further, that he had personally selected, and brought from London with him, one York and one Westphalian ham, which he ventured to think would meet all requirements.

'Only, what does her ladyship wish me to do with all that Spermaceti Oil, my lord?' asked the harassed Mrs Norton. 'There's not an oil-lamp in the house, barring the one that hangs in the kitchen, and Common Oil is what we burn in that, not Spermaceti, at seven shillings and sixpence the gallon!'

Having dealt as well as he could with this and other vexed questions, Mr Fancot was faced with the task of convincing his parent that to send one of the grooms to Hill Street for the purpose of obtaining from Mrs Dinting, or from Brigg, the hundreds of invitation cards she had forgotten to bring with her to Ravenhurst, and which would be discovered in the second drawer of her desk – or, failing that *cache*, in one of five other hiding-places – would be very much more costly than to order new ones from a Brighton stationer. He succeeded, but not without difficulty, Lady Denville being a little hurt by his failure to recognize her effort towards economy. It remained only for him to drop a tactful hint in the ear of the steward, to the effect that the scrawled directions received from my lady's bedchamber, while, banked up by lace-edged pillows, she consumed a light breakfast, should be brought to him before being carried out; and to approve the various bills of fare laid before him by Mr Dawlish. That artist, quick to perceive that my lord – doubtless because he contemplated marriage – had reformed his careless habits, lost no time in turning this improvement to good account. No one was more devoted to her ladyship; no one knew better what dishes to set before her to tempt her capricious appetite; no one was more willing to work himself to death in her interests; but (as he informed Mrs Norton, in a moment of condescension) when it came to planning a series of handsome dinners he preferred to lay his proposals before my lord, who, far from turning them topsy-turvy, and demanding game birds that were not in season in place of as tender a pair of turkey poults as anyone could wish for, could be trusted to cast no more than a cursory glance over the bills of fare before signifying his approval of them. However, said Mr Dawlish indulgently, there was no call for Mrs Norton to get into the fidgets: when she had been acquainted with my lady for as long as he had she would know that her starts never lasted above a day or two.

So, indeed, it proved. By the time the first guests arrived on Tuesday my lady was herself again, her final activity having been to drift through the flower-gardens, holding up a parasol to protect her complexion from the sun, and pointing out to the head gardener the blooms she wished to see in her six new containers. The effect was all that she had been sure it would be, for the gardener was expert in flower-arrangement; and since she watched him at work, several times choosing, and handing to him, a spray from the basket held by one of his satellites, and proffering a number of suggestions, she was convinced, by the end of the morning, that she had filled all the containers herself, with only a little assistance from him.

The first arrivals were the Hon. Cosmo and Mrs Cliffe, and Mr Ambrose Cliffe, their sole surviving offspring. They came in a somewhat antiquated travelling chariot, drawn by one pair of horses: a circumstance which caused my lady to exclaim: 'Good God, Cosmo, did you hire that shocking coach, or is it your own? I wonder you will be seen in such a Gothic affair!'

Mr Cliffe, who was a tall, spare man, some few years older than his sister, replied, as he dutifully kissed her cheek, that post-charges were too heavy for his modest purse. 'We are not all of us as fortunately circumstanced as you, my dear Amabel,' he said.

'Nonsense!' responded her ladyship. 'I dare say your purse is fatter than mine, for you never spend a groat out of the way. It is quite abominable of you to have brought poor Emma here, jumbling and jolting in a horrid old coach which *strongly* reminds me of the one Grandpapa had, and which always made Grandmama sea-sick! Dear Emma, how much I pity you, and how glad I am to see you – though not looking as stout as one would wish! I shall take you up to your bedchamber immediately, and see you laid down to rest before dinner.'

Mrs Cliffe, a flaccid woman, with weak blue eyes, and a sickly complexion, responded, with an indeterminate smile, and in a curiously flat voice, that she was pretty well, except for a slight headache.

'I shouldn't wonder at it if every inch of you ached!' said her ladyship, shepherding her into the house.

'Oh, no, indeed! If only Ambrose may not have caught cold!'

'My dear Emma, how could he possibly have done so on such a day as this?'

'His constitution is so delicate,' sighed Mrs Cliffe. 'He was sitting forward, too, and I am persuaded there was a draught. Perhaps if he were to swallow a few drops of camphor – I have some in my dressing-case –'

'If I were you I wouldn't encourage him to quack himself!' said Lady Denville frankly.

'No, dear, but your sons are so remarkably healthy, are they not?' said Mrs Cliffe, looking at her with faint compassion.

But as her ladyship was not one of those mothers who considered that delicacy of constitution conferred an interesting distinction on her children, the compassion was wasted. She said blithely: 'Yes, thank goodness! They never ail, though they did have the measles, and the whooping-cough, when they were small. They *may* have had chicken-pox too, but I can't remember it.'

Mrs Cliffe admired her lovely sister-in-law, but she could not help feeling that she must be a very heartless parent to have forgotten such an event in the lives of her sons. Perhaps Cosmo was right, when he said that Amabel cared for nothing but fashionable frivolities. But when Lady Denville presently left her, comfortably reposing on a day-bed, with a shawl cast lightly over her feet, a handkerchief soaked with her ladyship's very expensive eau-de-cologne in her hand, and the blinds drawn to shut out the sunshine, she decided that no one so kind and so attentive could be heartless, however fashionable she might be.

Meanwhile, Kit had led his uncle and his cousin into one of the saloons on the ground floor where various liquid refreshments of a fortifying nature awaited them. Although an engrained parsimony prompted Cosmo to stock his own cellar with indifferent wine, his palate was not so vitiated that he did not know good wine from bad. After a sniff, and an appreciative sip, his expression became almost benign, and he said, with a nod at Kit: '*Ah!*'

'A very tolerable sherry, coz!' said Ambrose, not to be outdone.

'Much you know about it!' said his father scornfully. 'Sherry, indeed! This is some of the Mountain-Malaga your uncle laid down – let me see! – ay, it must be thirteen or fourteen years ago! It wants another year or two yet, Denville, to be at its prime, for the longer the Spanish Mountain wines are allowed to mature the better they become. But it is very potable! Alas, what is now being sold as Malaga is a travesty of the Mountain wines I drank in my youth!' He took another sip, and favoured his nephew with a smile. 'I collect, my dear boy, that I shall shortly be called upon to offer you my felicitations. Very right! very proper! I live out of the world nowadays, but I understand that Miss Stavely is an unexceptionable female: I look forward to making her acquaintance. Your dear mother tells me that the match has Brumby's approval, so I must suppose that Miss Stavely's portion is handsome?'

'I regret, sir, that I can give you no information on that point, since I have no ideas what her portion may be,' said Kit, regarding him with disfavour.

Cosmo looked shocked, but said, after a moment's reflection: 'But it is not to be supposed that your uncle Brumby would favour the match if it were not so! To be sure, you were born to all the comfort of a handsome fortune, Denville, but it must cost a great deal of money – a *very* great deal of money! – to maintain an establishment such as this, and the house in London, to say nothing of the little place you own in Leicestershire. Then, too, your father, I dare say, made suitable provision for your brother, and that must mean a considerable diminution of your income.'

'As though Denville wasn't full of juice!' muttered young Mr Cliffe into his wineglass.

Happily, Cosmo did not hear this interpolation. He

seemed to take almost as much interest in his nephew's financial situation as in his own; and continued, for as long as it took him to drink three glasses of Malaga, to speculate on the probable yield of my lord's estates; the number of servants needed to keep so large a mansion in order; the cost of maintaining such extensive flower-gardens; and the extortionate rates demanded for houses in Mayfair. To do him justice, his interest, and his energetic plans for the reduction of his nephew's expenses, were entirely altruistic: he had nothing to gain; but almost as much as he liked to save money for himself did he like to evolve plans whereby other people's money could be saved. He was listened to politely by his nephew, and by his son with a mixture of rancour and embarrassment. That young gentleman, as soon as Cosmo had left the room, was so ill-advised as to beg Kit not to pay any heed to him. 'He always talks as if he was purse-pinched – it's his way! It's bad enough when he starts that tug-jaw at home, but when he does it in company it's beyond anything!'

Kit was not unsympathetic, for he could readily perceive that to a nineteen-year-old, unsure of himself, yet anxious to be thought all the go, Cosmo must be a severe trial; but he thought his cousin's speech extremely unbecoming, and somewhat pointedly changed the subject. It was to no avail. Ambrose continued to animadvert bitterly and at length on his father's shortcomings until Kit lost patience, and told him roundly that his complaints did him no credit. 'I don't wonder at it that my uncle should have taken your doings in snuff! Lord, could you find nothing better to do at Oxford than to visit the fancy-houses? As for rustication, let me tell you, cawker, that Eve –' He caught himself up, and swiftly altered the word he had been about to utter – 'that *even* Kit and I weren't rusticated because we had got into the petticoat line! In *our* day we left such stuff to the baggagery! As for boasting of having given some wretched ladybird a slip on the shoulder –'

'I didn't boast of it!' blurted out Mr Cliffe, blushing fierily. 'I only said –'

'Oh, yes, you did!' said Kit grimly. 'And if I were you I'd keep mum for that, halfling!'

Much discomposed, Ambrose muttered: 'Well, *you're* no saint, Denville! Everyone knows that!'

'No, and nor am I a Queer Nab, which is what you'll be, if you don't take care!' said Kit, with cheerful brutality. He laughed suddenly. 'Come, don't be such a gudgeon, Ambrose! You are making me forget I'm your host.'

'Well, considering they still talk of the things you and Kit did, when you was up, it's the outside of enough for you to be pinching at *me*!' said Ambrose, much injured.

'Do they? Famous!' said Kit, his eyes lighting with sudden laughter. 'I'll swear they don't say, though, that we wasted our time chasing the white-aprons!'

9

On the following day, towards the end of the afternoon, the Dowager Lady Stavely arrived at Ravenhurst, in an even more antiquated and ponderous travelling chariot than Mr Cliffe's, and accompanied by her granddaughter, her abigail, and her personal footman. Mr Fancot, notwithstanding his expressed wish to put as many miles as possible between himself and any member of the Stavely family, greeted their appearance on the scene with as much pleasure as was compatible with his fear that he might, in an unguarded moment, betray himself. For this, twenty-four hours spent in the company of his maternal relations were largely responsible. What Lady Denville mendaciously described as a cosily conversable evening had been followed by a singularly boring, and, at times, difficult day. Cosmo, himself the owner of a modest estate, had chosen, when civilly asked to say what he would like to do, to ride round his nephew's acres. During this expedition, on which Kit had felt himself bound to escort him, he had asked a great many pertinent questions to which Kit, who, as a younger son, had never concerned himself with the management or the revenue of his father's property, was hard put to it to answer. He was obliged to endure a homily from his uncle, who perceived, with regret, that report had not lied when it described the Sixth Lord Denville as a frippery young man, wholly abandoned to frivolity. Fortunately for the absent Evelyn's reputation, Mr Cliffe retired to the library after a substantial nuncheon, spread a handkerchief over his face, and sank into profound and audible slumber. Kit was left with the task of trying to entertain his cousin: no easy one, since young Mr Cliffe's sole desire was, as he expressed it, to take a bolt to Brighton. Asked what he wanted to do in Brighton, he replied vaguely that they might go for a toddle on the promenade, or perhaps take a look-in at a billiards-saloon. But as Kit, in the existing circumstances, was determined to give this haunt of fashion a wide berth; and would have shrunk, under any circumstances, from being seen in the company of a would-be dandy who presented to his jaundiced eye all the appearance of a counter-coxcomb, this scheme was blocked at the outset. Kit said that it behoved him to be on hand when the Stavelys arrived; and that if Ambrose wanted to play billiards on a summer's afternoon there was a very good table at Ravenhurst. In the end, as Ambrose said that he didn't know that he really wished to play billiards, he drove him upstairs to change his tightly fitting coat, his dove-coloured pantaloons, and his cut Venetian waistcoat for attire more suited to the country, and bore him off to shoot rabbits. Ambrose went unwillingly, saying, with a nervous laugh, that he was not a crack shot, like his cousin; but after he had been forcibly dissuaded from carrying his fowling-piece at an extremely dangerous angle, and had been given a lesson in how to load and fire it he forgot his affectations, and began to enjoy himself. He was much relieved to find his cousin so goodnatured, for he stood in secret awe of Evelyn, remembering a previous visit to Ravenhurst, as a schoolboy, when Evelyn, finding that he had neither the taste nor the aptitude for any form of sport, regarded him with contempt, and soon shrugged him off. It seemed to him that the passage of time had greatly improved Evelyn; and presently, emboldened by the patient encouragement he received, he confided that he rather thought he would like to be able to shoot well. 'Only the thing is, you see, that I never had the opportunity to learn, because m'father ain't a sporting cove.'

Realizing for the first time that Ambrose had grown up under disadvantages he had never himself experienced, Kit was inspired to suggest that while he was at Ravenhurst he should place himself in the hands of the head gamekeeper, who would be delighted to have a pupil to school. The idea took well; and as the proposal was shortly followed by a shot which accounted for one of a gathering of unwary rabbits Ambrose trod back to the house immensely set up in his own conceit, as convinced that he had aimed at that particular rabbit as he was that in less than no time he would be acknowledged by all to be a famous shot.

Half-an-hour after they had reached the house again, and just as Kit came downstairs, having changed his rough coat, his breeches, and his long gaiters for more formal attire, the Dowager Lady Stavely's impressive chariot was at the door and Norton, aided by my lady's footman, and with two of his own satellites in support, was tenderly handing her down from it. Kit arrived on the scene in time to hear the blistering reproof she addressed to her helpers: he gathered that her mood was unamiable, and was not surprised to be greeted with a pungent criticism of the state of the lane which led from the pike-road to the main gates. 'However,' she conceded magnanimously, 'you have a very tolerable place here – very tolerable indeed! I was never here before, so I'm glad to have seen it.' Her sharp eyes scanned the variegated façade. 'H'm, yes! I do not call it splendid, but a very respectable seat. You should root up all those rhododendrons beside the avenue: nasty, gloomy things! I can't abide 'em!'

'But think how beautiful they are when they are in bloom, ma'am!' said Cressy, who had just alighted from the carriage.

'All but the shabby-genteels are in London then, so much good do they do one!' said Lady Stavely sweepingly. She saw that her hostess was coming down the wide, shallow stone steps, and nodded to her. 'How-de-do? I've been telling Denville he should root up those rhododendrons on the avenue: they make it too dark.'

'Yes, don't they?' agreed Lady Denville. 'Like descending into Hell; only then, of course, one comes out into open ground, which is such an agreeable surprise. Let me take you into the house, ma'am: the sun is quite scorching!'

The Dowager uttered a cackle of amusement. 'Thinking of your complexion, are you? When you get to be my age you won't care a rush for it. We used to lay crushed strawberries on our faces, to clear the sunburn. Slices of raw veal, too, against wrinkles. Not that I ever did so: messy, I call it! I dare say you use all manner of newfangled lotions, but they don't do you any more good than the old-fashioned remedies did us.'

Lady Denville, who nightly applied distilled water of green pineapples to her exquisite countenance, and protected it during the day with Olympian Dew, replied without a blink that that was *very* true; and guided her guest towards the steps, offering the support of her arm. This was refused, the Dowager stating that she preferred the services of her footman. She also stated, when it was suggested to her that she might like to be conducted immediately to her bedchamber, that she was an old woman, and in no state to drag herself up any more stairs until she had recovered her breath and what little energy remained to her.

'Then you shall come into the Blue saloon, which is delightfully cool, ma'am,' responded Lady Denville, with unabated good-humour. 'I'll tell them to make tea, and that will revive you.'

'Well, it won't, for I shan't drink it!' said the Dowager. 'I'll take a cup of tea after dinner, but I won't maudle my inside with it at this time of day! What I *could* fancy – but it's of no consequence if you have none! – is a glass of negus.'

'To be sure! how stupid of me!' exclaimed Lady Denville, directing a look of agonized inquiry at her butler.

'Immediately, my lady!' he said, rising magnificently to the occasion.

Cressy, still standing at the foot of the steps, raised ruefully smiling eyes to Kit's face, and said softly: 'She is tired, you know, and that always makes her knaggy! I am so sorry! But she will be better presently.'

An answering smile was in his eyes as he said: 'I've a strong notion that somewhere – in one of the lumber-rooms, I fancy – there is a carrying-chair that was used by my grandfather, when he became crippled with the gout. Do you think –?'

'I do *not*!' she replied, on a choke of laughter. 'The chances are that she would take it as an insult. It will be best to leave her to your mother's management: depend upon it, she will charm her out of the mops! I think she would charm the most ill-natured person imaginable, don't you? And Grandmama is not that – truly!'

'Certainly not! A most redoubtable old lady, who instantly won my respect! Now, what would you like to do? Shall I hand you over to Mrs Norton, to be escorted to your bed-chamber, or will you take a turn on the terrace with me?'

'Thank you! I should like to do that. I caught glimpses

on the avenue of what I think must be a lake, and longed to get a better view of it.'

'That may be had from the terrace,' he said, offering his arm. 'I wish you might have seen it when the rhododendrons were in full bloom, however! Even your grandmama would own that their reflection in the water, on a sunny day, makes up for their gloominess now!'

'You wrong her, Denville! Nothing would prevail upon her to do so!' She turned her head, looking at him a little shyly, yet openly. 'I wish you will tell me if this visit of ours is – is quite what you wanted?'

He replied immediately: 'How could it have been otherwise?'

'Oh, easily! It was a stupid question to ask you, for you were obliged to give me a civil answer! The thing is that I have a lowering suspicion that Grandmama forced Lady Denville to invite us.'

'I believe it was she who hit upon the notion, but I can assure you that Mama was delighted with it. Can you doubt that I too am delighted?'

'Well, yes!' she replied unexpectedly. 'The thought has teased me that although I told you that I had not perfectly made up *my* mind, I didn't ask you to tell me whether you, perhaps, had misgivings too. When you left London, it occurred to me – I could not help wondering if – Oh, dear, my tongue is tying itself into knots! You see, I do understand how very awkward it must be for you, if you are wishing you had never offered for me! So don't stand on points, but tell me if you feel we should not suit, and leave it to me to settle the matter – which, I promise you, I can do, without the least fuss or noise!'

He put his hand over hers, as it lay on his arm. 'That is *very* kind and thoughtful of you!' he said gravely.

'Well, I know how difficult it is for gentlemen to cry off,' she explained. 'It has always seemed to me to be monstrously unjust, too, for you may quite as easily make a mistake as we females are held to do so frequently!'

'Very true! That is to say, I haven't yet had occasion to consider the matter, but I feel sure you are right.'

She smiled. 'Are you ever at a non-plus? That was charmingly said. But let us have no flummery, if you please! And don't be afraid that you will offend me! Tell me the truth!'

'The truth, Miss Stavely, without any flummery, is that the more I see of you the greater becomes my conviction that you are worthy of a better man than I am.'

She wrinkled her brow. 'Is that a civil way of telling me that you *would* like to cry off?'

'No. It is a way of telling you that you are a darling,' he said, lifting her hand, and lightly kissing it.

The words were spoken before he could check them, and with a sincerity which brought a wave of colour into Cressy's cheeks. He released her hand, thinking: *I must take care*; and: *I have never known a girl like this one.* Aloud, he said: 'Are you afraid to walk on the grass in those thin sandals, or will you let me show you the rose-garden? It is quite at its best – and I have just caught sight of my young cousin! He will almost certainly join us if we remain here, and I wouldn't for the world expose you to *that* trial until you have recovered from the fatigue of your journey!'

Her quick flush had faded; she laughed, falling into step beside him. 'Yes, indeed! I dare say we must have come quite thirty miles! Is your cousin so very dreadful?'

'Yes: half flash and half foolish!' he said, handing her down the unevenly flagged steps on to the shaven turf. 'We were used – my brother and I – to think him an irreclaimable jackstraw, and accorded him the roughest treatment on the rare occasions when we met him.'

'It seems to me that you still do so!'

'Not at all! I took him out to shoot rabbits this afternoon – my life in my hands! That's quite enough for one day. Seriously, he's a tiresome youth – what I should describe, if I were talking to one of my own sex, but not, of course, to *you*, as a shagbag.'

She said appreciatively: 'No, of course not! And how *would* you describe him to me?'

'As a quiz – and bumptious at that! But I'm beginning to think that the fault doesn't lie altogether at his own door. Are you acquainted with his father? my uncle Cosmo?' She shook her head. 'Ah, then that is another treat in store for you! He is one of mother's brothers, but she seems to suspect that he may be a changeling. Don't be surprised if he asks you what you paid for your gown, and then tells you where you could have had it made up more cheaply!'

She was in a little ripple of amusement. 'I won't! You can't think what a relief it is to me to know that you too have relations who put you to the blush! I'm covered with confusion every time I recall that *shocking* party in Mount Street, with poor dear Cousin Maria putting you out of countenance by saying in a voice to be heard all over London that you were *very* handsome; and that odious creature, Austin Lucton, trying to buttonhole you! My father was vexed to death when he heard that you *did* buy his horse! Is it a horrid commoner? Papa says that Austin can never judge a horse.'

'Oh, not a commoner!' he answered. 'Just a trifle short of bone! You may see him for yourself: I had him brought down here, and have been hacking him.'

'*Not* thinking him fit to go in Leicestershire!' she said. 'What can have possessed you to buy him? I fear your reputation will be sadly damaged!'

He chuckled softly. 'No, will it? That's famous!' He read a surprised question in her eyes, and added: 'No, I don't mean that! The truth is that I was obliged to purchase the animal – having kept your cousin waiting such an unconscionable time for my decision. Do you hunt, Cressy?'

She shook her head. 'No, I'm afraid I don't. I have been out once or twice with Papa, but not in the shires. You, I know, are what Papa calls one of the Tally-ho sort! I hope you won't require me to try to emulate you, for I am very sure I couldn't do so. I like to ride, but I am *not* an accomplished fencer! To own the truth, I find it very hard to throw my heart over a bullfinch, and I *hate* drop-fences!'

'Capital!' he said cheerfully. 'For my part, *I* hate hard-riding females! Of late years, I have had little opportunity –' He caught himself up, and continued smoothly – 'of observing the prowess of ladies on the hunting-field!' He stood aside, to allow her to pass through a rustic arch over-hung with trailing crimson ramblers. 'Here, ma'am, we enter into our celebrated rose-garden! Do you like it?'

'Oh, it is beautiful – exquisite!' she exclaimed, standing at gaze for a minute, before moving forward swiftly to inspect more closely a new specimen, just bursting into full flower.

'Tell Newbiggin so – he's our head gardener – and you will have made a slave for life! I should warn you, however, that my dear Mama is firmly convinced that she, and she alone, made this garden! And it is perfectly true that it was she who *conceived* the notion. She was immersed in plans when I left for Constantinople, but –'

'When you left for Constantinople?' she repeated, looking quickly up at him.

'To visit my brother,' he said glibly.

'Did you do that? How much I envy you!'

'Are you fond of foreign travel?'

'I have never done any – only in books!' she said. 'It was used to be my greatest ambition – to see the world a little – but Papa dislikes foreigners, and I never could persuade him to go even as far as to Paris. You visited your brother in Vienna too, didn't you? I wish you will tell me about it!'

There was no difficulty about this; and as they strolled companionably down the paths that separated the rose-beds Kit soon found that her reading had taught Cressy a great deal. She listened eagerly, interpolating an occasional question; and from time to time Kit paused to break

133

off a particularly fine bloom to give to her. When they made their way back to the house she held quite a bouquet, and said, conscience-stricken: 'If we should meet your gardener now he will become my enemy, not my slave! Tell me, Denville, did your father make the Grand Tour when he was young? Don't you wish you had grown up then, before the war, when it was thought to be part of a young man's education to travel abroad, learning to speak foreign languages, seeing how people live in other countries?'

'Except that if my father's Grand Tour is anything to judge by they went at too early an age, and were hedged about by tutors. As far as I could ever discover from the things my father told me, he went from one large city to another, armed with introductions to the ton, and spent his time between studying with his tutor and attending balls and routs – which he might as well have done in London!'

She said thoughtfully: 'Yes, but I have a melancholy suspicion that our fathers – and even more our grandfathers – had very little interest in the beauties of nature, and still less in the customs of the *people*. My own grandfather kept a diary of his Grand Tour, and it is composed almost entirely of great names, and social functions which he attended: I was never more disappointed, when Papa gave it to me to read! For he must have passed throughout the *grandest* scenery, you know!'

'Did he record that he took care to wear lambswool next the skin when travelling over an Alpine pass?'

She burst into laughter. 'Yes, he did! Oh, dear! How sad that our forebears should have had such opportunities, and should have wasted them so shockingly!'

They had reached the terrace-steps by this time. As they mounted them, Kit said: 'Have you taken Miss Clara Stavely's place in attendance on your grandmama, Cressy? My mother wasn't perfectly sure if she would be accompanying you, or not.'

'Oh, I'm sorry! I should have told her. Yes, I always go with Grandmama to Worthing at the end of the Season, so that Clara may enjoy what is known in the family as her *holiday*! In fact, she has gone to fetch and carry for my Aunt Caroline – and will very likely be required to take charge of the children as well, if I know my Aunt Caroline!' She smiled. 'Don't look so shocked! Let me tell you that my Aunt Elizabeth, who is the kindest creature imaginable, was used to think it as abominable as I can see you do that Clara should become a mere drudge. She invited her once to spend the summer in Hertfordshire, determined that she should enjoy a holiday of ease and comfort. Clara had nothing to do but be cosseted and amused – and had almost moped herself into a decline (as she later confided to me) when Aunt Eliza summoned her to come instantly to her aid, one of her children having thrown out a rash; her eldest son, my cousin Henry, having taken a toss, and broken his arm; and her housekeeper having been obliged to leave at a moment's notice to succour her ailing mother, who had been laid low with a palsy-stroke. Aunt Eliza told me that Clara packed her trunks in the twinkling of a bedpost, and was on her way to Lincoln while she, and her *very* attentive children, were still trying to prevail upon her to remain at Stoborough Hall! I collect that there was all to do in Lincoln, and I *know* how exacting is my Aunt Caroline, but I promise you that when Clara resumed her post beside Grandmama she was wonderfully refreshed!'

He was obliged to laugh at this lively history, but he said, cocking an eyebrow at her: 'Yes, I too have an aunt who – according to what my mother tells me – derives immense satisfaction from immolating herself on the altar of family duty. But I hope you don't mean to try to bamboozle me into believing that *you* are of this cut!'

'Not in the least!' she replied. 'Nor do I immolate myself. The worst I have to suffer when I go to Worthing with Grandmama is – is a certain tedium! And even that is alleviated by Grandmama's tongue.' He had opened a door that gave access to the terrace from the house, and she said, pausing before she stepped across the threshold: 'Thank you for my roses! Do you keep country hours at Ravenhurst? Will you desire one of the servants to take me to my room, if you please? It must be time I made myself ready for dinner.'

'We'll find my mother,' he replied. 'She will certainly wish to take you up herself.'

Lady Denville was not far to seek, for she was coming down the stairs as Kit conducted Cressy into the main hall. She was looking a trifle harassed, but when she saw Cressy her face brightened, and she came quickly down the remaining stairs to fold the girl in a scented embrace. 'Dearest child! I was wondering where you were, for I haven't exchanged above two words with you!'

'I beg your pardon, ma'am! Denville took me to see your rose-garden – and was so kind as to pluck these for me! Aren't they beautiful? The garden too, so charmingly laid out! We have nothing like it at Stavely.'

'It *is* pretty, isn't it?' agreed her ladyship. 'Such a labour as it was to make it! But I've never regretted it. Cressy, I must warn you that this is the *dreariest* party! It positively overpowers me to think that I should have invited you to it, poor child! What with my brother, prosing and moralizing in the most *boring* manner, and Emma growing *drabber* under one's very eyes, and speaking like a mouse in a cheese, not to mention Ambrose, whom anyone would take for a mere April-squire – '

'You didn't invite me, Godmother!' Cressy interrupted, laughing. 'I know very well I've been foisted on to you! And I defy any party of which you are a member to be dreary!'

'Yes, but I am already feeling excessively low and oppressed,' said her ladyship. 'And I was obliged to tell Norton to set dinner forward, because your grandmama particularly desired me not to expect her to keep late hours.

So we shall dine at six, my dear – though why one should dine in daylight merely because one is in the country I have *never* understood! However, it won't be so *very* bad, because I have ordered supper at eleven, when I do hope Lady Stavely will have retired!'

'You can't say I didn't warn you that I too have relations who put me to the blush, Cressy!' interpolated Kit.

'Oh, dear!' exclaimed Lady Denville, stricken. 'Well, doesn't it *show* you how disordered my senses are? Besides, Cressy knows that her grandmama always puts me in a quake!'

'Of course I do!' averred Cressy, her eyes alight with amusement. 'Was she very twitty, ma'am? Are you at outs with me for having left her to your management? I do beg your pardon, but I thought you would contrive to smooth down her bristles much more easily if I were not present. I expect you did, too!'

'Well, I don't know that I did that, precisely,' said Lady Denville, considering the matter, 'but I must own that when I took her to her room a few minutes ago she was not so out of reason cross! I don't mean to say that she was in high good-humour, but she very fortunately detected that the colour had faded a little from the brocade I chose for the curtains in the Blue saloon – which I never thought to be thankful for, K – Evelyn! because I had it sent from Lyons, and the cost put your father all on end. Indeed, I was quite provoked myself when I saw how sadly it had faded! But one never knows when what *seems* to have been a mistake will turn to good account: it put Lady Stavely in a *much* better humour when she was able to tell me what a peagoose I had been. Dearest Cressy, I think I should take you to your room *immediately*, for it won't do to keep your grandmama waiting for her dinner! They tell me you haven't brought your maid, so I will send Rimpton to you – and *don't*, my love, allow her to put on airs to be interesting! I wonder sometimes why I bear with her – but she is a wonderful dresser!'

Miss Stavely, though in no doubt of Miss Rimpton's skill, declined her condescending offices, saying that Grandmama's Jane would do all for her that was necessary. This was not of a nature to tax the skill of an abigail who was more a nurse than a dresser, for it consisted merely of hooking up a very becoming gown of light orange crape. This was done in the Dowager's room, and under her eye. She accorded the gown a certain measure of approval, but said that the skirt was too narrow, adding the time-honoured observation that she didn't know what the world was coming to, when females tried to make themselves look like hop-poles. Disdaining the modern fashion of high waists and clinging skirts, she was herself attired in a stiff black silk, worn over an underdress embroidered with silver thread. A cap of starched black lace was on her hair: mittens covered her arms; and in one hand she held a fan. Unlike her granddaughter, who wore the lightest of silk sandals, she had chosen from a large collection of out-moded shoes a pair with high heels, and paste buckles. Cressy told her mischievously that the only thing wanting was a patch on her cheek.

'Patches went out of fashion before you were born!' replied the Dowager crushingly. 'You may go now, Jane. No, give me my cane – the ebony one! Yes, that will do. And tell William to come up directly to support me down those slippery stairs!' She turned to survey Cressy, as the door closed behind the placid attendant. 'And where have you been, miss?' she demanded.

'Walking in the rose-garden with Lord Denville, ma'am,' said Cressy, undismayed by the sharpness of the question.

'H'm!' My lady scrutinized her own rouged countenance in the looking-glass, picked up a down puff with her twisted fingers, and gave her cheeks a further dusting of powder. 'Never thought to ask if I wanted your company!'

'I knew that you didn't, Grandmama,' responded Cressy, quizzing her intrepidly. 'You told me not to hang about you, unless I wished to fret you to flinders, which, I promise you, I don't! Furthermore, dear ma'am, I couldn't suppose that when you had Lady Denville to take care of you there was the smallest need for me to remain at your side.'

'Amabel Denville is nothing but a pretty widgeon!' declared the Dowager roundly. 'She always was, and she always will be!' She glared at her own reflection, her jaws working. 'One of these days she'll be like me: an old bag of bones! But I'll tell you this, girl! If any of my daughters had possessed a tenth part of her charm I'd have thanked God for it! Help me out of this chair! I ought to be in my bed, with a basin of gruel, but I'll come down to dinner, and if I feel able for it I'll have a game of backgammon with Cosmo Cliffe afterwards. But I dare say I shan't: I'm too old for all this junketing about the country! I only trust that if I'm carried off you'll remember it was for your sake I came here!'

This malevolent speech did not augur well, nor did the Dowager's mood grow more propitious until the party went in to dinner, when she became very much more mellow. For this her hosts had Mr Dawlish to thank. Not for nothing did this genius command an extortionate wage: he knew quite as well what to offer a very old lady as how to serve up a grand dinner of two full courses, consisting of half-a-dozen removes and upwards of thirty side dishes. The Dowager, revived by a soup made with fresh peas, allowed herself to be persuaded to try a morsel of turbot; followed this up with several morsels of a delicate fawn, roasted whole, and served with a chevreuil sauce; and ended her repast with a dish of asparagus, cut and delivered by the kitchen-gardener a bare ten minutes before Mr Dawlish was ready to cook it. This was so succulent that she was moved to compliment Kit on his cook. She informed him, in her forthright fashion, that she had eaten too much, and would probably be unable to close her eyes all night; but it was noticeable that when she left the dining-room she did so without assistance, and with a remarkable diminution of her previous decrepitude.

Although Kit had been willing enough to concede that Cosmo might entertain the Dowager by plying card-games with her, he had been quite unable to picture her enduring with even the appearance of complaisance his aunt's flat platitudes. Great was his astonishment, therefore, when, following his uncle and cousin into the drawing-room some time later, he found these two ladies seated side by side on the sofa, and engaged in interested converse. Since Lady Denville had had a card-table set up at the far end of the long room, and lost no time in sweeping the three younger members of the party to it, to play, under her aegis, such frivolous games as suggested themselves to her, it was not until he paid his mama a goodnight visit that Kit learned the reason for this sudden and extraordinary friendship. Nothing, declared her ladyship, had ever been more fortunate! Poor Emma, during the course of a very boring anecdote, had let fall a Name, which had instantly made Lady Stavely prick up her ears. After exhaustive discussion, which had appeared to Lady Denville to range over most of the noble houses in the country, and a fair proportion of the landed gentry, it had been established, to both ladies' satisfaction, that they were in some way related.

'But pray don't ask me how, dearest!' begged Lady Denville. 'I can't *tell* you how many cousins, and marriages, and mere connexions were dragged in: you cannot conceive how tedious! But it has led to that terrible old woman's taking a fancy to Emma, and I have every hope that we shall be able to fob her off on to your aunt!'

10

Lady Denville's hope was to some extent realized. Either because of the remote relationship between herself and Mrs Cliffe, or because the Dowager perceived in that biddable lady an excellent substitute for her daughter Clara, she chose to honour her with her approval, and lost no time in inducting her into the duties of companion-in-chief. Somewhat to Lady Denville's surprise, Poor Emma was perfectly willing to assume these. They were not, in fact, as arduous as might have been supposed, since the Dowager never left her bedchamber till noon, and admitted no one into it except her abigail; retired to it two hours before dinner; and spent the evening playing whist, or piquet, or backgammon with such members of the party as she considered to be worthy opponents, or partners. Mrs Cliffe was not numbered amongst these; and until the arrival of Sir Bonamy Ripple, three days after the rest of the guests had assembled, it was Kit who occupied the fourth place at the whist-table. He was a sound, if not a brilliant player, and once he had grasped the difference between long whist, which the Dowager preferred, and short, to which, as a member of the younger generation, he was accustomed, she had no serious fault to find with him. But as Lady Denville's play was divided between flashes of brilliance, and strange lapses (due, as she unacceptably explained to the Dowager, to her having been thinking of something else at just that moment), it was soon tacitly decided that she and her son should be perpetual partners against the Dowager and Cosmo Cliffe.

Emma's new duties, therefore, consisted merely of bearing the Dowager company during her unoccupied moments, and going with her, every fine afternoon, for a sedate drive round the neighbouring countryside; and as this regimen exactly suited her disposition no one felt her to be an object for compassion.

Ambrose, still fired with the hope of becoming a notable shot, spent every morning with the head gamekeeper, a longsuffering individual, who confided to Kit that if he succeeded in teaching Mr Ambrose to hit a barn-door at a range of twelve yards it would be more than he bargained for.

This, since Cosmo spent the better part of the day either

perusing the London papers in the library, or prowling about the estate, asking shrewd questions of bailiffs and farmers, and reporting detected extravagance to Kit, left Kit with the charge of entertaining Miss Stavely. On sunny days, they rode together, or played at battledore and shuttlecock; when it rained they played billiards, or sat in comfortable talk; once, at her request, he took her to the long picture-gallery, regaling her with an irreverent history of his ancestors, many of whose portraits lined the walls. She entered into the spirit of this, and capped with aplomb his top-lofty boast of a recusant priest (in the collateral) with an account of the Stavely who had blotted the escutcheon by having journeyed so far into Dun territory that he had seen nothing for it but to take to the High Toby.

Kit, acknowledging the superior distinction of this anecdote, wished to know if this enterprising scion had succeeded in making his fortune; but Miss Stavely informed him, with what he told her was odious pretension, that it was generally believed that her interesting forebear had perished on the scaffold, under the cognomen of Gentleman Dick.

'That's good,' he admitted. 'But take a look at old Ginger-hackle here! One of my great-great-uncles, and said to have murdered his first wife. Here she is, beside him!'

'Well,' said Cressy, subjecting the portrait of a languishing female to a thoughtful scrutiny, 'I shouldn't wonder at it if he did. Anyone can see that she was one of those complaining women, for ever having the vapours, or dissolving into floods of tears. And I have little doubt that that red head of his denotes an uncertain temper.'

But the picture which held Miss Stavely's interest longest was the Hoppner portrait of the Fancot twins, executed when they were schoolboys. 'How very alike you are!' she remarked, studying more closely than Kit appreciated what was held to have been one of Hoppner's best likenesses. 'There *is* a difference, when one looks more particularly into it. Your hair is brighter, and your brother is a trifle taller than you are. Something in the expressions, too . . . .'

'Do you think so? The seeming difference in height is merely the way in which we were posed, I fancy. As for the expression, the picture was never thought to be one of Hoppner's happier works,' said Kit, ruthlessly sacrificing the deceased artist's reputation. 'Come and look at Lawrence's portrait of my mother!'

She allowed herself to be drawn onward; but she cast another glance at the Hoppner before she left the gallery, and one surreptitious but searching one at Kit's profile. She said nothing, however, either then, or rather later, when the Dowager delivered herself of the opinion that Lord Brumby had wronged his elder nephew.

The Dowager was inclined to be indignant with his lordship. 'Depend upon it, Cressy, he's getting to be spiteful! It's often so with old bachelors. He dotes on the other boy, and is jealous of young Denville in consequence!'

'He said nothing to Papa about Denville that was in the least spiteful, ma'am,' Cressy ventured to interpolate. 'Indeed, he told Papa that although Denville had been a little wild he believed that nothing more than a – a suitable marriage was wanting to make him –'

'Stuff and nonsense!' exclaimed the Dowager, her eyes snapping. 'Henry Brumby's an old woman, and so I shall tell him! There's nothing of the profligate about the boy, and never was! I dare say he's had his adventures: why not? But I cut *my* wisdoms long before Brumby cut his, and if he thinks I don't know the signs of a loose-screw he very much mistakes the matter! There ain't one to be seen in Denville – and *that* you may believe, girl! I like him. Do you?'

This sudden question slightly discomposed Cressy, but upon being adjured to answer it, she said, blushing a little: 'Yes, I do. Much – much better than I did at the outset. But –'

'But what?' demanded the Dowager, as Cressy hesitated.

Cressy shook her head. 'Nothing, ma'am! That is – no, nothing!'

The Dowager looked narrowly at her, but said, after a moment: 'Early days yet! I don't mean to press you, so I'll say no more. You ain't a simpering miss, so you won't underrate the advantages of this match. You know as well as I do that Denville's a matrimonial prize: time was when I should have thought more of that than I do today. So was his father, and much good did it do silly little Amabel Cliffe when she caught him!' She sat ruminating for a moment, and then abruptly changed the subject, saying: 'I collect that Bonamy Ripple is coming to join us tomorrow. What a bag-pudding! However, I shall be glad to see him, for he plays a good game of whist, and knows all the latest on-dits.' She paused again, before adding, with the utmost reluctance: 'I'll say this for Amabel! – to be able to drag Ripple away from Brighton at this season is something indeed!'

But when Sir Bonamy lowered himself, with the assistance of two muscular footmen, from his travelling carriage next day no one would have supposed from his demeanour that the smallest force had been necessary to bring him away from the Pavilion to the seclusion of Ravenhurst. Radiating good-humour, he grasped Kit's hand with one of his own pudgy ones, and declared that this was 'something like!' Wheezing only a very little from the exertion of descending from the carriage, he stood looking about him, a not unimposing, if preposterous figure, in the nattiest of country raiment, with a voluminous drab driving coat hanging open from his shoulders, and a shaggy, low-crowned beaver set rakishly askew over his curled and pomaded locks. 'Very agreeable!' he pronounced. 'Very pleasing prospect! Do you know, my boy, I've never seen it in the summer before? Excellent! just the thing for recruiting nature! I feel as fresh as a nosegay already.'

Kit's eyes twinkled. 'I'm happy to welcome you here, sir!'

Sir Bonamy's little round eyes stared at him for an unwinking moment. 'Much obliged to you! Very prettily said!'

Recalling belatedly that his twin barely tolerated their mama's most devoted admirer, Kit skated smoothly over this, saying: 'But I should warn you that the exigencies of country life may perhaps put you quite out of frame! We dine at six, sir!'

'No need to warn me,' Sir Bonamy said, slowly mounting the shallow steps. 'I know the country habit! But you have a very good cook, and if one partakes of only a morsel by way of a nuncheon one is ready for one's dinner by six o'clock – with a mere snack for supper.'

'Oh, we shall offer you more than a snack!' promised Kit. 'You will certainly need a supporting meal after an evening spent in playing whist with the Dowager Lady Stavely!'

'So that's it, is it?' said Sir Bonamy, pausing at the top of the steps to get his breath back. His large frame was shaken by a chuckle. 'Now I know why you're happy to welcome me! Quite right! quite right! you leave the old lady to me! *Ah!*'

This last exclamation was evoked by the emergence from the house of his hostess, who gave him both her hands, and an embracing smile, saying: 'Dear Bonamy, I *knew* I might depend upon you! Infamous to have invited you to such a *dreadful* party, but I *needed* you!'

Kissing her hands, and continuing to hold them in his, Sir Bonamy said fondly: 'Now, my pretty – ! You know how happy it makes me to hear that! Ay, and you should know I couldn't think any party dreadful which *you* grace! Anything I can do to oblige you I'll do with alacrity. Just been telling Evelyn to leave Cornelia Stavely to me!'

'Yes, but there is a worse thing!' disclosed her ladyship. 'I know I should have divulged it to you before, but I dared not, for fear you should refuse to come.'

'No, no!' he replied, releasing one of her hands so that he

could pat the other. 'Nothing could have made me do so! Not even if you had invited the greatest bore in the country!'

'Well, that's just what I have done,' she said candidly. 'It's Cosmo!'

'Your brother Cosmo?' he asked.

'And his wife, *and* his son!' she said, making a clean breast of it.

'Well, well!' he said tolerantly. 'I'm not acquainted with them, and I dare say Cliffe won't fidget me very much. A dull dog, but there! No need to pay any heed to him, after all!'

'I knew I might depend on you!' said Lady Denville, withdrawing her hand from his, and tucking it into his arm. 'Now you shall come into my own drawing-room, and drink a glass of wine, while your man unpacks your trunks, and tell me all the latest crim. con. stories!'

Kit, realizing that his presence was unwanted, went off to look for Miss Stavely. He found her, after an extensive search, in the Long Drawing-room, engaged in arranging fresh flowers in two of his mama's new holders; and instantly demanded to be told who had set her to this task.

'No one,' she answered, her attention fixed on the exact placing of a tall lily. 'I asked Lady Denville if I might do it for her, and she gave me leave – so, you see, I am *not* meddling, or being odiously encroaching!'

'You know that's not what I meant. But you can't want to busy yourself with such matters! Mama assures me that there is nothing more exhausting.'

She laughed. 'Yes, so she told me. I don't find it anything but agreeable, however. Particularly here, where you have such a profusion of flowers. I've enjoyed myself uncommonly this morning, picking and choosing amongst them.'

'I'm glad, but I wish you will leave one of the servants to finish the bowls!'

'Certainly not! Why?'

'To ride with me,' he said, in a coaxing tone. 'It's not so hot today – and Mama's mare needs exercise!'

'Oh, dear!' she sighed. 'That's tempting, but – No, I must not! The invitation cards have come from Brighton, and I am going to help Lady Denville to send them out for the Public Day. She has settled to hold it next week, so there's no time to be lost.'

He was just about to offer his services when he remembered that his handwriting was very different from Evelyn's scrawl. He bit the words back, all at once realizing that a fresh danger threatened him. Sooner or later, he thought, one of his guests would ask him for a frank. He could write the one word, Denville, in a passable imitation of Evelyn's fist; but he felt it would be beyond his power to transcribe a full name and address. His father, rigidly meticulous, had always done so; he wondered if every peer and Member of Parliament adhered so strictly to the letter of the law. He rather fancied that most of them distributed their franks very freely; on the other hand he had an uneasy recollection of having read in some newspaper that franks were being subjected to close scrutiny by the Post Office, in an attempt to check the abuse of this privilege. He could only hope that Evelyn's signature was not yet well-known to any local postmaster; and decide that if the worst befell he would trade on the illegibility of Evelyn's writing, recommending the seeker after a frank to superscribe the letter himself, to ensure its safe arrival.

Cressy stood back, the better to survey her handiwork. 'I hope Lady Denville will like it,' she said. 'I think it is quite tolerable, don't you?'

'Just passable!' he said gravely.

She laughed. 'Let me tell you, sir, that I preen myself a little on my flower arrangements!'

'I can see that you do. If you won't ride with me, will you take a turn about the gardens with me?'

She glanced at the clock on the mantelpiece, and picked up her simple straw bergère hat. 'Yes, that would be very agreeable – for half-an-hour?'

He nodded. They went out together, and passed down the

terrace steps on to the lawn, and across it to a succession of shallow terraces backed by wide flower-borders on one side, and low stone parapets on the other. Cressy sighed. 'What a pity it is that dear Godmama doesn't care for the country! It is so beautiful here!'

No, Mama finds it a dead bore, unless the house is filled with entertaining guests.' He hesitated. 'Are you very fond of the country, Cressy?'

She considered the matter, wrinkling her brow in the way he had come to think charming. Then she said, with the flicker of a smile: 'That's a home question! When I'm here, and in such delightful weather, I wonder how I can support life in London. But the melancholy suspicion occurs to me that I am, *au fond*, a town-creature!' She glanced round at him, arching her brows quizzically. 'Does that cast you down? I recall that you told me, at that first encounter, that if you knew yourself to be master here you would choose to spend all but the spring months at Ravenhurst, or in Leicestershire. Don't be alarmed! I promise you I won't repine!'

He said nothing for a moment, for it flashed across his mind that her words had supplied him with the answer to the problem which had been troubling him. Evelyn, a far keener sportsman than himself, had always loved Ravenhurst for the congenial amusements it offered; and, perhaps from a natural aptitude for the life of a country landowner, perhaps because he had known all his life that it would one day be his own, he had taken much more interest in the management of the estates than had his twin. But his impetuous, autocratic temper made it impossible for him to bear with equanimity the humiliation of being master only in name; and that was why he had, apparently, plunged into the wild career of a regular dash, or Bond Street Spark. Kit could perceive, dispassionately, that this was folly, but he accepted it without criticism because it was a part of Evelyn, neither to be censured nor amended. The only thought in his head was that by hedge or by stile the Trust must be brought to an end. That Miss Stavely personified neither of these homely objects was a thought which had entered his head several days previously, and had taken such firm root there that it had swiftly become something to be taken for granted.

Watching him, Cressy said gently: 'Vexed, sir?'

His eyes, which had been looking frowningly ahead, travelled to her face, and smiled again. 'No, far from it!'

'In a little worry, then?'

'A little,' he acknowledged. 'For reasons which I can't, at present, explain to you. Bear with me!'

'Why, of course!' She strolled on beside him for a few paces. 'Did you wish to say something of a particular nature when you asked me to come into the garden?'

'No – that is, I have much to say to you of a very particular nature, but not yet!' He broke off, as the evils of his situation came home to him more forcibly than ever before. He felt himself to be at a stand, for, although every impulse urged him to disclose the truth to Cressy, to do so under the existing circumstances, and while he was uncertain of her mind, would be to run the risk of flooring not only himself but Evelyn as well.

That she was inclined, for some inscrutable reason, to prefer him to his twin, he knew; but he was no self-flatterer: he thought Evelyn his superior in all the qualities that might be supposed to captivate a lady; and he knew that in position and fortune Evelyn wholly eclipsed him. Cressy's affections were not engaged: that had been made plain to him at the outset, when he had consented to impersonate his twin for one, vital evening. Under no other circumstance would he have lent himself to such a hoax, but this now seemed to make the situation worse rather than better. Cressy, entering into a marriage of convenience, had shown herself willing to accept an offer which the ton would certainly think splendid. In Kit's view, that was a sensible thing to do: one could not have everything in an imperfect world, so if one was denied the best

149

thing of all it would be foolish not to accept an offer that carried with it the promise of ease and social distinction. Kit's own affections might be very thoroughly engaged, but it seemed incredible to him that Cressy, apparently impervious to Evelyn's charm, had fallen in love with him. She certainly liked him, but it would take more than mere liking to overcome the revulsion she must surely feel if he told her how outrageously she had been deceived. It did not so much as cross his mind that she need never be told: he was going to tell her the whole truth just as soon as he could do it, with Evelyn's knowledge, and when Cressy was no longer in the intolerable position of being a guest at Ravenhurst. The hoax, at no time acceptable to him, had begun to assume the colour of an unforgivable piece of chicanery. He would not have thought it surprising if Cressy, learning the truth, shook the dust of Ravenhurst from her feet with no more delay than would serve to put her grandmother in possession of the facts. Setting aside his own prospects, he thought there was scarcely a worse turn he could serve Evelyn. Such a break-up to the party would inevitably set tongues wagging, and wits to work; and though the Stavelys would be unlikely to repeat the story there was no dependence to be placed on the reticence of the servants. If only one amongst the score at Ravenhurst guessed the truth, the scandal, probably garbled out of recognition, would spread with the rapidity of a forest-fire. Better by far would it have been to have left Evelyn to make what excuses he could for his defection than to have set out to rescue him, and then to draw back from a task which proved to be harder and more distasteful than had been foreseen, leaving him in very much more serious straits. There was no intention of furthering his pretensions to Cressy's hand in Kit's head: loyalty to his twin might be strong, but it stopped short of helping Evelyn to marry, for expedience's sake, the girl he himself loved. Evelyn would never expect that of him; but Evelyn would expect – only that was the wrong word to use for what each of them knew to be a certainty – that in all other predicaments his twin would stand buff.

Cressy's voice intruded upon these reflections, telling him that the arrival that morning of the post with the previous day's London papers had ruffled the temper of one of his guests. She said this very gravely, but he was not deceived, and replied promptly: 'You terrify me! Tell me the worst!'

Her mouth quivered. 'It is very bad, I warn you! Your uncle has seen that the *Gazette* and the *Morning Post* have received the information that your mama has left London for Ravenhurst Park, and he is very much put out.'

He knew that Lady Denville had sent this notice to the two journals Evelyn was most likely to read; but what concern it was of Cosmo's he had no idea. Cressy, meeting the surprised question in his eyes with a decided twinkle in her own, said reproachfully: 'One would have supposed that dear Godmama would have thought it proper to have mentioned that she was entertaining visitors to Ravenhurst, amongst whom –'

'– are the Hon. Cosmo and Mrs Cliffe, *and* Ambrose Cliffe, all of whom their host wishes otherwise!'

'I don't think that was *precisely* how he feels the notice should have been phrased,' she said, in a considering tone.

He laughed. 'I'm very sure it's not! Feels he has been slighted does he? What the deuce does it matter to him? You'd think he must be some trumped up April-squire, wouldn't you?'

'I dare say it may come of his being a younger son.'

'No, that it does not!' he exclaimed, revolted.

She glanced speculatively at him. 'A younger son jealous of his elder brother's position, and one who has made no mark in the world,' she amended.

He had by this time recollected himself, and merely said: 'No, it comes from having a maggoty disposition and a vast quantity of self-importance.'

She told him that he was too severe, and passed easily to

an indifferent subject. They continued chatting companionably on a variety of topics until Cressy, hearing the stable-clock strike the hour, remembered her promise to her hostess, and was conscience-smitten by the realization that she must have kept her waiting for at least twenty minutes. This, she exclaimed, was the height of bad manners; and despite all Kit's amused assurances that his mother was more likely to have forgotten that she had planned to send out her invitation cards that morning than to complain of her young guest's want of conduct, she insisted on hastening back to the house. Kit went with her, offering her handsome odds against the chance that his mother would be found, as expected, in her own drawing-room. But she was found there, though with no thought of directing invitations in her head. She was standing in front of the gilded mirror hanging above the fireplace, surveying, with every sign of disapprobation, her own delightful reflection. A litter of crumpled wrapping-paper on the floor, an open box on the table, with a necklace composed of fine topazes set in fili-gree lying beside it, indicated that she had received a valuable package from London; sent, possibly, and at a moderate charge, through the medium of the Newhaven Mailcoach, and deposited, with the post, at the receiving office in Nutley; and more probably, as Kit knew, by a special messenger, at large cost.

It was difficult to perceive why Lady Denville was dissatisfied with her appearance, for she was attired in an underdress of deep gold, which matched her hair, veiled by a tunic of pale muslin, and the effect was at once dashing, and extremely becoming, but she speedily explained the matter. 'Was there anything ever more provoking?' she demanded. 'I purchased these horrid beads, because it struck me that they were just the thing to wear with this dress, and I even had them restrung to the exact length I required, and now I don't like them at all! In fact, I think them hideous!'

'Oh, no, no!' exclaimed Cressy. 'The most beautiful clear amber! How can you call them hideous, ma'am? You look charmingly!'

'No, Cressy, I do *not* look charmingly!' said her ladyship firmly. 'I don't know how it is, but no matter *how* dear they may be, there is something about beads which makes one look shabby-genteel. If I were to wear these, even Emma would think I bought made-up clothes in Cranbourne Alley!'

This seemed an unlikely contingency, but neither Kit nor Cressy ventured to say so. Kit, picking up the topaz necklace, asked, with a sinking heart, if she had bought it at the same time.

'Oh, no, dearest! I bought that *long* before!' she replied, elevating his spirits for a brief moment. '*Weeks* ago, when I chose the silk for this underdress! But you may see for yourself that the stones are made to look insipid, worn with this particular shade of yellow. I was afraid they would, but it is such a pretty necklace that I don't regret having purchased it. If I had some earrings made to match it, I could wear it with a pale yellow evening gown, couldn't I? But those amber beads I will *not* wear!'

'No, don't!' said Kit. 'Send them back to the jeweller!'

She considered this suggestion, but decided against it. 'No, I have a better notion! I shall give them to your cousin Kate! I don't suppose you remember her, but she is Baverstock's *second* daughter, and never has anything pretty to wear, because your *odious* Aunt Amelia won't spend a groat more than she need on her until she has snabbled a husband for Maria – which I shouldn't think she will ever do, for she's a plain girl, and has been out for three Seasons already.' She unclasped the amber string, and laid it aside, and said, smiling brilliantly upon her audience: 'So it turns out to be for the best, after all, and I must wear my pearls, until I find *just* what I have in mind! Did you want me particularly, my dears?'

'What did I tell you?' asked Kit, mocking Cressy. 'No, Mama: Cressy would have it that it was you who wanted her, to direct invitations for you.'

'I *knew* there was something I must attend to this morning!' said her ladyship, pleased with this feat of memory. 'Oh, dear, what a dead bore it is! I can't think why I didn't bring Mrs Woodbury with me, except, of course, that I shouldn't have known what to do with her here, for one couldn't expect her to dine in the housekeeper's room, precisely, and yet – But she is an *excellent* person, and writes all the invitations, and answers letters for me, and *never* forgets to remind me of the things I've arranged to do!'

Her eyes dancing, Cressy said: 'Never mind, ma'am! Only tell me the various directions, and I'll engage to be quite as excellent a secretary! You made out a list, didn't you, of all the people you wished to invite?'

'So I did! Not that I *wish* to invite any of them, because of all the tedious things imaginable Public Days are the worst! However, it would be very uncivil not to hold one, so we must make the best of it. Dear Cressy, how fortunate that you should have remembered that I made up that list! We have only to discover where I put it, and everything will be very simply accomplished – though I hope you don't think that I mean to let you do more than *assist* me! I wonder where I *did* put that list? *Not* in a safe place, for that is *always* fatal. Dearest K – *kindest* Evelyn!' she said, correcting herself with aplomb, 'perhaps, if you are not engaged elsewhere, *you* could direct some of the cards for me!'

'Nothing would afford me greater pleasure, love!' he replied, wondering how long it would be before his irresponsible parent unwittingly exposed him. 'But I *am* engaged elsewhere, and you know well that only you and Kit seem to be able to decipher my handwriting!'

The rest of the day passed without untoward incident. Cressy, assisted spasmodically by Lady Denville, directed the invitation cards; Sir Bonamy and Cosmo, after consuming a substantial nuncheon, slept stertorously in the library all the afternoon, their handkerchiefs spread over their faces; the Dowager enjoyed her usual drive with Mrs Cliffe; and Kit, finding his young cousin idling disconsolately in one of the saloons, ruthlessly bore him off for an inspection of the stables, and a tramp across the fields to the stud-farm, where one of my lord's brood mares had the day before given birth to a promising colt.

The evening was enlivened by the presence of the Squire, Sir John Thatcham, with his lady, and his two eldest offspring: Mr Edward Thatcham, just down from his second year at Cambridge; and Miss Anne, a lively girl, who had gratified her well-wishers by retiring from her first modest Season with a very respectable *parti* to her credit.

It might have been supposed that a party which included such ill-assorted persons as the Dowager, Sir John and Lady Thatcham, and Sir Bonamy Ripple was foredoomed to failure, for the Dowager, who arrogated to herself an old lady's privilege of being as uncivil as she chose to anyone whom she considered to be a bore, could almost certainly be depended on to snub the Thatchams; and Sir Bonamy was too much the idle man of fashion to meet with Sir John's approval. But, in the event, and due, as Cressy recognized with deep respect, to Lady Denville's unmatched qualities as a hostess, the party was very successful, the only member of it to feel dissatisfaction being Cosmo, who pouted a good deal when he discovered that his sister had excluded him from the whist-table, set up for the Dowager's edification in a small saloon leading from the Long Drawing-room. Having elicited the information that the Thatchams were very fond of whist, but liked to play together, Lady Denville settled them at the table with the Dowager and Sir Bonamy. No one could have guessed from Sir Bonamy's good-humoured demeanour that he was in the habit of playing whist in the Duke of York's company, for five pound points, with a pony on the rubber to make it worth while.

The rest of the party, with the single exception of Cosmo, who said that he was too old for such pastimes, gathered round a large table in the Long Drawing-room to play a number of games which the three youngest members of the party would, in their own homes, have condemned as being fit only for the schoolroom. But Lady Denville, who combined a genius for making her guests feel that she was genuinely happy to entertain them with an effervescent enjoyment of her own parties, rapidly infected the company with her own zest for such innocent pastimes as Command, Cross-Questions, and even Jack-straws. It was all very merry and informal, and when it culminated in a game of speculation Ambrose surprised everyone by displaying an unexpected aptitude for the game, making some very shrewd bids, and quite forgetting the languid air he thought it proper for a young man of mode to assume; and Cosmo, unable to bear the sight of his wife's improvident play, drew up his chair to the table so that he could advise and instruct her.

At ten o'clock, the Dowager, who had been behaving with great energy and acumen, winning several shillings, and sharply censuring Sir Bonamy for what she considered faults of play, suddenly assumed the appearance of extreme decrepitude, and broke up the game, saying that she was tired, and must go to bed. As soon as she emerged from the saloon, leaning on Sir Bonamy's arm, Lady Denville rose from the table, and went towards her, saying in her pretty, caressing voice: 'Going to retire now, ma'am? I hope you are not being driven away by the noise we have been making!'

'No, I've had a very agreeable evening,' replied the Dowager graciously. 'No need to leave your game on my account!' She nodded at Cressy. 'Stay where you are, child! I can see you're enjoying yourself, and I don't want you.'

'Enjoying myself! Nothing of the sort, Grandmama! I've fallen amongst sharks, and have lost my entire fortune! What Mr Ambrose Cliffe hasn't robbed me of has passed into Denville's possession: I wonder that you should abandon me to such a hard-bargaining pair!' said Cressy gaily.

'I dare say you'll come about,' said the Dowager. She allowed Lady Denville to take Sir Bonamy's place, and nodded generally. 'I'll bid you all goodnight. Happy to have made your acquaintance, Lady Thatcham: you play your cards very tolerably – very tolerably indeed!' She then withdrew, her ebony cane gripped in one claw-like hand, the other tucked in Lady Denville's arm. She favoured Kit, who was holding open the door for her, with a jocular command not to knock Cressy into horse-nails, but said somewhat snappishly to Lady Denville, as they went slowly along the broad corridor, that she didn't know why she troubled to escort her to her bedchamber.

'Oh, it isn't a trouble,' said Lady Denville. 'I like to go with you, ma'am, to be *quite* sure that you have everything just as you prefer it. One never knows that they won't have sent up your hot milk with horrid pieces of skin in it, or warmed the bed *far* too early!'

'Lord, Amabel, my woman takes good care of that!' said the Dowager scornfully. She added, in a grudging tone: 'Not but what you're a kind creature – and that I never denied!' She proceeded for some way in silence, but when the upper hall was reached, said suddenly: 'That was a good notion of yours, to set the young people to playing silly games. It ain't often I've seen that granddaughter of mine in such a glow of spirits. It's little enough fun she gets at home.'

'Dear Cressy! I wish you might have heard some of her drolleries! She had us all in whoops, and even succeeded in captivating that *dismal* nephew of mine!'

The Dowager uttered a crack of mirth. 'Him! I've no patience with whipstraws, playing off the airs of exquisites.' She paused outside the door of her bedroom. 'I'll tell you this, though, Amabel! I like your son.'

'Thank you!' Lady Denville said. Tears sparkled in her eyes. 'No one – *no one*! – was ever blessed with two such sons as mine!'

'Now, don't be a pea goose!' said the Dowager bracingly. 'I should like to know what there is to cry about in that! I shall be very well satisfied if Cressy likes him well enough to marry him, for he'll make her the kind of husband most of us wish for, and few of us have the good fortune to catch. Now, you be off, for whatever the rest of 'em want you may depend upon it that Ripple's thinking of nothing but his supper!'

Whatever secret longings Sir Bonamy may have been cherishing, he was far too well-mannered to allow these to appear. Lady Denville found him chatting urbanely with Lady Thatcham, who, under his benign influence, was fast coming to the conclusion that her husband's freely-expressed contempt of him (and every other member of the Prince Regent's set) was unjust. The game of speculation was coming to an end, with Cressy recovering some of her losses: a circumstance which she owed to the intervention of Cosmo, who had moved round the table to sit at her elbow. The stakes might be infinitesimal, but Cosmo could not bear to see her squandering her counters from what he called want of judgement, and what his disrespectful nephew later described as a want of huckstering instinct.

Informality was maintained at supper, for which lavish repast the Thatchams, in spite of demurring that a seven-mile drive lay before them, were persuaded to remain at Ravenhurst, but it did not extend to the dishes provided by

Mr Dawlish, which ranged from lobsters to a succulent array of tarts, jellies and creams, upon which the younger members of the party regaled themselves with unabashed greediness. The Thatchams took their leave, Mr Edward Thatcham, gazing with youthful admiration at his hostess, informing her that he had spent the *jolliest* evening, and reverently kissing her hand. Lady Denville took her sister-in-law and Cressy up to bed; and Kit returned to the supper-room, where the three remaining gentlemen were sitting amongst the broken meats: Ambrose in the sulks, because his father had reproved him for allowing Kit to give him a glass of Fine Old Cognac; Cosmo delivering himself of a monologue, addressed to Sir Bonamy; and Sir Bonamy savouring the bouquet of his brandy, and nodding occasionally from an amiable wish to lead Cosmo into believing that he was attending to him. He turned his little round eyes towards Kit, and said: 'Excellent supper! Very agreeable evening!'

'Thank you, sir! But the credit goes to my mother,' said Kit.

'Very true! Very true! Wonderful woman! Never anyone like her, my boy!' said Sir Bonamy, gustily sighing. He heaved himself round in his chair, groping in his pocket for his snuff-box. 'In such high beauty, too! Doesn't look a day older than when I first clapped eyes on her. Before your time, that was!'

Kit, recalling one of Fimber's repeated admonitions, produced the snuff-box which had been placed by that worthy in his own pocket, opened it, and offered it to Sir Bonamy, saying: 'Will you try some of my sort, sir?'

He knew immediately that in some way he had erred. Sir Bonamy's unnervingly expressionless gaze remained riveted to the snuff-box for several seconds, before travelling upwards to his face. It remained fixed for several more seconds, but Sir Bonamy only said: 'A pretty box, that. Purchased it in Paris, didn't you, when you went there to meet your brother once?'

'I believe I did,' acknowledged Kit, not a muscle quiver‚ ing in his face.

Sir Bonamy helped himself to a pinch. 'One of Bernier's,' he said. 'You showed it to me when you came home.'

He had, apparently, no further observations to make; but when, much later, he visited Kit in the huge room which was traditionally the bedchamber occupied by the Earls of Denville, Kit's dismay was not attended by surprise. Fimber had just eased him out of his coat; but Sir Bonamy had already escaped from the restriction of his corsets, and his rigidly starched shirt-points, and was attired in a dressing-gown of thick brocade, of such rich colouring and such voluminous cut that his appearance, at all times impressive, was almost overpowering. 'Came to have a word with you!' he announced.

Fimber, his face wooden, withdrew into the dressing-room; and Kit, feeling that his sheet-anchor had vanished, said: 'Why, certainly, sir! Is something amiss?'

'That snuff of yours is *dry*!' said Sir Bonamy, staring very hard at him.

'Good God, sir, is it? I do most humbly beg your pardon!'

'I'll drop a word of warning in your ear, my boy!' said Sir Bonamy, ignoring this interpolation. 'I don't know what sort of wheedle you're trying to cut, and I don't ask you to tell me, because it's no affair of mine, but if you want to bamboozle people into thinking you're young Denville, don't offer 'em dry snuff, and don't use two hands to open your box!'

'So that was it!' said Kit. 'I was afraid I had betrayed myself, but I didn't know how!'

'Damme, Kit, Evelyn set himself to copy Brummell's way of handling a snuff-box! One hand only, and no more than a flick of the thumb-nail to open it! You remember that!'

'I will, sir,' Kit promised. 'Thank you! You must feel that I owe you an explanation –'

Sir Bonamy checked him with an upraised hand. 'No, I

don't!' he said hastily. 'I've told you already it's no affair of mine! I'd as lief it wasn't, too, because it looks to me like a damned havey-cavey business.'

'It isn't quite as havey-cavey as it must seem,' Kit told him.

'If its *half* as havey-cavey as it seems I don't want to have anything to do with it!' replied Sir Bonamy, not mincing matters. 'And from what I know of you and Evelyn – not that I came here to pull a crow with you, for I didn't! What's more, you won't goad me into it, my boy, so don't think it! If Evelyn hasn't been able to wind me up in all the years he's been trying to do it, it stands to reason you can't.'

'But I don't wish to, sir!' expostulated Kit mildly.

'Now I come to think of it,' conceded Sir Bonamy, 'you never did take so much pepper in your nose at the sight of me as that whisky-frisky brother of yours, so I dare say that's true. As a matter of fact, that's what made me suspicious: you shouldn't have looked as if you was glad to see me! Ought to have known better: civil enough, young Denville, but pokers up a trifle!'

'Does he? I'll comb his hair for it!' said Kit. He smiled. 'In any event I shouldn't have done so: I'm by far too grateful to you for coming to support us! I knew, too, that I'd nothing to fear even if you did recognize me.'

'No, no, nothing at all!' Sir Bonamy assured him. 'But I'm not as young as I was, Kit, and it's no use thinking, if you've got hold of a wolf by one ear, that I'm going to grasp the other, because I won't do it! So don't you tell me anything! If your mother wishes me to know the whole she'll tell me fast enough, bless her!' He added uneasily: 'No need to edge her on to tell me, mind!'

Kit reassured him on this head; and he went off, feeling that he had done as much for his young friend as could have been expected of any man of his years and elevated position.

Lady Denville, when informed next day of this interlude,

not only went into a peal of laughter, but showed a regrettably mischievous desire to devise some way of entangling her hapless adorer in an imbroglio which she proudly claimed to be of her own making.

'No, Mama!' said Kit firmly. 'You'll do no such thing! We're devilish obliged to the old court card, and I won't have him roasted! No one could blame him for wanting to steer clear of this affair: if we save our groats without kicking up the very deuce of a scandal it's more than I'd bargain for!'

'I won't do anything you don't like, dearest,' she promised. 'But you mustn't be so downhearted!'

'Not *down*hearted! *Hen*hearted!'

'No, no, Kit!' she protested, dismayed to hear him make such an admission. 'Never *that*! Besides, why should you be? I own that there may be *difficulties* ahead, and, of course, our situation is often *most* awkward, but we shall come about!'

'What makes you think so, love?' he asked, regarding her in affectionate exasperation.

'One always does – and particularly when one thinks one is quite knocked up. Only consider how many times *I* have been in the briars! I have *always* contrived to bring myself home, even when my case appeared to be desperate! Now, why are you laughing, wicked one? It's *perfectly* true! The thing is that it's no use for us to fret ourselves over what can't be helped. Depend upon it, something will happen, or I shall have a notion suddenly, which will bring us off prosperously. I very often do, you know – really *nacky* ones!'

'I know you do,' he said. 'All I beg of you is that you won't have one without telling me!'

'Dearest, how can you be so foolish? I shall be *obliged* to tell you, because if I do think of a clever scheme you will have to bear your part in it.'

'That's exactly what I'm afraid of,' he said frankly.

'You're hipped, and I know why,' she said. 'It was the

lobster! I felt a trifle queasy myself, in the middle of the night, but I have some excellent powders, which Dr Ainslie gave me, so I swallowed one, and was right again in a trice. Come up to my dressing-room, poor boy, and I'll mix one for you!'

'No, Mama, it was *not* the lobster!'

'Very well, dearest, I won't tease you – though I assure you the powders aren't in the least nasty. Don't be in a worry, will you? When Evelyn comes home everything will be tidy again, remember!'

'You know, Mama, we have been saying that since the start of this masquerade – and God knows I wish he would come home! – but does it ever occur to you that when he does we shall find ourselves in a worse hobble than ever?'

'It *must* have been the lobster!' exclaimed her ladyship.

He laughed, but said: 'No, do, pray, consider, love! If Evelyn were to walk in today, what are we to do? I could disappear, but not even Ambrose would be deceived for more than half-an-hour – far less Lady Stavely! It's one thing to hoax people for an evening, quite another to do so in such circumstances as these! At the outset, none of them knew me very well and Lady Stavely not at all. But they know me now! They couldn't meet me at breakfast, and Evelyn at dinner, and not detect the difference between us!'

'No, very true!' she said, much struck. 'That *is* very awkward! I wonder why it should not have occurred to me? We must lose no time in trying to hit upon a – Oh, but I see just how to overcome the difficulty! Evelyn must pretend to be you, of course!'

Mr Fancot, declaring that he had now received a settler, went off, dutifully trying to think of some way of entertaining his male guests. Like the Dowager, Sir Bonamy (except under the press of extraordinary circumstances) never left his bedroom until noon; so when Kit learned from Norton that Mr Cliffe had gone out with Mr Ambrose, to see how he had come on under the gamekeeper's tuition, his thoughts turned, very naturally, to the ladies. His search for his aunt could not have been described as more than perfunctory; but he had the great good fortune, as he stood in the hall, wondering where to look for Miss Stavely, to see her coming down the wide staircase. She was charmingly dressed in a simple, high-necked gown of French muslin, but just as he was thinking how well she looked, he saw that there was a pucker between her brows, and a troubled expression in her eyes. He said quickly: 'What is it, Cressy? Something has happened to vex you?'

She paused looking down at him, and hesitated for a moment before answering. Then the crease disappeared from her brow, and she smiled, and descended the last stairs, saying: 'Well, yes! That is to say, it *has* vexed me, but not nearly as much as it has vexed Grandmama! I am afraid it has made her out of reason cross, but I *have* convinced her that it is absurd to lay the blame at poor Godmama's door! Or at Papa's! Neither of them would do such a thing! It is one of Albinia's high pieces of meddling, of course – trying to clinch the matter! I collect you haven't yet seen the London papers?'

He shook his head; and she held out to him the journal she was carrying. As he took it, he saw that it was folded open at a page largely devoted to social announcements and discreetly phrased on-dits. He looked quickly up, his brows asking a question. She answered it only by wrinkling her nose distastefully, and indicating with her forefinger the paragraph to which she wished to draw his attention. It stated, after enumerating the various persons of consequence to be found recruiting nature at Worthing, that the Dowager Lady Stavely (a well-known summer visitor to that elegant resort) was this year absent from the scene, having taken her granddaughter, the Hon. Cressida Stavely, to Ravenhurst Park, the principal seat of the Earl of Denville, where they were being entertained by the noble owner, and his mother, the Dowager Countess. The writer of this titillating paragraph understood, coyly, that an Interesting Announcement was shortly to be expected from this quarter.

'My mother never sent this to the paper!' Kit exclaimed, flushing with annoyance. 'Or anything that could have given rise to such a piece of impertinence!'

'No, of course she did not! I haven't the least doubt of its being Albinia's doing – trying to force my hand! Furthermore,' added Cressy, brooding darkly over it, 'I shall own myself astonished if I don't discover that she exerted herself to the utmost to persuade my father to insert a notice announcing that I had become engaged to marry the Earl of Denville! What a paper-skull she is! She should have known him better! You may imagine how much it has set up Grandmama's bristles!' She began to laugh. 'I don't know which has enraged her most: the detestably sly hint, or Albinia's impudence in having presumed to take it upon herself to give the *Post* information about *her* movements!'

Kit's eyes were kindling. 'And she thought that Mama – *Mama – ! –* would stoop to –'

She interrupted him, laying a hand on his arm, and saying quickly: 'Oh, pray, don't *you* rip up, Denville!' She gave a tiny choke of laughter. 'She did Godmama the justice to say, even in the height of her rage, that she would not have thought it of her, which is more than she said of poor Papa, when she decided it must have been *his* doing! In fact, she said that it was just like him! I assure you it is not, however.'

The angry look was fading, but as Kit glanced again at the paragraph his lips curled contemptuously. 'Insufferable! Your mother-in-law should have her neck wrung! As for the sneaking tattlemonger who composed this masterpiece –!' He tossed the paper aside. 'He took good care, you'll observe, to write nothing which I can either contradict or force him to apologize for!' His face softened, as he turned towards her again. 'I don't know why *I* should fly up into the boughs, when it is you who are the victim – except for that reason! My poor girl, I'm well aware of the embarrassment it must cause you to feel! Don't let it cut up your peace, or influence your decision!'

An odd little smile flickered for a moment in her eyes. 'No, I shan't do that. As for Albinia, I left Grandmama writing to her. You may depend upon it that it will be a thundering letter! I dare say she had liefer have her neck wrung than receive it. Indeed, I could almost pity her, for my father will be vexed to death, and although he is in general easy-going to a fault he flies into a worse passion than Grandmama, if one succeeds in putting him out of temper. The impropriety of this horrid piece of gossip will strike him most forcefully: I wish it may not lead to a serious quarrel between him and Albinia.'

'Do you? I'm not so charitable!'

'Well, she's such a pea-goose!' Cressy explained. 'One can't blame her for being foolish, or, I suppose, for being so jealous. One ought rather to feel compassion for her – or at least *try* to! – because she is bound to suffer a great deal of anguish.'

This view of the matter was not shared by Lady Denville, who, when she read the paragraph, was put into a flame. She went pink with anger, her eyes flashing magnificently. She turned them upon Kit, demanding in a trembling voice: 'How *dared* they? *Who* is responsible for this abominable piece of vulgarity!'

'Cressy believes that it was her mother-in-law. I feel as you do, Mama, but our only course is to ignore it.'

'That woman!' exclaimed her ladyship. 'I might have guessed as much! Do you see what she had the effrontery to call me? The *Dowager* Countess! *Dowager* –!'

He was taken aback. 'Well, yes, but –'

'And I know why!' raged her ladyship. 'She is a jealous, spiteful toad, and she knows that Stavely offered for me once, and still has a *tendre* for me! It would afford me very great pleasure to set her mind at rest! *Very* great pleasure! I'll have her know that if I had no fancy for Stavely when he was young, and passably goodlooking, I have less now! She is very welcome to a husband who will offer a carte blanche to some lightskirt the instant he becomes bored with *her* charms!'

Somewhat alarmed by this unusual venom, Kit made a quite unavailing attempt to soothe her. She interrupted him, requesting him not to put her out of all patience; and swept away, the offending newspaper clenched in her hand, to knock imperatively on the door of Lady Stavely's bed-chamber. Since nothing annoyed the Dowager more than to receive visitors before she chose to emerge from her seclusion, Kit waited for the inevitable disaster. It did not befall. The two ladies remained closeted together for a full hour, deriving great benefit from a free exchange of opinions on the character of Albinia Stavely. The only discordant note was struck by Lady Stavely, who bluntly informed her lovely hostess that however little she might relish the notion, she *was* Dowager Countess, and would be well-advised to accustom herself to this title.

'Which I cannot do, Kit!' Lady Denville said later, and in tragic accents. 'No one can say that I haven't borne up under a great deal of adversity, but this stroke is too much!'

The effect of the paragraph upon his maternal relations Kit dealt with summarily and conclusively. He told his aunt, who said that she had seen from the first how it was, that if his mother had dreamt that such an absurd construction would be placed on a visit from her favourite godchild she would never have invited her to Ravenhurst; and when his uncle, in a dudgeon, started to read him a lecture on the impropriety of allowing the news of his approaching nuptials to reach his relatives through the medium of the press, he put a swift end to any further re-criminations by saying, in a voice of cold and quelling civility: 'You may rest assured, sir, that when I contemplate matrimony I shall do myself the honour of informing you of the impending announcement.'

Ambrose, whose evil genius prompted him to quiz his cousin, was disposed of without finesse; and when Kit was able to exchange a private word with Cressy he told her not to waste a thought on an unpleasant, but evanescent annoyance. 'I fancy we shall hear no more about it,' he said.

12

He was permitted to dwell in this hopeful belief for rather less than twenty-four hours. Upon the following afternoon, driven indoors by a shower of rain, he was playing billiards with Cressy when Norton entered the room, and asked him in an expressionless voice if he might have a word with him.

'Yes, what is it?' Kit replied.

Norton coughed, and directed a meaning look at him. Unfortunately, Kit was watching Cressy, critically surveying the balls on the table, her cue in her hand. Their disposition was not promising. 'What a very unhandsome way to leave them!' she complained. 'I don't see what's to be done.'

'Try a cannon off the cushion!' he recommended. A second cough made him say, rather impatiently: 'Well, Norton? What do you want?'

'If I might have a word with your lordship?' Norton repeated.

Kit glanced frowningly at him. 'Presently: you are interrupting the game.'

'I beg your lordship's pardon!' said Norton, his meaning look becoming almost a glare. 'A Person has called to see your lordship.'

'Very well. Tell him I am at present engaged, and ask him to state his business!'

Cressy, who had raised her eyes from the table to look at the butler, said: 'Do go, Denville! I'll concede this game to you gracefully and happily, having already been beaten all hollow!' She smiled at Norton. 'I collect the business is urgent?'

'Well, yes, miss!' replied Norton gratefully.

By this time, Kit, his attention fairly caught, had realized that Norton was trying to convey an unspoken message to him. Since he had been assured by Fimber that the butler had no suspicion that he was not his noble master, he was puzzled to know why he was trying to warn him. He thrust his cue into the rack, made his apologies to Cressy, and preceded Norton out of the room. 'Well? Who is it?' he asked, as soon as the butler had shut the door behind him. 'What's his business with me?'

'As to that, my lord, I shouldn't care to say: the Individual being unwilling to divulge it to me.' He met Kit's questioning look woodenly, but added a sinister rider. 'I should perhaps mention, my lord, that the Individual in question is not of the male sex.'

Not by so much as the flicker of an eyelid did Kit betray his feelings. He asked curtly: 'Her name?'

'She calls herself Alperton, my lord,' responded Norton, at once disclaiming responsibility and revealing to the initiated the social status of the visitor. '*Mrs* Alperton – not a *young* female, my lord.' His gaze became fixed on some object over Kit's shoulder as he made his next tactfully worded disclosure. 'I thought it best to show her into the Blue saloon, my lord, Sir Bonamy and Mr Cliffe being in the library, as is their custom at this hour, and her not being willing to accept my assurance that you were not at home to visitors, but declaring to me her intention of remaining here until it should be convenient to you to receive her.'

It was now apparent to Kit that when he entered the Blue saloon he would be facing guns of unknown but almost certainly heavy calibre. His first alarming suspicion that some Cyprian whom Evelyn had taken under his protection had had the effrontery to present herself at Ravenhurst had been banished by the information that Mrs

Alperton was not a young female; and relief at the know-ledge that he would not be confronted by a female quite so intimately acquainted with Evelyn made it possible for him to nod, and to say coolly: 'Very well, I'll see her there.'

Norton bowed. 'Yes, my lord. Would you wish me to tell the postboy to wait?'

'Postboy?'

'A job-chaise, my lord, and one pair of horses.'

'Oh! Send him round to the stables: they'll look after him there.'

Norton bowed again, and led the way across the hall, and down a wide passage to the door leading into the Blue saloon. He held it open, and Kit walked into the room, his face schooled to an impassivity he was far from feeling.

His visitor was seated on a small sofa. She greeted him with a basilisk stare, and said, with terrible irony: 'Well, there! And so you *was* at home, after all, my lord!'

He advanced slowly into the middle of the room. His first thought was: *Ewe-mutton! no bread-and-butter of Eve-lyn's!* his second, that, incredible though it seemed, Mrs Alperton was a member of a certain sisterhood of elderly females known inappropriately as Abbesses. For this un-charitable belief her attire was largely responsible. His notions of feminine apparel were vague; had he been asked to describe what his mother was wearing that day he would have been unable to do so; but it struck him forcibly that Mrs Alperton's dashing and colourful raiment would never have been worn by a respectable, middle-aged female, and far less by a lady of quality. In spite of an elaborate array of metallic yellow locks, visible beneath a white satin cap, worn under a dome-crowned hat turned boldly up at the front, and with an ostrich plume curled over the brim to brush her forehead, he assessed her years at fifty. In fact, she was within a few months of Lady Denville's age; but although it was easy to see that in her youth she must have been a very prime article indeed, an over-lavish use of cos-metics, coupled with an addiction to spirituous liquors, had sadly ravaged a once-lovely countenance. Captious persons might consider that the size and brilliance of her eyes was marred by an avaricious gleam, but only those who had a predilection for slender women could have found fault with her well-corseted and opulent figure.

Whatever might have been her opinion of Mrs Alperton's taste, any woman would have recognized that she had taken great pains over her toilet, and thought it proper to wear, on a visit to a nobleman's seat, her bettermost dress and pelisse. Kit merely hoped, very devoutly, that he could succeed in getting rid of her before any of his guests set eyes on her; for a lilac pelisse, embellished with epaulets and cords, and worn over an open-bosomed robe of pink satin, struck him with horrifying effect. Pink kid half-boots and gloves, a lilac silk parasol, and a number of trinkets completed her costume; and she had lavishly sprayed her person with amber scent.

Kit paused by the table in the middle of the room, and stood looking down at her. 'Well, ma'am?' he said. 'May I know what brings you here?'

Her bosom swelled. '*May* you know indeed! Of course, you haven't a notion, have you? Oh, not the least in the world! Standing there, as proud as an apothecary, and holding up your nose at one which has kept company with gentlemen of the *highest* rank! *And* I've had grander servants than that niffy-naffy butler of yours waiting on me like slaves, my lord! I'm here to tell you that you can't jaunter about breaking a poor, innocent female's heart! Not without paying for it! Oh, dear me, no!'

'Whose heart have I broken?' asked Kit. 'Yours, ma'am?'

'Mine! That's a loud one!' she exclaimed. 'If I didn't break it for the Marquis, who treated me like a princess, never grudging a groat he spent on me, besides a handsome present when we parted, as part we did, and not a hard word spoken on either side, him knowing what was due to a lady –' She stopped, unable to find the thread of her argument, and demanded: 'Where was I?'

'You were saying,' supplied Kit helpfully, 'that you did not break your heart for the Marquis.'

'And nor I did! So it ain't likely I'd break it for a sprig scarce breeched, even if I were ten years younger than I am!' said Mrs Alperton, taking a telescopic view of her age. 'It's not *my* heart you've broke, but Clara's – though that's not to say mine don't bleed for her wrongs! Which is why I'm here today, my lord, and small pleasure to me, being jumbled and jolted in a yellow bouncer that has been used to travel in my own chaise, lined with velvet, and four horses, and outriders, besides, let alone the violence done to my feelings to think of being obliged to demean myself, which only a mother's devotion could have prevailed upon me to do!'

These last words effectually banished from Kit's mind an irresistible desire to discover the identity of the Marquis who had supported Mrs Alperton in such magnificent style. He had begun to think that the affair, whatever it was, might not be very serious; but he now realized that he had been indulging optimism too far. When Mrs Alperton, after groping in the pocket of her pelisse, brandished before his eyes a scrap cut from a newspaper he had no need to read it to know what it must be. For an awful moment the thought that Evelyn, in a besotted state of mind, had made the unknown Clara an offer of marriage flashed through his brain, and the vision of an action for breach of promise assailed him. It was strengthened by Mrs Alperton's next utterance. 'You are a serpent!' she told him. 'A knavish, deceiving man of the town that seduced that poor innocent with false promises!'

'Nonsense!' said Kit, maintaining his calm.

'Oh, so it's nonsense, is it? And I suppose you'll say next that you didn't give her a slip on the shoulder?'

He had no hesitation in answering this, for whatever folly Evelyn had committed it was impossible to believe that he had seduced an innocent damsel – or, indeed, that a daughter of Mrs Alperton's answered to that description. 'Most certainly I shall!' he said.

'When you took my Clara under your protection, my lord, you promised you'd care for her!'

'Well?'

The colour rose in her cheeks, causing them to assume a hue that nearly matched her pelisse, but which was at peculiar variance with the rouge she favoured. Her eyes narrowed; and she said menacingly: 'Trying to come crab over me, are you? Well, you won't do it, my fine sir, and so I tell you! You was able to put the change on that sweet, pretty lamb, but I'll have you know I'm more than seven, and I'm up to all the rigs!'

'I don't doubt it,' he said, smiling a little.

Her colour mounted still more alarmingly; but after glaring at him for several seconds she managed to get the better of her temper, and to say, abruptly abandoning her dramatic style for a more business-like approach: 'We'll have a round tale, if you please! You haven't been next or nigh Clara for close on a month, and when she wrote to you, as write she did, not a word did she get in reply from you, and her sick with apprehension, thinking you was ill, or had met with an accident! Not so much as a whisper did you see fit to vouchsafe, to warn her of the shocking sight which was to meet her poor, deluded eyes in this paper! She fell into hysterics on the instant, never dreaming but what you'd have told her, if you was meaning to get riveted, and acted gentlemanly by her!'

Considerably relieved to learn from this that Miss Alperton had apparently had no expectation of marrying Evelyn herself, Kit replied: 'That piece of gossip, ma'am, was published without my knowledge.' He was about to add that it was also without foundation, but he bit the words back, too uncertain of Cressy's intentions to venture to utter them. He said instead: 'Clara must know that I'm a poor hand at letter-writing, but I should have written to reassure her had I not meant to answer her letter in person. Circumstances intervened which have obliged me to postpone my visit to her –'

'Yes, and everyone knows what they are!' interrupted Mrs Alperton. 'What's more, anyone that isn't a knock-in-the-cradle knows better than to believe *that* bag of moonshine! Trying to shab off without paying down your dust, that's what you're doing, and you living as high as a coach-horse!'

'I don't, but you may tell Clara –'

'Oh, yes, you do!' said Mrs Alperton, a steely light in her eyes. 'No use thinking you can bamboozle me into believing your pockets ain't well-lined, my lord! for that's where you'll be made to turn short about! Full of juice your father was, and I'll be bound he cut up warm. And don't think I wasn't acquainted with him, because I was used to know all the swells, and very well pleased most of them were to get their legs under my mahogany, I can tell you!' She added, with dignity: 'Before I retired, that was. My dinners were thought to be first-rate, which I promise you they were, with a French chef, and no expense spared, the Marquis never grudging a penny, but telling me always to buy the best, and keeping the cellar stocked with his own wines.'

Breaking into this reminiscent spate, Kit said: 'You are labouring under a misapprehension, ma'am. I have not the remotest intention of *shabbing off*; nor shall I fail, when I contemplate matrimony, to inform Clara.'

'Why, that's just what you have done!' she exclaimed indignantly. 'Leaving her to read it in the newspaper, which only a heart of stone would have done!'

'I've told you already that what she read was mere gossip, and –'

'Yes, and I'll thank you not to waste your breath telling me again!' said Mrs Alperton fiercely. 'Nor to tell me that it's mere gossip that you've got Miss Stavely staying here with you at this very moment!'

'Miss Stavely, ma'am, is my mother's goddaughter, and is staying here as her guest, not mine!'

'Fancy that, now! Not that I thought other, for it's not to be supposed she'd have come if your mama hadn't invited her. And mighty fortunate she must think herself, for she must be twenty, if she's a day, and if Stavely means to come down handsomely it's more than I'd bargain for! *I* never knew him to be beforehand with the world! But whether she'd think herself so fortunate if she was to know the way you've treated my Clara is another pair of shoes, my lord!'

Kit stiffened imperceptibly, realizing, from the gloating smile on Mrs Alperton's lips, that this was not mere recrimination. Her object in coming to Ravenhurst was blackmail. This placed him in a position of extreme peril; for although a denunciation of his supposed perfidy would destroy the end she had in view he had seen enough of her to know that her hold over her temper was not strong; and he had little doubt that if he refused to comply with whatever demand she was about to make she would not hesitate to carry her threat into execution. Probably, since her voice became strident under the influence of emotion, Cressy would be by no means the only person at Ravenhurst to hear her disclosures. How to get rid of her without affording her the opportunity to kick up such a scene as he shuddered even to contemplate was a problem to which he could discover no certain answer. With the best will in the world to do it, he was powerless to silence her by presenting her with any such sum as she was likely to consider adequate: he could neither give her a draft on Evelyn's account, nor upon his own. The will, moreover, was entirely lacking. He had no means of discovering the extent of Evelyn's obligation; or whether Mrs Alperton was acting at her daughter's instigation. He suspected that no money given into her hand would ever reach Clara; and he was pretty sure that she had played no part in whatever bargain Evelyn might have struck with Clara. Not only would it be very unlike Evelyn to enter into sordid negotiations with his Aspasia's parent: it had been noticeable that throughout her discourse Mrs Alperton had refrained from making any such claim. Kit was determined to make no rash promises on his twin's behalf.

Something of this must have shown itself in his face, for Mrs Alperton, who had been closely watching him, said, on a rising note: 'And know it she shall, and so I warn you, my lord!'

'Tell me, Mrs Alperton,' said Kit, on a gentle note of mockery, 'am I expected to believe that you are Clara's mouthpiece? It seems strangely unlike her!'

It was a bow drawn at a venture, since, for anything he knew, Clara had inherited her mother's temper, but he saw from Mrs Alperton's face that he had hit the target. She looked angrily at him, but hardly hesitated before replying: 'Oh, dear me, no! Well do you know that the sweet creature, loving you so truly as she does, would allow herself to be trampled to death rather than throw the least rub in the way of anything you wanted to do, even if it killed her, which I am afraid for my life it will do, for never have I seen her so low and disordered – scarcely able to raise her head from the pillow, and done-up with weeping! I shouldn't wonder at it if she was to dwindle into a decline.'

Kit shook his head. 'You shock me, ma'am. Do you know, I had no notion she suffered from such a profound sensibility?'

He felt himself to be on safe ground, for his imagination boggled at the vision of Evelyn developing the smallest tendre for so lachrymose a female. Apparently he had again hit the target, for Mrs Alperton informed him, in a voice of suppressed fury, that he little knew how much Clara sank under agitating reflections, or how hard it was for her to wear a smiling face whenever he chose to visit her.

'If that's so, I should suppose her to be thankful to be rid of me,' he remarked, unable to repress an involuntary chuckle. He saw that Mrs Alperton was about to burst into further recriminations, and flung up a hand. 'No, no, enough, ma'am! You've performed your errand! I am excessively sorry to hear of Clara's distressing state, and I beg you will return to her bedside with all possible speed. Convey my deepest regrets to her that I have been the unwitting cause of her disorder, and assure her that as soon as it may be possible for me to do so I shall hasten to visit her.'

The issue seemed for a few moments to hang in the balance; but Mrs Alperton was made of resilient stuff. Abandoning all semblance of concern for her daughter's broken heart, she said roughly: 'Not till you come down with the derbies! *I* know your sort! A regular bounce, that's what you are, but you won't nurse my girl out of her due, not while I'm alive to protect her!'

'Mrs Alperton,' said Kit coldly, 'you are making a mistake! I don't run thin, but I am not a pigeon for your plucking! Clara will not find me ungenerous, but whatever may be the arrangement agreed upon it will be between her and me, and no one else.'

'Oh, will it indeed?' she ejaculated. '*Will* it? If that's your tone, my Lord Brass-face, I don't leave this house until I've opened my budget to Miss Stavely! Try to have me put out if you dare! And don't tell me she's gone out, and won't be back till nightfall, because if I believed you, which I don't, I'd wait till midnight, and longer!'

At this point an entirely unexpected voice made itself heard. 'What a fortunate circumstance that I haven't gone out!' said Miss Stavely. 'Did you wish to see me, ma'am?'

Since Kit had been standing with his back to the door, his person obscuring Mrs Alperton's view of it, neither of them had seen it open a little way, and Cressy slip softly into the room. Mrs Alperton started, and let her parasol fall to the floor; but Kit spun round, the nonchalance wiped suddenly from his face, to be succeeded by a look of consternation.

Smiling brightly upon him, Cressy advanced into the room. Involuntarily he put out a hand to check her, but she ignored it, and went to sit down in a chair facing Mrs Alperton across the empty hearth. 'Pray forgive me for interrupting you!' she said gracefully. 'But you were speaking rather loudly, you know, ma'am, and I could not help but hear a little of what you were saying. I collect you have something you wish to tell me?'

'No!' said Kit.

Mrs Alperton, her high colour abating, glanced speculatively at him, before resuming her study of Cressy. There was an uncertain look in her eyes; and it was plainly to be seen that she was unable to decide whether Cressy's entrance could be turned to pecuniary advantage, or whether it had effectually spiked her guns. She said slowly, and to gain time: 'So you're Stavely's girl, are you? You don't favour him much, by what I remember.'

Accepting this familiarity with unruffled calm, Cressy replied: 'No, I am thought to resemble my mother. Now, what is it that you wish to say to me, if you please?'

'As to that,' said Mrs Alperton, 'it's not my *wish* to say anything to you, not bearing you any ill-will, nor being one to tell tales, unless I'm pushed to it.' She transferred her gaze to Kit's face, and said: 'Maybe you'd prefer I kept mum, my lord?'

'But I shouldn't,' intervened Cressy.

Mrs Alperton paid no heed to this, but continued to watch Kit maliciously. He met her eyes, and his own hardened. 'I should infinitely prefer it,' he said, 'but I have warned you already that I am not a pigeon for your plucking! Take care what you're about, Mrs Alperton! The glue won't hold: you'll bowl yourself out.'

'Not before I've bowled you out!' she declared venomously. 'Which I'll be glad to do, for I'm a mother myself, and it would go to my heart to see an innocent girl deceived like my poor Clara has been! Ah, my dear, you little know what a cozening rascal has been casting out his wicked lures to you!'

Kit leaned his shoulders against the wall, folded his arms across his chest, and resigned himself.

'No, indeed!' agreed Cressy. 'Is Clara your daughter, ma'am?'

'My daughter!' said Mrs Alperton, in a throbbing voice. 'Seduced by that villain, and left to starve without so much as a leave-taking!'

'How very dreadful!' said Cressy. 'I must say I am astonished! I should never have thought he would have behaved so shabbily.'

Mrs Alperton was considerably taken aback. So too was Kit. He had hoped that Cressy would discredit the greater part of the story; but none of it was fit for the ears of a gently nurtured girl, and he had not dared to hope that she would not suffer a severe shock, attended by painful embarrassment. But neither he nor Mrs Alperton had taken into account the peculiar circumstances of her girlhood, or the undisguised gallantries of her father.

'Very improper indeed!' pursued Cressy. 'I do most sincerely pity her – and you, too, ma'am, for nothing, I dare say, could be more disagreeable than to feel yourself compelled to remind Lord Denville of his obligations.'

'No,' said Mrs Alperton, a little dazed. 'No, indeed!'

'But perhaps there is a misunderstanding?' suggested Cressy hopefully. 'The thing is that he is abominably forgetful, you know. You did very right to put him in mind of the matter, for I am persuaded he will do just as he ought, now that he has remembered it, won't you, sir?'

'Just as I ought!' corroborated Kit.

'Well, upon my word!' gasped Mrs Alperton. 'I never did, not in all my life! I'm telling you he's a *rake*, miss!'

'Yes, but do you think you should, ma'am?' asked Cressy diffidently. 'I perfectly understand your telling *him* so, but it doesn't seem to be quite the thing to tell *me*, for it is not in the least my affair – though I am naturally very sorry for your daughter.'

'I might have known it!' said Mrs Alperton terribly. 'It wouldn't make a bit of difference to you if he was a murderer, I dare say! Oh, the sinful hollowness of the world! That I should have lived to hear a lady of consequence – and single, too! – talk so bold and unblushing! Well, they didn't do so in *my* day, whatever they may have thought! Not those that held themselves up as the pink of gentility! And very right they shouldn't', she added, moved to a moment of sincerity. She seemed to be about to expatiate on this point, but changed her mind, and instead said, reverting to her original style: 'And me coming to warn you, believing you was but an innocent, and my heart wrung to think of you married to one such as he is! You'll live to regret it, my girl, for all his gingerbread, and his grand title!'

'Good God, I should think so indeed!' exclaimed Cressy. '*Marry* Lord Denville? But I've no such intention!'

Mrs Alperton was fast losing control of the situation, but she made a gallant attempt at a recover. 'Oh, you haven't? Then perhaps you'll tell me, Miss Stavely, what *this* means?'

Cressy, blinking at the scrap of print held up before her, presented for a moment all the appearance of one wholly bewildered. Then her puckered brow cleared, and she fell into laughter. '*Now* I understand!' she said. 'Do you know ma'am, I have been quite in a puzzle to know why you should have wished to talk to *me*? It seemed the oddest thing! But I see it all now! You have read that absurd paragraph in the *Morning Post*, which has had us all in whoops! Oh dear, was there ever anything so nonsensical? But it is a great deal too bad!' she said, resolutely schooling her countenance to an expression of gravity. 'I beg your pardon, ma'am! Infamous of me to laugh, when the tattling wretch who wrote that ridiculous farrago has been the cause of your being put to so much pain and inconvenience! How *very* kind it was in you to have come to see me! Indeed, I am excessively obliged to you, and shockingly distressed to think you should have undertaken such a disagreeable task for nothing.'

'*Not* going to marry him?' Mrs Alperton said incredulously. She looked from Cressy to Kit; and then, as she saw the smile in his eyes, as they rested on Cressy, said roundly: 'Humdudgeon! And I collect he's not nutty upon you either!'

'Oh, no! At least, I sincerely trust he is not, for I am persuaded we should not suit.'

'That's a loud one!' ejaculated Mrs Alperton, with a scornful crack of laughter. 'You won't gammon *me* so easily! Why, anyone could see –'

'Pray say no more!' begged Cressy, suddenly assailed by maidenly shyness. 'There is no possibility of my marrying Lord Denville, ma'am, as you will understand when I tell you that my affections are – are already engaged!'

There was a moment's frozen silence, during which Mrs Alperton seemed to wilt where she sat. Kit, withdrawing his intent gaze from Cressy's face, quietly left the room, feeling that she stood in no need of support, and that no time should be lost in summoning Mrs Alperton's chaise to the door. He despatched a footman on this errand, desiring him at the same time to send Challow up to the house.

That worthy arrived speedily. He evinced no surprise at the curt question which greeted him, but replied: 'Yes, sir, I do know where it came from. According to what the postboy told me, it was hired in Tunbridge Wells. And a regular saucebox *he* is, but he'd got no reason to tell me a whopper, so we may as well believe him as not. *Also* according to him, Master Kit, the party which hired it had quite an argle-bargle with Norton before he let her into the house, saying as how his lordship would regret it to his dying day if he didn't see her. Very full of it, the lad was! Well, it made me prick up my ears, as I don't need to tell you, but by what the lad *says*, the party was naught but an old griffin: not by any manner of means one of his lordship's convenients – asking your pardon, Master Kit, if I'm speaking too bold!'

'Not one of his convenients: her mother!' said Kit, his brows knit.

'You don't say!' exclaimed Challow, shocked. 'Whatever brought her here, sir?'

'It seems his lordship hasn't visited her daughter for nearly a month. She thinks he has abandoned her. I hoped that perhaps – But if she comes from the Wells we are no better off than we were before, for we know *that* wasn't where he went!'

'I'll take my affy-davy it wasn't,' asserted Challow. 'And a very good thing too if he *has* abandoned that one! All the same, Master Kit, it looks like you're in a case of pickles – if her ma's half the archwife the postboy says she is! Seems to me you'll have to hang up your axe.'

Kit's frown disappeared, and the ready laughter sprang into his eyes. 'Yes, it looked like a case of pickles to me too,' he admitted. 'In fact, I thought it was all holiday with me! But I was rescued in the very nick of time – and the archwife is about to depart: beaten at all points!'

13

When he re-entered the Blue saloon Kit gathered, from what he heard, that Mrs Alperton had been regaling Cressy with nostalgic reminiscences of her past glory. By the expression of sympathetic interest on Miss Stavely's serene countenance he was encouraged to hope that Mrs Alperton's frequently asserted regard for innocent girls had prompted her to withhold the more lurid details of her career, together with the information that she had been pretty well acquainted with Lord Stavely. Nor was he mistaken: Mrs Alperton had interrupted her narrative several times, with apologies for having allowed herself to run on more than was seemly; and she took care to assure Cressy that although she had more than once entertained Stavely at her parties their association had never ripened into anything beyond what she called company-acquaintance. She was describing these parties, explaining that however nobly born a gentleman might be there were times when he took a fancy for a bit of jollification, when Kit came in. Cressy had exercised a soothing influence upon her, but the sight of Kit brought her wrongs back to her mind. She cut short her reminiscences, and glowered at him.

'Denville, Mrs Alperton, as you may suppose, is anxious to return to her daughter,' said Cressy, before that lady could re-open hostilities. 'She has been telling me, too, how very ill-able she is to afford the post-charges, and I have ventured to say that I am persuaded you will see the propriety of discharging that obligation for her – since all the trouble and expense she has been put to was caused by your stupid forgetfulness!'

'I do indeed,' Kit replied. 'So much so that I have already attended to the matter. The chaise is at the door, ma'am: you will allow me to do myself the honour of escorting you to it!'

Mrs Alperton, rising from the sofa, favoured him with a stately inclination of her head, but observed with a good deal of bitterness that this was the least she had a right to expect, and pretty scaly at that. She then took gracious leave of Cressy, sniffed audibly at Kit, who was holding open the door, and stalked from the room.

He accompanied her out of the house, and very civilly handed her up the steps of the chaise, begging her, as he did so, to assure the afflicted Clara that she was not forgotten, and should not be left to starve.

But Mrs Alperton, somewhat exhausted by so much effort and emotion, had lost interest in her daughter's sorrows, and she merely cast Kit a look of loathing before sinking into a corner of the chaise, and closing her eyes.

Kit went back to the Blue saloon. Cressy was still there, standing where he had left her, with her back to the fireplace. She said seriously, as soon as he came in: 'She ought to have been offered some refreshment, you know. I did think of it, but I was in dread that at any moment someone might hear voices in here, and come in – Lady Denville, perhaps, or Mrs Cliffe.'

'I don't think Mama would have been any more perturbed than you were, but God forbid that my uncle should get wind of it!' He shut the door, and stood looking across the room at her. 'Cressy, what did you mean when you told that harridan that your affections were engaged?'

The colour deepened a little in her cheeks, but she replied lightly: 'Well, she talked so much like someone in a bad play that I became carried away myself! Besides, I had to say something to convince her! I could see she didn't quite believe me when I said I wasn't going to marry your brother.'

He let his breath go in a long sigh, and walked forward, setting his hands on her shoulders, and saying: 'You don't know how much I have wanted to tell you the truth! Cressy, my dear one, forgive me! I've treated you abominably, and I love you so much!'

Miss Stavely, who had developed an interest in the top button of his coat, looked shyly up at this. '*Do* you, Kit?' she asked. '*Truly?*'

Mr Fancot, preferring actions to words, said nothing whatsoever in answer to this, but took her in his arms and kissed her. Miss Stavely, who had previously thought him unfailingly gentle and courteous, perceived, in the light of this novel experience, that she had been mistaken: there was nothing gentle about Mr Fancot's crushing embrace; and his behaviour in paying no heed at all to her faint protest could only be described as extremely uncivil. She was wholly unused to such treatment, and she had a strong suspicion that her grandmother would condemn her conduct in submitting to it, but as Mr Fancot seemed to be dead to all sense of propriety it was clearly useless to argue with him.

Several minutes later, sitting within the circle of Kit's arm on the sofa lately occupied by Mrs Alperton, she said: '*Why* did you do it, Kit? It seems quite fantastic!'

'Of course it was – infamous as well! I beg your pardon, even though I can't be sorry I did it. If I hadn't come home that night, I might never have known you – or have known you only as Evelyn's wife!'

This terrible thought caused him to tighten his arm involuntarily. She soothed him by softly kissing his cheek, and by saying, as soon as she had recovered her breath: 'But I don't think I *should* have married Denville. I had so very nearly made up my mind not to when I met *you*! Then I thought – being so grossly deceived – that perhaps I would, after all. But *why* was I deceived?'

'I did it to get Evelyn out of a scrape,' he confessed. 'No one but Mama, and Fimber, and Challow knew I wasn't in Vienna; and in the old days, when we were prime for any lark, we often did exchange identities, and only those who knew us very well ever found us out. So I was pretty certain I could carry it off. But when I took Evelyn's place at that first dinner-party it was in the belief that it would be for one occasion only. If I had known that I should be obliged to maintain the hoax, nothing would have prevailed upon me to have yielded to Mama's persuasions!'

Her eyes danced. 'I knew it! She *did* persuade you!'

'Yes, but I must own,' said Kit scrupulously, 'that I put the notion into her head – not in the least meaning to do so, but by saying, in a funning way, that if Evelyn didn't come back in time to attend that party I should be obliged to take his place. Only to make her laugh! You see, I found her in the deuce of a pucker, because Evelyn was still absent, although he had been expected to return to London days earlier. I thought then that he had been delayed by some trifling hitch, so I consented to run that rig, though it went very much against the pluck with me. Can you understand, Cressy? The circumstances – the intolerable slight offered you if Evelyn failed to appear at a gathering assembled to make his acquaintance –!'

'Indeed I can!' she responded instantly. 'I don't blame you at all – I am even grateful to you for having spared me such a daunting humiliation! What *did* delay Evelyn?'

'I don't know.'

She had been leaning against his shoulder, but she sat up at this. 'You don't know? But – Where *is* Evelyn?'

'I don't know that either. That's the devil of it!' he said frankly. 'At the outset, I thought merely – not that he had forgotten his engagement in Mount Street, but that he had confused the date of it.'

'Very likely,' she agreed. 'He *does* forget, you know! People joke him about his shocking memory, and I am acquainted with one hostess who makes it a rule to send him a reminder on the day of her party!'

The rueful smile lit his eyes. 'Yes, but that's not it. He has been absent for too long. I think some accident befell him. That's why I came home in such a bang. I can't explain that to you, but we do know, each of us, when the other has suffered an injury. He knew it, a year ago, when I broke my leg – not the nature of the accident, but that I *had* sustained some hurt – and the express I sent him arrived only just in time to stop him posting off to Dover to board the next packet!'

'I remember,' she said. 'Godmama said it was the uncomfortable part of being a twin! And you felt that?'

He frowned slightly. 'Yes, I did. For several days, I – But it left me, that feeling, so completely that I wondered if my imagination had been playing me false. *Something* must have happened to him, but it wasn't a fatal accident, and I don't think he is any longer troubled in *mind*.'

'As he was when he steeled himself to make me an offer?' said Cressy, unable to resist temptation. 'Ah, well! I have been for too long at my last prayers to feel the least surprise at that!'

'Yes, love, indeed!' agreed Mr Fancot, unhandsomely refusing the gambit. 'So old cattish as you are!'

'Odious wretch!' Her brows drew together. 'Yes, but I still don't understand! Having so steeled himself, why did he go away at just that moment?'

'As far as we know,' replied Kit carefully, 'he went to redeem from Lord Silverdale, who was said to be in Brighton, a brooch which my mama had lost to him at play.'

'Oh!' said Cressy doubtfully. 'I see. That is, – yes, of course!'

'I should perhaps explain to you,' said Kit, in a kind voice, 'that when Mama staked this bauble, for a cool monkey, she had forgotten that it was merely a copy of one of the pieces she sold years ago.' He added, as she gasped: 'But pray don't think that Evelyn went off to Brighton so hurriedly at her instigation! Nothing could be farther from the truth! She considers that to redeem, for the sum of £500, a brooch worth only a few guineas is grossly improvident.'

Cressy struggled with herself for a desperate moment, but her feelings overcame her, and she went into a peal of mirth. 'Of course she does! I can almost hear her saying it! Oh, was there ever anyone so absurd and enchanting as Godmama?'

'Let me tell you, Miss Stavely,' said Kit severely, 'that this is *not* a diverting story! Are you ever serious?'

'Yes, in my own home. Amongst the Fancots, never! No one could be! I have had a – a bubble of laughter inside me ever since I came to Ravenhurst, and you have no idea how much I enjoy it! And when I recall that Godmama told me once that you are the *sober* twin, and think of this crazy masquerade –'

'But it is perfectly true!' he assured her. 'I *am* the sober twin! Mama would tell you that I am becoming prim and prosy, in fact, like my Uncle Brumby! The thing was, you see, that I couldn't help myself: what else *could* I do than help Evelyn out of a scrape?'

There was a warm twinkle in her eyes, but she responded gravely: 'Naturally you were obliged to do it. And did he recover the brooch?'

'We don't know. He certainly went to Brighton, and as

certainly returned here, for one night. He then sent Challow off to Hill Street, with all but his nightbag, saying that he would follow him within the next two days. He left Ravenhurst for an unknown destination, driving himself in his phaeton – and that is the last anyone has heard of him.'

She was startled, and exclaimed: 'Good God, what can have happened to him? Can you discover no trace?'

'I haven't tried to. When I came here it was with the intention of searching for him, not realizing what Challow lost no time in pointing out to me: that I'm hamstrung! So are we all. How can any of us set inquiries afoot for Evelyn while I am believed to *be* Evelyn?'

'I hadn't thought of that. But is there *nothing* to be done?'

'Nothing that I can think of. I hoped I might be able perhaps to discover some clue from Mrs Alperton, but *that* scent was false, and leads only to Tunbridge Wells, where Challow has already hunted for him. Cressy, I haven't thanked you for rescuing me from that harpy! I don't know what I should have done if you hadn't intervened – though I wouldn't have exposed you to such a scene for the world! What made you come into the room?'

'Well, I heard her ranting at you. I own, I suspected something of the sort when Norton looked so meaningly at you, and was so insistent that he must speak to you *alone*!'

'Good God! *Did* you?' he exclaimed, surprised.

She smiled faintly. 'Why, yes! I'm not quite without experience, you see. Oh, I don't mean that I have associated with women like Mrs Alperton – though I did once have an encounter with a – a lady of easy virtue! But that was quite by accident, and Papa never knew anything about it. The thing was that when my mother died Papa wouldn't permit any of my aunts to take charge of me, because he had always been so fond of me, and we were such good *friends*, ever since I can remember. So I stayed in Mount Street, with Miss Yate, who was my governess, and the dearest creature; and as soon as I was sixteen I came out of the schoolroom, and managed things, and looked after Papa – keeping him company, when he was at home, and *comfortable*, which he wasn't, after Mama died. So I pretty soon grew to know about – oh, the things girls *don't*, in general, know!' She laughed suddenly. 'If I had been the greatest nickninny alive, I *must* have guessed, from the veiled warnings of my aunts, that Papa's way of life was not – not perfectly respectable! I believe they thought that he might, at any moment, instal one of his fancies in Mount Street! Grandmama knew better, and was a great deal more blunt, when she explained matters to me, and told me how very improperly gentlemen of even the *first* consideration too often conduct themselves, and exactly how a lady of quality should behave in all circumstances – however mortifying these might be! I must own,' she added reflectively, 'that it gave me a very poor notion of my grandfather! And although I dearly love Papa I do know now why my mother was subject to fits of dejection, and – and I would *prefer* not to be married to anyone of a *rakish* disposition!'

'That's dished me!' observed Kit despondently.

'Yes, I was afraid you'd be sadly cast down!' she retorted. Her eyes narrowed in amusement. 'I wish you might have seen your own face, when I came into the room! Did you think I might add to the confusion by falling into a fit of the vapours?'

'Not quite that,' he answered, smiling, 'but I did think you must be very much shocked.'

'Oh, no! I knew that Denville had been a trifle in what Papa calls the *petticoat line*! What I did feel was that since you were *not* Denville you might very easily have found yourself in a fix –'

'Which I most certainly did!' he interjected.

She smiled at him, and said, quoting his own words: 'So what *could* I do but help you out of a scrape?'

He caught her hand to his lips. 'Oh, Cressy, you *are* such a darling!' he told her. 'Don't think badly of my twin!

I know it must seems as though he's a shocking loose-screw, but I promise you he's not!'

'No, of course he's not! You can't suppose that I believed the fustian nonsense Mrs Alperton talked, about his leaving Clara to starve! As for his having seduced her, I should think it very much more likely that it was Clara who seduced him! Kit, I know it is most improper of me to ask you, but *who* was the Marquis?'

'My dear, I haven't the least notion, and dared not inquire! I only know that he provided her with outriders, and stocked her cellars with wine from his own.'

'*And* a carriage drawn by cream-coloured horses! I *did* venture to inquire, but she said he was a Duke now, and turned respectable, and that she bore him no grudge, and so wouldn't take his character away.'

'What a pity! I dare say we shall never know now.' He sat frowning for a moment or two. 'I wonder if Evelyn *did* go after Silverdale? He has a place somewhere in the north, I collect. No, I don't think he would have done so without telling Mama.'

'He didn't. Sir Bonamy was talking about Silverdale yesterday, to Mr Cliffe – that is to say, he was talking about Brighton, and the people staying at the Pavilion. He mentioned Lord Silverdale: I heard him. Kit, cannot you think of *any* place where Denville might be? I do feel you ought to make a push to discover what has happened to him. You can't maintain this hoax for ever!'

'Oh, I shan't be obliged to!' he replied. 'He'll come back! Yes, I know it must seem odd in me not to be in flat despair: I think so myself, whenever I consider every appalling possibility; but I find, after conjuring up nightmares, that I don't believe one of 'em. Evelyn *could* not be dead, or in distress, and I not know it. And when he does come – Lord, we shall still be in the suds! This is the very devil of a hobble, Cressy!'

'But why? Of course it is bound to be a little awkward, but must it be so very bad? No announcement of my engagement to Denville has been made, and that horrid piece of printed gossip might just as well refer to you as Denville. Surely we must be able to contrive so that only our families need ever know that Denville made me an offer? Or if not that – I was forgetting that unfortunate dinner-party – at least my aunts and uncles need never know that you played that hoax on us all. We can tell the truth: that I met you, and found I liked you better!'

He smiled a little, but shook his head. 'That's not it. We are deeper in the suds than I think you know, love. Even assuming that your father would give his consent –'

'He will: Albinia will take good care of that!'

'I daren't assume so much. He must think me a poor exchange for Evelyn! I have neither his title nor his possessions, remember! *His* fortune is handsome; mine is merely genteel!'

'Well, Papa can scarcely take exception to that, for my fortune is merely genteel too. Of course, he may be disappointed when he learns that I am not going to be a Countess after all, so let us immediately decide what title you mean to adopt when you are raised to the peerage, like your uncle! That should reconcile him, don't you think?'

'To be honest with you,' he said apologetically, 'no, I don't! I can't help feeling that he might even doubt my ability to achieve such a distinction.'

'Papa is not very clever, but he's not such a goose as that! You may not be as wealthy as Denville, but I haven't the shadow of a doubt that you will make a much greater mark in the world than he will. Perhaps I ought to tell you that in preferring your suit to his I am governed by ambition. You, in course of time, will become the Secretary for Foreign Affairs –'

'In a year or two!' interpolated Mr Fancot affably.

Her lips quivered, but she continued smoothly: ' – and I shall go down to history as a great political hostess!'

'That's much easier to picture! Do you think you could be serious for a few moments, little love?'

She folded her hands demurely in her lap. 'I'll try, sir!' Then she saw that although he smiled there was trouble behind the smile, and she became grave at once, unfolding her hands to tuck one into his, warmly clasping it. 'Tell me!'

His long fingers closed over her hand, but he did not immediately answer her. When he did speak it was to ask her an abrupt question. 'What did Evelyn tell you, Cressy? You said that he had been very frank with you: how frank?'

'Perfectly, I believe. I liked him for it – for not pretending that he had fallen in love with me, which I knew he had not. He did it charmingly, too! Well, you know his engaging way! He explained to me how uncomfortably he was circumstanced, and that Lord Brumby would wind up the Trust if he entered into a suitable marriage. I thought it very understandable that his present situation should chafe him beyond bearing.'

'That was all he told you?'

'Why, yes! Was there some other reason?'

'Not precisely. His object was certainly to wind up that confounded Trust, which has irked him more than I guessed. But I *know* him, Cressy! – oh, as I know myself! – and I am very certain that he would never have proposed such a cold-blooded marriage merely to rid himself of shackles which *fretted* him. As I understand the matter, he was forced into this by the urgent need to get possession of his principal.'

'Do you mean that he is in debt?' she asked, considerably surprised. 'Surely you must be mistaken! I had thought, from what Papa told me, that the income he enjoys is very large indeed? *Could* he have run so deep into debt that he must broach his principal?'

He shook his head. 'No. Not Evelyn: Mama!'

She gave a gasp, but said quickly: 'Oh, poor Lady Denville! Yes, I see – of course I see! I should have known – that is, – Pardon me, but I have heard gossip! I discounted the better part of it. You must be as well acquainted with tattle-boxes as I am! *Detestable* creatures! I was aware too, that Godmama was – was a little afraid of Lord Denville; and of course I know that she is amazingly expensive! She told me herself that she was so monstrously in the wind that her case was desperate – but in such a droll way that I thought she was funning. And when your father died I supposed – I don't know why – that her affairs had been settled.'

'They were not. In justice to my father, I believe he didn't know in what case they stood. She never told him the whole – dared not! The blame for that must lie at his door!'

'Indeed it must!' she said warmly. 'Pray tell me the whole! You may trust me, I promise you! I love her too, remember! Is it *very* bad?'

'Do you think I would have breathed one word of this to you if I didn't trust you? I do, most implicitly, but I can't tell you how bad it may be until I've seen Evelyn. It would be useless to try to discover the answer from poor Mama, for I don't think she has the smallest notion how much she owes. It's plain enough it must be a larger sum than any of us suspected.'

She said diffidently: 'Would not Lord Brumby see the propriety of discharging her debts?'

'Yes, I think he would, but –' He paused, frowning. 'That was the thought that occurred to me. Not that she should have applied to my uncle, but that Evelyn might do so. But something she said to me – my uncle does not like her, you know – made me realize why Evelyn would not do that – or I either! It would be a betrayal.' He glanced up, with a twisted smile. 'We couldn't do it, you see. She would never betray us, and – well, we love her dearly! So you see why I said we are in the suds.'

She nodded. 'Very clearly! It is *most* awkward, and I don't immediately perceive by what means we are to come about. Unless your brother would consent to offer for some other eligible female?'

'That's the only solution I can think of,' he admitted. 'Unfortunately, my dear, *you* are, in my uncle's eyes, the most eligible of all females! He certainly knew that Evelyn meant to offer for you, and it may well be that Evelyn, or Mama, told him that he had done so, and had been accepted – subject to your grandmother's approval! Whatever his opinion of Evelyn may be, he's very full of starch, you know, and would find it impossible to believe that she would *not* approve of a marriage with the head of his house! He would be far more likely to think Evelyn incurably volatile, and by no means to be trusted with the control of his fortune. And even if he could be won over – No, I'll have no hand in thrusting my twin into a marriage of convenience! I wouldn't have furthered his engagement to you if I hadn't known he was committed already. So – so there we are, my darling! At Point Non-Plus!'

She nodded, and sat thinking, quite as troubled as he was. After a pause, she turned her eyes towards him, and said: 'You can do nothing till Evelyn comes back, can you? I understand that. And then?'

'Between us we must be able to come about. If I knew just how badly scorched Mama is – but even if I did I couldn't turn tail at this stage! Only think what a dust there would be if I were suddenly to announce that all this time I'd been hoaxing everyone! I can readily imagine your grandmother's delight at receiving such tidings: I should be ruining myself as well as Evelyn!'

'You might,' she conceded. 'One never knows, with Grandmama. She likes you, so that it's possible she would think it a very good joke. She will have to know the truth in the end, after all!'

'Yes, but not until Evelyn is here to explain why he was compelled – as I know he must have been – to behave so abominably.'

She thought this over. 'No. I was wondering if we might not make up some tale – but we should very likely be bowled out if we did. And I can't help feeling that it would be very much better if the Cliffes never do know that they were hoaxed.'

'Very much better! And how they are to be got rid of presents us with another problem. I have an uneasy suspicion that they mean to spend the rest of the summer at Ravenhurst.'

She laughed. 'Yes, but I am very sure Godmama won't allow them to do so! Kit, how many persons know the truth?'

'Besides those I've mentioned, only my old nurse, and Ripple. What made you find me out? Did I betray myself? Ripple, who has known me all my life, wouldn't have done so if I hadn't done something he knew Evelyn would never do.'

'Oh, no! You didn't betray yourself in any way you could help. I hardly know how it was – except that you are *not* quite like Evelyn, however much you appear to be his image. It puzzled me, when I first met you, but I thought you were perhaps a man of several moods. I might not have found you out if I hadn't seen that portrait, and if I hadn't been present when Godmama started to say Kit, and changed it suddenly to *Kind* Evelyn!'

'I thought you hadn't noticed that slip. I yield to none in my devotion to Mama, but a more caper-witted creature I hope I may never encounter! Let me tell you, my love, that her latest brilliant notion – a gem of high value, this one! – is that if Evelyn should suddenly return to us he must pretend to be me!'

That sent her off into another fit of laughter. 'Oh, she *is* so superb! Do you mean to tell her about *this*? I think we should, don't you?'

'No – emphatically!' said Kit, drawing her back into his arm. 'We'll keep our secret until Evelyn comes home!'

14

The following day was not destined to be ranked amongst Mr Fancot's happier memories. It included a picnic, arranged by Lady Denville for the entertainment of Cressy, Ambrose, the young Thatchams, the Vicar's elder daughter, and Kit himself; a singularly unsuccessful dinner-party; and a letter from Lord Brumby.

This was addressed to Evelyn, and it did nothing to raise Kit's hopes of being able to solve the problem which had kept him awake for a considerable part of the night. It was written in an amicable spirit, but it made Kit's heart sink. Lord Brumby had seen the paragraph in the *Morning Post*, and, while he expressed himself austerely on the impropriety of it, he was glad to learn from it that his nephew's affairs were prospering so well. He had received from his old friend, Stavely, a gratifying account of the excellent impression Evelyn had made in Mount Street; and he entertained no doubt that this must be strengthened during Miss Stavely's stay at Ravenhurst. His congratulations might be premature, but he believed he need not hesitate to offer them, since it would be strange indeed if his dear Denville, who (as he was well aware), possessed the gift of being able to make himself very agreeable, when he chose to do so (underscored), should fail to win a lady already favourably disposed towards his suit.

That made Kit grin appreciatively, but the next sheet, however acceptable it might have been had it been addressed to himself, lowered his spirits still more. It was devoted to praise of Miss Stavely. No one, in Lord Brumby's opinion, could be a more eligible bride. Her fortune was not large, but it was respectable; her lineage was impeccable; and from all he had seen and heard of her she was eminently fitted for the position offered her. His lordship ventured to predict for his nephew a future of domestic bliss, un-attended by such youthful volatility as he had been obliged, in the past, to deprecate.

He ended this missive with a brief paragraph which, under other circumstances, might well have encouraged optimism in Mr Fancot's breast. *'I must not conclude, my dear Denville, without informing you that I have received a very comfortable account of your brother from Stewart, who writes of him in such terms as must, I know well, afford you as much gratification as they afford me.'*

Mr Fancot, reading these lines in unabated gloom, put up his uncle's letter, and went off to superintend the final preparations for an expedition of pleasure to Ashdown Forest.

This, being attended by all the ills, including a shower of rain, which commonly beset all fresco entertainments, was spoilt for Kit from the outset by the inability of the Vicar's daughter to ride. She was driven to the rendezvous in the landaulet, which also carried the picnic-hampers; and Miss Stavely, the doyenne of the party, bore her company: a graceful act of self-abnegation which would have confirmed Lord Brumby in his high opinion of her excellence, but which won no encomiums whatsoever from Mr Fancot.

The dinner-party, which followed hard upon his return from this expedition, sent him to bed in a state of exhaustion. Lady Denville, in her praiseworthy desire to make the Dowager Lady Stavely's visit to Ravenhurst agreeable, had been inspired to beg the pleasure of Lord and Lady Dersingham's company to dinner; and this couple, whom she described to Kit as antiquated fogies who belonged to the Dowager's set, had felt themselves obliged to accept her invitation. In the event, her inspiration was proved to be far from happy, as Sir Bonamy, when he learned of the high treat in store, correctly prognosticated. 'Maria Dersingham?' exclaimed that amiable hedonist, his eyes starting from their sockets. 'No, no, my pretty! You can't be serious! Why, she and the old Tartar here have been at outs these dozen years and more!'

The truth of these daunting words was confirmed within five minutes of the Dersinghams' arrival. Nothing could have been more honeyed than the civilities exchanged between two elderly and redoubtable ladies of quality; and nothing could have struck more terror into the bosoms of the rest of the company than the smiling remarks each subsequently addressed to the other. The only person to remain unaffected was Mrs Cliffe, whose unshakeable conviction that her sole offspring would shortly succumb to an inflammation of the lungs, contracted in Ashdown Forest during a shower of rain, occupied her mind to the exclusion of all other considerations; and the only two persons who derived enjoyment from the party were the contestants themselves, who showed signs of alarming revivification at every hit scored.

It was in a state of prostration (as he informed Cressy, when he contrived to snatch a brief moment or two alone with her) that Kit retired to bed shortly after eleven o'clock. He was certainly very much too tired to tease his brain by trying to hit upon a solution to the problem that confronted him; and, in fact, fell asleep within a very few minutes of Fimber's drawing the curtains round the enormous four-poster bed, and leaving the room.

He was dragged up, an hour later, from fathoms deep, by a hand grasping his shoulder, and shaking it, and a voice saying: 'Oh, *do* wake up, Kester! *Kester!*'

Only one person had ever called him that. Still half-asleep, he responded automatically, murmuring: 'Eve. . . !'

'Wake up, you gudgeon!'

He opened his eyes, and blinked into the laughing face of his twin, illuminated by candlelight. For a moment he stared; then a slow smile crept into his eyes, and he said, a little thickly, and stretching out his hand: 'I knew you couldn't have stuck your spoon in the wall!'

His hand was taken by his twin's left one, and strongly grasped.

'I thought you would,' Evelyn said. 'What brought you home? Did you know I'd damned nearly done so?'

'Yes. And that you were in some kind of a hank.'

The grasp tightened on his hand. 'I hoped you wouldn't guess that. Oh, but, Kester, it's *good* to see you again!'

'Yes,' agreed Kit, deep, if drowsy, affection in his smile. 'Damn you!' he added.

'I'm sorry: I'd have sent you word if I hadn't been knocked senseless,' said Evelyn penitently.

Emerging from the last clinging remnants of sleep, Kit became aware of some awkwardness in the clasp on his hand. He then saw that it was being held by Evelyn's left one, and that his right lay in a sling. 'So you did suffer an accident!' he remarked. 'Broken your arm?'

'No: my shoulder, and a couple of ribs. That's nothing!'

'How did you do it?'

'Took a corner too fast, and overturned the phaeton.'

'Cawker!' said Kit, sitting up. He released Evelyn's hand, yawned, stretched, cast off his nightcap, vigorously rubbed his head, and then, apparently refreshed by these activities, said: 'That's better!' and swung his legs out of bed.

Evelyn, lighting all the candles with which Lady Denville lavishly provided every bedroom in the house, said: 'You must have made a pretty batch of it tonight! It took me five minutes to waken you.'

'If you knew what sort of an evening I *have* been spending, or just half the things I've been yearning to do to you, you skirter, you'd take damned good care not to set up my bristles!' said Kit, shrugging himself into an elegant dressing-gown. 'When I think of the bumble-bath I've been pitched into, and what I've endured, all for the sake of a crazy, rope-ripe –'

'Well, if that's not the outside of enough!' exclaimed his

twin indignantly. '*I* didn't pitch you into a bumble-bath! What's more, I'll have you know that's my new dressing-gown you're wearing, you thieving dog!'

'Don't let such a trifle as that put you in a tweak!' retorted Kit. 'The only things of yours which I am *not* wearing are your boots!'

These amenities having been exchanged, the dressing-gown securely fastened, and his feet thrust into a pair of Morocco slippers, Kit advanced, to grasp his brother's left shoulder, and turn him towards the light thrown by a branch of candles on the dressing-table. 'Let me look at you!' he said roughly. His eyes keenly scanned Evelyn's face; he said: 'You've been in pretty queer stirrups, haven't you? Still out of frame! And not because of a few broken bones! Eve, why didn't you *tell* me the worry you were in?'

Evelyn put up his hand to pull Kit's from his shoulder. He said, wryly smiling: 'It's no bread-and-butter of yours, Kester. Did Mama tell you?'

'Yes, of course. As for it's being no bread-and-butter of mine –'

'How is she?' interrupted Evelyn.

'Very much herself!'

'Bless her! At least I knew *she* wouldn't get into a stew!'

'She isn't in a stew, because I told her I knew you weren't dead; but she was in the deuce of a twitter when I reached London,' said Kit, with some severity.

Evelyn cocked a quizzical eyebrow at him. 'No, was she? Well, that's a new come-out! Her spirits worn down by anxiety, I collect? Doing it much too brown, Kester! I've never known Mama to be in a worry for more than ten minutes at a time!'

'No,' Kit admitted, 'but this was something out of the way! Why the devil didn't you send her a message?'

'I couldn't: I was out of my senses for days, and when I did come to myself I wasn't in any case to be thinking of sending messages. If you'd ever suffered a deep concussion, you'd know what I felt like!'

'So that was it! Here, sit down! What we need is some brandy: I'll go and fetch up the decanter!'

'I brought it up with me, *and* a couple of glasses,' said Evelyn, nodding towards a chest against the wall. 'All right and tight with you, old fellow?'

'Yes, except for this damned hobble we're in,' Kit replied, pouring out two generous measures of Fine Old Cognac. He handed one of the glasses to Evelyn, and sat down on the day-bed confronting the chair in which Evelyn had disposed himself. 'Where have you sprung from?' he asked. 'And how the devil did you get into the house?'

'Oh, Pinny still has her key to the nursery-wing! She gave it to me, and I walked from her cottage as soon as I thought it would be safe. I'm putting up there for the night. I was driven over, after dark. No one saw me.'

'Driven over from where?' demanded Kit.

Evelyn had tilted his glass, and was watching the glint of the candlelight on the brandy. 'A place called Woodland House. You wouldn't know it: it's a few miles south of Crowborough. Belongs to a Mr and Mrs Askham.'

'*Crowborough?*' Kit ejaculated. 'Do you mean to tell me you've been within ten miles of Ravenhurst all this time?'

Evelyn nodded, shooting him a sidelong look which held as much mischief as guilt. 'Yes, but I told you – I had concussion!'

'I heard you!' said Kit grimly. 'You came round this morning, jumped out of bed, and posted home, as bobbish as ever! Since when have you run sly with *me*, Eve?'

'No, no, I'm not running sly! It's just that it's a long story, and – and I was wondering where to begin!'

'Well, begin by telling me what took you to Crowborough of all unlikely places!'

'Oh, I didn't go to Crowborough! I went to Networth. You know, Kester! – a village not far from Nutley, where John-Coachman went to live with his married daughter, when my father pensioned him. Goodleigh told me, when I was here, that he's grown pretty feeble, and keeps asking after us both. So I drove over to see the poor old chap. Lord, Kester, do you remember how he was used to have one of the carriages pulled out into the yard, and sit us up on the box-seat, and teach us how to handle the whip?'

'Of course I do! But you didn't get rid of Challow because you were going to see old John!'

'Oh, no! That was by the way – or not so very much out of it! I was bound for Tunbridge Wells, and thought I might just as easily take the pike-road from Uckfield as –'

'Clara!' uttered Kit.

'Yes, that's right, but how in thunder did you know? If that meddling busybody, Challow, has been nosing out what's no concern of his, I'll be *damned* if I'll keep him any longer! The way he and Fimber cluck after me, like a couple of hens with one chick, is enough to drive me out of my mind!'

'Yes, I know, but I didn't learn about Clara from him. He knew you'd got a ladybird in Tunbridge Wells, but not who she was, or where she lived. Just as well! He'd have been in a rare taking, if he'd known she was in bed with a broken heart, all on your account!'

Evelyn gave a shout of laughter. 'Clara? I wish I might see it! She wouldn't shed a tear for me, or anyone else!'

'On the contrary! She hasn't ceased to shed tears since the news of your perfidy burst upon her. She fell into hysterics first – fit after fit of'em!'

'*Will* you stop pitching your gammon? I don't want to be made to laugh: it hurts! Clara's the merriest little game pullet alive – full of fun and gig, and don't give a rap for anyone! As for breaking her heart over me, I'll lay you any odds you like my place in it has been filled by now. I fancy

I know who's got it, too. Where did you pick up this bag of moonshine?'

'From her loving parent – thank you very much, brother!'

'*What?*' Evelyn sat up with an unwise jerk which made him wince. 'Do you mean that rusty old elbow-crooker came here to find me? Kester, you didn't let yourself be bit, did you?'

'Only to the tune of paying the postboy.'

'Well, thank God for that! Lord, Clara would rend her to flinders if she got wind of it! I only met her once, and that was enough for me!'

'It was enough for me too,' said Kit.

'Poor twin!' Evelyn said remorsefully. 'You must have had the devil of a time with her!' His eyes began to dance. 'I'd give a monkey to have seen you, though! Did she gab for ever about the days of her glory?'

'I should rather think she did! Who was the Marquis who kept her in style?'

'I don't know: might have been almost any Marquis, by what I've heard. You wouldn't think she'd been a regular high-flier, would you? She was: old Flixton told me she was a dasher of the first water when she was young. Devil of a temper, but as full of fun as Clara is. The bottle was her undoing: that's why it's low tide with her now, for, according to Clara, she was pretty well-inlaid when she retired! Clara don't live with her, but she looks after her. Which reminds me that I never did get to Tunbridge Wells, and I must. I owe Clara something for the good times we've had together. That's all over now, and I expect she knows it, but I'll tell her myself.' He chuckled. 'As corky a squirrel as you could wish for! Wrote to beg me to send her an express if I was dead, so that she could get her blacks together!' He drank the rest of his brandy, and set the glass down beside his chair. 'Where the deuce was I, when you led me off on to Clara?'

'On the way to Networth, to visit John-Coachman.'

'Oh, yes! Well, I did that all right and tight, and then I took the lane that joins the pike-road at Poundgate. That's where I overturned – just short of Poundgate, and not fifty yards from Woodland House. Mrs Askham happened to be coming out of the gate, and saw it, and the long and the short of it was that she had me carried up to the house, and – and there I've been ever since.' He looked at Kit, warmth in his eyes, 'They couldn't have done more for me if I'd been one of their sons, Kester. I can't tell you how – how *good* they are, or how kind! I didn't know anything about it, of course, but Mr Askham rode off himself to fetch their doctor, and even had the grays led into the stable, and saw to it that they were looked after as well as they would have been here. No broken legs, thank God! And no bad scars – thanks to Mr Askham!'

'Well, that's good, but why didn't he send them a message here? He surely must have known how anxious everyone must be!'

'Yes, yes, but he didn't know who I was! *I* couldn't tell them! Mrs Askham was in a regular stew over it, thinking what would be *her* feelings, if it had happened to Jeffrey, or Philip! They are her two elder sons. I haven't met Jeffrey: he's a parson; but Philip was there – a very good fellow! he's up at Cambridge. Then there's Ned. He's still at Rugby, but he's army-mad. And, in the nursery –'

'Yes, I dare say!' said Kit, ruthlessly interrupting this enthusiastic catalogue. 'But what I want to know is why these excellent people didn't think to take a look inside your card-case! If you were going to see Silverdale – yes, I know about that! – you *can't* have forgotten to take it with you!'

'No, no, I *did* remember to do that!' Evelyn assured him. He cast another of his guilty looks upon his twin, but his eyes were brimful of laughter. 'The thing was that there weren't any cards in it! Now, Kester, *don't* comb my hair! I was in a hurry, but I *did* remember to assure myself that the case was in my pocket, and – dash it, I won't let you rake me down! I am your elder brother, *and* the head of the family, so just you keep your tongue between your teeth!'

'God help the family!' retorted Kit, the laughter reflected in his own eyes. 'Of all the paperskulls –! Was there *nothing* to tell the Askhams who you are?'

'No, what should there be? I'd only my nightbag with me, and you don't suppose I flaunt about the country with my crest blazoned on my sporting carriages, do you?'

'No, but when you came round? They must have asked you what your name was!'

'Yes, they did – at least, Mrs Askham did, when I came round the first time. I don't remember it, and they say I slipped off again, but it seems that Mrs Askham asked me what my name was, and though I didn't answer until she'd asked me several times, in the end I said "Evelyn". Very likely I thought I was at Harrow, and saying my catechism! I don't know! But when I really did come to my senses I found they were calling me Mr Evelyn. At first, I didn't care what they called me. Then, when I got to be more myself, and knew how many days had passed, and that I must have lurched myself with the Stavelys, it didn't seem to signify. Well, Kester, I was all to pieces, and they didn't encourage me to talk, because Dr Elstead had warned them not to do so! And later – I didn't want to tell them.' He paused, studying his right hand, lying in the sling, the flicker of a reminiscent smile playing about the corners of his mouth. After a moment, as Kit waited, in some bewilderment, he looked up, and for the first time in his life met his twin's eyes with a little shyness in his own. 'Kester, when I woke up the second time, and looked round, wondering where the devil I was – I saw an angel!'

'You saw *what*?'

'Sitting in a chair, and watching me,' said Evelyn, in a rapt voice. 'With eyes of such a clear blue – oh, like

the sky! and *shining* – I can't describe them to you! And
the sweetest, tenderest mouth – and pale gold hair, like
a halo! I almost thought myself dead, and in heaven! And
then she rose up out of the chair, and said, in her soft,
pretty voice: "Oh, you are better!" With such a smile as
only an angel *could* have!'

'Oh, did she?' said Kit, no longer bewildered. 'As though
we weren't in a bad enough tangle already! And what else
did she say?'

'Nothing,' replied Evelyn simply. 'She vanished!'

This was rather too much for even the most devoted
twin to accept with complaisance. 'Stubble it!' commanded
Kit wrathfully. 'If you don't stop talking as if you'd rats
in your upper storey, Eve, I'll go back to Vienna tomorrow,
and leave you to get yourself out of this hobble as best you
may!'

'*Kester!*' exclaimed Evelyn, in accents of deep reproach.

Kit's lips quivered, but he said sternly: 'Cut line!'

Evelyn laughed. 'Well, she *seemed* to vanish! She went
away to fetch Mrs Askham back into the room. She had
been set to watch me, you see – they never left me alone
until I came to myself, and Nurse had gone off to her dinner, and Mrs Askham had been called away, which was
why Patience was there. After that, I only saw her when
she brought up a glass of milk for me, or some such thing,
and then only for a moment, and never alone, of course,
for Mrs Askham guards her strictly, until that curst saw-
bones – no, I don't mean that! He was a famous fellow!
– until I was allowed to leave my bed. James – Mrs Askham's man-servant – was used to help me dress, and to
support me downstairs, for I was as weak as a cat for days!
Fit for nothing but to lie on a sofa, which they carried into
the garden for me, and to watch the children at their play!'

'Also to talk to the angel, I collect!' said Kit dryly. 'Is
she a daughter of the Askhams?'

'The eldest daughter. Yes, *then* I was able to talk to

her, but always – always with Mrs Askham there, or Nurse, or the children! It didn't signify – they were right to guard her! And though *I* knew, the instant I clapped eyes on her, that it was bellows to mend with me, she is so – so divinely innocent, Kester, I couldn't suppose that she felt the same! They might have left us alone for hours: I – I wouldn't have said a word to her that might have startled her! She's such a shy little bird – no, not shy, precisely! So open, and confiding! So unaffected, so –'

'Innocent,' supplied Kit, as his besotted twin hesitated for a word.

'Yes,' agreed Evelyn. 'Did you – did you ever meet a girl, Kester, who made you feel that – that the only thing you wanted to do in life was to protect her – shield her from so much as a draught?'

'No,' replied Kit. He added tactfully: 'Not yet!'

'I hope you may!' Evelyn said, in all sincerity. The next instant, he frowned, and shook his head. 'No, I don't! Not in your style!'

'It doesn't sound to me as if she was quite in yours,' Kit ventured to suggest.

A brilliant smile answered him. 'I didn't know, until I saw Patience, what *was* my style! How could I? I never met a girl that even faintly resembled her!'

There did not seem to be anything to be said in reply to this. Kit merely asked: 'Are the Askhams still labouring under the impression that you are Mr Evelyn?'

'No. Before I came away, I made a clean breast of it to Mr Askham. I told him about that damned Trust, and – and how I had meant to bring it to an end – Oh, not *why*, of course! – and – well, all of it, except what concerned Mama! I dare say it may seem odd to you that I should do so, but you won't think it when you've met him, Kester! He is a man of strong principle, and considerable pride, but he wants neither sense nor feeling, and one can talk to him, as if he were – I was about to say one's father, but the lord knows we could never talk anything but commonplace to Papa, could we? He was very much surprised, of course, and he didn't like it above half, but in the end I managed to get him to say that although he must forbid me to say anything to Patience, until I'd settled my affairs, and that neither he nor Mrs Askham had ever wished Patience to make an *unequal marriage* – such stuff! – he wouldn't forbid me to come to the house again, if I was seriously attached to Patience, and if he believed her affections to be engaged also. I couldn't hope for more, and I think Mrs Askham will stand my friend – though she gave me the devil of a scold! I would have left Woodland House then – thinking it was what I ought to do, besides knowing I must see you as soon as possible – but Mrs Askham wouldn't hear of it, because the doctor came to see me that day, and told her to keep me quiet for another day or two.'

'Oh, so you knew I was here, did you?'

'Good God, Kester!' exclaimed Evelyn. 'You may be the clever twin, but you haven't *all* the wits in the family! Of course I knew it, the instant I saw that thing in the *Morning Post!* If old Lady Stavely and Cressida had gone to stay with Lord Denville at Ravenhurst, it was as plain as anything could be that you'd come home, and had stepped into my shoes!' His voice changed suddenly, with his mood. 'I know why you did it. Only to get me out of a scrape! You couldn't have done anything else – but O God, I wish you hadn't! It was bad enough before, but I could have gone to Cressy – told her the truth – *then*! There was never any pretence between us, and she has a great deal of sense – not one of your simpering die-aways! But *now*, when she's been staying at Ravenhurst, and that curst newspaper has set everyone's ears acock –! And even if that hadn't happened, there is still Mama to be considered! Kester, what am I to *do*?'

'I don't know,' said Kit frankly. 'But I can relieve your

mind of one thing! I've played you false, Eve! *I* am going to marry Cressy!'

Evelyn had sunk his brow on to his clenched fist, but at these words he raised his head, staring at Kit, as if he could scarcely believe his ears. '*You* are going – Does she know, then? That you're not me?'

'Yes, of course she does. She has known for longer than I guessed. And let me tell you, my lord, that when I took your place at the dinner-party you skirted she had very nearly made up her mind to refuse your very obliging offer! For all your lordship's charm and address! You can't think how set up I am in my own esteem to know that *one* person prefers me to my engaging brother!'

'I said she had a great deal of sense!' retorted Evelyn, laughing at him. 'I could tell you of some others who share her preference, but you're much too puffed-up already, so I shan't. But, Kester, no more funning! You mean it?'

'Well, of course I mean it, you gapeseed!'

Evelyn seemed to be thinking it over. He said slowly: 'Yes, Cressy *is* your style, isn't she? Oh, twin, I do wish you happy, and I see that you will *suit*! She's a most agreeable girl: I like her very well myself – though I can't conceive how you should fall in love with her!'

Kit opened his mouth to make the obvious retort, but shut it again. He had never before hesitated to speak his mind to Evelyn, but he perceived that their relationship had undergone a subtle change. The bond between them was as strong as ever, but there were some thoughts they would no longer give utterance to. So all he said was: 'Very likely not. But don't fly into alt too soon, Eve! We may have unravelled one knot in this tangle, but it seems to me that we are still in pretty bad loaf. I know you wouldn't have offered for Cressy if you hadn't thought the case desperate. What I *don't* know is *how* desperate it is. To what tune is Mama down the wind?'

The cloud descended again on to Evelyn's brow. He re-

plied curtly: 'About £20,000 – as near as I can discover.'

There was a frozen silence. Then Kit got up, and went
to pick up the decanter. 'I think, Eve,' he said carefully,
'that we had best have a little more cognac!'

15

Evelyn picked up his glass, and held it out. 'I daresay you
need it more than I do,' he observed, 'I shouldn't have
thrown the total at you like that.'

'For how long have you known?'

'Oh, some time now! Not all at once, however. I don't
know that I have the total sum yet, but I think it isn't more
than that.'

'How much of it is owed to tradesmen?'

'The least part – though there's a pretty staggering
amount owing to Rundell & Bridge, and there's no saying what she may owe her dressmaker. Rundell & Bridge
don't dun her: they're far too long-headed! I should think
they must have been jewellers to the Earls of Denville ever
since they set up their sign, wouldn't you? And I shouldn't
wonder at it if they have a pretty shrewd notion that if
Mama don't pay them now, *I* shall, later! I can't tell about
Céleste: you see, Kester, poor Mama doesn't *understand*!
The ready just – just slides through her fingers! *She*
don't know where it goes to, and I'm damned if I do! You
never know what she may do next, either! I suppose we
always knew that she was in debt, but it wasn't until some
time after my father died that I discovered how far she'd
run into Dun territory, or that she's been borrowing money
for years!' He laughed, but not very mirthfully. 'Poor
darling! If you gave her a century tomorrow, because she
was all to pieces, and being dunned by the harpy who de-
signs her hats, the chances are she'd give it away to one of

her indigent old friends! And even if she *does* settle the most pressing of her debts with the money she's borrowed, she don't see – and you can't make her! – that she's no more in the clear than she was before! You might not know this – I didn't, until a year or two ago, and there's not another soul on earth I'd tell it to.'

'Of course not.' Kit stood frowning down at the glass cupped between his hands. 'I *didn't* know, but I've learnt a good deal since I stepped into your shoes. By the way, Eve, my feet are bigger than yours, so I *didn't* step into your shoes!'

'Thank God for that, clodcrusher!'

Kit smiled, rather abstractedly. He said, after a slight pause: 'Does it ever occur to you that it was a case, rather, of Poor Papa?'

'No!'

The word was uttered explosively. Kit glanced up quickly, and saw in Evelyn's eyes an expression of implacable hatred, which startled him. 'Well, don't eat me!' he said lightly. 'I only meant –'

'I know what you meant! And it doesn't occur to me! Nor would it occur to you, if you knew all I learned from Mama when this – this business first crashed upon me! She was seventeen when my father married her! As innocent as Patience, but not reared as Patience was! What she told me about that household –! All Grandmother Baverstock ever cared for was that her daughters should be taught accomplishments, so that they might make good marriages! As for *economy*, Cosmo is the only Cliffe I ever heard of who knows how to hold household! My father – *years* older than she was! – fancied himself to be in love with her! *Love*? He was dazzled by her face, and her captivating ways, and had no more love for her than I have for Cressida Stavely! *That* was soon over! Everything in Mama which makes her so lovable he disliked! Cold, selfish –! Kester, he drove her off – pokered up when she showed her affection, in that impulsive way she has! It was not *the thing* for Lady Denville to allow the world to suspect she had a heart! Can you wonder at it that she turned from him, let herself be drawn into – Well, never mind! You don't understand that, Kester, but I do, and I tell you that whatever sins or follies Mama has committed are to be laid at my father's door!'

'Take a damper!' Kit advised him. 'I'm entirely at one with you in believing that Papa was grossly to blame; but dearly as I love Mama I *can* see how maddening she must have been to a man of his cut! You think he could have taught her to hold household: you may be right, but I doubt it. Now, don't fly up into the boughs again! None of that signifies today: it's past mending. What we have to do, Eve, is to find a way to tow her off Point Non-Plus *now*. I know she stands in Edgbaston's debt, and in Child's. Anyone else?'

'Yes, several people's – including Ripple!'

'Well, *he* isn't dunning her, at all events,' said Kit thoughtfully.

Evelyn's angry flush had faded, but it surged up again. 'What difference does that make? Are you suggesting that I should permit Mama to remain in debt to him? Or anyone else! Would *you* be content to turn a blind eye to such obligations?'

'No,' confessed Kit. 'They must all be paid, of course, but not all immediately. It's the devil of a sum to raise, Eve!'

'Fiddle! I could do it in the twinkling of a bedpost, if I could but persuade my uncle to wind up the Trust!'

Kit shook his head. 'You must know he won't. He's not going to like this proposed marriage of yours.'

'Then he should! He's been preaching sobriety to me from the day my father died! If I would become less *volatile* he would gladly wind up the Trust! If he wasn't cutting a sham – and I acquit him of that! – he should welcome my marriage to such a girl as Patience!'

'Unfortunately,' said Kit, grimacing, 'he is enthusiastically welcoming your marriage to Cressy. You had a letter from him this morning. I'll give it to you.'

'I don't want it. Does he imagine that with my heart given to Patience marriage to Cressy would make me less volatile?'

Kit looked a little quizzically at him. 'What he will imagine, Eve, is that you're as volatile as ever you were, and will soon have formed a lasting passion for another lady!'

'He'll discover his mistake! I don't deny I've fancied myself in love a dozen times, or that I didn't think even the liveliest of my flirts a dead bore, after a few weeks of dangling about her! To own the truth, when I offered for Cressy, I'd reached the conclusion that I *was* volatile! Hence Clara – and several other bits of muslin! Then I met Patience, and knew that I had never been in love before. She's not dashing, or lively, or full of fun and wit, and I dare say you might not consider her to be as beautiful as some others I could name. But I have been constantly in her company, and the very notion that I could think her a dead bore is so absurd – so fantastic – Oh, I can't explain it to you, Kester!'

'Listen, Eve!' Kit said. 'You needn't explain it to me! I know, and if I didn't it would make no odds! All that concerns us is the light in which my uncle will look upon the marriage. There's never been any hiding of teeth between us, so I'll tell you without roundaboutation that my uncle will be at one with Askham in thinking it a most unequal match. Which, from what you've told me, I collect that it is, if one looks at it from a worldly point of view.'

'Dash it, Kester, I haven't fallen in love with the daughter of a Cit, or a mere smatterer. Her birth may not be noble, but it is as respectable as my own! The Askhams are not *fashionable*, but they are well-connected, so if you

213

are picturing to yourself a family of – of dowdy provincials, you're fair and far off! Askham is a man of culture, his wife a most superior woman, and Patience herself as much beyond my touch as any star in the sky! As for fortune, my uncle has said himself it's unimportant!'

Kit, well aware that his twin was placing too liberal a construction on Lord Brumby's words, asked bluntly: 'What *is* her fortune?'

Evelyn flushed. 'She has none! Oh, that's to say none that my uncle would consider worth the mention! Askham is not affluent. You may say that he was born to an independence! I should describe his circumstances as comfortable rather than handsome, and his family is large. He told me frankly that he could not dower Patience with anything more than a sum that would seem paltry to me; and I told him, as frankly, that I'm not hanging out for an heiress, and should think myself fortunate to win Patience if she hadn't as much as a grig to call her own!'

'I dare say! But if you think to make a hand of it by telling all that to my uncle it must be midsummer moon with you! Good God, his notion of what is due to your consequence is as top-lofty as ever Papa's was, and pretty near as stiff-rumped!'

'*Damn* my consequence! When I think that if it were not so imperative for me to get possession of my fortune I shouldn't care a straw for my uncle's opinion – But it *is* imperative!'

'I've been thinking about that,' said Kit. 'Not in Dun territory on your own account, are you?'

'Of course I'm not! However volatile I may be!' Evelyn snapped.

'Then it's merely a question of Mama's debts, and I think –'

He was interrupted by a sudden crack of laughter from his twin. 'The word I like is *merely*!' Evelyn told him.

'– and I think,' repeated Kit, 'that the best way out of the difficulty is for me to settle them.'

There was a moment's astonished silence before Evelyn demanded: 'Have you run mad, Kester? You can't surely be bosky after a couple of brandies!'

'Neither mad nor bosky. It hadn't occurred to me until a minute ago, and I fancy it didn't occur to you either: we've been forgetting that legacy of mine, Eve!' He walked across the room to set down his glass, and came back to the day-bed. 'I haven't been able to go into things with the lawyers yet, but I collect the stocks ought to realize something in the neighbourhood of £20,000. There are no strings tied to the bequest, so –'

'So that makes everything as right as a ram's horn! I wonder that I shouldn't have thought of it myself. We'll call it a wedding-present, shall we?'

Kit grinned, but said: 'Now, don't be a gudgeon, twin! If you –'

'*I* a gudgeon?' gasped Evelyn. 'Well, if that don't beat the Dutch!'

'Gammon! I've as much right as you to rescue Mama!'

'You haven't, and you know it! The obligation was my father's, and it has descended to me! Try playing off your tricks on someone who *ain't* your twin, you unconscionable humbug!'

'Call it a loan!' suggested Kit. 'It was only a windfall, remember! My father left me very well provided for, and I don't stand in need of it. You can pay it back to me when you're thirty, after all!'

'Oh, do stop talking such slum, Kester!' begged Evelyn. 'You might just as well, for there's no power on earth that would make me consent to such a scheme! Would *you* consent to it, if our positions were reversed?'

'No, I don't suppose I should,' Kit admitted.

'Well, I *know* you wouldn't!' Evelyn got up. 'I must be off, or poor old Pinny won't get a wink of sleep: she means to undress me! Kester, could you spare me Challow tomorrow? I want him to drive me to Brighton. I didn't see Silverdale, you know, and I must. He's got a damned mischief-making tongue, and if he were to discover the truth about that brooch it would be all over London within a sennight.'

'You didn't see him! I hoped that that business at least had been settled.'

'I couldn't. I found he was visiting the Regent. That was a facer to start with! I've never exchanged more than half-a-dozen words with the Regent in my life, and that was at the levée my father dragged us both to at our come-out! Well, is it likely I should be acquainted with him? He's old enough to be my father, and Papa never was one of his set. I hadn't thought it would be difficult to get my name sent in to Silverdale, but it was *dashed* difficult – particularly when I took out my card-case, and found it empty! I shouldn't wonder at it if they thought I was an imposter, at the door! In any event, they said that his lordship had gone into the country that day. I don't know if it was true, or not, but there was no arguing the point, so I desired them, with haughty composure (though not by half as haughty as theirs!), to inform his lordship that I was sorry to have found him absent, but should hope to have the good fortune to see him when I returned to Brighton, within a sennight or so. I couldn't remain in Brighton, you see, because I wanted to visit Clara before returning to London, and I was a trifle pressed for time. Which reminds me, Kester! Send Fimber down to me tomorrow, will you? I want some clothes to wear, my snuff, and some visiting-cards! He can help me to dress, too.'

'I'll do that, but you won't need your cards, and you won't need Challow. You're not going to Brighton, so don't think it! For one thing, we can't have two Denvilles at large – and one of them with his arm in a sling! For another, you're in no case to be jauntering about. I'll go, if you'll tell me exactly what you want me to say to Silverdale, and how I'm to redeem the brooch. If it's by a draft on the Bank, can you write it?'

'I should think I might be able to, but it isn't. By rag-money, because I am acting on Mama's behalf, and it is *she* who is to redeem the brooch. I've got a roll of soft in my nightbag, and Fimber can bring it to you tomorrow. Kester, will you do it for me? I ought not to permit you to, but by now Brighton is probably as full as it can hold of people who know us, and I do see that it won't do for me to be in two places at once – and in *one* of them with a broken shoulder! That's the sort of thing that *always* gets to be known! And I dare say,' he added, in a thought-ful tone, 'that you know much better than I do how to force your way into royal residences!'

'One of my chief duties!' agreed Kit. 'Sit down again while I put on some clothes, and I'll go with you to Pin-ny's cottage, and put you to bed. You can give me your roll of soft, too.'

'You'd much better go to bed yourself,' said Evelyn, sitting down on the arm of the chair. 'I can manage very well, you know. But I'd liefer be undressed by you than Pinny – and we've the devil of a lot to discuss still!'

'We aren't going to discuss anything tonight,' said Kit, tossing his dressing-gown on to the bed. 'Too late – and you're worn to a bone, Eve!'

'Oh, no! Just a trifle out of curl still, that's all! Shall I go and wake Mama up?'

'No, don't! You'd stay talking to her till daylight. I'll tell her first thing, and I should think she'll be at Pinny's a good hour before breakfast!'

'No, no Kester! Mama don't leave her room until an hour *after* breakfast!'

'She does when we have our Aunt Emma staying with us!' replied Kit, grinning, as he stepped into a pair of breeches. 'My aunt is an early riser! Did Pinny tell you that we are enjoying the rare felicity of entertaining her, and my uncle, and our beloved cousin?'

'She did! Also that Ripple is one of the party! What the

devil do you mean by inviting that bag-pudding to Raven-hurst?' demanded Evelyn.

'I didn't: it was Mama's doing – but I've no objection. He's not such a bag-pudding as we were used to think, you know. He and Cressy are the only ones – other than Fimber and Challow, of course – who have yet found me out! You must teach me your way of opening a snuff-box, Eve! I made a mull of that – and the snuff in it was dry!'

'Oh, *shame!*' Evelyn exclaimed. He produced his snuff-box from his pocket, and flicked it open. 'Thus!'

'Oh, very deedy!' said Kit approvingly. 'Lefthanded, too!'

'Good God, twin, I *never* use my right hand!' Evelyn said, shocked.

Kit chuckled, but said, as he knotted a handkerchief round his neck: 'Why do you hold the old fellow in such dislike? I know we were used to think him a bobbing-block, but there's no harm in him that I can discover; and you must own that he's good-natured!'

'He makes Mama ridiculous!' Evelyn said resentfully.

'Oh, I don't know that! He may be barrel-bellied, but he's a tremendous swell! When you think of the position he's held ever since *I* can remember, and his wealth, which I understand to be staggering, it's more of a triumph for Mama, to have kept him tied to her apron-strings all these years!' said Kit cheerfully. 'I'll tell you this, Eve! I'd liefer by far have him dangling after her than one or two of the other insinuating court cards I saw in Mount Street! That fellow, Louth, for one! If ever I saw a loose-screw –! I'd have given something to have tipped him a settler!'

Evelyn said quickly: 'Yes, so would I, but there's nothing in it, Kester! There has never been anything since we were children, when she was so lonely, and unhappy – she told me herself, begging me not to judge her harshly! *I* judge her harshly –!'

Kit looked across at him, a question in his eyes. 'Matlock?'

'Yes. Didn't you know?'

Kit shook his head. 'No. That is, I've sometimes wondered, looking back, and remembering things that happened then. Poor little Mama! How should either of us judge her, who have had *all* her love? Did my uncle know?'

'Can you doubt it?' said Evelyn savagely.

'I suppose not. Well, that settles it! Whatever else we may do to bring her about, we will *not* approach him in the matter!'

'I should rather think not! But, Kester –' He broke off, looking at Kit with a remorseful gleam in his eyes. 'I wish I hadn't told you that! I can't think how I came to do so, except that I didn't recollect that you've been away since we came down from Oxford. It doesn't seem like that, does it? I wish you will forget I told you: you may, you know!' The remorse faded, his irrepressible smile leaping into his eyes. '*She* has done so! Of course, if anything were to happen to recall it to her mind, she would remember, but not otherwise! *For, after all, dearest,*' he continued, in exact and loving imitation of his wayward parent, '*it happened a very long time ago, and crying over spilt milk is such a melancholy thing to do!*'

16

Lady Denville did not, after all, visit her prodigal son before breakfast, being strongly urged by Kit not to do so, on the grounds that she would in all probability wake him from a deep sleep, induced partly by exhaustion, and partly by a posset brewed by Nurse Pinner from some recipe known only to herself.

Kit had visited his mama while she was still attired in her filmy dressing-gown. The stately Miss Rimpton was deftly arranging her burnished locks *à la Tite*, and although she might be said, by the slight curtsy she dropped him, to have acknowledged the right of my lady's son to intrude upon his mama's toilet, her face remained set in lines of austere disapproval. Lady Denville might welcome his supposed lordship with cordiality, but in Miss Rimpton's opinion no gentleman, however nearly related, should be permitted to set eyes on her until she had passed out of her dresser's expert hands. She said repressively: 'One moment, my lady, if you please!' and went on pinning up her mistress's hair in an unhurried way which was designed to put Kit in his place. It succeeded very well, since when she presently withdrew, having desired her ladyship to ring the bell when she should be ready to receive her further services, he exclaimed: 'You know, that woman frightens me to death, Mama!'

'Yes, isn't she odious?' agreed Lady Denville. 'But a positive *genius*! What is it you want, dearest? Don't tell me something dreadful has happened!'

'Not a bit of it!' he replied, quizzing her. 'Can't you guess?'

'No, wicked one! How should I – Kit! You don't mean – Oh, is it *Evelyn*?' She flew up out of her chair, as he nodded. 'Oh, thank God! Where is he? When did he arrive?'

'Last night, after we had all gone to bed. He let himself in with Pinny's key. He wanted to come and wake you, but I wouldn't allow him to do so.'

'Oh, Kit, how could you? You must have *known* I should have been only too glad to have been awakened!'

'Yes, love, I did, but I also knew that if he did wake you it would be hours before I could drag him off to bed! Which I was determined to do, because he's not in very plump currant yet. Nothing to alarm you! – He overturned his phaeton, broke his shoulder and a couple of ribs, and seems to have suffered a pretty severe concussion.'

'Oh, my poor, poor darling!' she cried. 'Where is he? Tell me instantly, Kit!'

'He's with Pinny. I went back with him there in the small hours, to help him to undress, and I promise you she's taking good care of him!'

'Yes, yes, of course she is, but I must go to him at once! Ring the bell for Rimpton, dearest! You must make my excuses to your aunt – say I have the headache, and am still in bed! Yes, and the quails! Dawlish procured them from Brighton, because Bonamy particularly likes them, but so does Evelyn, and perhaps he might be tempted to eat them, even if he fancies nothing else. So tell Dawlish to put two of them in a basket, with some asparagus, and –'

But at this point Kit intervened, representing to her very kindly, but with considerable firmness, firstly, that Evelyn's presence must remain a secret; secondly, that any such order would inevitably lead to his discovery; thirdly, that this difficulty would *not* be overcome by telling Dawlish that the quails and the asparagus were for Nurse Pinner's consumption; and fourthly, that he had been strictly enjoined by Nurse not to let anyone disturb Evelyn until he had had his sleep out. 'So sit down again, Mama, and let me tell you what happened to Evelyn!' he said. 'You will be able to stay with him much longer, if you go down *after* breakfast, for you can tell my aunt that you are obliged to visit Pinny, because she's out of sorts, and no one will think it in the least odd of you. Besides, if I know Evelyn, he'll want to be shaved before he receives visitors! I sent Fimber down to the cottage, with some of his gear, an hour ago, so with both Pinny *and* Fimber to cosset and scold him you may be very sure he won't be neglected!'

'He will need me to protect him!' she said, laughing.

However, she did sit down again; and Kit embarked on the task of recounting a slightly expurgated version of his twin's adventures. 'For you'll do it much better than I could, Kester!' had said Evelyn coaxingly.

This confidence was not misplaced. Mr Fancot, bred to diplomacy, omitted all reference to Tunbridge Wells; slid gracefully over the peculiar behaviour of his twin in having shaken off his devoted groom; and managed to make Lady Denville so impatient to learn the exact circumstances of the accident that it never occurred to her to wonder what could have induced Evelyn to have chosen so roundabout a way to London in preference to the direct pike-road which he could have rejoined, after his visit to John-Coachman, merely by retracing his route for a couple of miles to Nutley. Long before Kit ventured to introduce Miss Patience into his recital, her ladyship was so brimful of gratitude to Mrs Askham for the tender care she had lavished upon Evelyn that it seemed doubtful whether she would be able to restrain her impulsive desire to have herself driven to Woodland House before she had even set eyes on Evelyn. 'How can I wait to thank her?' she demanded, tears sparkling in her eyes. 'How can I ever repay her? Oh, she must be the noblest creature alive! But for her he might have *died*, Kit!'

While he did not share this extreme view of the case, Kit was very ready to encourage it, and to slip in a word or two designed to imbue Lady Denville with the conviction that in Mr Askham she would discover a gentleman of culture, and respectable ancestry. She said she had no doubt at all that he and his wife were excellent persons.

She was not in the least surprised to learn that Evelyn had forgotten to assure himself that his card-case did, in fact, contain some cards: it was just the sort of mischance, she said, that might be depended upon to overtake one at precisely the wrong moment; and she found nothing to wonder at in Evelyn's having asserted that his name was Evelyn, rather than Denville. 'For, you know, dearest, a great many people *do* call him Evelyn! I think, perhaps, it is because he is that *kind* of man, and so very unlike your father, whom no one ever addressed as William! Do you recall that before Papa died it was only the merest acquaintances who called Evelyn Martinhoe? But, oh, Kit, if only the Askhams had known that he was Denville! They must have sent a message instantly, and you need never have pretended *you* were Denville, for no one could have expected Evelyn to attend a dinner-party when he was out of his senses! Oh, dear, Kit, I meant it for the best, but only think what has come of it! Try as I will, I cannot feel the least degree of certainty that Cressy won't recognize the difference between you! Even if I could hit upon a way of accounting for his suddenly being obliged to keep his arm in a sling! So, instead of *rescuing* him, I have very likely *ruined* him!'

Courageously facing the worst of his task, Mr Fancot said: 'No, Mama, you haven't. I was about to tell you that he no longer wishes to marry Cressy. The fact is –'

She interrupted him, demanding in a voice of deep foreboding: 'Who is it?'

'It's Miss Askham, Mama. Evelyn has fallen tail over top in love with her, and it's she he means to marry, I shall leave it to him to tell you about her, but she seems to be a – a most unexceptionable girl!'

'Oh, *no*, Kit!' she uttered imploringly. 'When he has already *offered* for Cressy! Dear one, *don't*, I beg of you, imagine that I mean to pinch at him, for no one knows better than I do that it is impossible to find a fault in *either* of you – indeed, I have always been so very sorry for *other* parents whose sons are so sadly inferior to mine! – but I cannot but think it a *pity* that Evelyn should fall in love *quite* so often, and nearly always with such ineligible girls!'

'Yes, Mama,' he agreed, regarding her in affectionate amusement. 'But consider how impossible it would be to find a girl in any way worthy of either of us!'

'Now you are being absurd!' said her ladyship, with great dignity.

He laughed. 'No, how can you say so? In all seriousness, love, I have a strong notion that this is a very different affair from all Evelyn's former fits of gallantry. I do believe that he has formed a lasting attachment, and so, I think, will you, when you have talked to him. From what he told me, Miss Askham is wholly unlike any other of his flirts – and, I should have supposed, lacking in the qualities which he has hitherto found so captivating. He told me that she was neither dashing nor full of wit, but that the mere thought that he might grow bored with her seemed to him *fantastic*! Well, Mama, my own taste is – is for a girl of a different cut, but it flashed across my mind, as I listened to Evelyn, that perhaps Miss Askham may be the very thing for him. I'll say no more on that head, but leave you to judge for yourself. As for her eligibility from the worldly standpoint – no! It must be thought an unequal marriage, though I collect that Evelyn would have no reason to blush either for Miss Askham, or for her family. They are not persons of consequence, nor are they affluent, but they seem to be of unquestionable gentility.'

Lady Denville had been listening intently to this, a look of doubt on her face, and she now said anxiously: 'Kit, you don't think that they *did* know who Evelyn was, and – and drew him in?'

'No, I don't, Mama,' he said decidedly. 'I own, that *was* my first thought, but if that was their intention they went a mightly queer way to work to bring it about! Mrs Askham never permitted her daughter to be alone with Evelyn from the moment that he recovered his senses; and it seems that Askham is no more in favour of the match than – than my Uncle Henry will be! Evelyn made a pretty clean breast of the whole business to him; and while he didn't forbid Evelyn ever to cross the threshold again, he *did* forbid him to make any attempt to fix his interest with Miss Askham while his affairs are in such a tangled state.'

'Ah, *that* gives me a very good opinion of him!' said her ladyship quickly. 'I shouldn't like it at all if Evelyn wished to marry *too* far beneath him, but I don't give a straw for *consequence*! As for your Uncle Henry, it has nothing whatsoever to do with him, and so I shall tell him, if he has the impertinence to object to a marriage which has *my* approval! The only thing is –' She paused, hesitating for a moment, her brow puckered. Then she directed an inquiring, not entirely unhopeful look at Kit, and said tentatively: 'Dearest, do you think perhaps *you* would like to marry Cressy? I can't but feel that *one* of you ought to do so, when I reflect on the excessively awkward situation she has been placed in, poor child!' She added hastily, as Kit fell into uncontrollable laughter: 'Not that I wish to press you! Only that the thought has frequently crossed my mind that you and she would deal admirably together!'

'That thought has crossed our minds, too, Mama!' he replied unsteadily. 'I *should* like to marry Cressy, and, since she feels she might like to marry me, it is precisely what I hope to do, and what I was just about to divulge to you!'

'Then Cressy knows already! Oh, wicked one, wicked one not to have told me!' cried her ladyship, her countenance transformed. 'Dearest, nothing could delight me more! She is the very girl I would have chosen for you, if I hadn't already chosen her for Evelyn, which was a very foolish mistake, but *not*, thank goodness, one that can't be remedied! I *knew* something would happen to bring us about! Oh, my darling Kit, I wish you so *very* happy!'

Kit thanked her, but ventured to point out to her that her felicitations were a little premature, since several difficulties still blocked the way to a happy issue. She acknowledged the truth of this, but with unabated cheerfulness, saying: 'To be sure, but they are only trifling ones! We shall be obliged to confess the whole to Lady Stavely, for one thing, and I don't think we dare hope that she won't cut up dreadfully stiff, do you? Of course, we *could* keep it a secret from her, but I am much inclined to think it would be wrong to do so.'

'Yes, Mama, so am I!' agreed Kit.

She nodded. 'I knew you would say so. Because if Evelyn is determined to marry Miss Askham it would be bound to put Lady Stavely in a *much* worse pet when she saw the notice of his engagement in the Gazette, and had been thinking all the time that he was promised to Cressy! And, of course, Stavely may not be quite pleased, but you may depend upon it that that odious creature, Albinia Gillifoot, will take good care he gives his consent.'

'Yes, Mama, very possibly. But there is a far worse obstacle confronting us,' Kit said gently. 'When you say that Evelyn's marriage has nothing to do with my uncle, are you not forgetting the circumstances which prompted Evelyn to offer for Cressy?'

She stared at him, the bewilderment in her face slowly changing to consternation. She looked stricken for an instant, but even as he stretched out his hand to her, in quick remorse, she made a recover. She clasped his hand, giving it a reassuring squeeze, and said, gallantly smiling at him: 'Are you remembering my tiresome debts? Oh, my darling, you must *neither* of you waste a moment's thought on them! As though I could be so *monstrous* as to set anything so paltry against the happiness of my sons! Besides, I've been in debt for years and years, and have grown to be perfectly accustomed to it! I shall bring myself about. Well, of course I shall! I have *always* contrived to do so, even when matters seemed to be quite desperate!' She gave his hand a pat, and released it. 'So now that we have settled *that*, dearest, you must go away, because it must be ten o'clock already, and I am not yet fully dressed.'

Mr Fancot, never one to waste his time in argument which he knew to be futile, abandoned his attempt to bring his parent to a sense of the size and urgency of her embarrassments. Bestowing a fond embrace upon her, he informed her – just in case he might previously have omitted to do so – that he loved her very much; and left her to Miss Rimpton's ministrations.

He found the Cliffes and Cressy assembled in the breakfast-parlour; and it said much for his ability to shine in the world of diplomacy that not even Cressy suspected that while he responded with every appearance of interest and amiability to the various utterances of his relations his mind was preoccupied with two problems. The first, and more immediate, was how to gain access to Lord

Silverdale, and to this he found a possible answer. The second seemed to be insoluble.

Lady Denville, presently joining the party, bade everyone good-morning; hoped, in her pretty, solicitous way, that her sister-in-law had slept well; and said, as she took her seat at the table: 'Dearest Cressy! This afternoon we must have a delightful cose together, you and I!'

As the sparkling glance that accompanied these words was as eloquent as it was mischievous, Kit intervened, asking, with all the heartiness of a host bent on arranging every detail of the day, what his guests would like to do that morning.

Attention was certainly drawn away from Lady Denville, but the responses Kit received must have disappointed such a host as he was trying to impersonate. But as his only desire was to snatch a private interview with Cressy, he was very well satisfied with them. His cousin said moodily that he didn't know; Cosmo, whom the humdrum pattern of an ordinary day in a country house exactly suited, said that he would read, and write letters until the post came in; Cressy, who was having much ado not to laugh, kept her eyes lowered, and did not attempt to speak; and Mrs Cliffe, who was anxiously watching her son, returned no answer, but suddenly declared that Ambrose might say what he chose but she was persuaded that he had a boil forming on his neck. All eyes turned involuntarily towards Ambrose, who reddened, shot a glowering look at his mama, and said angrily that it was no such thing. He added that he had the headache.

'Poor boy!' said Lady Denville, smiling kindly upon him. 'I dare say if you were to go for a walk it would soon leave you.'

'Amabel, I must beg you not to encourage Ambrose to expose himself!' said Mrs Cliffe. 'There is a wind blowing, and I am positive it is *easterly*, for I myself have a touch of the tic, which I never get but when there is an east wind! It would be *fatal* for Ambrose to stir out of doors when he is already not quite the thing, for with his constitution, you know, any disorder is very likely to lay him up for a fortnight!'

'*Is* it?' said Lady Denville, gazing at her nephew with the awed interest of one confronted with some rare exhibit. 'Poor boy, how awkward it must be for you, to be obliged to remain indoors whenever the wind is in the east! Because, so often it *is*!'

'Well, well, we need not make mountains out of molehills!' said Cosmo testily. 'I don't deny that his constitution is sickly, but —'

'Nonsense, Cosmo, how can you talk so?' exclaimed his sister. 'I'm sure he isn't sickly, even if he has got a little headache!' She smiled encouragingly at Ambrose, sublimely unconscious of having offended all three Cliffes: Ambrose, because, however much he might dislike having an incipient boil pointed out, he was proud of his headaches, which often earned for him a great deal of attention; Cosmo, because he had for some years subscribed to his wife's view of the matter, finding in Ambrose's delicacy an excuse for his sad want of interest in any manly sport; and Emma, because she regarded any suggestion that her only child was not in a deplorable state of debility as little short of an insult.

'I fear,' said Cosmo, 'that Ambrose has never enjoyed his cousins' robust health.'

'Your sister cannot be expected to understand delicate constitutions, my dear,' said Emma. 'I dare say the twins never suffered a day's illness in their lives!'

'No, I don't think they did,' replied Lady Denville, with a touch of pride. 'They were the *stoutest* couple! Of course, they did have things like measles and whooping-cough, but I can't recall that they were ever *ill*. In fact, when they had whooping-cough, one of them — was it you, dearest? — climbed up the chimney after a starling's nest!'

'No, that was Kit,' said Mr Fancot.

'So it was!' she agreed, twinkling at him.

'But how *terrible*!' exclaimed Emma.

'Yes, wasn't it? He came down looking exactly like a blackamoor, and brought so much soot down with him that everything in the room seemed to be covered with it. I don't think I ever laughed so much in my life!'

'*Laughed?*' gasped Emma. 'Laughed when one of your children was in danger of falling, and breaking his neck?'

'Well, I don't think he could have done *that*, though I suppose he might have broken his legs, or got stuck in the chimney. I do remember wondering how we were to get him out if he did stick tight. However, it would have been a great waste of time to get into a worry about the twins, because they were for ever falling out of trees, or into the lake, or off their ponies, and nothing dreadful ever happened to them,' said Lady Denville serenely.

Mrs Cliffe could only shudder at such callous unconcern; while Ambrose, quite mistakenly supposing that these reflections were directed at his own, less adventurous, career, fell into obvious sulks.

Lady Denville, having disposed of the tea and bread-and-butter which constituted her breakfast, then excused herself, saying, as she got up from the table: 'Now I must leave you, because Nurse Pinner seems not to be very well, and it would be too unkind in me not to visit her, and perhaps take her something to tempt her appetite.'

'Some fruit!' said Kit hastily.

She gave a little chuckle, and said, irrepressible mischief in her voice: 'Yes, dearest! *Not* quails!'

'Quails!' ejaculated Cosmo, shocked beyond measure. 'Quails for your old *nurse*, Amabel?'

'No, Evelyn thinks some fruit would be better.'

'*I* should have thought that some arrowroot, or a supporting broth would have been more suitable!' said Emma.

That set her incorrigible sister-in-law's eyes dancing wickedly. 'Oh, no, I assure you it wouldn't be! *Particularly* not the arrowroot, which – which she abominates! Dear Emma, how uncivil it is in me to run away, as I must! But

I am persuaded you must understand how it is!' Her lovely smile embraced her seething younger son. 'Dearest, I leave our guests in your hands! Oh, and I think a bottle of port, don't you? So much more supporting than mutton-broth! So will you, if you please, –'

'Don't tease yourself, Mama!' he interrupted, holding open the door for her. 'I'll attend to that!'

'To be sure, I might have known you would!' she said, wholly unaffected by the quelling look she received from him. 'You will know just what will be most acceptable!'

'I sometimes wonder,' said Cosmo, in accents of the deepest disapproval, as Kit shut the door behind her ladyship, 'whether your mother has taken entire leave of her senses, Denville!'

Mr Fancot might be incensed by his wayward parent's behaviour, but no more than the mildest criticism was needed to make him show hackle. '*Do* you, sir?' he said, dangerously affable. 'Then it affords me great pleasure to be able to reassure you!'

Mr Cliffe's understanding was not superior, but only a moonling could have failed to read the challenge behind the sweet smile that accompanied these words. Reddening, he said: 'I imagine I may venture, without impropriety, to animadvert upon the conduct of one who is my sister!'

'*Do* you, sir?' said Kit again, and with even more affability.

Mr Cliffe, rising, and going towards the door with great stateliness, expressed the hope that he had rather too much force of mind to allow himself to be provoked by the top-loftiness of a mere nephew, who was, like many other bumptious sprigs, too ready to sport his canvas; and withdrew in good order.

Mindful of the charge laid upon him, Kit then turned his attention to his aunt, with polite suggestions for her entertainment. She received these with a slight air of affront, giving him to understand that her day would be spent in laying slices of lemon-peel on her son's brow, burning pastilles, and – if his headache persisted – applying a cataplasm to his feet. He listened gravely to this dismal programme; and with a solicitude which placed a severe strain upon Miss Stavely's self-command, and caused Ambrose to glare at him in impotent rage, suggested that in extreme cases a blister to the head was often found to be beneficial. Apparently feeling that he had discharged his obligations, he then invited Miss Stavely to take a turn in the shrubbery with him. Miss Stavely, prudently refusing to meet his eye, said, with very tolerable composure, that that would be very agreeable; and subsequently afforded him the gratification of realizing (had he been considering the matter) that she was eminently fitted to become the wife of an Ambassador by containing her bubbling amusement until out of sight of the house, when pent-up giggles overcame her, and rapidly infected her somewhat harassed escort.

Mr Fancot, the first to recover, said: 'Yes, I know, Cressy, but there is nothing to laugh at in the fix we are *now* in, I promise you! I imagine you've guessed already that my abominable twin has reappeared?'

'Oh, yes!' she managed to utter. 'F-from the moment G-Godmama said – said: *Not quails!* with *such* a quizzing look at you!'

Mr Fancot grinned, but expressed his inability to understand why no one had ever yet murdered his beloved mama. Miss Stavely cried out upon him for saying anything so unjust and improper; but she became rather more sober as she listened to the tale of Evelyn's adventure. She did indeed suffer a slight relapse when kindly informed of her noble suitor's relief at learning that he had been released from his obligations; but she was quick to perceive all the difficulties of a situation broadened to include an alternative bride for his lordship of whom so rigid a stickler as his uncle would certainly not approve.

'Oh, dear!' she said distressfully. 'That *is* unfortunate! What is to be done?'

He responded frankly: 'I haven't the least notion! Do you bend your mind to the problem, love! *My* present concern is to recover that confounded brooch!'

She nodded. 'Yes, indeed! I do feel that that is of the first importance. I am not myself acquainted with Lord Silverdale, but from anything I have ever heard said of him I am much afraid that your brother is very right: he is – he is shockingly malicious! Papa told me once that he is as hungry as a church mouse, but can always command a dinner at the price of the latest and most scandalous on-dit. And if he is one of the Prince Regent's guests – Kit, do *you* know how to obtain a private interview with him?'

'No,' replied Kit cheerfully, 'but I fancy I know who can supply me with the answer to that problem!'

'Sir Bonamy!' she exclaimed, after an instant's frowning bewilderment.

'Exactly so!' said Kit. He added proudly: 'Not for nothing am I Mama's son! I too have nacky notions!'

17

A luncheon, consisting of sundry cold meats, cakes, jellies, and fruit, was always served at noon in the apartment known as the Little Dining-room; and it had been Kit's intention to have lain in wait for Sir Bonamy to issue forth from his bedroom, in the hope of being able to exchange a few words with him before he joined the other guests downstairs. But owing to the extraordinarily swift passage of time it was not until the stable-clock had struck twelve that either Mr Fancot or Miss Stavely could believe that they had been in the shrubbery for over an hour. A glance at Kit's watch, however, sent them hurrying back to the house, where they found the rest of the party, with the single exception of the Dowager, already discussing luncheon. Although Mr and Mrs Cliffe later agreed that modern damsels were permitted a regrettable freedom which would never have been countenanced when they were young, no one made any comment on the tardy and simultaneous arrival of the truants, Lady Denville even going so far as to smile at them.

Ambrose had allowed himself to be persuaded by his mother to partake of a few morsels of food, to keep up his strength; but the Dowager had sent down a message by her maid, excusing herself from putting in an appearance until later in the day. 'Nothing to cause alarm!' Lady Denville told Cressy. 'Her maid says that she passed a wakeful night, and so finds herself just a trifle down pin today.'

'I thought she would,' said Sir Bonamy, putting up his quizzing-glass the better to inspect a raised chicken-pie. 'Too much cross-and-jostle work last night!' He looked up to shake his head in fond reproof at his hostess. 'You shouldn't have invited Maria Dersingham, my lady!'

'I am so *very* sorry, Cressy!'

But Cressy, with a cheerfulness which Mrs Cliffe considered to be very unbecoming in a granddaughter, assured Lady Denville that, although the excitement of encountering her ancient ally and present enemy might have been a little too much for her, Grandmama had much enjoyed the evening.

'So she did!' nodded Sir Bonamy. 'Mind you, it was touch-and-go until we came to the calves' ears! That's when she took the lead in milling. Wonderful memory your grandmama has, my dear Miss Stavely!' His vast bulk shook with his rumbling laugh. 'Popped in as pretty a hit as I hope to see over Maria Dersingham's guard! By the bye, my lady, that was a capital Italian sauce your cook served with the calves' ears!'

It was left to Lady Denville to express the sentiments of the rest of the company, which she promptly did, saying: 'Yes, but what happened about calves' ears, Bonamy?'

'No, no!' he replied, still gently shaking. 'I'm not one to go on the high gab, my lady, and I'll tell no tales! I'll take a mouthful of the pie, Denville, and just a sliver of ham!'

Interpreting this in a liberal spirit, Kit supplied him with a large wedge of pie, and flanked it with half-a-dozen slices of ham. Mrs Cliffe, who had never ceased to marvel at his appetite, turned eyes of mute astonishment towards her sister-in-law, who told Sir Bonamy severely that a little fruit, and a biscuit (if he was ravenous), was all he ought to permit himself to eat in the middle of the day. She added that she herself rarely ate any nuncheon at all.

'Yes, yes, but you have not so much to keep up!' said Sir Bonamy, blenching at the thought of such privation.

'Well, if you didn't eat so much you wouldn't have so much to keep up either!' she pointed out.

Her brother, strongly disapproving of this candid speech, directed a quelling look at her, and pointedly changed the subject, saying that he trusted she had found Nurse Pinner suffering from no serious disorder. 'Nothing infectious, I hope?'

'Oh, no! Just a trifle out of sorts!' she replied.

'Infectious!' exclaimed Mrs Cliffe. 'My dear sister, how can you tell that it is not? How imprudent of you to have visited her! I wish you had not done so!'

'Nonsense, Emma! A mere colic!'

Mrs Cliffe's fears seemed to have been allayed. Kit saw, with some foreboding, that his mama had become suddenly a little pensive, and quaked inwardly. Never, he reflected, did she look more soulful than when she was hatching some outrageous scheme. He tried to catch her eye, but she was looking at Cressy, who had finished her nuncheon, and was sitting with her hands folded patiently in her lap.

'Dear child, you wish to go upstairs to see your grand-mama!' she said. 'You know we don't stand on ceremony, so run away immediately! Give her my love, and tell her how much I hope to see her presently; and then come to my drawing-room – that is, if Lady Stavely can spare you, of course!' She waited until Cressy had left the room, and then addressed herself to Kit. 'Dearest, your uncle's asking me if Pinny's disorder is infectious puts me in mind of something I think I should tell you – oh, and Ambrose too, perhaps! I wouldn't mention it in Cressy's presence – not that I think she would have taken fright, for she has a great deal too much commonsense, but she might speak of it to Lady Stavely, and I would not for the world cast *her* into high fidgets! It is all nonsense, but I wish you will neither of you go into the village just at present! Though you may depend upon it if there *is* an epidemic disease there one of servants will contract it, and spread it *all* over the house. However –'

But at this point she was interrupted, Mrs Cliffe demanding in palpitating accents: '*What* disease? For heaven's sake, Amabel, tell me this instant!'

'Why, none at all, Emma!' replied her ladyship, laughing. 'It is only one of Pinny's tales! Merely because one or two of the villagers complain of sore throats she *will* have it that they have contracted scarlet fever! Such stuff!'

'*Scarlet fever* –!'

'Oh, my dear Emma, there is not the least occasion for any of us to fly into a fuss!' Lady Denville said earnestly. 'Pinny always thinks that if one has nothing more than a cold in the head one is sickening for a fatal complaint! Why she once said there was *typhus* in the village!' She broke off, wrinkling her brow. 'Well, now I come to think of it, she was quite right! But this is a very different matter, and I do beg of you not to take fright!'

She had said enough. Mrs Cliffe, pallid with dismay, declared distractedly that nothing could prevail upon her to remain another hour in such a plague-stricken neighbourhood. Amabel might think her timorous and uncivil, but she must understand that every consideration must yield to the paramount need to remove her only son out of danger.

Lady Denville, to Kit's intense admiration, managed to beseech her not to fly from Ravenhurst, without in any way lessening her alarm; Cosmo, when dramatically appealed to, wavered; and Ambrose, who had been dragged to Ravenhurst against his will, and had been wishing himself otherwhere from the moment he had crossed the threshold, seized the first opportunity that offered of lending his mother his support. He did not think the air at Ravenhurst salubrious; he had not cared to mention it before, but he had been feeling out of sorts for several days. A hint that a few weeks spent at Brighton might prove beneficial was well taken by Mrs Cliffe, but met with a flat veto from Cosmo, visibly appalled by the very thought of sojourning at so expensive a resort. In the end, and after much argument, it was settled that they should go to Worthing, where, according to what Mrs Cliffe had learnt from the Dowager, there were several excellent boarding-houses which provided an extraordinary degree of comfort at very moderate charges. Here, protected from the chilling blasts of the north and east winds by the Downs, Ambrose would be able to bathe, or to ride along the sands, without running the risk of contracting an inflammation of the lungs. There were also three respectable libraries, at two of which newspapers and magazines were received every morning and evening; and at least one very reliable doctor, of whom the Dowager spoke in terms of rare encomium.

Had it been possible, Cosmo would have returned with his wife and son to his own home; but since he had graciously lent this for the summer months to a distant and far from affluent cousin, who was too thankful to have been offered, free, a country residence large enough to accommodate his numerous progeny to cavil at being obliged to pay the wages of Cosmo's servants, this was impossible. With the utmost reluctance, and only when the wife of his bosom had announced that he might remain at Ravenhurst, if he chose to run the risk of contracting scarlet fever, but that nothing would prevail upon her to expose her only child to such a danger, did he consent to remove that very day to Worthing's one hotel, and then only on condition that no time should be lost, on arrival at this elegant hostelry, in seeking less expensive quarters.

It was not to be expected that Mr Ambrose Cliffe, hankering after the amusements afforded by Brighton, would be entirely satisfied by the decision to spend the summer months at a small place patronized largely by such elderly persons as disliked the racket of Brighton; but as he had never had much hope of persuading his father to look for lodgings in Brighton, and knew that Worthing was a mere ten or eleven miles distant from the more fashionable resort, he raised no objection.

Throughout the discussion, which was punctuated by charming, if mendacious, entreaties from Lady Denville that her relations should remain at Ravenhurst, in defiance of a rumour which she was *positive* was ill-founded, Sir Bonamy, with the utmost placidity, continued to work his way through the various dishes set upon the table. Only when Mrs Cliffe, hurrying away to prepare for the journey, turned to take her leave of him, did he heave himself out of his chair, or betray the smallest interest in the scarifying story set about by his hostess. She, declaring her intention of rendering dear Emma every assistance in the arduous task of packing her trunk, shepherded the three Cliffes out of the room, but turned back, exclaiming that she had forgotten to pick up her reticule, for the purpose of confiding hurriedly to her son and her cicisbeo that it was all a hum, but that she had felt that the Cliffes *must* be induced to go away.

'Yes, yes, my pretty, *I* knew you were up to your tricks!' said Sir Bonamy fondly. 'I never thought you'd endure having that brother of yours here above a sennight. Told you he was a devilish dull dog!'

'Yes, *isn't* he? But *that's* not it! I invited him because I thought it would make it less awkward for Kit, but it turns out that he makes it much *more* awkward, now that Evelyn has returned! I can't stay to explain it to you, but Kit will do so!'

She then flitted away in the wake of Mrs Cliffe, and Sir Bonamy, lowering himself into his chair again, drew a dish of peaches and nectarines towards him, pausing only, before making a careful selection from amongst them, to inform Kit that there was no need for him to explain anything to him, 'Just as soon you didn't, my boy! Nothing to do with me!' he said, delicately pinching one of the peaches.

'I won't,' promised Kit. 'But I've been wanting to have a word with you, sir! I believe you may be able to help me.'

Sir Bonamy, casting him a glance of acute suspicion, said: 'I shouldn't think so – shouldn't think so at all! Not if it has anything to do with this havey-cavey rig you're running!'

'Nothing at all,' replied Kit reassuringly. 'It is merely that I find myself faced with a – a social problem on which I am very sure you can advise me.'

'Oh, if that's all –!' said Sir Bonamy, much relieved. 'Very happy to be of service, my boy!' He picked up his fruit knife, adding, with a simplicity which robbed his words of self-consequence: 'You couldn't have applied to a better man!'

'Just so!' agreed Kit. 'It's quite a small matter, but it has me in rather a puzzle. If you stood in my shoes, sir – or, rather, in my brother's – and you wished to visit someone who happened to be staying at the Pavilion, how would you set about it?'

Sir Bonamy raised his eyes from the peach, which he had begun to strip of its skin, and stared very hard at Kit. 'Who?' he demanded.

'One of the Prince Regent's guests, sir.'

'I wouldn't,' said Sir Bonamy, turning back to his peach. 'You don't want to get mixed up in that set. Couldn't if you did. I'm the only one of Prinny's friends Denville is acquainted with, so what does *he* want with any of 'em?'

'A trifling matter of business, which I wish to discharge for him.'

'Well, if that's all, my advice to you is to wait until he leaves the Pavilion,' said Sir Bonamy, dissecting his peach with finicking care.

'Unfortunately, the matter is rather urgent, sir.'

'Oh, it is, is it? Sounds to me as if that brother of yours has been getting himself into trouble! Not been playing cards in that set, has he?'

'No, he has not – which you must surely be in a better position than I am to know!' replied Kit, a little stiffly.

Sir Bonamy nodded, conveying a quarter of the peach to his mouth. 'I didn't think he had, but one never knows what these young cocks of the game will get up to next. Too rackety by half! Now, you needn't bite my nose off! Who is it you want to visit at the Pavilion? Can't help you if I don't know.'

'Lord Silverdale. On a matter of business, as I have said.'

Sir Bonamy slowly consumed another quarter of the peach. 'Well, if I were you, Kit, I'd tell Evelyn not to enter on any business with Silverdale. Don't mind telling you that Prinny's got some mighty queer cronies! He's one of 'em. A shocking loose-screw, my boy! Never a feather to fly with, either, and has a damned nasty tongue in his head. Cuts up more characters in an evening than I would in a twelvemonth.'

'Nevertheless, sir, it is imperative that I should see him.'

Sir Bonamy turned his eyes towards him, and stared at him for several unwinking moments. 'Oh! Now, look 'ee, my boy! If it has anything to do with the ruby brooch your mother lost to him at play, you leave well alone! Ay, and tell your brother to do so too!'

'So you know about that, do you, sir?'

'Yes, yes, of course I know!' said Sir Bonamy. 'I was there! Saw her stake it, and so did everyone else. A silly thing to do, for her luck was quite out, but nothing in it to make Evelyn get upon his high ropes! All open and above-board, you know, and everyone joking her about it, and saying it was just like her to throw her jewelry after her guineas. Why, even Silverdale himself couldn't brew any scandal-broth out of it! So just you forget it, Kit, and tell Evelyn to take a damper!'

'I can't do that, sir. I feel quite as strongly as Evelyn does that the brooch must be redeemed.'

'Oh, I shouldn't try to do that!' said Sir Bonamy, putting the nectarine he had been considering back in the dish.

'But you must surely perceive –'

'No, I don't. If you was to ask me, I should say it was a good thing your mother did lose it! It never became her, you know. In fact, I can't think what made her take a fancy to it, for she don't in general make mistakes of that nature. But she can't wear rubies! Anything else, but not rubies or garnets! Don't you try to get it back for her! Tell Evelyn to buy her another – sapphires or emeralds. She'll like it just as well!'

'Probably better,' agreed Kit, smiling.

'There you are, then!' said Sir Bonamy. 'Damme, Kit, you've cut your eye-teeth! Don't you go stirring coals! Stupid thing to do, because you may depend upon it Silverdale sold it weeks ago!'

'I am very sure he didn't,' said Kit.

'You know nothing about it! Silverdale's going to pigs and whistles, and that brooch was worth a monkey if it was worth a groat.'

Kit hesitated before saying: 'I fancy I needn't hide my teeth with you, sir. It isn't worth more than a pony – if as much. It is nothing but trumpery: a copy of the real brooch.'

'Nonsense!' said Sir Bonamy testily.

'I wish it were nonsense, but I'm afraid –'

'Well, it is nonsense. Good God, you don't suppose Silverdale's a flat, do you? Because he ain't!'

'I don't suppose it occurred to him that my mother would have staked it, if –'

'No, and nor did she!' interrupted Sir Bonamy. 'Told you I was there, didn't I? If you think I'd have let her put up a piece of trumpery, you've got less rumgumption than they give you credit for: more of a beetlehead than one of the tightish clever sort! The only advice I'm giving you is to tell young Denville to stop trying to raise a dust!'

He shot Kit an angry glare, and found that he was being steadily regarded. 'Mama told me herself that she had sold that brooch, sir,' said Kit. 'I recall, furthermore, that she also told me that you had several times sold trinkets for her.'

'Well, I didn't sell that brooch for her.'

'Did you ever sell *any* of her jewelry, sir?'

'Now, look 'ee, Kit. I've had enough of you trying to nose out what's no concern of yours!' said Sir Bonamy, in a blustering tone. 'Damme if you're not getting to be as bad as your brother! Well, I won't have it! Couple of impudent halflings I knew when you was fubsy, muffin-faced brats in the same cradle! What your mother saw in you I never could make out!'

Kit could not help laughing, but he said: 'That's all very well, sir, but it won't do, you know. It is very much our concern – and you know that too!'

Sir Bonamy, who was looking hot and harassed, groped for his snuff-box, and fortified himself with a liberal pinch.

'Now, you listen to me, my boy!' he said. 'You've no reason to meddle, either of you! No one knows anything about the business, and never will, so if you're afraid of its leaking out and starting a scandal –'

'Believe me, sir, I'm not in the least afraid of that, and nor will Evelyn be!'

'For God's sake, Kit, don't go blabbing it all to Evelyn!' begged Sir Bonamy, alarmed. 'It's bad enough having to put up with you poking and prying into my business, without having that young make-bait buzzing round me like a hornet! I knew your mother before you was born or thought of, and, what's more, if it hadn't been for Denville, *I* might have been your father! Mind you, I'm damned glad

I'm not, for of all the resty, top-lofty, whisky-frisky young jackanapes you're the worst!'

'Yes, sir,' said Kit meekly. 'But you can't expect us to allow my mother to stand in your debt!'

Sir Bonamy's little round eyes started at him, and his cheeks began to assume a purple hue. 'Oh, I can't, can't I? Bumptious, that's what you are, my boy! Next you'll be asking me to render up an account! Well, that's where you'll be bowled out, because I won't do it, and it's not a bit of good pestering your mother about it, because she don't know, bless her heart!'

'Sir, we *can't* let it rest like that!'

'Well, you'll learn your mistake! You can tell Evelyn it's none of his business, because it all happened before your father died. And don't you try to pay me for that curst brooch, for I won't have it! Good God, boy, what the devil is it to me, a miserable monkey?'

'If it was you who bought the Denville necklace, sir, Mama must be thousands in your debt!'

'Well, that's nothing to me either! Thought you knew that!'

'Everyone knows you're as rich as Golden Ball, sir, but it's beside the point.'

'No it ain't,' said Sir Bonamy crossly. 'You've got no right to stop me spending my blunt anyway I choose – not that I'd put it beyond you to try!'

'Sir, I do beg of you –'

'No, no, you keep your tongue between your teeth, Kit! Getting to be a regular jaw-me-dead! You'll only come to fiddlestick's end, and so I warn you! It was no fault of Evelyn's that your mother ran aground, and there was nothing he could have done about it when she was near to being blown up at Point Non-Plus! Little enough I could do either, for she never would take a penny from me unless she was forced to, and then I had to call it a loan, and charge her interest!'

'Which you never demand!'

'No, of course I don't! But I'm not at all sure that I oughtn't to have done so,' said Sir Bonamy reflectively. 'She's got no more notion of business than a kitten, but she don't like to be beholden. Frets her more than you might guess!' He chuckled. 'Bless her, she thinks all's right and tight if she can pay interest! She don't tell me much more than she told your father, and I've got my suspicions that she's borrowed money from others besides me. Well, I know she has, and that's where I'm at a stand, because she won't let me give her the rhino to pay her debts, and *I* can't redeem 'em without raising a nasty dust. She's got it fixed in her head that there's no harm in borrowing from people who don't hesitate to dun her for the interest she owes 'em, but that it's wrong to come to me. No use arguing with her: all she does is talk balderdash about imposing on me. And when I told her she ought to know there was nothing I wouldn't do for her, she said she did know it, and it made it worse!' He sighed. 'I dare say you don't like it – in fact, I know you don't – but I'm devoted to her – always have been, always shall be – but there's no understanding her!'

'I think I do understand what's in her mind when she doesn't like to hang on your sleeve, sir. You're mistaken in thinking that I don't like your devotion to her: we were used to be jealous of you, I think, but that was when we were muffin-faced brats! What could either of us feel, in the light of what I've learnt today, but thankful for it that you were devoted to her, and – and most obliged to you?'

Sir Bonamy looked rather gratified, but said shrewdly: 'You speak for yourself, my boy! You ain't speaking for Evelyn, and if you think you are you don't know him as well as I thought you did!'

'I know him as I know myself,' Kit replied, 'and I am speaking for him. I haven't said he'll like it: he won't and nor do I. He won't stomach it. Good God, sir, how could either of us accept such a situation with complaisance? It was my father's duty to discharge Mama's debts. He didn't do so, and Evelyn will tell you that he inherited his obligations as well as his fortune.'

'Well, I'd as lief he didn't tell me,' responded Sir Bonamy. 'I don't want to have him ranting at me as well as you. What's more, he'll be wasting his breath, for he hasn't inherited your father's fortune yet, and from what I've seen of his carryings-on he ain't likely to get Brumby to wind that Trust up a day before he must! I'll tell you this too, Kit: when he does get control of his fortune he'll have enough to do to settle the rest of your mother's debts without adding what she's borrowed from me to 'em!'

18

There was no more to be got from Sir Bonamy, who went off to enjoy his usual afternoon sleep in the library, saying that he was glad not to have that fidgety fellow, Cliffe, sharing the room with him any longer. Kit made no attempt to detain him. Every feeling might revolt against allowing his mother to be so deeply indebted to a man upon whom she had no claim, and who stood outside the family, but he could perceive no way either of forcing Sir Bonamy to state the sum of her obligation to him, or of discharging the debt, if he surmounted that first obstacle.

The Cliffes were gone within an hour of rising from the nuncheon table; and Kit waited only to see them off before going across the park to Nurse Pinner's cottage. He found Fimber, whom he had sent there earlier with a couple of bottles of wine, engaged in rather more than usually acrimonious hostilities with Nurse, and for once at a disadvantage, since the noble object of their jealousy was once more, and for the first time since her retirement, restored to Nurse's fond and despotic care. Fimber had scored a point in having his services in helping his lordship to dress preferred to Nurse's; but he had been obliged to yield to her superior skill in bandaging; to endure, in tight-lipped silence, her sharply authoritative warnings and instructions when he eased my lord into his shirt and coat; and to suppress his wrath at my lord's tacit refusal to send her out of his tiny bedroom while he was dressed. She bustled in and out, full of interference, and addressing her nursling with such endearments as she had used during his childhood, so that the only course open to his valet was to adopt an attitude of meticulous respect towards a young gentleman whom he was burning to scold and to cross-question.

When Kit walked into the parlour, Fimber bowed, and immediately informed him that he would find his lordship in the garden. He added, dropping his voice in the manner of one imparting a confidence whose significance was known only to himself and Kit, that he would find his lordship a trifle on the fidgets.

'Lord bless the man, what else was to be expected?' Nurse exclaimed scornfully. 'Do you go out to him, Master Kit! And if he is to go up to the house this evening, as her ladyship wishes, you may bring him back here, though there's not a bit of need, for I can help him out of his coat better than you or Fimber. Nor I don't want Fimber to come fussing round him at that hour of night, keeping him awake till all hours, with brushing his clothes, and I don't know what besides, in the finicking way he has!'

'Well, we can talk about that later, Pinny,' Kit said pacifically. He added, with the flicker of an eyelid at the outraged valet: 'Better get back to the house now, Fimber, or Norton will begin to wonder what's become of you.'

He then made good his escape into the small, enclosed garden at the back of the cottage, where he found Evelyn moodily winding his way along the narrow paths which separated various beds filled with vegetables and currant bushes. Nurse had carried a chair out, and placed it in the shade of an apple tree; an open book lay on the ground beside it, with a clutter of newspapers and magazines.

Kit said cheerfully: 'I wouldn't be in your shoes for

something, twin! There's a pitched battle going on in the parlour!'

Evelyn was looking moody, but he laughed. 'Oh, I don't mind that! They've been skirmishing over me ever since you sent Fimber here. The thing is that every time he starts to give me one of his thundering scolds Pinny comes back into the room, so he's obliged to stop, because by the mercy of God neither combs my hair if the other is present. I can't think why not, but I can tell you I'm thankful for it! Has Mama managed to send the Cliffes packing? She said she meant to, if she could only hit upon a means of doing it. Did she?'

'Can you doubt it? I've just been waving farewell to them.'

'Mama is wonderful! How did she contrive to make them shab off?'

'By telling them that there was *not* an outbreak of scarlet fever in the village. I was afraid, when she began to talk of sickness, she was going to make it small-pox, which would have been doing it *too* brown. If you're coming up to the house tonight, I'd best meet you in the nursery-wing, to make sure the coast is clear. Lady Stavely goes to bed at ten and the servants won't come into the drawing-room once the tea-tray has been taken away.'

Evelyn nodded. 'Yes, very well. Kester, I think I'll go to Tunbridge Wells tomorrow. That's one piece of business I *can* settle – and if I stay cooped up here for much longer I shall go mad!'

'I should think you might,' agreed Kit. 'But you can't go to Tunbridge Wells, for all that.'

'Oh, for God's sake, Kester, don't *you* start talking fustian about my broken shoulder!' Evelyn exclaimed irritably.

'I wasn't thinking about your shoulder. The fact is, Eve, you can't go anywhere until I've disappeared. How are you to get there? Challow can't drive you there in the curricle, because for one thing, someone would be bound to see you,

and recognize you; and, for another, he can't take the curricle out secretly, you know.'

'But he can take it out at your orders, and bring you here
in it,' Evelyn pointed out, an impish gleam in his eyes.
'Then, dear twin, *you* can take my place here, in hiding,
and *I* can go to Tunbridge Wells!'

'Leaving my guests to fend for themselves! I would, if
the matter were of any particular urgency, but as it
doesn't seem to be – no!'

Evelyn sighed. 'I suppose not. But you'll have to leave
them, if you mean to go to Brighton in my stead.'

'I don't. I came to talk to you about that,' Kit said. 'Let's
sit down!'

He dragged Evelyn's chair up to a wooden bench, and
himself sat on the bench. 'You won't like this,' he warned
Evelyn, 'but you've got to know it.' He drew from his
pocket the roll of bills Evelyn had given him, and handed
it to him. 'Here are your flimsies: they won't be needed.
The brooch was not counterfeit. I doubt whether any of
Mama's jewelry is – not even the necklace she says she
sold on your behalf.'

Evelyn frowned at him, flushing slightly. 'What the devil
do you mean? She told me herself she had sold the brooch,
and had had it copied!'

'Yes, that's what she told me. But she also told me that
she had several times employed Ripple to sell trinkets for
her, which I imagine you didn't know.'

'You may be very sure I didn't.'

'Well, the long and the short of it, Eve, is that Ripple
never sold anything for her. He gave her the price of that
brooch and what he told her was a copy of it.'

Evelyn stiffened, his hand closing on the roll of bills so
tightly that his knuckles whitened. His eyes blazed for an
instant, then he lowered them to his clenched hand, and
opened his fingers. 'Why didn't you give him this, then?'

Kit shrugged, half-smiling. 'You may be able to: I found
I couldn't.'

'Kester, he had no *right* –!'

'No.'

'It is intolerable!' Evelyn said, in a suffocating voice. 'How much does Mama owe him?'

'I don't know. He wouldn't tell me.'

'He will tell me!'

'He won't, Eve. Or anyone. I think you had better hear what passed between us.'

Evelyn nodded, his lips compressed. But when Kit reached the end of his unquestioned recital, the white, angry look had left his face, and although he still frowned there was a softer light in his eyes. He did not speak immediately, but a rather bitter smile curled his lips, and presently he said: 'My father left me one thing I forgot to mention last night – humiliation! I shan't be rid of that until I've repaid Ripple.'

'It isn't in your power to repay him, twin.'

'Not yet. But it will be – when I'm thirty, if not before. I must talk to him.'

'Of course – but he bade me tell you it was none of your business, since it all happened during my father's lifetime, when you *couldn't* have rescued Mama. And further,' Kit said, with a twinkle, 'that he didn't want to have you buzzing round him like a hornet.'

Evelyn laughed, but ruefully. 'No, no, how could he think I would?'

'Well, he knows you don't like him! What's more he told me that you hadn't been able to wind him up in all the years you'd been trying to do it, so that it wasn't likely *I* could!'

Evelyn pulled a grimace. '*Not* so bacon-brained, after all. I suppose I have tried to draw wool, now and now. I don't dislike him precisely – or I shouldn't, if he didn't dangle after Mama, calling her his pretty, talking of his devotion, when even *she* knows how many mistresses he's had in keeping! But I never suspected him of *this*! I own, I thought it was all a hum: that he pretended to feel an unalterable attachment to Mama because to be *her* most favoured cicisbeo added to his consequence.'

'Yes, so did I,' Kit agreed. 'I think now, however, that he *is* devoted to her, in his way. Good-natured, too, and certainly generous – though he says himself that a few thousands here and there meant nothing to him.'

'I must see him!' Evelyn said, in a fretting tone. 'He has placed me under an obligation, and however much I – I hate it, I am very sensible of it, and must tell him so, and make it plain to him that I hold myself responsible, in my father's place, for Mama's debts.'

'You will do as you think right,' Kit said equably. 'We have also to consider, you, and Mama, and I, where you should go to until I am safely out of the country. You can't remain cooped up here, and while Lady Stavely is known to be at Ravenhurst you can't go to London, or to Brighton.'

'It's a pity I didn't break my neck instead of my shoulder. That would have solved all our problems,' remarked Evelyn. He turned his head to look at Kit, and added quickly: 'No, no, I don't mean that! Only funning, Kester!'

'Not one of your more diverting jokes, brother,' replied Kit. 'I mean it hasn't sent me into whoops, precisely!'

'I know, I know! don't rake me down!' Evelyn begged, in a penitent voice. 'The fact is, I'm blue-devilled!'

Kit nodded, but said: 'Very likely. Of course we're in the deuce of a hobble, but we shall bring ourselves off! When did we ever fail to?'

Evelyn smiled at him. 'True! Don't let us talk about my affairs: I'll retire to Leicestershire. Let's discuss yours instead! I suppose you can't immediately announce your engagement to Cressy, but I'm strongly of the opinion that you should see Stavely before you go back to Vienna, and get his consent. I've been considering that, and I think I should go with you to Mount Street.'

'I don't know that, but I agree that I must see Stavely as

soon as may be possible. But my affairs are simpler than yours, and don't call for discussion, Eve.'

'Mine are beyond discussion,' Evelyn answered. 'I've had plenty of time for thought, and I can see that my case is pretty hopeless. You said as much last night, didn't you?'

'I neither said it nor thought it.'

'Well, you said that my uncle will be opposed to my marriage to Patience Askham, and that is the same thing. I've tried to think he might not dislike it, but of course he will. How could I ask Patience to wait for six years? Even if I were sure that she loved me! I haven't – I haven't tried to fix her interest, and as things are – No, even if her father would permit me to declare myself, I mustn't do it.'

'If ever I knew such a fellow!' exclaimed Kit, in a rallying tone. 'Either you're in alt, or in flat despair!' He laid a hand on Evelyn's knee, and gripped it. 'You're not *quite* knocked up, you gudgeon! I shall try to see my uncle before I leave England, and though I don't yet know just what I shall tell him you may depend upon it that *your* part in my story will be positively saintly!'

'If you try to pitch it as rum as that, he'll smell out a hoax immediately!' Evelyn interrupted, laughing in spite of himself.

'Not at all! I fancy you sacrificed your own interests to further mine – and that he *will* believe. It won't do to say anything about Miss Askham, and I don't mean to. You *will* have to wait for a period, but not for very long, if you will but stop committing what he calls extravagant follies. Spend more of your time here, twin, and interest yourself in the estate! In fact, interest yourself to such a pitch that he'll be only too glad to relinquish his authority! Urge improvements, demand information – pester him! Add a melancholy air to your demeanour, as though you had suffered a disappointment, and ten to one he'll be so much concerned that he'll greet with relief your engagement to Miss Askham!'

He spoke with a gay confidence which amused Evelyn,

and served, for the moment, to put up his spirits; but he was not himself convinced. He knew his uncle's inflexible nature too well to believe that he could be easily persuaded; nor was he able to entertain any hopes that he would look with favour upon Evelyn's marriage to one whom he would infallibly consider a nobody. Knowing his twin, he entertained almost as little hope that Evelyn would adhere for any length of time to the line of conduct he had suggested to him. His disposition was too impetuous, his spirits too volatile, to enable him to wait, enduring boredom and frustration with patience. He would fall into one of his fits of despair, and seek alleviation in sprees and revel-routs.

It was therefore in a mood of considerable anxiety that Kit at last left his twin, and walked slowly back to the house, cudgelling his brain to discover a way to overcome difficulties which bore all the appearance of being insuperable. He began to feel almost as depressed as Evelyn, and was not cheered by the intelligence, imparted to him by Norton, upon his entering the house, that Miss Stavely had driven out with the Dowager. By way of solace, Norton offered him the newspapers, the post having come in some time previously.

It had brought no letters for Evelyn, but several for Lady Denville, and two franked by Lord Stavely, and addressed to his mother and his daughter.

Cressy was carrying her letter when she entered Lady Denville's drawing-room, and she said, as she shut the door: 'Godmama, I have had such good news from Papa! Albinia was brought to bed on Tuesday, and was delivered of a son! Papa is so delighted! He writes very briefly – just to tell me that it is a very fine child, and Albinia going on prosperously, in spite of a difficult labour.' She broke off suddenly perceiving that Lady Denville had been crying. She went swiftly forward, falling on her knees beside her ladyship's chair, and saying: 'What is it? Dearest, dearest Godmama, what has happened?'

Lady Denville made a huge effort to pull herself together, responding, with a valiant smile: 'Why, nothing in the world, dear child! What was that you said? Your father has a son? Well, that is charming – at least, I suppose one must say it is, though for my part I consider he should have been content with his daughter, for it isn't as though he had no brothers to succeed him, and I *cannot* think that any son of Albinia Gillifoot's will be anything but an *odious* child!'

Cressy gave an involuntary giggle, but said: 'Never mind that! Only tell me what has happened to distress you, ma'am!' Her eyes fell upon a closely written sheet of paper, lying on the table at Lady Denville's elbow. 'You have received disturbing news, ma'am? I do most sincerely trust you – you haven't suffered a bereavement? One of your sisters, or your brothers?'

'Oh no, nothing of that nature!' Lady Denville assured her. 'Much, much worse! Of course, I should be excessively sorry to hear that any of them had died, but I shouldn't cry about it, because I hardly ever see any of them, and Baverstock and Amelia I positively dislike! To own the truth, it made me feel very low when I saw Evelyn this morning. Just when Kit had made me so happy, too! Dearest Cressy, indeed I am overjoyed! You are the very wife for my darling Kit, and so I've been thinking for the past sennight!'

Emerging from her ladyship's scented embrace, Cressy blushed, laughed, and said: 'Thank you, ma'am! I hope I may prove you right! I only know that he is the very husband for me! But why did it make you feel low to see Evelyn? Do you fear he may be worse injured than Kit thinks?'

'Oh no, I shouldn't think so! To be sure, he does look rather pulled, poor lamb, but *that's* nothing! Cressy, did Kit tell you about Miss Askham?'

'To be sure he did! I understand she is a very beautiful and – and sweet girl!'

'Well, she *may* be,' said Lady Denville doubtfully. 'But her name is Patience!'

'How pretty!' said Cressy, in encouraging accents. 'Rather – rather Quakerish, and refreshingly unusual!'

'Do you think so?' Lady Denville grew still more doubtful. 'But I fear she *is* Quakerish, Cressy, and, try as I will, I *cannot* feel that she will suit Evelyn! You know, my love – and I can say this to you *now*, without any hiding of the truth! – the girls he has previously fallen in love with have *all* been very lively and dashing!'

Cressy smiled. 'But he has quite quickly fallen *out* of love with them, hasn't he, ma'am? Perhaps – being so dashing himself? – a quiet, gentle girl will suit him much better. I believe it is often so.'

'Yes, that is what Kit says. Kit thinks that *this* time Evelyn has formed a *lasting* passion, and of course Kit knows him as no one else does. But if he wanted a *quiet* girl I can't conceive why he couldn't have fallen in love with you, dearest! It seems so capricious of him! Not that I grudge you to Kit, for Evelyn is *not* my favourite son, whatever Kit may say. I love them both equally, and so he knows! The thing is that Evelyn is closer to me, because we have always lived together; but Kit is so much more dependable, and the *greatest* comfort to me! And I should think,' she added reflectively, 'that he will make a charming husband.'

'Yes, so do I,' agreed Cressy, her eyes warm with amusement. She clasped one of Lady Denville's hands, and ventured to say: 'I feel, too, that Miss Askham will make a charming wife.'

'No,' said her ladyship decidedly. 'Not *charming*, Cressy! A *good* wife, I dare say – in fact, I am sure of it, and it does make me feel very low, because she sounds to me to be such an *insipid* girl!'

Cressy patted her hand. 'Oh no, I am persuaded you won't think her so! I expect she is shy merely.'

Lady Denville looked at her in an awed way. 'Cressy,

she has been reared on the strictest principles, and her mama is *full* of propriety, and Evelyn says that they are all of them truly good and saintly! Indeed, he described Patience to me as an *angel*! Well, dearest, I wouldn't for a moment deny that that is – is *most* admirable, but I find saintly persons excessively uncomfortable, and I *cannot* live with an angel!'

'But must you live with her, ma'am?'

'No, and I don't mean to. I told Evelyn so, when he offered for you, for it *never* answers! Only, when I began to think of living by myself – Cressy, do you think I could afford to do so? I should be obliged to buy a house, for I don't feel I *could* hire one; and I will *not* live in some dreadful, shabby-genteel quarter of the town, or miles and miles from anywhere, like Upper Grosvenor Place, where poor Augusta Sandhayes removed to when Sandhayes lost a great deal of money on 'Change and said they must hold household. And only think of the cost of the servants, and the carriages, and – and all the things I never *have* paid for!' Her eyes filled. 'And when I consider that I have never been able to keep out of debt when I didn't pay for such things, how could I possibly do so when I shall be obliged to?'

The question was unanswerable. Cressy sat back on her heels, a very thoughtful expression in her eyes, but she said nothing. The truth of Lady Denville's words had struck home. She had not previously considered the matter; but she was well enough acquainted with her ladyship to realize that the income necessary to maintain her in the style to which she was accustomed must be far in excess of even the most handsome jointure. She realized, too, having a great deal of commonsense, that it would be folly to suppose that she would reduce her expenditure: she was quite incapable of doing so.

As though she had read the thought in Cressy's mind, Lady Denville said: 'It is of no use to tell me I must practise economy, because I can't! Whenever I have tried to do

so it has only led to *much* more expense. Denville's sister
– a most disagreeable woman, my love, besides being a
nipcheese, which is much worse than being extravagant,
because it makes everyone uncomfortable, on account of
not employing a second footman, and serving horrid dinners – was used to prick at me, and instruct me in habits
of economy, and I perceived *then* that I could never bring
myself to practise such habits. I must own I could only be
thankful when she died, for she never met me but what she
asked me how much my dress had cost, and then said that
I could have had one made for less than *half* the price. I
know I could, but nothing would induce me to. You see,
Cressy, ever since my come-out, people have said I was
the best-dressed woman in London, and whenever I have
gone to a party they looked to see what I was wearing, and
how my hair was dressed, and – and copied me. I've led
fashion, and I still do, so I *couldn't* go to parties now, looking like a dowd! It is *not* that I am vain – at least, I don't
think I am – but – well, I can't explain it to you! I dare
say you might not understand – though you are always
very well dressed yourself, dear one!'

'I do understand,' Cressy said. 'Yes, and I couldn't bear
it if you were even the tiniest bit less – less exquisite, and
nor could Evelyn and Kit! Godmama, you mustn't set up
your own establishment! Even if you could afford to do so,
I am persuaded you wouldn't like it. Consider how much
you would miss having a gentleman to – to *manage* for
you, and escort you to parties!'

'Well, I shouldn't miss *that*,' said her ladyship candidly,
'because I should still have *plenty* of gentlemen to escort
me!'

'Yes, but no host for your own parties!' Cressy pointed
out.

'No,' Lady Denville agreed. 'That is the worst thing
about being a widow. But in every other way it is most
agreeable, I find. In fact, *far* more agreeable than being a
wife! At least, it is for me, but not, of course, for you,

dearest!' she hastened to add, with one of her lovely smiles. It faded; she looked stricken all at once, and older; and said: 'I was forgetting. You see, it is of no consequence.' Two large tears welled over her eyelids, and rolled unheeded down her cheeks. She said sadly: 'I have been such a *bad* mother, and I love them so very much!'

Cressy burst out laughing. 'Godmama! Oh, I beg your pardon, but it is too absurd! Why, they adore you.'

Lady Denville carefully wiped the tears away. 'I know they do, and I can't think why they should – though I don't think I have ruined *Kit*'s life. But when I saw Evelyn today – then I knew what a detestable parent I am!'

'He never said so!'

'Oh no, poor darling! But he asked me to forgive him for – for having failed at such a crisis, and left me in the lurch, and it almost broke my heart, because if it weren't for my *crushing* debts, he could marry Patience *tomorrow*. I begged him not to think of them, but although he laughed, and turned it off, he was obliged to own that he *does* think of them, and – and has no hope of being able to marry Patience for years and years – which is as good as to say Never! Because it would be folly to suppose that his Uncle Brumby will approve of such a match, you know. And then he tried to joke me, saying that it was not my fault at all, but his, for having made his father think him too volatile to be trusted to manage his affairs, and that was almost more than I could bear, Cressy! Only, when he saw how distressed I was, he rallied me, in his enchanting way, saying that we were both blue-devilled, and that things weren't so very bad, because even though it might not be in his power to discharge my debts at present, he knew he could compound with my creditors, or some such thing, and so there was nothing for me to worry about, or him either. I dare say you will think it very foolish of me to have believed he could do it, but – but when Evelyn sets out to coax me out of the hips, he is so very gay and persuasive that one cannot help feeling reassured! And I *did* feel that perhaps *something* could be done, if people knew they would be paid back as soon as Evelyn is thirty, and I was quite *cheerful* when I left him. And then the post came in, and – and brought me a *shattering* letter!' She ended on a sob and dabbed at her eyes again. 'Mr – well, never mind his name! You wouldn't know him, but he lent me rather a *large* sum of money some years ago, when I was quite at my wits' end. I *truly* believed I should be able to give it back to him at the next quarter, when my allowance was paid, but it turned out to be otherwise. Indeed, it was *wholly* impossible, as I was obliged to explain to him. But I *did* contrive to pay him the interest, and invited his daughter to one of my parties, besides taking her for *two* drives with me in the Park, and introducing her to *hosts* of people, so what more *could* I do? And now he has written me a long letter, saying that *much* as he sympathizes with me, he cannot afford to continue in this way, because he has had a great many expenses which have been a sad drain on his purse, and so he must, though with the utmost reluctance, beg me to refund the sum he lent me. And, which I find more upsetting than anything, and *quite* outweighs his civility, he didn't even get a frank for his letter, so that I have had to pay *two shillings* for it! At least, *someone* did, probably Norton, but it is the same thing – except that it will be poor Evelyn who will pay it in the end, when he pays all the household accounts.'

With only the faintest tremor in her voice, Cressy replied gravely: 'A – a want of delicacy in him, to be sure, ma'am!'

'Exactly so! And in general, you know, he is a very gentlemanlike person.' She sighed. 'I shall be obliged to repay him, but Evelyn is to know nothing about it. No, and not Kit either, mind that, Cressy! I *trust* you not to mention it to him!'

'Very well, ma'am, but – but *can* you repay the sum?' asked Cressy diffidently.

'Yes,' Lady Denville replied, 'All my debts – *all* of them!' She rose, and picked up the offending letter, and carried it to her tambour-topped writing-desk, and put it away in one of the drawers. She said, in a constricted tone: 'I have quite made up my mind to it. I ought to have done so when Denville died, but I could not bring myself to it. But *now* I can, and I will, because however bad a mother I have been there is *nothing* I wouldn't do for my beloved sons! Now, pray, Cressy, don't tell Kit that I cried a little!'

Cressy got up from her knees. 'I won't tell him anything you don't wish me to, Godmama, but won't you tell *me* how you mean to pay your debts, and – and why it makes you so unhappy?'

'Well, to own the truth, dearest, it utterly sinks my spirits only to *think* of going to live abroad, with a sensible female companion – but I dare say I shall soon grow accustomed!' said her ladyship, gallantly smiling.

'Going to live abroad with a – But *why?*' demanded Cressy, in bewilderment.

'Henry will insist on it. I *know* he will! Once before, when the twins were babies, he and Louisa – his sister – persuaded Denville that that was the only thing to be done with me, because – Oh, there were so many reasons, but it is a long time ago now, and it never happened, because the continent became quite unsafe, on account of Napoleon, which is why I never *could* dislike him as much as others did! But now the war is over, and people who find themselves run off their legs, like poor Brummell, go and live at horridly cheap places, where there are no parties, or gaming, or races, or anybody one knows!'

Cressy said indignantly: 'Lord Brumby couldn't be so inhuman!'

'Yes, he could,' answered her ladyship. 'Either that, or the Dower House here – and very likely he won't even offer me the Dower House, because he will think it is situated too close to Brighton, or that he couldn't stop me going up to London, once my debts were paid.'

'Well, *one* thing is certain!' said Cressy, her eyes kindling.

'Neither Evelyn nor Kit would countenance such an arrangement!'

'No,' agreed her ladyship. 'Not if they know about it, and that is a *very* comforting thought! But I shall say that I would *like* to go abroad for a time, when Evelyn is married. And perhaps I shall be able to visit you and Kit, so it won't be so very bad!'

After a slight pause, Cressy said slowly: 'I think it would be *very* bad. Not at all the thing for you, Godmama! You would find living with a respectable female a dead bore.'

'I know I shall,' sighed Lady Denville. 'And if it has to be my sister Harriet, it will be *worse* than a bore!'

'Oh no, that wouldn't do at all!' Cressy said decidedly. She glanced at her ladyship, and gave a little laugh. 'You mustn't live with *any* female, ma'am! Consider, you have been used always to live with a gentleman! I know myself that one can't easily accustom oneself to female companionship when that has been the case. That was why I was ready to accept Evelyn's offer, even though I didn't love him.'

'Yes, but –' Lady Denville broke off, an arrested expression on her face. Watching her, Cressy saw the mischievous look creep into her eyes. Suddenly she gave a tiny gurgle of laughter, and turned, and impulsively embraced Cressy. 'Dearest, you have put a – a notion into my head! It is *too* absurd, and I am not at all sure – or even if – Well, I must *think*! So go away now, dear child, and don't say a word to *anyone* about the talk we've had!'

'No, I won't, I promise you,' Cressy said. 'I am going to drive out with Grandmama for an hour. Papa's letter has wonderfully restored her! She is *aux anges*, and is even prepared to forgive Albinia for having married him. I am strongly of the opinion that *now* is the moment to tell her that Kit is Kit, and not Evelyn, and if she continues in this benign humour I mean to do it!'

19

Sir Bonamy, waking from his afternoon nap, yawned, sighed, and refreshed himself with a pinch of snuff. He then picked up the *Morning Post*, which Norton, tiptoeing into the room, had laid on a table at his elbow, and cast a lacklustre eye over its columns. The only items of interest to him were contained on the page devoted to the activities of the ton; and, since London, in July, was almost deserted, these consisted mostly of such arid pieces of information as that Lady X, with her three daughters, was visiting Scarborough; or that the Duchess of B— was taking the waters at Tunbridge Wells. Brighton news occupied most of the space; and Sir Bonamy read, nostalgically, that His Royal Highness the Prince Regent had entertained a party of distinguished guests at the Pavilion, dinner, to which a select company had been invited, having been followed by a brilliant soirée, with music. Sir Bonamy could not have been said to have shared his royal crony's taste for music, but he would have enjoyed the dinner, to which he would most certainly have been bidden. Then he read that His Royal Highness the Duke of York was expected to arrive at the Pavilion at the end of the week; and this so painfully sharpened his nostalgia that he decided that the end of the week should also see the return of Sir Bonamy Ripple to the Pavilion.

He had responded without hesitation to Lady Denville's summons, flattered by it, and willing, in his goodnatured way, to do her least bidding. He had looked forward to some agreeable tête-à-têtes with his hostess; he knew that her cook was second only to his own; and he vaguely supposed that the rest of the company would consist of congenial persons with whom he would be able to play whist for high stakes every evening. His devotion to her ladyship had become so much a habit that he would not have refused her invitation even if he had known that his fellow-guests would be unfashionable people with whom he had nothing in common; but he had been as much daunted as surprised when he discovered that one of the ton's most successful hostesses had invited to Ravenhurst such a small and dull collection of guests.

Sir Bonamy was no lover of the pastoral scene, in general confining his visits to the country to several weeks spent during the winter at various great houses, where he could be sure of meeting persons who were congenial to him, and of being amused by such diversions as exactly suited a grossly fat and elderly dandy of his sedentary disposition; and a very few days spent at Ravenhurst had been enough to set him hankering after the delights of Brighton. There had been few opportunities for elegant dalliance with Lady Denville; playing indifferent whist for chicken-stakes bored him; and the discovery that he had unwittingly stepped into a masquerade made him feel profoundly uneasy. There was no saying what devilry the Fancot twins might be engaged in, and to become involved in what bore all the appearance of a major scandal was a fate which he shuddered to contemplate.

He had laid aside the *Morning Post*, and was wondering what excuse he could offer Lady Denville for bringing his visit to an end, when the door was softly opened, and she peeped into the room.

As soon as she saw that he was awake, she smiled, and said: 'Ah, here you are! Dear Bonamy, do let us go for a stroll together! I don't believe I've had as much as five minutes alone with you since the day you arrived.'

As he hoisted himself out of his chair, she came across the room with her light, graceful step, looking so youthful that he exclaimed: 'Upon my word, Amabel, you don't look a day older than you did when I first saw you!'

She laughed, but said wistfully: 'You always say such charming things, Bonamy! But, alas, you're offering me Spanish coin!'

'Oh, no, I'm not!' he assured her, kissing her hand. 'Never any need for that, my pretty! Not an *hour* older!'

'So many years older!' she sighed. 'I daren't reckon them. Do you care to come into the garden with me? Cressy has driven out with her Grandmama, so at last I am free to do what I choose! My dear, how prosy and dreadful Cosmo has become! Thank you for bearing with him so nobly! I don't know what I should have done without you!'

'Oh, pooh, nonsense!' he said, beaming fondly down at her. 'Always a joy to me to be able to serve you! As for Cosmo – well, thank *you* for ridding me of him!' He rumbled a laugh. 'Scarlet fever indeed, you naughty puss! I thought you were pitching it a trifle too rum, but, lord, he's the biggest flat I ever knew, for all he thinks himself up to everything!' He drew her hand through his arm and patted it. 'If he knew you as well as I do, my pretty, you'd have been gapped!'

'But he doesn't,' she pointed out. 'I don't think anyone does.'

He was so much gratified by this that he could only heave an eloquent sigh, squeezing her arm, and growing pink in the face. Lady Denville guided him out of the house, and disengaged her hand to open her frivolous parasol. She then slipped it back within his crooked arm, and walked slowly along the terrace with him to the shallow steps, saying: 'How delightful this is! I have been so much harassed that it is a struggle to support my spirits, but it always does me good to talk to you, my best of friends.'

'It does *me* good only to *look* at you, my love!' he responded gallantly, but with a slightly wary look in his eye.

'Dear Bonamy!' she murmured. 'Such a detestably dull party to have invited you to! I knew you wouldn't fail, too, which makes it quite shameless of me to have made such a demand on your good nature! I *do* beg your pardon!'

'No, no! Happy to have been of assistance to you!' he said, quite overcome.

'I expect you are longing to get back to Brighton,' she

sighed. 'I don't wonder at it, and only wish I were going there too, for I do *not* like the country, except for a *very* little while!'

'Come, come, Amabel, what's this?' he expostulated. 'Of course you are going to Brighton! Why, you told me yourself that Evelyn had hired the same house on the Steyne which you had last year!'

'Yes, and doesn't it seem a *waste*? But Evelyn *cannot* go there until his shoulder has mended – he was in an accident, you know, which is why Kit was obliged to take his place – and he says he shall go to Leicestershire, to Crome Lodge, and only think how dismal for him, poor lamb, at this season! I *must* accompany him. Besides, he is in low spirits, because – but I don't mean to burden you with my troubles!'

'Never a burden to me! There's nothing I wouldn't do for you, Amabel, but the thing is that Evelyn wouldn't like it if I were to meddle in his affairs. Better not tell me what sort of a scrape he's got himself into, for you know he don't like me above half, and I'll be bound he'd fly up into the boughs if he got to know you'd taken me into your confidence!' said Sir Bonamy firmly.

'I am afraid that even you couldn't unravel *this* tangle,' she agreed, with another sigh.

'I'm dashed sure I couldn't! You leave it to Kit, my pretty! *He* don't want for sense! In fact,' he said, with a sudden burst of candour, 'it's surprising how longheaded he's grown to be! Never thought there was a penny to choose between 'em, your boys, but I shouldn't wonder at it if Kit turns out to be a sure card.'

It was on the tip of her ladyship's tongue to utter a hot defence of her beloved elder-born son, but she bit back the words, and replied meekly that Kit had always been the more reliable twin. They had crossed the lawn by this time, to where a rustic seat had been placed in the shade of a great cedar, and she now suggested that they should sit down there, out of the sunshine. Sir Bonamy hailed this with

263

relief, for he was already uncomfortably hot, and had grave fears that his rigid shirt-points were beginning to wilt. He lowered himself on to the seat, beside her ladyship, and mopped his brow. Lady Denville, looking deliciously cool, shut up her parasol, and leaned back, observing that there was nothing so exhausting as walking in such sultry weather. She then fell silent, gazing ahead with so much melancholy in her expression that Sir Bonamy began to feel perturbed. After a long pause, he laid one of his pudgy hands on hers, and said: 'Now, my pretty! You mustn't let yourself get into the hips! Depend upon it, Kit will make all tidy!'

She gave a little start, and turned her head to smile at him. 'I wasn't thinking of that. I was – oh, *remembering*! Do you ever look back over the years, Bonamy? It does sink one's spirits a little: so long ago! so many mistakes! so much unhappiness! But there are happy memories too, of course! Do you recall the first time we met?'

'Ay, as if it were yesterday, and so I shall to the end of my life! All in white, you were, my lovely one, with your glorious gold hair glinting under just a light powder, and your eyes like sapphires! I fell in love with you the instant I saw you – swore I'd win your hand, or remain a bachelor! Which I have done! And, what's more, I was never tempted to break that oath! For no man, my pretty, that loved you,' said Sir Bonamy earnestly, conveniently forgetting the several articles of virtue whom he had subsequently maintained at enormous expense, 'could ever feel the smallest tendre for any other female!'

Lady Denville, recalling one veritable Incognita, and at least three high-flyers, who had enjoyed Sir Bonamy's protection, stifled a giggle, and said soulfully: 'And Papa married me to Denville! We danced together, didn't we? And the next day you sent me a bouquet of white and yellow roses – so many that there was no counting them! That should be a happy memory, but it makes me want to cry. Not that I mean to do so,' she added, with one of her dancing gleams of mischief, 'for there is *nothing* so tedious as a female who turns herself into a watering-pot! I've never done that, have I?'

'Never!' he declared, raising her hand to his lips.

'Well, I hope it will be set down in my favour in the judgement-book, and I do feel it may be, for I haven't had a happy life. One shouldn't speak ill of the dead, and I *perfectly* realize that poor Denville had as much to bear as I had – well, *almost* as much! The truth is that we were each of us deceived in the other, and should never, never have been married!' She wrinkled her brow. 'I've often wondered why he believed himself to have fallen in love with me, for he disapproved of me amazingly, and he was so cold – so formal – that even now it makes me shiver to remember it!'

'Ah, my poor pretty!' said Sir Bonamy, much moved. 'If you had married me, how happy we should both have been!'

Her eyes quizzed him laughingly. 'Well, *I* might have been, but perhaps *you* would have been as much provoked by me as Denville was! Consider my shocking want of *management*, and *economy*, and my fondness for gaming, and my dreadful debts!'

Sir Bonamy snapped his fingers in the air. '*That* for such fiddle-faddle! Your debts? Pooh! – an almond for a parrot! Let me settle them! Over and over I've told you I'm able to stand more of the nonsense than you ever dreamed of, my lovely one. It don't do to be prating like some counter-coxcomb, but I'm no chicken-nabob. Well, I'm not a nabob at all, of course: I inherited my fortune, and how much I'm worth I can't tell you, for it don't signify: even you couldn't spend the half of it!'

'Good gracious, Bonamy, you *must* be rich!' she countered.

'I am,' he said simply. 'Richest man in the kingdom, for I fancy I have a trifle the advantage of Golden Ball. Much good it does me! I had as lief be living on a mere competence, for I've not a soul to spend it on, Amabel, and it didn't win me the only thing I wanted. You may say it's of no consequence – no consequence at all!'

Since she was well aware that he lived in the height of luxury, maintaining, in addition to his mansion in Grosvenor Square, establishments at Brighton, Newmarket, York and Bath (to which slightly outmoded resort he occasionally retired, when his constitution demanded rehabilitation); stabling teams of prime cattle on no fewer than five of the main post-roads; and gaming for preposterous stakes either at Watier's, or at Oatlands, the residence of his extremely expensive crony, the Duke of York, she had no overmastering desire to avail herself of this permission. But, although her lips quivered, and there was just the suspicion of a choke in her voice, she responded, with a shake of her head: 'No, indeed! How *very* sad it is, my dear friend! How *empty* your life has been! How lonely!'

'Ay, so it has!' he agreed, struck for the first time in many years by the truth of this sympathetic remark. He took her hand again, pressing it in his own very warm and slightly damp one, and said with great earnestness: 'All the use I ever had for my wealth was to bestow it upon you, my dear! It's yours for the asking, and always will be. Only let me take your debts on my shoulders! Let me –'

She interrupted him, raising her beautiful eyes to his face, and saying: 'Bonamy, are you – after all these years – asking me to marry you?'

There was a stunned pause. Sir Bonamy's round eyes stared down into hers. They were never expressive, but they were now more than ordinarily blank; and the rich colour faded perceptibly from his pendulous cheeks. Twenty-six years earlier he had been a suitor for her hand; during the years of her marriage he had been her constant and devoted *cavaliere servente,* and very agreeably had those years slipped past. She was indeed the only woman he had ever wished to marry; but although the disappointment he had suffered when the late Lord Baverstock had preferred the Earl of Denville's offer to his had been severe it had not been very long before his cracked heart had mended sufficiently for him not only to appreciate the advantages of his single state, but to offer a carte blanche to a charming, if somewhat rapacious, ladybird, universally acknowledged to be a dasher of the first water. But throughout this left-hand connexion, and the many which had succeeded it, he had maintained his devotion to the lovely Countess of Denville, earning for himself the envious respect of his less favoured contemporaries, and, in due course, the reputation of being a man who, having once lost his heart, would never again offer it (with his enormous fortune) to any other lady. After a couple of years, even the most determined matron, with marriageable daughters on her hands, considered it a waste of time to throw out lures to him, and observed his light, elegant flirtations without a flicker either of hope or of jealousy.

Such a state of affairs exactly suited his indolent, hedonistic disposition. He had settled down into a state of opulent bachelordom, enjoying every luxury which his wealth could provide, rapidly becoming the intimate of the Prince of Wales, and of his scarcely less expensive brother, the Duke of York; abandoning the struggle to overcome a tendency to corpulence; and achieving, by his impeccable lineage, his amiable manners, his lavish hospitality, the genius of his tailor, and the favour of the most admired lady in the land, the position of being a leader of fashion, and one whom any ambitious hostess was proud to include amongst her guests.

Credited by his world with an undying passion for his first love, it had never until this moment occurred to him to question his own heart; and had it been suggested to him that his original infatuation had gently but inevitably declined into fondness he would have been much affronted. But now, staring down into Lady Denville's beautiful face, an even more beautiful kaleidoscope of his comfortable untrammelled existence intervened.

Lady Denville's soft laughter recalled him from this vision; she said, in a voice of affectionate chiding: 'Oh, Bonamy, what a complete hand you are! A Banbury man, no less! You *don't* wish to marry me, do you?'

He pulled himself together, declaring valiantly: 'The one wish of my heart!'

'Well, you didn't look as if it was! Confess, now! You've been shamming it – all these years!'

He rejected this playful accusation with vehemence. 'No, that I haven't! How can you say such a thing, Amabel? Haven't I stayed single for your sake?'

A provocative smile hovered about the corners of her mouth; she seemed to consider him. 'That's what you *say*, but are you perfectly sure it wasn't for your own sake, abominable palaverer that you are, my dear?'

He was so indignant at having a doubt cast on his fidelity that the colour surged up into his face, and he almost glared at her. 'No! I mean, yes! I *am* sure! Upon my word, Amabel –! Have I ever formed an attachment for anyone but yourself? Have I –'

'Often!' she said cordially. 'First, there was that *ravishing* creature, with black curls and flashing eyes, who was used to drive in the park in a landaulet behind a pair of *jet*-black horses, *perfectly* matched, and *such* beautiful steppers that everyone said they must have cost you a fortune! Then there was that *languishing* female – the one with the flaxen hair, who was *certainly* of a consumptive habit! And after her –'

'Now, that will do!' interposed Sir Bonamy, aghast at these accurate recollections. 'Bachelor's fare! Good God, Amabel, you should know that they don't mean anything, those little connexions! Why, your own father – Well, well, mum for that!'

The laughter was quenched in her eyes; she turned her head away, and said in a low voice: 'And Denville. Did it mean nothing? It seemed to me to mean so much! What a goose-cap I was!'

'Amabel!' pronounced Sir Bonamy, controlling himself with a strong effort, 'I have never permitted myself to utter a word in dispraise of Denville, and I'll keep my tongue between my teeth *now*, but had you married *me*, the most dazzling bird of Paradise amongst the whole of the muslin company would have thrown out her lures in vain to me!'

'But it is too late,' she said mournfully. 'I've worn out your love, my poor Bonamy! I read it in your face, and *indeed* I cannot wonder at it!'

'Nothing of the sort!' he replied stoutly. 'You misunderstood! I had come to believe that my case was hopeless – can you wonder at it that I was knocked acock? My heart stood still! Was it possible, I asked myself, that its dearest wish might yet be granted? A moment's rapture, and my spirits were dashed down again, as I realized how absurd it was to think that at my age I could win what was denied me when I was young, and – I fancy – not an ill-looking man!'

'Very true! Even then you had a decided air of fashion – though it wasn't until *much* later that you became of the first stare!'

'Well, well!' he said, visibly gratified, 'I was always one who liked to have everything prime about me, but propriety of taste, you know, comes to one in later years! But I am growing old, my pretty – too old for you, I fear! Alas that it should be so!'

'Fudge!' said her ladyship briskly. 'You are three-and-fifty, just ten years older than I am! A very comfortable age!'

'But of late years I have grown to be a trifle portly! I don't ride any more, you know, and I get fagged easily nowadays. Ticklish in the wind, too – I might pop off the hooks at any moment, for I have palpitations!'

'Yes, you eat too much,' she nodded. 'My poor dear Bonamy, it is high time you had me to take care of you! I have thought for years that your constitution must be of *iron* to have withstood your excesses, and so it is, for you don't even suffer from the gout, which Denville did, although for every bottle *he* drank you drank two, if not three!'

'No, no!' protested Sir Bonamy feebly. 'Not *three*, Amabel! I own I eat more than he did, but recollect that he was of a spare habit! Now, I have a large frame, and I must eat to keep up my strength!'

'So you shall!' said her ladyship, smiling seraphically upon him. 'But *not* to send yourself off in an apoplexy!'

Regarding her with eyes of fascinated horror, he played his last ace. 'Evelyn!' he uttered. 'You are forgetting Evelyn, my pretty! Ay, and Kit too, I dare say, though he don't seem to hold me in such aversion as Evelyn does! But you must know Evelyn wouldn't stomach it! Why, he never sees me but he looks yellow! Well do I know there ain't a soul you dote on more, and *never* would I cause a rift between you!'

Wholly unimpressed by this noble self-abnegation, she replied: 'You couldn't! Besides, he is going to be married!'

'What?' he ejaculated, momentarily diverted. 'But it's as plain as a pack-saddle the gal's head over ears in love with Kit!'

'Yes, and was there ever anything so delightful? Dear Cressy! she might have been *made* for Kit! Evelyn has formed what he declares to be a lasting passion for quite another sort of girl. Kit believes it may well be so, but she sounds to me to be positively *Quakerish*! The daughter of a mere country gentleman – *perfectly* genteel, but only picture to yourself how ineligible Brumby will think her! – and one of those *pale*, saintly females, reared in the *strictest* respectability!'

'You don't mean it!' gasped Sir Bonamy, staggered by this disclosure.

'I *do* mean it!' she asserted, tears sparkling on her curling eyelashes. She brushed them hurriedly away. 'Evelyn thinks I shall love her, but I have the most melancholy conviction that I shan't, Bonamy! And, what is more, I don't think she will love me, do you?'

'No,' he replied candidly. 'Not if she's Quakerish! You wouldn't deal well at all!'

'Exactly so! I *knew* you would understand! Evelyn declares I must continue to live in Hill Street, but that I was determined not to do, even if he had married Cressy! I had quite made up my mind to it that I must retire to an establishment of my own, and dwindle into a mere widow, until *you* came here, my dear friend, only because I begged you to, and not wanting to leave Brighton in the *least*, which I know very well you didn't, and it struck me, like a flash of lightning, that *never* had you wavered in your attachment to me, and *never* had you received the smallest reward, or even looked for one, for all your goodness to me, and your *exceeding* generosity!'

'I see what it is!' he exclaimed. 'Kit blabbed to you that I didn't have that brooch of yours copied, silly chub that he is! Now, put it out of your mind, my pretty! Yes, yes, you think you must make a sacrifice of yourself, but I won't permit you to do so!'

She interrupted him, staring at him with widened eyes. 'You *didn't* – Do you mean to tell me that I lost the *real* brooch to Silverdale? And you gave me £500 for it, saying that – Bonamy, did you sell *any* of my jewelry? Kit has never breathed a word of this! Bonamy – *did* you?'

'No, no, of course I didn't!' he answered, much discomposed. 'Now, is it *likely* I'd let you sell your jewels, and replace 'em with paste and pinchbeck? It was nothing to me, Amabel, so, if Kit didn't tell you, you may forget it, and oblige me very much!'

'Oh, Bonamy!' she cried, impulsively stretching out her hands to him, 'how good you are! How much, much *too* good!'

He responded instinctively, and, the next instant, found himself clasping a fragrant armful to his massive bosom. Lady Denville, adapting her slim form, not without difficulty, to his formidable contour, lifted her face invitingly. His senses swimming, Sir Bonamy tightened his hold about her, and fastened his lips to hers. At the back of his mind lurked the conviction that he would regret this yielding to temptation, and the premonition that the sybaritic pleasures of his life stood in jeopardy; but never before had he been encouraged to venture more than a chaste salute upon her ladyship's hand, or, upon rare occasions, her cheek, and he surrendered to intoxication.

He came to earth again when she gently disengaged herself, saying: 'How comfortable it is to reflect that we need neither of us look forward to a lonely old age, which I have always thought the most *lowering* prospect!'

His countenance would not have led anyone to suppose that he was deriving much comfort from this reflection, but he replied heroically: 'You have made me the happiest man on earth, my beautiful!'

The irrepressible laughter, inherited from her by her sons, bubbled up. 'No, I haven't: I've thrown you into gloom! But I *shall* make you happy. Only consider how alike are our tastes, and how very well we are acquainted! Naturally it will seem strange at first, because you are so much accustomed to being a bachelor. To own the truth, I didn't think I should ever marry again, for I have enjoyed being a widow amazingly! But I am persuaded it will be the best thing for everyone! *Particularly* for Evelyn!'

'I hope he may think so!' Sir Bonamy said gloomily.

'It isn't of the least consequence if he doesn't, because it *will* be. I dare say he won't care *nearly* as much now that his mind is full of his angelic Patience. In any event, he's at the end of his rope, poor love, on account of my wretched debts, which he is determined to discharge, and which he would never be able to do until he is thirty, if he marries Patience, because you may depend upon it Brumby will *utterly* disapprove of the match! But if he were not obliged to pay my debts that wouldn't signify in the least, and although he made me promise I would never again borrow money from you, he *couldn't* refuse to let you pay the debts if I were your wife, could he?'

'Well, it won't make a ha'porth of odds if he does!' said Sir Bonamy, accepting without resentment this unflattering reason for the marriage proposed to him, but regarding his prospective bride with tolerant cynicism. 'I might have known that resty young bellows-blower of yours was behind this!'

'Yes, but how *fortunate,* Bonamy, that my affairs had come to such a pass that I was obliged to consider the advantages of marrying you! But for that I might never have thought of it!' she said. '*Or* have perceived how much more comfortable I should be if I did marry you! It is all very well *now* to be a widow, but only think how dismal when I begin to grow hagged, and have to cover up my throat, because it looks exactly like the neck of a plucked hen, and I've no flirts left to me! And then, of course, I thought of *you,* my poor Bonamy, and my heart was *wrung*! I, at least, have my beloved sons, and I *might* become wrapped up in my grandchildren – though it seems *most* unlikely, and quite sinks my spirits – but what, my dear, will be left to *you,* when your friends drop off –'

'Eh?' exclaimed Sir Bonamy, startled.

'*Or* die!' continued her ladyship inexorably. 'And you find yourself alone, with no one to care a straw what becomes of you – except that odious cousin of yours, who will very likely *push* you into your grave! – and your whole life *wasted*? Dear Bonamy I cannot endure the thought of it!'

'No!' he said fervently. 'No, indeed!'

She smiled brilliantly upon him. 'So you see that it will be much better for you too!'

'Yes,' he agreed, horrified by the picture she had delineated. 'Good God, yes!'

20

It was not many minutes before Cressy, dutifully accompanying the Dowager on a sedate drive, realized that an open carriage was hardly the place for an exchange of confidences. The Dowager, with a magnificent disregard for the coachman and the footman, perched on the box-seat in front of her, knew no such reticence, and discoursed with great freedom on the birth of an heir to the barony, animadverting with embarrassing candour, and all the contempt of a matriarch who had brought half-a-dozen children into the world without fuss or complications, on sickly young women who fancied themselves to be ill days before their time, and ended by suffering cross births and hard labours. For herself, she had no patience with such nonsense.

But although she expressed the fervent hope that the heir would not grow up to resemble his mama, it was evident that Albinia (in spite of her hard labour) had grown considerably in her esteem. Lord Stavely's first wife had been of the Dowager's choosing, but although she had, naturally, held her up as a pattern of virtue and amiability, she had never been able, in her secret heart, to forgive her for having failed to present her lord with an heir. But Albinia, whom Lord Stavely had married without so much as a by-your-leave, had produced (if his lordship's ecstatically scribbled letter were to be believed), a bouncing boy, sound in wind and limb, and weighing almost nine pounds; and this feat, notwithstanding her own subsequent exhaustion, raised her pretty high in the Dowager's esteem. But not so high as to exempt her from censure for her alleged inability to nurse her child. The inescapable duty of a mother to suckle her offspring was one of the Dowager's hobby-horses; and originated from the shocking discovery that the wet-nurse engaged to supply the wants of her second son (unhappily deceased), had been strongly addicted to spirituous liquors. The Dowager informed her granddaughter, in a very robust way, that she had already written to recommend hot ale and ginger to Albinia.

Cressy bore this with tolerable equanimity, but when the Dowager abruptly deserted the subject of the proper sustenance of the Honourable Edward John Francis Stavely, to warn her that the appearance of this young gentleman on the scene made it imperative for her to withdraw from Mount Street to an establishment of her own, she laid a hand on her outspoken grandmother's knee, and warningly directed her attention to the stolid, liveried backs on the box of the landaulet.

The Dowager appeared to appreciate the propriety of this reminder. She said: 'Drat these open carriages! I never could abide 'em! Coachman! Drive back to Ravenhurst!'

She reinforced this command by digging him in the back with her cane, an indignity which he suffered with perfect good humour, having decided, days previously, that she was a rare old griffin, full of pluck, and game to the scratch.

'I want to talk to you, Cressy,' she said grimly. 'It's high time you emptied the bag! So we'll go back, and you'll come with me to my room, and give me a round tale before I take my nap!'

'Yes, ma'am: certainly!' responded Cressy, with smiling composure.

The Dowager favoured her with a searching glance, but refrained from comment. She beguiled the rest of the drive with roseate plans for the future Lord Stavely's career, in which agreeable occupation she was much encouraged by Cressy; but although this put her into great good humour, it was with marked asperity that she commanded Cressy, as soon as she had removed her sable-plumed bonnet, and sunk into the winged chair, thoughtfully placed in her bedroom by her hostess, to declare herself, and without any roundaboutation.

'And don't put on any simpering, missish airs, girl, for I abominate 'em!' she added sharply.

'Now, that, Grandmama, is most unjust!' said Cressy, in deeply injured accents. 'I have a great many faults, but I am *not* a simpering miss!'

'No,' acknowledged the Dowager, always mollified by a fearless retort, 'you're not! Come here, child!'

Cressy obeyed her, sinking down at her feet, and folding her hands with a meekness belied by the twinkling look she cast up at her formidable grandparent. 'Yes, ma'am?' she said innocently.

'Baggage!' said the Dowager, in no way deceived, but palliating the severity of this remark by pinching Cressy's cheek. 'Now, you listen to me, girl! You'll find that this brat of Albinia's has put your nose out of joint, so, if you take my advice, you'll bring all this paltering of yours to an end, and accept Denville's offer. I said I wouldn't press you, and I stand by my word; but I know Albinia, and I tell you to your head that if you found her hard to deal with before she gave birth to a son you'll find her insupportable now that she's puffed up in her own conceit! What's more, she won't rest until she's rid of you: make up your mind to that! As for your father, he's fond of you, but he won't take your part: he's a weak man – none of my sons ever had an ounce of spunk between them! Took after their father, more's the pity! Bag and baggage policy was all you could look for in any of 'em.'

'Well, I shouldn't wish Papa to take my part, ma'am – or, rather, I know that it would be very improper to encourage him to do so!'

'It wouldn't fadge if you did. If Albinia ain't a shrew I'm much mistaken!'

'Impossible!' Cressy said, laughing at her.

The dowager's fierce eyes gleamed, but she said: 'None of your impudence, miss! Not that I'm often mistaken, for I haven't lived to be an old woman without learning to know one point more than the devil, as they say.' Her eyes softened, as she looked down into Cressy's face. 'Never mind that! I've more fondness for you than for anyone, child, and I want to see you established, and happy. I told you at the outset I set no store by Denville's rank or fortune, and no more I would have, if I'd discovered him to be the frippery young care-for-nobody Brumby thinks him. Not but what he's a prize catch, and has had 'em all on the scramble for him ever since his come-out! However, I've lived long enough to know that it ain't by any means everything to land a big fish, and not a word of censure would you have heard from me, Cressy, if you'd had a preference for some lesser gentleman – provided, of course, that his birth matched your own, and he was up to the rig!'

'You like him, don't you, Grandmama?' said Cressy.

'Yes, I do – not that it signifies! A very proper man, I call him, and one that knows what's o'clock, and ain't afraid to look one in the face, and give one back as good as he gets!' the Dowager replied, with a dry chuckle. 'No want of proper spunk in *him*, for all his engaging manners! But what I want to know, my girl, is whether *you* like him?'

'Oh, yes! I think everyone does,' Cressy responded. 'He is very charming!'

'I'd a notion you thought so!' remarked the Dowager caustically.

'Oh, I do! But I am not very well-acquainted with him yet, you know,' said Cressy pensively.

'I know nothing of the sort!' declared the Dowager, staring down at her under frowning brows. 'Pray, how much better acquainted with him do you expect to be, miss?'

'*Much* better, ma'am! But however well-acquainted with him I may be I shall never marry him!'

'Well, upon my word!' uttered the Dowager, her eyes snapping. 'Have you taken leave of your senses, girl, or are you no better than a common flirt? You've lived in his pocket above a sennight – smelling of April and May, the pair of you! and very well pleased I've been to see it! I wasn't in favour of the match at the outset, and I know very well *you* were of two minds, Cressy! Which was why I brought you here! I'll thank you to tell me why, if you was ready enough to accept his offer at the outset, you've changed your mind! What, in heaven's name, do you look for in your husband, wet-goose? As handsome a young man as I've clapped eyes on this many a day, with a well-formed person, excellent style, easy manners, an address many an older man might envy, superior understanding, and

277

a smile *I* could not have withstood when I was a girl, and you choose to turn niffy-naffy! Good God, Cressy, have you windmills in your head? You told me you had made up your mind to a *mariage de convenance*, but if you don't know he's nutty upon you, you're no better than a moonling, and I wash my hands of you!'

Cressy, a mixture of guilt and amusement in her face, possessed herself of one of these hands, and nursed it to her cheek. 'Indeed I'm not a moonling, Grandmama!' she said, her voice quivering on the edge of laughter. 'I told you the truth, moreover! I *did* think that such a marriage would be preferable to remaining in Mount Street, and Denville never pretended that he felt any warmer affection for me than I felt for him! As for being *nutty* upon me, he never was, and never will be! Which I am heartily glad of, dear ma'am, because *I* tumbled quite – quite *desperately* in love with his brother, and *he* is the man I am going to marry, whatever you, or Papa, or anyone may say!'

The Dowager's claw-like hand closed on hers like a vice. '*What?*' she demanded. 'Denville's *brother?*'

Cressy raised glowing eyes to hers. 'His brother, Grandmama. You have never met Denville. Kit is so like him that even I was deceived at first! But there is no comparison! I – I *felt* the difference when he came to Mount Street in Denville's place, to meet you; and that was why I was willing to come here with you!' She drew the Dowager's twisted hand to her mouth, and kissed it. 'You will perceive the difference, because you're so wise, ma'am, and so discerning! Oh, I can't tell you how happy it makes me to know that you think so well of Kit!'

'You're out!' interrupted the Dowager harshly, snatching her hand away. 'Jackanapes!' she uttered, her jaws working. 'So he's been making a May game of me, has he? A more impudent imposture I never heard of, not in all my days!'

Cressy smiled lovingly at her. 'You will discover him to

be in perfect agreement with you, ma'am, for that is precisely what he thinks. He entered into it against his will, and would have escaped from it had *you* not proposed this visit to Lady Denville! I must try to make you understand the circumstances – the bond that exists between him and Denville! But I am much inclined to think that no one who was not born a twin could wholly understand the – the strength of that bond!'

'What I understand, and without difficulty, is that he's a cozening rascal who knows just how to bring you round his finger, nickninny!' retorted the Dowager, in no way appeased.

'Well, he hasn't tried to do so, but I haven't the least doubt that he *could*!' admitted Cressy, unabashed. 'I have no more knowledge than you, Grandmama, of what it means to be a twin, but I collect that, if they are as close as Kit and Evelyn, each knows when the other is in trouble, or has suffered a physical injury; and neither would hesitate, no matter what the cost, to fly to the other's rescue. It seems,' she said slowly, knitting her brows, 'that they can't *help* but do so!'

'Does it indeed?' snorted the Dowager. 'Well, perhaps you'll explain to me, my girl, what trouble Denville was in which caused his brother to practise this abominable cheat!'

'Yes, indeed I will, ma'am!' Cressy said, with disarming readiness. She chuckled. 'It is quite fantastic, you know, but for my part I have never enjoyed anything more in my life! Only a Fancot *could* have embarked on such a crazy adventure – and only Kit could have carried it with such a high hand! *He* doesn't want for proper spunk, Grandmama!'

'Cut no wheedles for my benefit!' commanded the Dowager, 'A round tale is all I wish to hear!'

It was not quite a round tale which Cressy, disposing herself more comfortably at her knee, recounted; for it underwent certain expurgations; but it was true in all its essentials, and the Dowager listened to it in silence. It could not have been said that there was any relaxing in her countenance; but she appeared, several times, to be afflicted with a tic, which twitched the muscles in her cheek; and once, when Cressy, knowing her love of a salted story, ventured to describe the encounter with Mrs Alperton, she was seized by a choking fit, which, glaring at her granddaughter, she ascribed to asthma. But when the tale was told she declared that a more disgraceful one she had never heard, adding shrewdly: 'I notice that that pretty, silly gadabout whom you choose to call your dearest Godmama don't figure in it! Trying to put the change on me, ain't you? You may hang up your axe, Cressy! *I'm* not a pea-goose, and never was, so if you mean to tell me she wasn't at the back of it, spare your breath!'

'Why, of course she was, ma'am!' said Cressy, all wide-eyed innocence. 'It was her notion that Kit should take Evelyn's place just for that one evening, and to save his face! Surely I told you so?'

'Ay! You told me!' said the Dowager sardonically. 'What you *haven't* told me is why it was so mightily important to Denville to have the Trust wound up!'

'But can you wonder at it, Grandmama? Only think how irksome it must be to him!'

'Don't talk flummery to me, girl!' said the Dowager irascibly. 'I have it on the best of authority that his revenues don't bring him a penny less than £16000 a year, and Henry Brumby told me himself that his debts were paid out of the estate when his father died!' Her eyes narrowed. 'His mother's debts, eh? You needn't put yourself to the trouble of denying it! It's common knowledge she's been at a standstill these dozen years and more! Means to settle 'em, does he? Well, I don't think the worse of him for that, but what such a caper-witted, fly-away wastethrift has ever done to deserve so much devotion I shall never know, if I live to be a hundred!' Her crooked fingers worked amongst the folds of her silken skirt. Cressy said nothing; and after a moment or two, she brought her piercing gaze back to the girl's face. 'A pretty piece of business you've made of it, between you!' she said scathingly. 'Understand me, miss! I'll have no scandal attached to *our* name! Good God, it must be common knowledge by now that you stand upon the brink of an engagement to Denville! What do you imagine your father will have to say, when he learns of this?'

'He will await *your* decision, Grandmama,' Cressy answered calmly. 'You know that as surely as I do! I hope it may be in my favour – in Kit's favour! – because I love you both, and to marry without your approval couldn't but throw a cloud over my happiness.' She raised her eyes, giving the Dowager look for look. 'But in less than a twelve-month, ma'am, I shall come of age, and neither you nor Papa will have the power to prevent my marriage to Kit!'

'If,' said the Dowager, after a pregnant silence, '*I* had ever dared to speak so to *my* grandmother, I should have been soundly whipped, and confined to my bedchamber on bread-and-water for a sennight!'

The gravity vanished from Cressy's face. 'No, would you, ma'am? How *very* brave *your* parents must have been!'

'Hussy!' said the Dowager, putting up her hand to hide her quivering mouth. 'Don't think you can come over *me* with your impertinence! Pull the bell! I am out of all patience with you, and fagged to death as well! Look at the time! I should have been laid down on my bed half-an-hour ago! Not an hour left before I shall be obliged to rig myself out for dinner, and not a wink of sleep shall I get, thanks to you, you ungrateful, abandoned, unnatural baggage! Go away! And don't flatter yourself that you've won my support, because you haven't!'

Retiring discreetly from the presence, Cressy closed her eyes in momentary thankfulness, before running down the stairs in search of Mr Fancot. Admirably though she had concealed it, it had been with considerable trepidation that she had admitted the Dowager into the secret of the hoax practised upon her. The result of her disclosure had, so far, been more hopeful than she had allowed herself to expect. At no time had she indulged her fancy with the thought that her tyrannical grandparent would instantly bestow her blessing on a union which, besides being undeniably inferior to the one first submitted for her approval, bore all the signs of being attended by exactly the sort of scandalous on-dits which were most obnoxious to a high-bred dame of her age and generation; she had rather entertained a lively fear that the Dowager would fly into a towering rage, which might even impel her to sweep herself and her granddaughter off to Worthing that very day. She had certainly, and justifiably, taken a violent pet; but, to Cressy's experienced eye, no thought of proceeding to extremes had so much as crossed her mind. Even more significantly (and very much to Cressy's relief), she had not instantly summoned her hostess to account for her perfidy. Instead, and in a querulous voice which belonged to a vexed and bewildered old lady rather than to an infuriated despot, she had abused her erring granddaughter, not for having lent herself to a disgraceful hoax, but for having caused her to lose half-an-hour's sleep. Grandmama, thought Cressy shrewdly, wanted time for reflection; and that circumstance alone was enough to encourage optimism in the initiated. The battle was by no means won; Grandmama might yet prove hard to handle; but she had undoubtedly been amused by certain aspects of the outrageous story unfolded to her; and equally undoubtedly she had taken a strong fancy to Mr Christopher Fancot. In Cressy's judgement, all now depended upon that resourceful gentleman's ability to discover a discreet way of extricating himself and her from a situation which gave every promise of affording the ton matter for unlimited gossip and conjecture.

She ran him to earth in the library, but he was not alone.

Even as she spoke his name, she saw that Sir Bonamy was present, and she drew back, murmuring an apology.

Kit was standing with his hand on the back of a chair, confronting Sir Bonamy, seated on a sofa, his hands on his knees, and an expression of resignation on his countenance. Kit turned his head quickly, saying in rather an odd voice: 'Don't go, Cressy! Sir Bonamy knows the truth about us, and won't object, I believe, to my disclosing to you the – unexpected news which he has just broken to me.'

'No,' said Sir Bonamy, preparing to heave himself to his feet. 'No sense in objecting to it. Mark me if it ain't all over the county before the cat can lick her ear!'

'Pray don't get up, sir!' Cressy said, coming across the room to lay a restraining hand on his arm. 'What is this news? Don't keep me on tenterhooks, Kit! I c-can see that it is *good* news!'

Mr Fancot's eyes narrowed in sudden suspicion. He said in a measured tone: 'Sir Bonamy informs me that my mother has accepted an offer of marriage from him.'

'*No!*' cried Cressy. 'Is it so indeed? Oh, my dear sir, let me be the first to felicitate you!'

'Much obliged to you! Hardly know whether I'm on my head or my heels, but I don't need to tell you I'm the happiest man on earth! That,' said Sir Bonamy doggedly, 'goes without saying!'

'Of course it does! It must seem to you like a fairy story!'

'Ay, that's it! Sort of thing one never thought would happen to one. What I mean is,' he corrected himself hastily, 'something I'd ceased to hope for!'

Kit had been looking decidedly grim, but Cressy, stealing a glance at him, was relieved to see that his ready sense of humour had been roused by the dejected picture presented by his parent's successful suitor, softening the lines about his mouth, and bringing the laughter back into his eyes. But he said, with perfect gravity: 'You must find it hard to realize your good fortune, sir.'

'Yes, well, I do!' confessed Sir Bonamy. 'At my time of

life, you know, a thing like this takes some getting used to! Yes, and another thing! I can't but ask myself if your mother will be happy, married to me! Now, tell me, Kit! do you think she might regret it?'

'No,' said Kit. 'I am very much inclined to think, sir, that you will neither of you regret it.'

'Well, I must say, Kit, that's very handsome of you – very handsome indeed!' exclaimed Sir Bonamy, visibly astonished. 'There's no question of *my* regretting it, of course, but damme if I ever thought to hear you say such a thing to me! To tell you the truth, I thought you'd cut up pretty stiff!'

'I could hardly wish for a kinder or more indulgent husband for her!' Kit said, smiling. 'You'll cosset her to death!'

'Ay, so I will! But did you wish *any* man to marry her?'

'No, certainly not *any* man, but one who loved her, and could be trusted to take care of her, yes! What I do *not* wish is to see her setting up an establishment of her own – and getting her affairs into heaven only knows what sort of a tangle!'

'No, by God!' ejaculated Sir Bonamy. 'I hadn't thought of that, but you're very right, my boy! It wouldn't do at all! At least I shan't have *that* to worry about!'

'You won't have anything to worry about!' Cressy assured him. 'Will you think me very saucy if I say that never did a knight more thoroughly deserve to win his lady than you, dear sir?'

'No, no!' protested Sir Bonamy, much discomposed. 'Nonsense! Very obliging of you to say so, but no such thing! As a matter of fact, I'm a baronet.'

'To me,' said Cressy, avoiding Kit's eye, 'you have always seemed like a knight of ancient chivalry!'

'What, one of those fellows who careered all over, looking for dragons? Well, whatever put such a silly notion as that into your head, my dear girl? Rigged out in armour, too! Why, it makes me hot only to think of it! Not the style of thing I care for at all, I promise you!'

'Ah, you misunderstand me! It wasn't dragons I had in mind but your unswerving faithfulness to Godmama! You have been her sworn knight throughout the years!'

'Baronet,' interpolated Kit unsteadily.

'I've so often thought how lonely you must have been,' pursued Cressy, ignoring this frivolity. 'In that great house of yours, quite alone, and – as it must have seemed to you – with nothing to look forward to!'

'Very true! Except that one grows accustomed, you know, and I don't live in it *alone* precisely.'

'You have servants, of course, but what do they signify? So very little!'

Sir Bonamy, who employed an enormous staff which included three cooks wholly indispensable to his comfort, thought that they signified a great deal, but refrained from saying so.

'But now how different it will be!'

'I know it will,' he agreed, with a deep sigh.

'And, oh, how you will be envied!' she said, hastily changing her note. 'They will be ready to murder you, all Godmama's disappointed suitors! I can't but laugh when I picture to myself the chagrin of certain of their number when you walk off with her from under their noses!'

It was plain that this aspect had not previously occurred to him. He considered it, puffing out his cheeks a little, as he always did when anything pleased him. 'Yes, by Jupiter!' he said. 'They *will* be ready to murder me! The loveliest, most sought-after woman in the ton, and she chose me! A triumph that, eh? Lord, I'd give a monkey to see Louth's face when he reads the advertisement! *He'll* be ready to murder me, if you like!' A less agreeable thought occurred to him: he said gloomily: 'Yes, and I know of someone else who'll be fit to cut my liver out, and that's young Denville! I was forgetting him. Kit, if this marriage was to cause a breach between him and your mother, she'd break her heart, and I'd give her up sooner than do that!'

'Don't worry, sir: it won't!' Kit replied. 'I can't promise that Evelyn will take very readily to the marriage, but never fear! he'll come round, and under no circumstances would he become estranged from Mama. That you may depend on!'

'I dare say you know best,' said Sir Bonamy, accepting his fate. He rose ponderously to his feet. 'Time I went up to change my dress!'

'We don't change this evening, sir: General Oakenshaw drove over an hour ago to pay his respects to my mother, and she has persuaded him to remain to dine here.'

'You don't mean it! Why, I thought that old spider-shanks had gone to roost years ago!' exclaimed Sir Bonamy. 'Well, well, what a day this has been! One surprise after another! I won't put on my evening rig, but I must change my coat, and I don't know but what I won't take a little rest before dinner, just to pluck me up, you know!'

'And perhaps a cordial?' suggested Kit.

'No, no, I don't want a cordial! The thing is that I've had a lot of excitement today, which I ain't accustomed to, and I feel a trifle fagged! A short nap will set me to rights again!'

'As you wish, sir,' said Kit, holding open the door for him, and bowing him out of the room.

Shutting it again, he turned to find that Cressy had collapsed into a chair, in fits of laughter. She uttered, between gusts: 'Oh, Kit! Oh, Kit! I thought I should die! *Poor* Sir Bonamy!'

'You and your knights!' he said.

That sent her into a fresh paroxysm. 'Baronets!' she wailed. 'Wretch that you are! That was nearly my undoing! Oh, don't make me laugh any more! It positively *hurts*!' She mopped her eyes. 'But it *will* be a happy marriage, won't it? When he has accustomed himself to the idea?'

'I should think it might well be, if he can be brought up to the scratch. What I want to know, my love, is whether this was one of Mama's nacky notions, or yours? Out with it, now!'

'Kit, how can you suppose that I would venture to suggest to Godmama that she should marry Sir Bonamy, or anyone else?'

'I don't. But I strongly suspect that it was you who put the idea into her head! Well?'

Her mirth ceased. 'Not quite that. I own, however, that it did spring from something I said, and that I hoped it might. Are you vexed with me?'

'I don't know. No, of course I'm not, but – Cressy, is she doing this for Evelyn's sake?'

'Not entirely. I think for her own as much as his. I can't tell you what passed between us, for what she said to me was in confidence. I will only tell you that I found her in great distress, and discovered that she meant to – oh, to make a perfectly dreadful sacrifice for Evelyn! – and that when I left her she was wearing her *mischief-look*! Kit, I do most sincerely believe that she *will* be happy! She is very fond of Sir Bonamy, you know, and always on *comfortable* terms with him! And above all she must not live alone! You yourself said so. You had her quite incurable extravagance in mind, but what has been very much in my mind is my conviction that she would be miserably unhappy.'

'Yes, I feel that too. But what of Ripple? You wouldn't describe him as radiant, would you?'

She laughed. 'Well, perhaps not *radiant*, precisely! Now don't set me off again, I implore you! The thing is that he has been perfectly content with his lot for years, and has suddenly realized – I *think*! – that he doesn't in the least wish to change it! It must have been a great shock to him, but he will very soon become reconciled to the idea, for he does dote on her, you know! He will be very proud of her, too, and positively *revel* in squandering enormous sums on her. Oh, dear, look at the time! I must go, or I shall be late for dinner! Kit, who is this General Godmama has invited to dine with us? I wish she had not, for there is something else I must tell you. I have broken it to Grandmama that you are not Denville.'

'Good God! You have been busy, haven't you? I thought it was agreed that that should be left to me to do?'

She shook her head. 'Believe me, Kit, it wouldn't have answered!'

He lifted an eyebrow at her. 'Wouldn't it? Am I to understand that *your* efforts have been crowned by success?'

'Well, I don't know – and I must own that nothing could be more unfortunate than this General!' she said seriously. 'It is bound to put her out of temper, to be obliged to keep her tongue between her teeth all the evening, for you may depend upon it she will have decided just how she means to rattle you down. However, there's no denying that she has a pronounced tendre for you, and I am very hopeful that if you can but hit upon a scheme to bring us all off from this mingle-mangle without anyone's knowing what *really* happened she will be very much inclined to relent.'

'I should think she might well!'

She looked inquiringly at him. 'I must own that it seems very difficult to me, but I wondered if you have *already* some such scheme in your mind? *Have* you?'

'Frankly, my loved one, no!'

'Oh!' she said, slightly dashed. 'I must admit that it has *me* at a standstill, but I did think that perhaps *you* might have discovered just how to do the trick neatly!'

'I can see you did,' he replied, regarding her in rueful amusement. 'Believe me, adorable, it is only with the *utmost* reluctance that I shatter an illusion so flattering to myself! But, sooner or later, the truth will out! Better, I dare say, to make a clean breast of it immediately! Cressy, my darling, if your mind is set on becoming the wife of a brilliant diplomatist, cry off at once! For I must confess to you that I too am wholly at a standstill!'

Her gravity melted into laughter. 'Oh, Kit, you *detestable* creature! How dare you think me such a widgeon as to cherish *illusions*? I *know* that you'll do the trick!'

Mr Fancot, having dealt suitably with this moving declaration of his loved one's faith in his superior intellect, said affably, still holding her in his arms: 'To be sure I shall! After all, I have twenty minutes to consider the problem before we sit down to dinner, haven't I? As for the task of breaking the news of Mama's approaching nuptials to Eve – not to mention cajoling him into accepting it with at least the *semblance* of complaisance! – twenty *seconds,* I dare say, will be time enough for me!'

Miss Stavely, a gurgle of laughter in her throat, but blatant adoration in her eyes, said: 'More than enough – my darling, my *darling*!'

21

Dinner at Ravenhurst, that evening, was not destined to be ranked amongst Lady Denville's more successful parties. She, indeed, deriving consolation from the reflection that no one for whose opinion she cared a rush would ever know anything about it, sparkled with all her usual brilliance; but her harassed son showed signs of preoccupation; Miss Stavely was in a quake; the Dowager, too long-headed to denounce, in the presence of a stranger, the irreclaimable hedge-bird seated beside her, at the head of the table, was understandably filled with a thwarted rage which caused her to snap the nose off anyone so unwise as to address her; and General Oakenshaw was revolted by the discovery that his ancient rival (whom he variously stigmatized as a chawbacon, a bag-pudding, a ludicrously fat Bartholomew baby, and a contemptible barber's block) was not only an honoured guest at Ravenhurst, but was apparently on terms of the most regrettable intimacy with his hostess.

The only person, in fact, who enjoyed the party was Sir Bonamy Ripple.

He had joined the rest of the company without the smallest expectation of enjoyment. The recuperative nap to which he had pinned his faith had been denied him: he had been unable to close his eyes; and he arose from his uneasy couch feeling as blue as megrim, and much inclined to suspect that he had received notice to quit. But when he entered the saloon in which the remaining members of the party were gathered his sinking spirits revived. Lady Denville, ravishingly beautiful in a golden satin gown, came towards him, bewitching him with her lovely smile, and murmuring, as she held out her hands to him: 'Bonamy, my dear!'

'Amabel!' he breathed. 'Well, upon my word! Exquisite, my pretty! *Exquisite!*'

'Truly? Then I'm satisfied! No one is a better judge than you of what becomes me!'

He was so much overcome by this tribute that words failed him, and he was obliged to content himself with kissing both her hands. Straightening himself from a bow which caused his Cumberland corset to creak ominously, he became aware of General Oakenshaw, and realized, with immense satisfaction, that that distinguished gentleman was observing this passage with blatant revulsion. From that moment his subsequent enjoyment of the evening was assured. Raising his quizzing-glass to his eye, he ejaculated: 'God bless my soul! *Oakenshaw!*' Then allowing his quizzing-glass to fall, he surged forward, holding out his hand and saying, with an apologetic air which deceived no one: 'My dear sir! You must forgive me for not immediately recognizing you! But when one begins to grow old, you know, one's memory fails! How many years is it since I last had the pleasure of shaking your hand? Ah, well! best not inquire too closely into *that,* eh?'

'*My* memory has not failed!' countered the General. 'I recognized you the instant you came into the room! Still as fat as a flawn, I perceive!'

'No, no, my dear old friend!' said Sir Bonamy, with unabated joviality. 'It is like your kind heart to say so, but I am *much* fatter than that! But you haven't changed a jot! Now I look at you more closely I see that you are still the same old – *what* was it they used to call you? Sheep-biter! No, no, what am I thinking of? *That* wasn't it! Spidershanks! Ay, how could I have forgotten? *Spider-shanks!*'

This interchange, while it wonderfully refreshed Sir Bonamy, afforded no pleasure at all to anyone else, with the possible exception of the Dowager. She, indeed, uttered a sharp crack of laughter, but whether this arose from amusement, or from an unamiable wish to vent her spleen on someone, whether she was acquainted with him, or (as happened to be the case) had never met him before in her life, was doubtful.

By the time dinner came to an end, even Lady Denville, whose delightful insouciance had been maintained, without apparent effort, throughout the meal, felt that the sooner her courtly but ancient admirer took his departure the better it would be for everyone; and she issued a softly spoken direction to Norton to bring in the tea-tray not a moment later than half-past eight. Since Cressy had been unable to warn her that the Dowager was in possession of her guilty secret, she was unprepared to meet the attack mounted against her by that formidable octogenarian the instant the door of the Long Drawing-room had been shut, and made no attempt to defend herself. All she did was to bow her shining head before the storm, saying wretchedly: 'I know, I know, but *indeed* I never meant to cause so much trouble! It was my fault – all of it! Say what you like to me, ma'am, but pray, *pray* don't lay the blame at poor Kit's door!'

In the event, this spiritless behaviour stood her in excellent stead, as Cressy, on the brink of picking up the cudgels in her defence, providentially realized. The Dowager said crossly: 'For heaven's sake, don't start to cry, Amabel! You're a pea-goose, and always were, and that's all there is to it! As for your precious Kit, you may leave him to fight his own battles! He has enough effrontery for anything!'

From this, Cressy, who had been doing her best to entertain the General when the Dowager exchanged a brief but pungent discourse with Mr Fancot during the course of dinner, deduced, thankfully, that he had not sunk beyond recall in her grandmother's opinion.

'I have something to say to you, young man!' had said the Dowager, in a voice which was not less intimidating for being discreetly lowered.

'I know it, ma'am,' he had responded. 'I only wish that I could think of anything more to say to you than *Forgive me!* but I can't.'

'I collect,' she said, glaring at him, 'that you fancy you have only to smile at me to bring me round your thumb!'

'Indeed I don't!' he replied, looking startled.

'Just as well! Next you'll have the audacity to say you regret your conduct!'

'No, no, ma'am! You are far too much up to snuff to swallow such a plumper as that! How *could* I regret it?'

'For two pins,' she informed him, 'I'd box your ears, Master Jack-sauce!'

That was the sum of their interchange. There was nothing in the scathing glance the Dowager cast at Mr Fancot to encourage him to suppose that she was at all mollified; but when the gentlemen later entered the Long Drawing-room it was noticeable that there was a hint of softening in her eyes, when they rested on the reprobate's well-formed person.

The General showed no disposition to outstay his welcome. Pleading a fifteen-mile drive, he took his leave as soon as he had drunk one cup of tea. Kit escorted him downstairs to his waiting carriage, and was just about to tell

Norton to send Fimber to him when he perceived that that faithful, if censorious, henchman was standing on the half-landing, where the graceful staircase branched to left and right. 'Good! I want you!' he said, treading swiftly up the stairs, and grasping Fimber by the arm. 'Fimber, I must have a word with my brother!' he said, under his breath. 'I told him ten o'clock, but her ladyship ordered tea to be brought in earlier, and the coast should be clear in a very few minutes. Go down to the cottage, will you, and bring his lordship up to my room!'

'His lordship, Mr Christopher,' said Fimber, 'as I was about to tell you, is already in your room – or, as I should say, his *own* room.' Having delivered himself of this reproof, he unbent, saying confidentially: 'Which was imprudent, sir, as I told him, but can you wonder at it, knowing what he is, and the way Mrs Pinner frets him to fiddlestrings, carrying on as if he was in short coats, and scolding as I am sure *I* should think it very improper to do!'

'Well, that's a new come-out!' retorted Kit. 'Let me know when Norton has taken away the tea-tray, you old humbug!'

He found his twin moodily flicking over the pages of the latest number of the Gentleman's Magazine. Evelyn looked up quickly, his frown changing to a smile. 'Now, don't scold, Kester! I've had enough of that from Fimber! Talk of jobations! But when it came to a glass of hot milk before being tucked up in bed at eight o'clock there was nothing for it but to escape from Pinny!' He rose, and began to pace restlessly about the room. 'I've thought till my brain reels, Kester, but it's hopeless!'

'Oh, no, it isn't!' replied Kit. 'Something has happened which entirely alters the situation. Tell me one thing, Eve! If you were not faced with the burden of our treasured parent's debts, and were free to marry Miss Askham, would you be prepared to endure the Trust until such time as it may take you to convince my uncle that you are very well able to manage your own affairs?'

'Yes, I dare say, but since I *am* faced with that burden –'

'No, you're not, brother!' interrupted Kit.

'Oh, am I not?' said Evelyn, a flash in his eyes. 'I have already told you, Kester, that I will not, under any circumstances whatsoever, permit you to saddle a responsibility which is mine, and mine only!'

'I'm not going to saddle it, so come down from your high ropes! Now, listen, Eve! I have some news for you which I know very well you won't like, but which you must stomach. Mama has accepted an offer of marriage from Ripple.'

'*What?*' Evelyn exclaimed thunderously. 'It isn't possible!'

'You'd have been even more incredulous had you been present when he made the announcement to me. Lord, Eve, I wish you *had* been present! He couldn't have been cast into greater gloom if he had received a death sentence! My own view of the matter is that it wasn't he who made the offer, but Mama.'

'Oh, my God, no!' Evelyn said, shuddering. 'How *could* she do such a thing? How can *you*, Kester, think that I would let her make such a sacrifice? Just what sort of a contemptible skirter do you believe me to be? Don't spare me!'

'I shan't, if you don't stop behaving like a Tragedy Jack!' replied Kit. 'For God's sake, twin, take a damper! I didn't relish the notion either, but it will do, you know. I haven't lived with Mama for as long as you have, but for long enough to realize that she's no more fitted to live alone than a babe unborn! I know you think she'll continue to live with you, but you may take it from me that she won't. Well, what do you imagine will be the outcome, if she sets up an establishment of her own?'

'I know, I know, Kester, but –'

'I should rather think you might! Now consider what her life will be, if she marries Ripple!'

Their eyes met, and held, across the space that lay

between them, Evelyn's holding an arrested look, Kit's very steady. It was he who broke the silence. 'We always thought him a bobbing-block, didn't we, Eve? Well, so he is, but he's been a pretty firm friend to Mama! He isn't *in love* with her now, but Cressy's right when she says that he dotes on her. There's very little he wouldn't do for her, and the more she wastes the ready the better pleased he'll be! Furthermore, twin, he'll take better care of her than ever you or I could! I fancy that such loose fish as Louth will be speedily put to rout!'

There was a long silence. 'If I thought that she would be happy – Oh, no, Kester, no! She's doing it to smooth my path, and for no other reason!'

'Yes, I think she is,' agreed Kit imperturbably. 'But if you imagine that she's sacrificing herself, you're fair and far off! It's Ripple who is the sacrifice: Mama's in high gig! I tell you, in all seriousness, Eve, that if you drive a spoke into this wheel you'll be doing her the worst turn you could!'

'Kester, you *know* I wouldn't –!' He broke off, as the door opened, and Fimber entered the room, and said impatiently: 'Yes, what is it?'

'The tea-tray has been removed, sir,' said Fimber, addressing himself pointedly to Kit. 'I have taken it upon myself to instruct Norton – informing him that such was your desire, Mr Christopher – to set out the brandy in the library. He will have no occasion, therefore, to enter the Long Drawing-room again this evening. I should perhaps add that, according to what he tells me, Lady Stavely has not yet retired, but is playing piquet with Sir Bonamy. I shall hold myself in readiness to accompany his lordship to Mrs Pinner's cottage in due course.'

'That,' said Evelyn bitterly, as Fimber withdrew, 'is what I have to endure! What now, Kester?'

'Now,' said Kit, 'you are going to meet Lady Stavely, God help you! You are also going to felicitate poor old Ripple; and finally you are going to try and discover a way out of this scrape which will *not* set the ton by the ears!'

'There isn't one!'

'There *must* be one!' said Kit firmly. 'My life's happiness depends upon it!'

'Then you find it!' recommended Evelyn. '*I'm* not the clever twin! Kester, what's the old lady like? How do I deal with her?'

'Boldly! She's a tartar!'

'Lord, I wish I'd never come home!' said Evelyn. 'Don't you dare to abandon me! I'm all of a twitter already!'

'Courage, brother!' said Kit, opening the door into the Long Drawing-room.

They entered the room together, and paused for a moment on the threshold. The Dowager, who had just picked up the cards dealt her by Sir Bonamy, laid them down again, staring at the twins in astonishment. She did not speak, but the sudden gleam in her eyes informed her granddaughter that she was not unappreciative of the picture quite unconsciously presented by the Fancot twins.

Apart, they were held to be very fine young men; together, with the candlelight glinting on their burnished heads, they were so striking that the Dowager, like many before her, was dazzled into thinking them the most handsome men she had ever beheld.

'Evelyn, my dear one!' exclaimed Lady Denville, springing up from the sofa, and going towards him with her light, graceful step, and her hands held out in welcome.

He took one in his own left hand, and kissed it, murmuring wickedly: 'You *are* smart tonight, love! Dressed like Christmas beef!'

She chuckled, and would have led him forward, but he put her gently aside, and advanced down the room alone, to where the Dowager sat. If he was in a quake, no trace of it was apparent in his bearing. He bowed, and with a smile quite as disarming as Kit's, said: 'I owe you an apology, Lady Stavely. But *indeed* I couldn't help it!'

In spite of herself, her lips twitched, and she put out her hand. 'So you are Denville, are you?' she said. 'H'm!

You'd better beg my granddaughter's pardon, young man!'

'Why, yes!' he agreed, his mother's mischievous look in his eyes; and turned towards Cressy, holding out his hand. 'So I do, Cressy – but you are very well rid of me, you know!' She had risen to her feet, and as she laughed, giving him her hand, he kissed it, and then her cheek, saying: 'I wish you every happiness, my dear!'

'Thank you! May I return that wish?' she said demurely.

The smile in his eyes acknowledged the sly allusion, but he replied audaciously: 'Indeed, I am excessively happy to have you for a sister!' He turned his head. 'Kester!'

Kit strolled forward, but his eyes were on Cressy, warmly appreciative. Evelyn said: 'If I have any right to this hand, may I bestow it on my brother, Miss Stavely? He is much more worthy of it than I am – but that I needn't tell you!'

'Thank you, twin, that will do!' said Kit, receiving the hand, and clasping it strongly.

Evelyn laughed, and turned away to confront Sir Bonamy. He looked down at him, laughter dying, and his smile a little rigid. 'Kit tells me, sir, that I must offer you my felicitations.'

Sir Bonamy, regarding him with all the wariness of one faced with a cobra, said: 'Yes, yes! Very much obliged to you, Denville! That is – if you have no objection!'

'Eh?' exclaimed the Dowager. She looked sharply from Sir Bonamy to Lady Denville. 'So *that's* it, is it? Upon my word!'

'Yes, ma'am,' corroborated Lady Denville sunnily. 'That's it! Sir Bonamy has done me the honour to ask me to marry him, and I have accepted his offer.'

'You have, have you? Well,' said the Dowager trenchantly, 'if that's so, it's the only sensible thing I've ever known you do, Amabel!'

Sir Bonamy, paying no heed to this, seized the opportunity to say, in an urgent undervoice: 'Not if you dislike it, Denville! Naturally, it's the dearest wish of *my* heart, but no need for you to take snuff! Only have to tell me! For I wouldn't come between you and your mother for the world!'

Over his hapless head the twins' eyes met for an instant of unholy joy. No more than Kit could Evelyn resist the appeal of the ludicrous; the rigidity melted from his smile; he produced his snuff-box from his pocket, unfobbed it with an expert flick, and offered it to Sir Bonamy, saying: 'Take snuff? Yes, indeed! Will you try my sort, sir?'

'Well, that isn't precisely what I meant, but – thank you, my boy! I've often wondered what your mixture is – a touch of old Havre, I fancy, and a suspicion – no more – of French Prize, added, of course, to –'

'Just so, sir – and you will not find it *dry*!'

Sir Bonamy, helping himself to a pinch, was shaken by one of his rumbling laughs. 'Ah, that was where I was a trifle too knowing for Kit! Told you about it, did he? He hasn't your deft way of opening his box, either!'

'Oh, he will never acquire that!' said Evelyn. 'His taste is for cigars!'

'*No!*' uttered Sir Bonamy, profoundly shocked.

The Dowager broke in impatiently on this digression. 'Now, listen to me,' she commanded, driving her cane into the carpet with an imperative thud. 'Very pretty talking, all of this, but if you think – any of you! – that I'll give *my* consent to this havey-cavey business you very much mistake the matter!'

'But, Grandmama!' interposed Cressy, releasing Kit's hand, and sitting down beside the Dowager. 'You told me more than once that you liked Kit! Why, this very day you said that he was *a very proper man*, and were ready to eat me for seeming to be unwilling to accept his offer! You said I was no better than a moonling!'

'Hold your tongue, girl! I'll have you know that there has never been any scandal attached to the Stavelys, and I'll have no hand in helping you to create one! A fine piece of work this is!'

'Well, of course, it *is* a little awkward,' agreed Lady Denville, 'but I dare say it will soon be forgotten!'

'That,' said the Dowager witheringly, 'is an observation only worthy of such a jingle-brain as you are, Amabel!'

A flush rose to Evelyn's lean cheeks; but before he could speak Sir Bonamy forestalled him. 'Perfectly true!' he pronounced, fixing the Dowager with his round-eyed stare. '*I* never knew a scandal that wasn't precious soon ousted by another! What's more,' he added, pointing a stubby finger at her, and wagging it, 'if it hadn't been for that dashed silly notice in the *Morning Post* there ain't a soul worth a rush who would have known anything about this affair!'

'Yes!' Evelyn struck in. 'Who was responsible for that notice? Not you, Mama!'

'No, indeed!' Lady Denville replied indignantly. 'I may be jingle-brained but *never* have I been guilty of *vulgarity*!'

'No one said you had!' said the Dowager testily, and for once in her life disconcerted. 'We all know it was Albinia who was responsible for that! Not that it's proved against her, mind, but *I'm* not one to blink what's as plain as the nose on your face! It was her doing, no question about it! I wrote instantly to tell her that I knew it, and not one word has she dared set down on paper in reply! And if she thinks that because she has given Stavely an heir she'll hear no more of the business she will very soon learn her mistake! *But*,' pursued the old lady, making a gallant recovery, 'I'll thank you all to remember that pretty well every member of the family believes that it was *you*, Denville, whom they was invited to meet in my son's house, and *you* who had made her an offer!'

'What of that?' demanded Sir Bonamy, continuing to fret the Dowager with his unnervingly blank stare. 'It ain't to be supposed *they'll* spread it about that they was hoaxed! They'll do what you bid 'em, my lady!'

'Not all of them!' replied the Dowager unexpectedly. 'Stavely saw fit to gather his relations together stock and block, and there were several sprigs there I never saw before in my life, and don't wish to see again!'

'That's *very* true!' said Lady Denville. 'Only think of that tiresome young man who pestered Kit to buy a horse which I *know* poor Evelyn doesn't want to own!'

'Lucton!' ejaculated Evelyn. 'Kester, you didn't?'

Kit, who had seated himself a little apart from the rest of the group, replied briefly: 'Nothing else I could do.'

'Gudgeon!' said Evelyn. 'An abominable screw! Why didn't you consult Challow?'

He won no answer at all to this inquiry, Kit having relapsed into frowning abstraction. He took no part in the lively discussion that followed, although once or twice he showed that he was not wholly deaf to it by raising his eyes from contemplation of his own clasped hands to glance thoughtfully at one or other of the disputants. If the Dowager was brought to own that, despite his perfidy, she would be very well pleased to see her granddaughter married to Kit, only that hitherto pattern of superior sense and propriety herself maintained, in what the Dowager did not scruple to inform her was an unbecomingly highty-tighty manner, her unshakeable indifference to public opinion. Lady Denville was fully alive to the necessity of concealing (by unexplained means) the true facts of the case from the world; Evelyn, knowing that these could only be extremely prejudicial, if not fatal, to his twin's career, came down heavily on the Dowager's side; and threw Sir Bonamy into disorder by demanding whether he, an experienced exponent of the established mode, was sincere in declaring that no one would think anything more of the hoax than that it was a very good joke.

'But it's something you have frequently done before!' urged Cressy. 'Would people be so very much shocked?'

'I should hope they would be!' replied Evelyn tartly. 'Good God, Cressy, I'd a better opinion of your understanding! Of course we have done it before, but only for the sport of it! That was one thing: this is quite another!'

'Oh, dear, that is *exactly* what Kit said!' exclaimed Lady Denville guiltily. 'I ought never to have asked him to do it! It is all my wretched fault – only I was *fully* persuaded that *you* would have done the same thing for *him*!'

The swift change in his expression betrayed the difference that lay between his own mercurial temperament and Kit's more evenly balanced one. The frown of fretting anxiety vanished; a zestful gleam, compound of recklessness and amusement, heightened the brilliance of his eyes; he burst out laughing. 'You were right, love!' he told his mother. 'I would! In a crack!' He threw a challenging look at the Dowager. 'You might as well blame my brother for drawing breath as for coming to my rescue, ma'am: he couldn't help himself! Nor could I! But *he*, if I know him, took my place that evening only for that reason, and with extreme reluctance; whereas *I*, standing in his shoes, should have had no reluctance whatsoever! I don't know that I should have carried it off as well as he must have done, but I should certainly have enjoyed the fling, which he, even more certainly, did *not*!'

'No doubt!' she retorted. 'It didn't need your uncle Brumby to tell me that your brother's worth a dozen of you, young man!'

'Oh, anyone could have told you that, ma'am!' he said cheerfully. 'Indeed, I know of only two persons who would deny so obvious a truth: Kester himself, and my mother – who considers us *both* to be above criticism! Well, we are not, but you may believe, Lady Stavely, that neither he nor I would have entered into this particular hoax had we known that it would ever become known, or that we should be obliged to maintain the imposture! My brother presented himself to you that evening in the belief that either I had forgotten the date of the engagement, or had been delayed by some hitch, or accident, and must surely reappear at any moment. In fact, I had suffered an accident which knocked me senseless for days. When I did recover consciousness, and realized that the date of my engagement was past, I thought I must have ruined myself, and – to own the truth! – I was too pulled and battered to care! Had I known that my brother was in England, and desperately trying to save my face – but I didn't know it, until I saw the notice in the newspaper! By that time he had not only been forced to keep up the pretence – which, once having entered into, he couldn't abandon without, as he believed, serving me the worst possible turn – but he had fallen in love with Cressy, and she with him. But what I wish you will understand, ma'am, is that at the outset he had no other thought than to save my face!'

'And mine!' Cressy interpolated. 'That thought also was in his mind, and in Godmama's mind too, and whatever the outcome I should have been grateful to them for sparing me the humiliation I must have suffered had he *not* presented himself in your stead that evening!'

'Very noble!' said the Dowager. She added, in the querulous tone of a very old lady rapidly approaching exhaustion: 'I don't want to hear any more of your glib-tongued pittle-pattle! Find a way out of this abominable scrape that won't set every tongue wagging, and Cressy may marry your brother with my goodwill! And that's my last word!'

'Well, if that's so, a way *must* be found!' said Evelyn. 'But the only way *I* can see is for Kester to continue to be me, and for me to be him!'

The Dowager threw him a contemptuous glance; Cressy laughed; and Sir Bonamy paid no heed. But Lady Denville said earnestly: 'No, no, dearest, that would *never* do! Only think how awkward it would be for you in Vienna, trying to make everyone believe you were Kit, when I dare say you don't know *anything* about foreign affairs, or even who anyone *is*!'

'For heaven's sake, don't be such a widgeon!' snapped the Dowager, quite exasperated. 'And if you can think of nothing better to do in this pass, Denville, than to cut silly jokes –'

'Not at all!' said Evelyn incorrigibly. 'Kester could perform his part without the least difficulty, but Mama is far from being a widgeon! She has detected, in a flash, the flaw in my scheme! I had never the least turn for politics –'

'Or I,' interposed Kit, getting up, 'for the management of estates!' He came forward, and said, addressing himself to the Dowager: 'May I make a suggestion, ma'am? I know how tired you must be, but – but I think it just possible that there *is* a way out of the tangle.'

'*Ah!*' breathed Cressy, raising her eyes to his in a glowing look of confidence. 'I knew you would find it – oh, I *knew* it, my dearest dear!'

22

'Well, it's to be hoped he has!' said the Dowager irascibly.

'But of course he has!' said Evelyn, shocked by her evident want of faith in his twin's ingenuity. 'Go on, Kester! Tell us!'

Kit could not help laughing, but he coloured a little, and said: 'I will, but I'm afraid the scheme I have in mind is pretty make-shift. I *think* it covers all the difficulties, but I may have left something out of account: the devil of it is there are so many of them!' He glanced round the circle. 'Well – it seems to me that the most urgent need is to restore Evelyn to his rightful position. That can't be accomplished here, but I see no reason for him to bury himself in Leicestershire: he need go no further than to Hill Street. Brigg won't suspect anything, for he's a great deal too shortsighted; and I fancy Dinting won't either, because I took good care to keep out of her way when I was in Hill Street myself.'

'What about my shoulder?' interrupted Evelyn.

'How are the London servants to know when, or how,

you broke it? They *do* know here, so you'll overturn that phaeton of yours tomorrow, on your way to London – which will account for your arrival in a hired chaise.'

'Now, hold a minute, Kester!' said Evelyn. 'What the devil should I be doing, jauntering up to London, when I'm known to be entertaining guests here? Dash it, even my uncle wouldn't believe I was as freakish as that!'

'You are going up to London to meet *me*, twin. I shall send Challow to fetch the letters from the receiving-office tomorrow, and he will bring me a packet-letter from myself. Whereupon Mama will be cast into transports, and I – faithfully imitating your well-known impetuosity, Eve! – shall set out for London in your curricle, taking Challow with me, and picking you up at Pinny's cottage. There you'll take his place – and we'll hope to God we can get to East Grinstead without anyone's recognizing you!'

'I'll keep my hat over my eyes, and wind a muffler round my chin,' promised Evelyn. 'What's the significance of East Grinstead?'

'Well, you don't ever stop for a change there, do you?'

'What, a bare six or seven miles from here? No, of course I don't!'

'So however well they may know you at the toll-gate, they *don't* know you at the posting-houses. I propose to leave the curricle at one of them, and to accomplish the rest of the journey in a job-chaise. Challow will have to walk to East Grinstead as soon as it begins to get dark, and drive the curricle up to London tomorrow. Fimber will follow us, with your baggage: no difficulty about that! I must remember to ask him where he deposited my own baggage, by the bye. You'll set me down, when we get to London, and arrive in solitary state in Hill Street, where, in due course, I also shall arrive – in a hack, having, for some inscrutable reason, journeyed up from the coast on the stage-coach.'

'Not the stage: the Mail!' interrupted Cressy.

'Yes, that's much better!' Kit agreed. 'Thank you, love!'

'And then?' she asked.

'I must see your father, and disclose the truth to him. If I can persuade him to pardon the deception, and to give his consent to our marriage, I think I can contrive to turn the affair into an unexceptionable romance. If not –' He stopped, and said, after a moment: 'I don't know, Cressy, and can't bring myself to face that possibility!'

'Well, that don't signify!' said the Dowager, who had been listening to him intently. 'He'll consent fast enough when he learns that *I* do!'

'May I tell him that, ma'am?'

'I said you might marry Cressy with my goodwill, if you could find a way out of this scrape without setting tongues wagging, and I'm a woman of my word! How do you mean to do it?'

He smiled. 'I don't ma'am: it would be a task quite beyond my capability!'

'Beyond anyone's, my boy,' said Sir Bonamy. 'There's bound to be a deal of talk: no getting away from that!'

'None at all, sir. The only thing to be done is to sell the world a bargain! – I beg your pardon, ma'am! – to publish a Banbury story, which the tattle-boxes may discuss to their hearts' content without doing any of us an ounce of harm.'

'Another of your hoaxes, eh? I thought as much!' said the Dowager, eyeing him with a certain grim respect.

'The last one, I promise you!' he said. 'And only with your approval, ma'am!'

'You've as much effrontery as your brother!' she told him. 'Out with it!'

'Yes, ma'am! Little though any of you may know it, my love for Cressy is of long standing. I met her when I was last in England, and formed an enduring passion for her, which, however, I – er – kept locked in my breast!'

'Why?' demanded Cressy, blinking in bewilderment.

'I knew my case to be hopeless. Your father would not have entertained my suit, nor did I feel that my circumstances were such as would enable me to support you in the style to which you were accustomed.'

'You *were* modest, weren't you?' said Evelyn.

'Certainly I was! Noble, too, don't you think?'

'No,' replied Evelyn frankly. 'Buffleheaded!'

'Dear one, Evelyn is perfectly right!' said Lady Denville. 'You couldn't have been such a goose! Depend upon it, everyone must know that you came into a comfortable fortune when your father died!'

'Let the boy alone!' commanded the Dowager. '*Stavely* thought it not large enough: I'll attend to *that*! Go on!'

'I'm much obliged to you, ma'am! Well, I withdrew, never dreaming that my passion was reciprocated, and that I was dashing Cressy's hopes to the ground.'

'Oh, Kit, no!' Cressy uttered imploringly. 'Don't tell me I hadn't the wit to throw out even *one* lure!'

'No, no!' he assured her. 'You had too much maidenly reserve to do so! And far too much pride to let anyone suspect your secret. You resolutely thrust me out of your mind.'

'No, I didn't: I wondered if Evelyn wouldn't suit me just as well. After all, he's as like you as he can stare!'

'That's an even better notion,' said Kit approvingly. 'We now arrive at the point where we stand on unassailable ground. My godfather died, leaving his entire fortune to me. I built the whole story round that circumstance, because it is precisely what *did* happen! Naturally, this altered the complexion of the affair. I came home, full of hope, to find you on the brink of becoming betrothed to my brother. We met, our feelings were too strong to be mastered, and either Evelyn discovered us locked in a fond embrace, or we disclosed our touching story to him – whichever you fancy, Eve! – whereupon he too succumbed to an attack of nobility, and gracefully retired from the lists.'

'Only if I can also have too much pride to let anyone suspect my secret!' stipulated Evelyn. 'Not even for you am I going to languish with a broken heart, Kester!'

Sir Bonamy, who had listened in rapt interest to the tale, said: 'Well, if ever I knew you had it in you, Kit! Why, I shouldn't wonder at it if you could write a book, or a play, or some such thing!' He perceived, with faint surprise, that Cressy had collapsed into helpless giggles. 'I'm bound to say I don't see what there is to laugh at: in my opinion you made a dashed moving thing of it, my boy! You know, Amabel, I begin to think he'll go a long way after all!'

'I *know* he will!' she responded proudly. 'I've frequently told you that Kit was *always* equal to anything!'

Kit's lips twitched at these tributes, but he was looking at the Dowager. 'Will it do, ma'am?'

She was not attending, and vouchsafed no answer. He waited; and after a short interval she said abruptly: 'I'll write to Stavely: no sense in leaving anything to chance! You'll give the letter to him, and take care he reads it! I never in my life listened to a sicklier, stupider story, but, from what I've seen of you, all you would do, if I was to tell you I wouldn't have it, would be to think of something even more outrageous! Cressy, you may give me your arm! I'm going to bed, for I'm fagged to death!' She bade the assembled company a cursory good night, but informed Kit, holding open the door for her, that she would thank him not to get himself hanged while she was still alive, and able to feel the shame of being connected with a gallows-bird. After that, she allowed him to kiss her hand, and withdrew, leaning heavily on Cressy's arm.

'Kester, if you do indeed mean to spread this story, we must give it a new touch! You could no more tell it as it stands than I could. Anyone who knows us would guess we were cutting a sham!'

'Good God, *we* aren't going to spread it!' replied Kit. 'That's the last thing we should do, if it happened to be true! There's no need to dress it up. We have only to put Fimber and Challow in possession of the bare bones of it, and leave them to tell it as they please. Give Challow half-an-hour amongst his cronies at the Running Footman, and I'll lay you any odds you like that there'll be upwards of a dozen garbled versions spreading all over London within a day! Lord, how many times has Challow favoured you with a choice morsel of gossip? If Stavely consents to Cressy's marriage, he'll be only too glad to adopt the story; and I don't mean to tell Mama what sort of touch to give it!'

'Oh, no!' agreed Lady Denville. 'I know *just* how I shall tell it, if anyone ventures to ask me any questions, when the advertisement of the engagement appears! Of course, only my particular friends *will* venture, but I know one who will, and it won't matter a rush if not another soul does!'

'For my part,' said Sir Bonamy firmly, 'I shall say I ain't on the high gab!'

'That's the ticket, sir!' said Kit, grinning at him. 'Give 'em a set-down!'

'Yes, but do you think it might give people *quite* a wrong notion?' suggested Lady Denville. ' Could you, perhaps, say that it is a – a most *touching* romance?'

'I *might* do that,' conceded Sir Bonamy, having subjected the proposition to careful consideration.

'What do you think Evelyn should say, Kit?' asked her ladyship anxiously.

'Nothing whatsoever!' he replied.

'That's fortunate!' remarked his twin.

'All Evelyn has to do,' said Kit, answering the doubtful question in her ladyship's eyes, 'is to behave exactly as he would if the story were true! Poker up, assume an air of distant civility, look down his nose – *You* know what he is when he gets on his high ropes, Mama!'

'And how, you uppish Jack-in-the-pulpit, do *you* mean to answer the curious?' inquired Evelyn.

'If it please your lordship – or even if it doesn't! –' retorted Kit, 'I shan't be obliged to answer them, because by the time the news is out, I shall be in Vienna! Now, don't eat me! Before I make good my escape, I am going to divulge my apocryphal story to the person for whose benefit it was principally designed. And if you imagine, Eve, that –' He broke off, as the door opened, and looked quickly round.

But it was Cressy who came into the room, and, as she told him, only to bid him goodnight, and to tell him that she had left the Dowager chuckling. 'I said I was positive you would make a stir in the world, and that's what set her off: she said she hadn't a doubt you would, and fell into such a fit of choking that I was in the greatest dread that it would carry her off! Kit, only a Fancot *could* have fabricated such a story! Of all the – No, I will *not* start laughing again!' Her hands were clasped in his, and her slender fingers tightened. 'When shall I see you again?' she asked, looking up into his face.

'Tomorrow, love,' he answered, smiling tenderly down at her.

'Ah, yes, but after that?'

'As soon as I can contrive it. That's something I must discuss with your father. If the abominable Albinia could be cajoled into thinking she would enjoy a trip abroad – But we won't pin our hopes to that chance! Stewart, I'm persuaded, would give me leave in August.'

She said, resolutely smiling: 'Not so very long, then! We shall leave for Worthing almost immediately. I suppose, you couldn't – No, of course not!'

He shook his head. 'I've still something to do, love, and I've lingered too long already.'

'Cressy, my dear, forgive me if I run away!' interposed Lady Denville. 'I have suddenly remembered that I have something *most* important I must say to Evelyn, before he goes back to Pinny!'

Evelyn, instantly and accurately interpreting this as an excuse hurriedly conjured up to leave Kit alone with his prospective bride, responded without hesitation. Sir Bonamy was a little harder to move, but it was not long before he grasped that her ladyship was trying to convey a silent message to him, and no time at all, after that, before complete enlightenment dawned upon him. 'Oh!' he said, hoisting himself to his feet: 'Yes, yes, my pretty! To be sure! I'll bid you goodnight, my dear Miss Stavely! It's been a tiring day, you know – devilish tiring!'

'Yes, indeed!' said Kit, perceiving that his love was once more in dire straits. 'Eve, wait for me!'

'Why, Kester, of course! What's an hour to me? Don't hesitate to wake me if I should happen to have fallen asleep!' responded his twin, strategically retiring in Sir Bonamy's wake, and closing the door behind him.

It was not, however, many minutes before Kit joined him. 'Hell-hound!' Kit said, entirely without rancour. 'Eve, I racked my brains to hit upon a way to speed *your* affair, but it can't be done! The only way to enable us to get there with both feet is for me to marry Cressy before you allow my uncle even to know that Miss Askham exists.'

'I might have guessed you'd stab me in the back!' said Evelyn mournfully. 'First you tried to usurp my place; then you stole my bride – Kester, remember my shoulder, remember I'm the head of the family, you unnatural brute!'

'*Will* you be serious?' demanded Kit wrathfully.

'I swear I will be, if only you won't talk balderdash! Good God, you great gudgeon, I haven't yet so much as made the smallest push even to fix Patience's interest!'

'I know that, but I know you too, twin! However, it can't be helped, and if you join Mama in Brighton presently you won't be so far off that you can't visit the Askhams, will you?'

'No, Kester, I shan't. So, now that that's off your mind, let us consider *your* affairs! I've an uneasy conviction that you should have been in Vienna days ago. Yes?'

'Yes,' Kit admitted, 'I don't think Stewart will cut up stiff, however, so don't tease yourself! I made my godfather's death my excuse for wanting leave of absence, and couldn't have hit on a surer card! He almost *ordered* me not to hesitate to extend my furlough, if I found myself unable to settle my affairs as soon as I'd thought I should. So, as I hadn't the smallest notion where you were, or how long it would be before you reappeared, I took the precaution of writing to him, before I left London, telling him that I'd found things in the deuce of a tangle! Never mind that! What I was going to tell you when Cressy came into the room, was that the moment I've settled things with Stavely, I'm going to post off to present my uncle with my moving story. That ought to make all tidy!'

'Make all tidy –! You'd ruin yourself with him!'

'Not a bit of it!' said Kit cheerfully. 'You think that because you can't deal with him no one can, but that's where you're out! You leave him to me – but for God's sake, don't forget the part you played in the epic! Perhaps I'd better write it down for you.'

'Perhaps you had,' agreed Evelyn. 'After all, there's no saying what I might do, when you aren't here to – Listen! That's not Fimber's step!'

He got up, as a knock fell on the door, and prepared to slip behind the bed-curtains. Kit strode over to the door, and opened it, to find Sir Bonamy standing outside, his nightcap already on his head, and his uncorseted form swathed in his gorgeous dressing-gown. 'Oh, it's you, sir!' Kit said. 'Come in! Is there anything amiss?'

'No, no, I wouldn't say there was anything *amiss*!' replied Sir Bonamy. 'The thing is –' He broke off, as his eyes fell upon Evelyn. 'I thought you was alone!' he told Kit. 'Well, well, never mind! It wasn't important!'

Evelyn, stunned by the monstrous figure presented by Sir Bonamy *en déshabillé*, said faintly: 'Don't go on my account, sir! Or shall I go?'

'No, no! I haven't anything private to say! I dare say you'll think it of no consequence – well, no more it is! Just one of those trifling things one gets to thinking about in the middle of the night! Ay, and worse! Damme, if I didn't dream I was *eating* it last night! Never had such a nightmare in my life! I thought I'd have a word with you, Kit, before you go off to Vienna. Well, you've been very civil – *very* civil and amiable, and you've a deal of influence with your mother, and if you would just drop a word in her ear I should be devilish obliged to you! Mind, I don't mean I shan't like being married to her, because, in a great many ways, I rather think I shall. But not if she means to give me biscuits and soda-water!'

'*D-does* she?' asked Evelyn, in a shaking voice.

'Of course she doesn't!' said Kit.

'I wouldn't say that,' said Sir Bonamy. 'You remember her telling me I ought to live on biscuits and soda-water?'

'I can't say I do, sir, but if she did she was only funning, I promise you!'

'Ah, but you never know what notions a female will take into her head! What's more, they always get their own way! Ask Evelyn, if you don't believe me! You ain't much in the petticoat-line yourself, I fancy.'

'N-not very much, sir!' acknowledged Kit. 'I'll take your word for it, however, and – and won't fail to speak to Mama!'

Sir Bonamy, much moved, shook him warmly by the hand, and thanked him with heartfelt sincerity, saying that he could now seek his bed without dreading a recurrence of his hideous nightmare. He then surged out of the room, just as Lady Denville, looking like a water-nymph, in a dressing-gown composed of layer upon layer of diaphanous material dyed every shade of green, emerged from her own bedchamber. He shrank instinctively, but she positively recoiled, gasping: 'Great heavens –! *Bonamy!*'

Overcoming his discomposure, he said, putting a bold face on it: 'Not wearing my corsets! I know you don't like 'em: you told me so!'

Recovering from her initial shock, she floated up to him, laying a fragile hand on his arm, and saying: 'Dearest friend, you must be mistaken! How *could* I have said such a thing?'

'No, I'm not,' asserted Sir Bonamy, fixedly regarding her. 'You begged me to give up strait-lacing!'

'I must have been mad!' said her ladyship.

'And,' continued Sir Bonamy, hope in his eyes, 'you said I creaked!'

'Now, *that*,' conceded her ladyship, 'I *do* recall! But don't give it another thought, my dear! I have grown *perfectly* accustomed to it! *Never* abandon your Cumberland corset, I beg of you!'

'You know what, my pretty?' said Sir Bonamy, care wiped from his brow. 'You've taken a weight off my mind! Damme, I *am* the happiest man alive! Bless you, my lovely one!'

Lady Denville, emerging unruffled from an overwhelming embrace, dismissed him in the kindest way to his allotted bedchamber, and joined her sons, saying, as she entered the room: '*Poor* Bonamy! I am quite shocked to think that I never before realized how much he *needs* me to take care of him!'

'I don't th-think he realizes it either, M-mama!' said Kit.

'No, not *yet*, but I promise you he will! Naturally, it came as a dreadful shock to him, but *already* he is beginning to grow more cheerful!' She added, as this drew wails from her distressingly afflicted sons, each of whom was clinging to a heavily carved bedpost: 'Wicked ones, wicked ones, you are *not* to laugh at him!'

'Only give me leave to tell him you won't f-feed him on biscuits and soda-water!' gasped Kit.

At that, her own enchanting ripple of laughter bubbled up. 'Oh, poor lamb! As though I could be so inhuman! I should think it would kill him! Tell him that I shan't interfere in *any* way! I shall, of course, but he will never know it, so you needn't scruple to say that, dearest!'

It was Evelyn who laughed the most at this, and inevitably, he whose laughter quite suddenly vanished. He said vehemently: 'Don't do it, Mama, don't do it! You can't! You must know you can't!'

She replied quite seriously: 'That is exactly what I thought myself, when I made up my mind that I *would* do it! But, do you know, my dear one, the more I think about it the more I believe that I shall positively *enjoy* being married to Bonamy! That's what I came to tell you, because I know you don't like it, and I haven't been able to snatch a word with either of you since it happened! And suddenly it occurred to me that I shan't be a Dowager after all! You can't think what a relief that is to me!' She drew his handsome head down, and kissed him. 'So now you'll let Fimber take you back to Pinny, my dearest, and you won't worry about anything, because there is nothing more you *can* worry about! Kit came to the rescue, just as he – just as he –' Her voice cracked, and she turned swiftly to hug her younger son convulsively. 'Oh, my darling!' she said. '*Thank you*! I'm not going to say another *word*, because I should cry if I did, and I look *hideous,* when I do that! Good night, my precious ones!'

The twins were left confronting one another. 'You'll grow accustomed to it, Eve,' said Kit, faintly smiling. 'She *will* enjoy being married to him!'

'Yes,' said Evelyn. He raised his eyes to Kit's, and a reflection of Kit's smile glimmered in them. 'I don't propose to embarrass you, Kester, by enlarging on what our beloved parent said – or, mercifully, left unsaid!'

'Well, thank God for that!' said Kit.

'Just so! I do hope we shall never be obliged to *say* anything to each other!'

'Why the devil should we?'

'I haven't the least idea. Give the bell a tug, Kester! I'm going to bed! In the words of our future father-in-law, it's been a tiring day!'

'*Devilish* tiring!' instantly responded his twin.

THE PRIVATE WORLD OF
Georgette Heyer

JANE AIKEN HODGE

Lavishly illustrated from Georgette Heyer's
family archives and from Regency sources, Jane
Aiken Hodge's affectionate life of the bestselling
novelist should delight her many
thousands of admirers.

216 pages with 24 pages in full colour and black
and white photographs throughout.

Published by The Bodley Head at £10.95.

Georgette Heyer
The Grand Sophy £1.75

Fresh from the ballrooms and battlefields of Wellington's Europe,
the dashing, unconventional Sophy disrupts her aunt's staid
London household. With wit and brisk commonsense she sets
about extracting her cousins from their various tiresome
entanglements — and in doing so meets her own destiny.

Bath Tangle £1.75

Lady Serena's rage when she found that her father's death had
placed her marriage prospects and fortune in Lord Rotherham's
control was understandable. Soon Serena, her childhood
sweetheart, her lovely young stepmother and Lord Rotherham are
all involved in a tangle — which is intriguingly resolved.

Pistols for Two £1.75

All the gallantry, villainy and elegance of the years when
Europe's first gentleman held court at Carlton House are brilliantly
recaptured in eleven lively episodes featuring the bucks, rakes and
blades of the Regency — and their high-spirited beauties.

Cotillion £1.75

The future of vivacious Kitty Charing was assured by her
whimsical stepfather, Mr Penicuik, provided she married one of
the handsome beaux now seeking her hand. But Kitty was in no
hurry to conclude such a contract. She intended to go to London,
where anything might happen — and very often did.

Cousin Kate £1.95

When Kate Malvern, unable to find another post as governess, is swept off to Staplewood by her rich aunt Minerva, she is delighted and grateful. But, once in the country, Kate discovers surprising reasons for Minerva's generosity – including the need to cope with her handsome, but sullen and moody, cousin Torquil.

Devil's Cub £1.75

Duellist and gamester, the young Marquis of Vidal had fairly earned the sobriquet 'Devil's Cub' – a tribute to the wilder excesses of his father, the Duke of Avon. When Mary Challoner discovers Vidal's plan to abduct her lovely half-sister she dons cloak and mask in a daring impersonation, and finds herself bound for France with the most notorious rake in Georgian London.

The Corinthian £1.75

Sir Richard Wyndham, every inch a man of the Regency, was wandering home, just a trifle befuddled, through the London dawn. He was pondering with some distaste his forthcoming betrothal. A lovely young girl disguised as a boy, falling into his arms from an upper window, provided him with the escape route he was looking for.

Susan Howatch
Cashelmara £3.50

Three generations of drama, passion and turmoil . . .

A glorious, full-blooded novel, brimming with memorable characters, which centres on Cashelmara, the coldly beautiful Georgian house in Galway, ancestral home of Edward de Salis.

Charged with emotion, the fast-moving plot follows the turbulent fortunes of an aristocratic Victorian family through half a century of furious encounters, ill-advised liaisons and bitter-sweet interludes of love.

Penmarric £3.50

The magnificent bestseller of the passionate loves and hatreds of a Cornish family.

'I was ten years old when I first saw the inheritance and twenty years old when I saw Janna Roslyn, but my reaction to both was identical. I wanted them.'

The inheritance is Penmarric, a huge gaunt house in Cornwall belonging to the tempestuous, hot-blooded Castallacks ; Janna Roslyn is a beautiful village girl who becomes mistress of Laurence Castallack, wife to his son . . .

Daphne du Maurier
Rebecca £1.95

'Last night I dreamt I went to Manderley again . . .'

One of the most appealing heroines in all of fiction, with a special magic that enthrals every reader . . .

Rebecca is known to millions through its outstandingly successful stage and screen versions ; and the characters in this timeless romance are hauntingly real.

Brilliantly conceived, masterfully executed, Daphne du Maurier's unforgettable tale of love, mystery and suspense is a story-telling triumph that will be read and re-read.

Fiction

☐ The Chains of Fate	Pamela Belle	£2.95p
☐ Options	Freda Bright	£1.50p
☐ The Thirty-nine Steps	John Buchan	£1.50p
☐ Secret of Blackoaks	Ashley Carter	£1.50p
☐ Hercule Poirot's Christmas	Agatha Christie	£1.50p
☐ Dupe	Liza Cody	£1.25p
☐ Lovers and Gamblers	Jackie Collins	£2.50p
☐ Sphinx	Robin Cook	£1.25p
☐ My Cousin Rachel	Daphne du Maurier	£1.95p
☐ Flashman and the Redskins	George Macdonald Fraser	£1.95p
☐ The Moneychangers	Arthur Hailey	£2.50p
☐ Secrets	Unity Hall	£1.75p
☐ Black Sheep	Georgette Heyer	£1.75p
☐ The Eagle Has Landed	Jack Higgins	£1.95p
☐ Sins of the Fathers	Susan Howatch	£3.50p
☐ Smiley's People	John le Carré	£1.95p
☐ To Kill a Mockingbird	Harper Lee	£1.95p
☐ Ghosts	Ed McBain	£1.75p
☐ The Silent People	Walter Macken	£1.95p
☐ Gone with the Wind	Margaret Mitchell	£3.50p
☐ Blood Oath	David Morrell	£1.75p
☐ The Night of Morningstar	Peter O'Donnell	£1.75p
☐ Wilt	Tom Sharpe	£1.75p
☐ Rage of Angels	Sidney Sheldon	£1.95p
☐ The Unborn	David Shobin	£1.50p
☐ A Town Like Alice	Nevile Shute	£1.75p
☐ Gorky Park	Martin Cruz Smith	£1.95p
☐ A Falcon Flies	Wilbur Smith	£2.50p
☐ The Grapes of Wrath	John Steinbeck	£2.50p
☐ The Deep Well at Noon	Jessica Stirling	£2.50p
☐ The Ironmaster	Jean Stubbs	£1.75p
☐ The Music Makers	E. V. Thompson	£1.95p

Non-fiction

☐ The First Christian	Karen Armstrong	£2.50p
☐ Pregnancy	Gordon Bourne	£3.50p
☐ The Law is an Ass	Gyles Brandreth	£1.75p
☐ The 35mm Photographer's Handbook	Julian Calder and John Garrett	£5.95p
☐ London at its Best	Hunter Davies	£2.95p
☐ Back from the Brink	Michael Edwardes	£2.95p

☐	**Travellers' Britain**	⎫ Arthur Eperon	£2.95p
☐	**Travellers' Italy**	⎭	£2.95p
☐	**The Complete Calorie Counter**	Eileen Fowler	80p
☐	**The Diary of Anne Frank**	Anne Frank	£1.75p
☐	**And the Walls Came Tumbling Down**	Jack Fishman	£1.95p
☐	**Linda Goodman's Sun Signs**	Linda Goodman	£2.50p
☐	**Scott and Amundsen**	Roland Huntford	£3.95p
☐	**Victoria RI**	Elizabeth Longford	£4.95p
☐	**Symptoms**	Sigmund Stephen Miller	£2.50p
☐	**Book of Worries**	Robert Morley	£1.50p
☐	**Airport International**	Brian Moynahan	£1.75p
☐	**Pan Book of Card Games**	Hubert Phillips	£1.95p
☐	**Keep Taking the Tabloids**	Fritz Spiegl	£1.75p
☐	**An Unfinished History of the World**	Hugh Thomas	£3.95p
☐	**The Baby and Child Book**	Penny and Andrew Stanway	£4.95p
☐	**The Third Wave**	Alvin Toffler	£2.95p
☐	**Pauper's Paris**	Miles Turner	£2.50p
☐	**The Psychic Detectives**	Colin Wilson	£2.50p
☐	**The Flier's Handbook**		£5.95p

All these books are available at your local bookshop or newsagent, or can be ordered direct from the publisher. Indicate the number of copies required and fill in the form below   **11**

....

Name..
(Block letters please)

Address..

_____

Send to CS Department, Pan Books Ltd, PO Box 40, Basingstoke, Hants
Please enclose remittance to the value of the cover price plus:
35p for the first book plus 15p per copy for each additional book ordered
to a maximum charge of £1.25 to cover postage and packing
Applicable only in the UK

While every effort is made to keep prices low, it is sometimes
necessary to increase prices at short notice. Pan Books reserve
the right to show on covers and charge new retail prices which
may differ from those advertised in the text or elsewhere